Kevin J. A~~~~~~~~~~~~~~~~~~~~~~~~~~~~~~~~~~~l novels,
forty-seven of which have appeared on national or international
bestseller lists. He has over twenty million books in print in thirty
languages. He has won or been nominated for numerous prestigious

THE MAMMOTH BOOK OF
NEBULA AWARDS SF

Edited by
KEVIN J. ANDERSON

ROBINSON

Constable & Robinson Ltd
55–56 Russell Square
London WC1B 4HP
www.constablerobinson.com

First published in the USA as *The Nebula Awards Showcase 2011*
by Tor, a division of Tom Doherty Associates, LLC, 2011

First published in the UK by Robinson,
an imprint of Constable & Robinson Ltd, 2012

A copy of the British Library Cataloguing in
Publication Data is available from the British Library

ISBN: 978-1-78033-429-5 (paperback)
ISBN: 978-1-78033-430-1 (ebook)

Printed and bound in the UK

1 3 5 7 9 10 8 6 4 2

COPYRIGHT ACKNOWLEDGMENTS

CONTENTS

INTRODUCTION

Kevin J. Anderson

For forty-five years, the members of the Science Fiction and Fantasy Writers of America (SFWA) have been reading, pondering, dickering over, and selecting the most exceptional works in the genre. Each year, they present the prestigious Nebula Award for Best Novel, Novella (17,500–40,000 words), Novelette (7,500–17,500 words), and Short Story (less than 7,500 words). The first ceremonies, in 1965, honored works by Frank Herbert, Brian W. Aldiss, Roger Zelazny, and Harlan Ellison. Not a bad start.

Throughout each year, the fifteen hundred or so members of SFWA send in recommendations to call attention to works they find worthy of consideration. If a story or novel receives enough recommendations within a year of publication, the work is included on that year's Preliminary Ballot. The full members of SFWA vote on the shortlisted works to winnow them down to four candidates in each category (a special jury can also add works that they feel slipped through the cracks), and that's the final Nebula ballot, from which the winners are chosen.

Hence, the contents of this *Showcase*.

The genre's rival award, the Hugo, is chosen by the readers and fans, the equivalent of the People's Choice Awards. The Hugo and Nebula audiences' tastes don't always agree, but both awards are an impressive feather in an author's cap. For me, the final ballots serve another vital purpose: providing SF and fantasy readers with a cream-of-the-crop reading list.

When I grew up as a kid in small-town Wisconsin, with a whole section of the public library devoted to science fiction (as denoted by little rocket stickers on the spines), it was hard to know where to start. The section was daunting and huge – *six whole shelves* filled with science fiction books! I could have begun at the top and worked my way down, which would have made me very familiar with Asimov, Bradbury, and Clarke, but I would never have made it to Zelazny. Obviously, not a good system.

Instead, I turned to the Nebula Awards anthologies for a selection of each year's best work; from there, with a checklist of past Nebula novel winners, I was steered toward such masterpieces as *Ringworld*, *The Forever War*, *Rendezvous with Rama*, *Man Plus*, *Gateway*, *Stardance*, and many others. I studied the works, learned from them, and (most of all) enjoyed them.

By age twelve I was already an aspiring writer sending stories out in the mail, and starting my pile of rejection slips. My interest in writing did not go unnoticed, and teachers began to encourage me. I got connected with a local book-review service and found myself with as many free novels as I could read, so long as I turned in reviews afterward. (I was only fifteen at the time, and "book review" felt more like a "book report.") The book review editor encouraged me to attend a local science fiction convention in Madison, Wisconsin – WisCon. He even loaned me the $15 membership fee. That was where I met my very first real-live New York editor, David Hartwell. I was just a high-school kid, too shy to talk much, and I wondered if all professional editors wore such strange neckties. (Hartwell, by the way, is also Tor's editor for this very book, and we have worked together on other projects as well.)

After graduating from the University of Wisconsin, I moved away from the Midwest – still wanting to be an author – and took a job in the San Francisco area as a technical writer for a large research laboratory. There I discovered a much wider world of fandom, other like-minded aspiring authors, writers' workshops, and frequent conventions. I attended my first Nebula Awards ceremony in 1985 at the swanky Claremont Hotel in Oakland, California (nobody told me I wasn't supposed to wear my battered Star Wars T-shirt), where I watched Orson Scott Card receive the Nebula for *Ender's Game*.

I published my first professional stories, sold my first novel, then three more novels, joined SFWA as a full member – and suddenly authors and publishers began sending me novels and stories to consider for the Nebula Award. Instead of just looking at each year's nominees and winners as a list of good fiction to read, I could cast my vote, add my recommendation to books and stories that I found particularly noteworthy. It was a heady responsibility (and a tough task for a relatively slow reader). Just keeping up with all the *best* writing was nearly impossible.

Each year's *Nebula Awards Showcase* certainly helps.

Tastes and styles have changed over the years, but the works that are recommended and nominated by SFWA members always form a melting pot of science fiction and fantasy: bold ideas, excellent world-building, clear and precise prose, or mind-bending experimental writing – the whole gamut.

This volume is no different. Reading these stories, you will find a wide range of colorful fantasy, experimental speculative fiction, steampunk, edgy near-mainstream, and hard SF. The tales will take you from the distant past, to a skewed modern day, to the far future, as well as to sideways points in between. Tor Books has generously allowed us the space to include not only the winning works in the three short-form categories, but also all of the nominees in the Novelette and Short Story categories. I guarantee that you'll love something here.

Let the Science Fiction and Fantasy Writers of America show you our best.

FINAL 2009
NEBULA BALLOT

Short Story

"Hooves and the Hovel of Abdel Jameela," Saladin Ahmed (*Clockwork Phoenix 2*, Norilana Books, July 2009)

"I Remember the Future," Michael A. Burstein (*I Remember the Future*, Apex Publications, November 2008)

"Non-Zero Probabilities," N. K. Jemisin (*Clarkesworld*, November 2009)

"Spar," Kij Johnson (*Clarkesworld*, October 2009)

"Going Deep," James Patrick Kelly (*Asimov's Science Fiction*, June 2009)

"Bridesicle," Will McIntosh (*Asimov's Science Fiction*, January 2009)

Novelette

"The Gambler," Paolo Bacigalupi (*Fast Forward 2*, Pyr Books, October 2008)

"Vinegar Peace (or, the Wrong-Way, Used-Adult Orphanage)," Michael Bishop (*Asimov's Science Fiction*, July 2008)

"I Needs Must Part, the Policeman Said," Richard Bowes (*The Magazine of Fantasy & Science Fiction*, December 2009)

"Sinner, Baker, Fabulist, Priest; Red Mask, Black Mask, Gentleman, Beast," Eugie Foster (*Interzone*, February 2009)

"Divining Light," Ted Kosmatka (*Asimov's Science Fiction*, August 2008)

"A Memory of Wind," Rachel Swirsky (Tor.com, November 2009)

Novella

The Women of Nell Gwynne's, Kage Baker (Subterranean Press, June 2009)

Arkfall, Carolyn Ives Gilman (*The Magazine of Fantasy & Science Fiction*, September 2009)

Act One, Nancy Kress (*Asimov's Science Fiction*, March 2009)
Shambling Towards Hiroshima, James Morrow (Tachyon, February 2009)
Sublimation Angels, Jason Sanford (*Interzone*, October 2009)
The God Engines, John Scalzi (Subterranean Press, December 2009)

Novel

The Windup Girl, Paolo Bacigalupi (Night Shade Books, September 2009)
The Love We Share Without Knowing, Christopher Barzak (Bantam, November 2008)
Flesh and Fire, Laura Anne Gilman (Pocket, October 2009)
The City & The City, China Miéville (Del Rey, May 2009)
Boneshaker, Cherie Priest (Tor, September 2009)
Finch, Jeff VanderMeer (Underland Press, October 2009)

The Ray Bradbury Award for
Outstanding Dramatic Presentation

Star Trek, JJ Abrams, Roberto Orci and Alex Kurtzman (Paramount, May 2009)
District 9, Neill Blomkamp and Terri Tatchell (Tri-Star, August 2009)
Avatar, James Cameron (Fox, December 2009)
Moon, Duncan Jones and Nathan Parker (Sony, June 2009)
Up, Bob Peterson and Pete Docter (Disney/Pixar, May 2009)
Coraline, Henry Selick (Laika/Focus, February 2009)

Andre Norton Award for
Young Adult Science Fiction and Fantasy

Hotel Under the Sand, Kage Baker (Tachyon, July 2009)
Ice, Sarah Beth Durst (Simon & Schuster, October 2009)
Ash, Malinda Lo (Little, Brown and Company, September 2009)
Eyes Like Stars, Lisa Mantchev (Feiwel and Friends, July 2009)
Zoe's Tale, John Scalzi (Tor Books, August 2008)
When You Reach Me, Rebecca Stead (Wendy Lamb Books, July, 2009)
The Girl Who Circumnavigated Fairyland in a Ship of Her Own Making, Catherynne M. Valente (Catherynne M. Valente, June 2009)
Leviathan, Scott Westerfeld (Simon Pulse, October 2009)

SHORT
STORY

HOOVES AND THE HOVEL OF ABDEL JAMEELA

Saladin Ahmed

FROM THE AUTHOR: "Hooves and the Hovel of Abdel Jameela" is actually a prosification of a very short poem I wrote years ago. The poem consisted entirely of a single image – an old man somewhere in the medieval Islamic world defying the narrow-minded by declaring his love for a hooved woman. Translating this image into a story, of course, introduced deeper demands in terms of plot and character. These demands eventually led to the story that appears here. Most of the characters' names, by the way, are vaguely allegorical or otherwise playful – "Abdel Jameela," for instance, might be roughly translated as "servant (or slave) of beauty."

As soon as I arrive in the village of Beit Zujaaj I begin to hear the mutters about Abdel Jameela, a strange old man supposedly unconnected to any of the local families. Two days into my stay the villagers fall over one another to share with me the rumors that Abdel Jameela is in fact distantly related to the esteemed Assad clan. By my third day in Beit Zujaaj, several of the Assads, omniscient as "important" families always are in these piles of cottages, have accosted me to deny the malicious whispers. No doubt they are worried about the bad impression such an association might make on me, favorite physicker of the Caliph's own son.

The latest denial comes from Hajjar al-Assad himself, the middle-aged head of the clan and the sort of half-literate lout that passes for a Shaykh in these parts. Desperate for the approval of the young courtier whom he no doubt privately condemns as an overschooled sodomite, bristle-bearded Shaykh Hajjar has cornered me in the village's only café – if the sitting room of a qat-chewing old woman can be called a café by anyone other than bumpkins.

I should not be so hard on Beit Zujaaj and its bumpkins. But when I look at the gray rock-heap houses, the withered gray vegetable-yards, and the stuporous gray lives that fill this village, I want to weep for the lost color of Baghdad.

Instead I sit and listen to the Shaykh.

"Abdel Jameela is not of Assad blood, O learned Professor. My grandfather took mercy, as God tells us we must, on the old man's mother. Seventy-and-some years ago she showed up in Beit Zujaaj, half-dead from traveling and big with child, telling tales – God alone knows if they were true – of her Assad-clan husband, supposedly slain by highwaymen. Abdel Jameela was birthed and raised here, but he has never been of this village." Shaykh Hajjar scowls. "For decades now – since I was a boy – he has lived up on the hilltop rather than among us. More of a hermit than a villager. And *not* of Assad blood," he says again.

I stand up. I can take no more of the man's unctuous voice and, praise God, I don't have to.

"Of course, O Shaykh, of course. I understand. Now, if you will excuse me?"

Shaykh Hajjar blinks. He wishes to say more but doesn't dare. For I have come from the Caliph's court.

"Yes, Professor. Peace be upon you." His voice is like a snuffed candle.

"And upon you, peace." I head for the door as I speak.

The villagers would be less deferential if they knew of my current position at court – or rather, lack of one. The Caliph has sent me to Beit Zujaaj as an insult. I am here as a reminder that the well-read young physicker with the clever wit and impressive skill, whose company the Commander of the Faithful's own bookish son enjoys, is worth less than the droppings of the Caliph's favorite falcon. At least when gold and a Persian noble's beautiful daughter are involved.

For God's viceroy the Caliph has seen fit to promise my Shireen to another, despite her love for me. Her husband-to-be is older than her father – too ill, the last I heard, to even sign the marriage contract. But as soon as his palsied, liver-spotted hand is hale enough to raise a pen . . .

Things would have gone differently were I a wealthy man. Shireen's father would have heard my proposal happily enough if I'd been able to provide the grand dowry he sought. The Caliph's son, fond of his brilliant physicker, even asked that Shireen be wedded to me. But the boy's fondness could only get me so far. The Commander of the Faithful saw no reason to impose a raggedy scholar of a son-in-law on the Persian when a rich old vulture would please the man more. I am, in the Caliph's eyes, an amusing companion to his son, but one whom the boy will lose like a doll once he grows to love killing and gold-getting more than learning. Certainly I am nothing worth upsetting Shireen's coin-crazed courtier father over.

For a man is not merely who he is, but what he has. Had I land or caravans I would be a different man – the sort who could compete for Shireen's hand. But I have only books and instruments and a tiny inheritance, and thus that is all that I am. A man made of books and pittances would be a fool to protest when the Commander of the Faithful told him that his love would soon wed another.

I am a fool.

My outburst in court did not quite cost me my head, but I was sent to Beit Zujaaj "for a time, only, to minister to the villagers as a representative of Our beneficent concern for Our subjects." And my fiery, tree-climbing Shireen was locked away to await her half-dead suitor's recovery.

"O Professor! Looks like you might get a chance to see Abdel Jameela for yourself!" Just outside the café, the gravelly voice of Umm Hikma the café-keeper pierces the cool morning air and pulls me out of my reverie. I like old Umm Hikma, with her qat-chewer's irascibility and her blacksmithish arms. Beside her is a broad-shouldered man I don't know. He scuffs the dusty ground with his sandal and speaks to me in a worried stutter.

"P-peace be upon you, O learned Professor. We haven't yet met. I'm Yousef, the porter."

"And upon you, peace, O Yousef. A pleasure to meet you."

"The pleasure's mine, O Professor. But I am here on behalf of another. To bring you a message. From Abdel Jameela."

For the first time since arriving in Beit Zujaaj, I am surprised. "A message? For me?"

"Yes, Professor. I am just returned from the old hermit's hovel, a half-day's walk from here, on the hilltop. Five, six times a year I bring things to Abdel Jameela, you see. In exchange he gives a few coins, praise God."

"And where does he get these coins, up there on the hill?" Shaykh Hajjar's voice spits out the words from the café doorway behind me. I glare and he falls silent.

I turn back to the porter. "What message do you bear, O Yousef? And how does this graybeard know of me?"

Broad-shouldered Yousef looks terrified. The power of the court. "Forgive me, O learned Professor! Abdel Jameela asked what news from the village and I . . . I told him that a court physicker was in Beit Zujaaj. He grew excited and told me beg upon his behalf for your aid. He said his wife was horribly ill. He fears she will lose her legs, and perhaps her life."

"His wife?" I've never heard of a married hermit.

Umm Hikma raises her charcoaled eyebrows, chews her qat, and says nothing.

Shaykh Hajjar is more vocal. "No one save God knows where she came from, or how many years she's been up there. The people have had glimpses only. She doesn't wear the head scarf that our women wear. She is wrapped all in black cloth from head to toe and mesh-masked like a foreigner. She has spoken to no one. Do you know, O Professor, what the old rascal said to me years ago when I asked why his wife never comes down to the village? He said, 'She is very religious'! The old dog! Where is it written that a woman can't speak to other women? Other women who are good Muslims? The old son of a whore! What should his wife fear here? The truth of the matter is—"

"The truth, O Shaykh, is that in this village only *your* poor wife need live in fear!" Umm Hikma lets out a rockslide chuckle and gives me a conspiratorial wink. Before the Shaykh can sputter out his offended reply, I turn to Yousef again.

"On this visit, did you see Abdel Jameela's wife?" If he can describe the sick woman, I may be able to make some guesses about her condition. But the porter frowns.

"He does not ask me into his home, O Professor. No one has been asked into his home for thirty years."

Except for the gifted young physicker from the Caliph's court. Well, it may prove more interesting than what I've seen of Beit Zujaaj thus far. I do have a fondness for hermits. Or, rather, for the *idea* of hermits. I can't say that I have ever met one. But as a student I always fantasized that I would one day *be* a hermit, alone with God and my many books in the barren hills.

That was before I met Shireen.

"There is one thing more," Yousef says, his broad face looking even more nervous. "He asked that you come alone."

My heartbeat quickens, though there is no good reason for fear. Surely this is just an old hater-of-men's surly whim. A physicker deals with such temperamental oddities as often as maladies of the liver or lungs. Still . . . "Why does he ask this?"

"He says that his wife is very modest and that in her state the frightening presence of men might worsen her illness."

Shaykh Hajjar erupts at this. "Bah! Illness! More likely they've done something shameful they don't want the village to know of. Almighty God forbid, maybe they—"

Whatever malicious thing the Shaykh is going to say, I silence it with another glare borrowed from the Commander of the Faithful. "If the woman is ill, it is my duty as a Muslim and a physicker to help her, whatever her husband's oddities."

Shaykh Hajjar's scowl is soul-deep "Forgive me, O Professor, but this is not a matter of oddities. You could be in danger. We know why Abdel Jameela's wife hides away, though some here fear to speak of such things."

Umm Hikma spits her qat into the road, folds her powerful arms, and frowns. "In the name of God! Don't you believe, Professor, that Abdel Jameela, who couldn't kill an ant, means you any harm." She jerks her chin at Shaykh Hajjar. "And you, O Shaykh, by God, please don't start telling your old lady stories again!"

The Shaykh wags a finger at her. "Yes, I *will* tell him, woman! And may Almighty God forgive you for mocking your Shaykh!" Shaykh Hajjar turns to me with a grim look. "O learned Professor, I will say it plainly: Abdel Jameela's wife is a witch."

"A witch?" The last drops of my patience with Beit Zujaaj have dripped through the water clock. It is time to be away from these people. "Why would you say such a thing, O Shaykh?"

The Shaykh shrugs. "Only God knows for certain," he says. His tone belies his words.

"May God protect us all from slanderous ill-wishers," I say.

He scowls. But I have come from the Caliph's court, so his tone is venomously polite. "It is no slander, O Professor. Abdel Jameela's wife consorts with ghouls. Travelers have heard strange noises coming from the hilltop. And hoofprints have been seen on the hill-path. Cloven hoofprints, O Professor, where there are neither sheep nor goats."

"No! Not cloven hoofprints!" I say.

But the Shaykh pretends not to notice my sarcasm. He just nods. "There is no strength and no safety but with God."

"God is great," I say in vague, obligatory acknowledgment. I have heard enough rumor and nonsense. And a sick woman needs my help. "I will leave as soon as I gather my things. This Abdel Jameela lives up the road, yes? On a hill? If I walk, how long will it take me?"

"If you do not stop to rest, you will see the hill in the distance by noontime prayer," says Umm Hikma, who has a new bit of qat going in her cheek.

"I will bring you some food for your trip, Professor, and the stream runs alongside the road much of the way, so you'll have no need of water." Yousef seems relieved that I'm not angry with him, though I don't quite know why I would be. I thank him then speak to the group.

"Peace be upon you all."

"And upon you, peace," they say in near-unison.

In my room, I gather scalpel, saw, and drugs into my pack – the kid-leather pack that my beloved gifted to me. I say more farewells to the villagers, firmly discourage their company, and set off alone on the road. As I walk, rumors of witches and wife-beaters are crowded out of my thoughts by the sweet remembered sweat-and-ambergris scent of my Shireen.

After an hour on the rock-strewn road, the late-morning air warms. The sound of the stream beside the road almost calms me.

Time passes and the sun climbs high in the sky. I take off my turban and caftan, make ablution by the stream, and say my noon prayers. Not long after I begin walking again, I can make out what must be Beit Zujaaj Hill off in the distance. In another hour or so I am at its foot.

It is not much of a hill, actually. There are buildings in Baghdad that are taller. A relief, as I am not much of a hill-climber. The rocky path is not too steep, and green sprays of grass and thyme dot it – a pleasant enough walk, really. The sun sinks a bit in the sky and I break halfway up the hill for afternoon prayers and a bit of bread and green apple. I try to keep my soul from sinking as I recall Shireen, her skirts tied up scandalously, knocking apples down to me from the high branches of the Caliph's orchard trees.

The rest of the path proves steeper and I am sweating through my galabeya when I finally reach the hilltop. As I stand there huffing and puffing my eyes land on a small structure thirty yards away.

If Beit Zujaaj Hill is not much of a hill, at least the hermit's hovel can be called nothing but a hovel. Stones piled on stones until they have taken the vague shape of a dwelling. Two sickly chickens scratching in the dirt. As soon as I have caught my breath a man comes walking out to meet me. Abdel Jameela.

He is shriveled with a long gray beard and a ragged kaffiyeh, and I can tell he will smell unpleasant even before he reaches me. How does he already know I'm here? I don't have much time to wonder, as the old man moves quickly despite clearly gouty legs.

"You are the physicker, yes? From the Caliph's court?"

No "peace be upon you," no "how is your health," no "pleased to meet you." Life on a hilltop apparently wears away one's manners. As if reading my thoughts, the old man bows his head in supplication.

"Ah. Forgive my abruptness, O learned Professor. I am Abdel Jameela. Thank you. Thank you a thousand times for coming." I am right about his stink, and I thank God he does not try to embrace me. With no further ceremony I am led into the hovel.

There are a few stained and tattered carpets layered on the packed-dirt floor. A straw mat, an old cushion, and a battered tea tray are the only furnishings. Except for the screen. Directly opposite the door is a tall, incongruously fine cedar-and-pearl latticed folding screen, behind which I can make out only a vague shape. It is a more expensive piece of furniture than any of the villagers could afford, I'm sure. And behind it, no doubt, sits Abdel Jameela's wife.

The old man makes tea hurriedly, clattering the cups but saying nothing the whole while. The scent of the seeping mint leaves drifts up, covering his sour smell. Abdel Jameela sets my tea before me, places a cup beside the screen, and sits down. A hand reaches out from behind the screen to take the tea. It is brown and graceful. *Beautiful*, if I am to speak truly. I realize I am staring and tear my gaze away.

The old man doesn't seem to notice. "I don't spend my time among men, Professor. I can't talk like a courtier. All I can say is that we need your help."

"Yousef the porter has told me that your wife is ill, O Uncle. Something to do with her legs, yes? I will do whatever I can to cure her, Almighty God willing."

For some reason, Abdel Jameela grimaces at this. Then he rubs his hands together and gives me an even more pained expression. "O Professor, I must show you a sight that will shock you. My wife . . . Well, words are not the way."

With a grunt the old man stands and walks halfway behind the screen. He gestures for me to follow then bids me stop a few feet away. I hear rustling behind the screen, and I can see a woman's form moving, but still Abdel Jameela's wife is silent.

"Prepare yourself, Professor. Please show him, O beautiful wife of mine." The shape behind the screen shifts. There is a scraping noise. And a woman's leg ending in a cloven hoof stretches out from behind the screen.

I take a deep breath. "God is Great," I say aloud. This, then, is the source of Shaykh Hajjar's fanciful grumbling. But such grotesqueries are not unheard of to an educated man. Only last year another physicker at court showed me a child – born to a healthy, pious man and his modest wife – all covered in fur. This same physicker told me of another child he'd seen born with scaly skin. I take another deep breath. If a hooved woman can be born and live, is it so strange that she might find a mad old man to care for her?

"O my sweetheart!" Abdel Jameela's whisper is indecent as he holds his wife's hoof.

And for a moment I see what mad Abdel Jameela sees. The hoof's glossy black beauty, as smoldering as a woman's eye. It is entrancing. . . .

"O, my wife," the old man goes on, and runs his crooked old finger over the hoof-cleft slowly and lovingly. "O, my beautiful wife . . ." The leg flexes, but still no sound comes from behind the screen.

This is wrong. I take a step back from the screen without meaning to. "In the name of God! Have you no shame, old man?"

Abdel Jameela turns from the screen and faces me with an apologetic smile. "I am sorry to say that I have little shame left," he says.

I've never heard words spoken with such weariness. I remind myself that charity and mercy are our duty to God, and I soften my tone. "Is this why you sent for me, Uncle? What would you have me do? Give her feet she was not born with? My heart bleeds for you, truly. But such a thing only God can do."

Another wrinkled grimace. "O Professor, I am afraid that I must beg your forgiveness. For I have lied to you. And for that I am sorry. For it is not my wife that needs your help, but I."

"But her – pardon me, Uncle – her hoof."

"Yes! Its curve! Like a jet-black half-moon!" The old hermit's voice quivers and he struggles to keep his gaze on me. Away from his wife's hoof. "Her hoof is breathtaking, Professor. No, it is *I* that need your help, for I am not the creature I need to be."

"I don't understand, Uncle." Exasperation burns away my sympathy. I've walked for hours and climbed a hill, small though it was. I am in no mood for a hermit's games. Abdel Jameela winces at the anger in my eyes and says "My . . . my wife will explain."

I will try, my husband.

The voice is like song and there is the strong scent of sweet flowers. Then she steps from behind the screen and I lose all my words. I scream. I call on God, and I scream.

Abdel Jameela's wife is no creature of God. Her head is a goat's and her mouth a wolf's muzzle. Fish-scales and jackal-hair cover her. A scorpion's tail curls behind her. I look into a woman's eyes set in a demon's face and I stagger backward, calling on God and my dead mother.

Please, learned one, be calm.

"What . . . what . . ." I can't form the words. I look to the floor. I try to bury my sight in the dirty carpets and hard-packed earth. Her voice is more beautiful than any woman's. And there is the powerful smell of jasmine and clove. A nightingale sings perfumed words at me while my mind's eye burns with horrors that would make the Almighty turn away.

If fear did not hold your tongue, you would ask what I am. Men have called my people by many names – ghoul, demon. Does a word matter so very much? What I am, learned one, is Abdel Jameela's wife.

For long moments I don't speak. If I don't speak this nightmare will end. I will wake in Baghdad, or Beit Zujaaj. But I don't wake.

She speaks again, and I cover my ears, though the sound is beauty itself.

The words you hear come not from my mouth, and you do not hear them with your ears. I ask you to listen with your mind and your heart. We will die, my husband and I, if you will not lend us your skill. Have you, learned one, never needed to be something other that what you are?

Cinnamon scent and the sound of an oasis wind come to me. I cannot speak to this demon. My heart will stop if I do, I am certain. I want to run, but fear has fixed my feet. I turn to Abdel Jameela, who stands there wringing his hands.

"Why am I here, Uncle? God damn you, why did you call me here? There is no sick woman here! God protect me, I know nothing of . . . of ghouls, or—" A horrible thought comes to me. "You . . . you are not hoping to make her into a woman? Only God can . . ."

The old hermit casts his eyes downward. "Please . . . you must listen to my wife. I beg you." He falls silent and his wife, behind the screen again, goes on.

My husband and I have been on this hilltop too long, learned one. My body cannot stand so much time away from my people. I smell yellow roses and hear bumblebees droning beneath her voice. *If we stay in this place one more season, I will die. And without me to care for him and keep age's scourge from him, my sweet Abdel Jameela will die, too. But across the desert there is a life for us. My father was a prince among our people. Long ago I left. For many reasons. But I never forsook my birthright. My father is dying now, I have word. He has left no sons and so his lands are mine. Mine, and my handsome husband's.*

In her voice is a chorus of wind chimes. Despite myself, I lift my eyes. She steps from behind the screen, clad now in a black abaya and a mask. Behind the mask's mesh is the glint of wolf-teeth. I look again to the floor, focusing on a faded blue spiral in the carpet and the kindness in that voice.

But my people do not love men. I cannot claim my lands unless things change. Unless my husband shows my people that he can change.

Somehow I force myself to speak. "What . . . what do you mean, change?"

There is a cymbal-shimmer in her voice and sandalwood incense fills my nostrils. *O learned one, you will help me to make these my Abdel Jameela's.*

She extends her slender brown hands, ablaze with henna. In each she holds a length of golden sculpture – goatlike legs ending in shining, cloven hooves. A thick braid of gold thread dances at the end of each statue-leg, alive.

Madness, and I must say so though this creature may kill me for it. "I have not the skill to do this! No man alive does!"

You will not do this through your skill alone. Just as I cannot do it through my sorcery alone. My art will guide yours as your hands work. She takes a step toward me and my shoulders clench at the sound of her hooves hitting the earth.

"No! No . . . I cannot do this thing."

"Please!" I jump at Abdel Jameela's voice, nearly having forgotten him. There are tears in the old man's eyes as he pulls at my galabeya, and his stink gets in my nostrils. "Please listen! We need your help. And we know what has brought you to Beit Zujaaj." The old man falls to his knees before me. "Please! Would not your Shireen aid us?"

With those words he knocks the wind from my lungs. How can he know that name? The Shaykh hadn't lied – there *is* witchcraft at work here, and I should run from it.

But, Almighty God, help me, Abdel Jameela is right. Fierce as she is, Shireen still has her dreamy Persian notions – that love is more important than money or duty or religion. If I turn this old man away . . .

My throat is dry and cracked. "How do you know of Shireen?" Each word burns.

His eyes dart away. "She has . . . ways, my wife."

"All protection comes from God." I feel foul even as I steel myself with the old words. Is this forbidden? Am I walking the path of those who displease the Almighty? God forgive me, it is hard to know or to care when my beloved is gone. "If I were a good Muslim I would run down to the village now and . . . and . . ."

And what, learned one? Spread word of what you have seen? Bring men with spears and arrows? Why would you do this? Vanilla beans and the sound of rain give way to something else. Clanging steel and clean-burning fire. *I will not let you harm my husband. What we ask is not disallowed to you. Can you tell me, learned one, that it is in your book of what is blessed and what is forbidden not to give a man golden legs?*

It is not. Not in so many words. But this thing can't be acceptable in God's eyes. Can it? "Has this ever been done before?"

There are old stories. But it has been centuries. Each of her words spreads perfume and music and she asks, *Please, learned one, will you help us?* And then one scent rises above the others.

Almighty God protect me, it is the sweat-and-ambergris smell of my beloved. Shireen of the ribbing remark, who in quiet moments confessed her love of my learning. She *would* help them.

Have I any choice after that? This, then, the fruit of my study. And this my reward for wishing to be more than what I am. A twisted, unnatural path.

"Very well." I reach for my small saw and try not to hear Abdel Jameela's weird whimpers as I sharpen it.

I give him poppy and hemlock, but as I work Abdel Jameela still screams, nearly loud enough to make my heart cease beating. His old body is going through things it should not be surviving. And I am the one putting him through these things, with knives and fire and bone-breaking clamps. I wad cotton and stuff it in my ears to block out the hermit's screams.

But I feel half-asleep as I do so, hardly aware of my own hands. Somehow the demon's magic is keeping Abdel Jameela alive and guiding me through this grisly task. It is painful, like having two minds crammed inside my skull and shadow-puppet poles lashed to my arms. I am burning up, and I can barely trace my thoughts. Slowly I become aware of the she-ghoul's voice in my head and the scent of apricots.

Cut there. Now the mercury powder. The cauterizing iron is hot. Put a rag in his mouth so he does not bite his tongue. I flay and cauterize and lose track of time. A fever cooks my mind away. I work through the evening prayer, then the night prayer. I feel withered inside.

In each step Abdel Jameela's wife guides me. With her magic she rifles my mind for the knowledge she needs and steers my skilled fingers. For a long while there is only her voice in my head and the feeling of bloody instruments in my hands, which move with a life of their own.

Then I am holding a man's loose tendons in my right hand and thick golden threads in my left. There are shameful smells in the air and Abdel Jameela shouts and begs me to stop even though he is half-asleep with the great pot of drugs I have forced down his throat.

Something is wrong! The she-ghoul screams in my skull and Abdel Jameela passes out. My hands no longer dance magically. The shining threads shrivel in my fist. We have failed, though I know not exactly how.

No! No! Our skill! Our sorcery! But his body refuses! There are funeral wails in the air and the smell of houses burning. *My husband! Do something, physicker!*

The golden legs turn to dust in my hands. With my ears I hear Abdel Jameela's wife growl a wordless death-threat.

I deserve death! Almighty God, what have I done? An old man lies dying on my blanket. I have sawed off his legs at a she-ghoul's bidding. There is no strength save in God! I bow my head.

Then I see them. Just above where I've amputated Abdel Jameela's legs are the swollen bulges that I'd thought came from gout. But it is not gout that has made these. There is something buried beneath the skin of each leg. I take hold of my scalpel and flay each thin thigh. The old man moans with what little life he has left.

What are you doing? Abdel Jameela's wife asks the walls of my skull. I ignore her, pulling at a flap of the old man's thigh-flesh, revealing a corrupted sort of miracle.

Beneath Abdel Jameela's skin, tucked between muscles, are tiny legs. Thin as spindles and hairless. Each folded little leg ends in a miniscule hoof.

Unbidden, a memory comes to me – Shireen and I in the Caliph's orchards. A baby bird had fallen from its nest. I'd sighed and bit my lip and my Shireen – a dreamer, but not a soft one – had laughed and clapped at my tender-heartedness.

I slide each wet gray leg out from under the flayed skin and gently unbend them. As I flex the little joints, the she-ghoul's voice returns.

What . . . what is this, learned one? Tell me!

For a long moment I am mute. Then I force words out, my throat still cracked. "I . . . I do not know. They are – they look like – the legs of a kid or a ewe still in the womb."

It is as if she nods inside my mind. *Or the legs of one of my people. I have long wondered how a mere man could captivate me so.*

"All knowledge and understanding lies with God," I say. "Perhaps your husband always had these within him. The villagers say he is of uncertain parentage. Or perhaps . . . Perhaps his love for you . . . The crippled beggars of Cairo are the most grotesque – and the best – in the world. It is said that they wish so fiercely to make money begging that their souls reshape their bodies from the inside out. Yesterday I saw such stories as nonsense. But yesterday I'd have named *you* a villager's fantasy, too." As I speak I continue to work the little legs carefully, to help their circulation. The she-ghoul's sorcery no longer guides my hands, but a physicker's nurturing routines are nearly as compelling. There is weakness here and I do what I can to help it find strength.

The tiny legs twitch and kick in my hands.

Abdel Jameela's wife howls in my head. *They are drawing on my magic. Something pulls at—* The voice falls silent.

I let go of the legs and, before my eyes, they begin to grow. As they grow, they fill with color, as if blood flowed into them. Then fur starts to sprout upon them.

"There is no strength or safety but in God!" I try to close my eyes and focus on the words I speak but I can't. My head swims and my body swoons.

The spell that I cast on my poor husband to preserve him – these hidden hooves of his nurse on it! O, my surprising, wonderful husband! I hear loud lute music and smell lemongrass and then everything around me goes black.

When I wake I am on my back, looking up at a purple sky. An early morning sky. I am lying on a blanket outside the hovel. I sit up and Abdel Jameela hunches over me with his sour smell. Farther away, near the hill-path, I see the black shape of his wife.

"Professor, you are awake! Good!" the hermit says. "We were about to leave."

But we are glad to have the chance to thank you.

My heart skips and my stomach clenches as I hear that voice in my head again. Kitten purrs and a crushed cardamom scent linger beneath the demon's words. I look at Abdel Jameela's legs.

They are sleek and covered in fur the color of almonds. And each leg ends in a perfect cloven hoof. He walks on them with a surprising grace.

Yes, learned one, my beloved husband lives and stands on two hooves. It would not be so if we hadn't had your help. You have our gratitude.

Dazedly clambering to my feet, I nod in the she-ghoul's direction. Abdel Jameela claps me on the back wordlessly and takes a few goat-strides toward the hill-path. His wife makes a slight bow to me. *With my people, learned one, gratitude is more than a word. Look toward the hovel.*

I turn and look. And my breath catches.

A hoard right out of the stories. Gold and spices. Jewels and musks. Silver and silks. Porcelain and punks of aloe.

It is probably ten times the dowry Shireen's father seeks.

We leave you this and wish you well. I have purged the signs of our work in the hovel. And in the language of the donkeys, I have called two wild asses to carry your goods. No troubles left to bother our brave friend!

I manage to smile gratefully with my head high for one long moment. Blood and bits of the old man's bone still stain my hands. But as I look on

Abdel Jameela and his wife in the light of the sunrise, all my thoughts are not grim or grisly.

As they set off on the hill-path the she-ghoul takes Abdel Jameela's arm, and the hooves of husband and wife scrabble against the pebbles of Beit Zujaaj Hill. I stand stock-still, watching them walk toward the land of the ghouls.

They cross a bend in the path and disappear behind the hill. And a faint voice, full of mischievous laughter and smelling of early morning love in perfumed sheets, whispers in my head. *No troubles at all, learned one. For last night your Shireen's husband-to-be lost his battle with the destroyer of delights.*

Can it really be so? The old vulture dead? And me a rich man? I should laugh and dance. Instead I am brought to my knees by the heavy memory of blood-spattered golden hooves. I wonder whether Shireen's suitor died from his illness, or from malicious magic meant to reward me. I fear for my soul. For a long while I kneel there and cry.

But after a while I can cry no longer. Tears give way to hopes I'd thought dead. I stand and thank Beneficent God, hoping it is not wrong to do so. Then I begin to put together an acceptable story about a secretly wealthy hermit who has rewarded me for saving his wife's life. And I wonder what Shireen and her father will think of the man I have become.

Saladin Ahmed was born in Detroit. He has been a finalist for the Campbell Award for Best New Science Fiction or Fantasy Writer and the Harper's Pen Award for Best Sword and Sorcery / Heroic Fantasy Short Story. His fiction has appeared in magazines and podcasts including *Strange Horizons, Orson Scott Card's InterGalactic Medicine Show, Beneath Ceaseless Skies, Apex Magazine,* and *PodCastle,* and has been translated into Portuguese, Czech, and Dutch. His fantasy novel *Throne of the Crescent Moon* is forthcoming from DAW Books. His website is www.saladinahmed.com.

I REMEMBER THE FUTURE

Michael A. Burstein

FROM THE AUTHOR: When Apex Publications decided to publish a collection of my award-nominated short stories, I asked the readers of my LiveJournal if they could help me come up with an appropriate title. My high school friend Andrew Marc Greene suggested the title *I Remember the Future* as a fitting one for the type of stories I tend to write. I agreed, but that meant writing a new story with that title as well. I kept running the phrase "I Remember the Future" over and over in my head, but no story idea came to mind. And then on the afternoon of Tuesday, March 18, 2008, we heard the news that Arthur C. Clarke had died. (Oddly, because Clarke lived in a time zone farther east, he died on Wednesday, March 19, but those of us living in the West heard the news on Tuesday. It's almost like time travel.)

Late that night, as I stared into a mirror and thought about how the last of the Big Three was gone, I suddenly realized what this story had to be about. I quickly shared the idea with my wife, Nomi, and then jotted down a bunch of notes so I wouldn't forget it. I also called Janna Silverstein, since I needed to tell another science fiction and fantasy writer about the epiphany I just had, and it was too late to call anyone on the East Coast. "I Remember the Future" is about an elderly science-fiction writer named Abraham Beard (the name is a joke between my high school friend Charles Ardai and me, as we both have used it for writers or editors who are characters in our stories). Abraham has spent his life writing of various hopeful futures, and he is disappointed that none of them have come to pass. He reaches out to his adult daughter Emma, to connect with the future one last time, but Emma and her own family are moving away, and she rejects his overtures as being too little, too late. From Emma's perspective, her father spent far too much of his life pursuing his writing career with his head lost in the clouds and too little time connecting with his family. Abraham acknowledges this in the story when he says, "I consider once again telling her what I've told her before: that times were tough, that money was tight, and that Sheila and I both had to work to support Emma properly. But then I recall the many times I shut the door of my home office on Emma to meet a deadline, and I realize that the chance for apologies and explanations has passed far into the mists of time." As the story ends, Abraham connects with his other progeny, the characters he created in his infinite worlds.

The story is somber but hopeful. I had fun writing the selections from Abraham's own novels that I worked throughout the narrative, as I had to capture the feel of science fiction from the various decades of the twentieth century. The story also tackles head-on the minor controversy that nowadays many science fiction and fantasy writers are looking to the past more than to the future; the story suggests that we should embrace that past rather than reject it. As Shakespeare said in *The Tempest*, "What's past is prologue."

"I Remember the Future" isn't my first foray into recursive science fiction meant to honor those writers who came before us; my Hugo nominees "Cosmic Corkscrew" and "Paying It Forward" also show my interest in this theme.

"I Remember the Future" is dedicated to Arthur C. Clarke.

I REMEMBER THE FUTURE.
The future was glorious once. It was filled with sleek silver spaceships, lunar colonies, and galactic empires. The horizon seemed within reach; we could almost grasp the stars if we would but try.

I helped to create that future once. We created it out of our blood, sweat, and tears for a penny a word. We churned that future out onto reams of wood pulp paper, only to see the bitter acids of the decades eat it away. I can still smell the freshness of that world, amidst the stale odors left in the libraries, real ink on real paper.

But I despair that no one else does.

Smith turned to Angela, whose face was obscured by the glass plate of her helmet. Despite the higher gravity and the bulkiness of his environmental suit, he felt like jumping a hundred feet into the vacuum.

"Angela, look!"

"What is it?" she asked. She reached over with her gloved hands to take the object from him.

"Gently," he said as he handed over the sheet. "It's paper. Real paper."

Angela took it and handled it almost reverently. Once again, she looked around the large cavern at the many inscribed marble columns, flashing her light into every dark corner.

"Paper? That dead wood stuff you told me about? Made from trees?"

Smith nodded. "It's true. We've found the ancient lost library of New Earth. And maybe, just maybe, in these volumes we'll find the final clue that will lead us to the location of the original human home world."

—Abraham Beard,
The Searchers (1950)

The day after my diagnosis, Emma comes to visit me at home. When she rings the bell, I get up from my seat in the living room, where I've been watching *Forbidden Planet* on DVD for the past hour, and I shuffle over to the front door at the end of the hall.

A cold wind blasts me as I creak open the door. I shiver momentarily as Emma strides past me.

As I shut the door, she opens the hall closet and lets her hands dance upon the hangers. She ignores the empty wooden ones and selects a blue plastic one.

"It's the middle of the day and you're still in your bathrobe?" she asks me as she slips off her overcoat.

"I'm retired and it's the weekend," I say. "Why should I get dressed up?"

"Because your only daughter is coming to visit? Oh, never mind." She hangs up her coat.

"Where's Frank and the kids?" I ask her.

She sniffs. "They decided to stay at home."

The kids decided to stay at home. My grandchildren, Zachary and Kenneth. Or Zach and Ken, as Emma told me they prefer to be called. I haven't seen them in months. "They didn't feel like schlepping out to Queens?"

"It's too cold."

"So why the visit?"

Emma purses her lips and glances at the floor. "I thought it would be nice to see you."

I know there must be more to it than that, but I don't press it. Emma will tell me in her own sweet time. "Are you hungry?" I ask as we walk to the living room. "Do you want something to eat?"

She smiles. "What are you going to offer this time? A red pepper? A clementine?"

As it so happens, the refrigerator crisper holds many peppers and clementines, but I refuse to give Emma the satisfaction. "I thought you might want some ice cream."

"Ice cream?" she asks with bemusement. "Sure, I'd love some ice cream. Where is it?"

"It's in the freezer," I tell her, although it should be obvious. Where else does one keep ice cream?

The first thing Larry noticed was the cold. It filled the core of his being, then slowly began to recede as tendrils of warmth entered his body.

Then he noticed a faint-white light blinking in the distance. Either the light became larger or it moved closer, and it continued to pulsate in a regular rhythm.

And finally he heard a hiss, the sound of air leaking quickly across a barrier. He tried to breathe and felt as if his lungs were filled with liquid. He tried again —

— when suddenly a door swung open, and Larry realized that he was floating vertically in a round glass chamber. The gelatinous liquid surrounding him quickly drained, and Larry fell into the arms of two men in silver jumpsuits.

"Easy now," the taller one said. "Your muscles need time to adjust."

Larry shook off their support. "I'm fine," he croaked. He coughed up some fluid and spoke again. "I don't need any help."

"If you say so," the taller man said.

"I do, indeed," Larry answered. He stretched out of his stoop, and although his legs felt like they would give way, he refused to give these strangers the satisfaction of seeing him fall.

"Where am I? What's going on?" he asked.

"All in due time," the shorter man said in a thin, reedy voice.

Larry turned to stare at him. "I am Larry Garner, the richest man on Earth, and I demand you tell me what's going on, now!"

The two men looked at each other, and the shorter one shrugged. "Usually, we give people more time to adjust, but if you insist —"

"I do!"

"You're in the future," the man said. "It's two thousand years since you died."

Larry fainted.

—Abraham Beard,
The Unfrozen (1955)

"Earth to Dad? Hello? Are you there?"

Emma is waving a hand in front of my face.

"Sorry," I say. "I was just thinking. My mind—"

"Was elsewhen. Yeah, I've heard that before."

I realize that we are sitting in the dining room and that Emma has scooped two bowls of ice cream, one for each of us. I pick up my spoon and take a bite. It's butter pecan.

I hate butter pecan, but I bought some for when Zach and Ken were last here.

The ice cream is very badly freezer-burned. It's so cold against my tongue that it hurts. I put the spoon down into the bowl and watch Emma eat her ice cream.

"You can take the rest of it when you leave," I say. "The kids might enjoy it."

Emma gives me a half-smile. "Even with the cold outside, it'll probably still melt before I get it home."

"Oh," I say.

We sit in silence for a few moments, the only sound the tick of the analog clock in the other room, the clock my wife, Sheila, bought when we got married, the clock that hangs above the flatscreen television set that Emma and Frank gave me for my last birthday.

"So, how are things?"

"Things are good."

"The kids doing well at school?"

"Yeah." Emma smiles. "Zach did a PowerPoint presentation on blogging for one of his teachers."

I nod and try to keep my face neutral, but Emma sees right through me. "You disapprove?"

"It's not that," I say. "It's just—"

"I know what it is. Rant number twenty-three."

"I'm not that predictable."

She crosses her arms. "Fine. Then what were you thinking?"

I pause for a moment, but she doesn't sound sarcastic so I say, "When I was growing up, the future seemed so full of possibilities."

"We have possibilities, Dad."

I shake my head. "We've turned inward. All of us have. We used to dream of a world as big as the sky. Now we're all hunched over our tiny screens."

Emma rolls her eyes. "Like I said, rant number twenty-three. Within three sentences, you're going from the Internet to the lack of a manned space program again."

"You don't think it's a problem?"

"It's just that I've heard it before."

"The more true something is, the more it bears repeating."

"Nothing bears repeating if you can't do anything about it." She sighs. "I mean, seriously, what did you ever expect me to do at the age of twelve when you first warned me about the eventual heat-death of the universe?"

The starship *HaTikvah* had finally made it to the edge of the universe. A hopeful mood filled the souls of the fifty thousand humans and aliens who occupied the ship, each the last of their kind.

On the bridge, Captain Sandra McAllister spoke into her intercom. "Fellow sentients," she said, "this is the proverbial 'it.' The universe is ending, the embers of the stars are fading into nothing, and in a moment we'll tap into the power of Black Hole Omega. If all goes according to plan, we'll break out of our dying universe and into a new one, one that's young and vibrant. Our own personal lives will continue, but more importantly, we will continue to exist in order to be able to remember all of those who came before us."

McAllister turned to her first officer and said, "Any time you're ready, Jacob. Push the button."

Jacob nodded and reached out with his spindly fingers to the Doorway Device. But just as he was about to depress the red button, a blast rocked the ship.

"What was that?" he cried out.

Virilion, the ship's robotic helmsman, replied in a croak, "It's the Nichashim! They've come to stop us!"

McAllister narrowed her eyes. "Like hell they will," she said. "Virilion, fire at will! Blast them out of our sky!"

—Abraham Beard,
Fire and Ice (1980)

"Dad? Dad?"

"You don't need to shout."

"You were gone again," she says.

"Perhaps," I say, "I'm turning inward because I'm getting old."

For the first time since she came into the house today, Emma looks worried. "You're not that old, Dad."

I smile at Emma to keep her from noticing the wetness I feel in my eyes. "That's nice of you to say, but it's not true. I *am* old."

"You're only as old as you feel. You told me that once."

I shake my head. "It's hard to feel young when so many of my colleagues are gone." *First Robert, then Isaac, now Arthur,* I think, although I don't say it aloud. I know Emma too well; she might laugh at me for placing myself among such giants.

Instead, she doesn't seem to know what to say in response. She fidgets for a few seconds, eats some more ice cream, and then changes the subject.

"Listen, Dad, I'm here because I have news."

"Funny, so do I. You go first."

"Are you sure?"

"Yes, I'm sure. What is it?" I ask.

She takes a deep breath and looks me in the eye. "We're moving to California."

Jackie looked at the gleaming silver spaceship with portholes running all up and down its sides. She felt more excited than she ever had before in her six years of life. Soon, her family would leave behind this polluted, depressing planet for a new world filled with cool green fields, rich with possibilities.

Jackie's mother and father held tightly onto her hands as the three of them walked in the line out onto the launching pad. The hoverlift floated next to them, carrying their luggage, while Jackie's robot dog kept running ahead and back toward Jackie, matching her excitement.

Finally, after what seemed like hours but Jackie knew was only minutes according to her chronometer, Jackie and her parents made it to the open hatch of the spaceship. A stewardess, her hair dyed platinum blonde, stood at the doorway greeting the immigrants with a big smile. She took their tickets and welcomed them aboard.

"Is this really it, Dad?" Jackie asked.

Her father removed the pipe from his mouth and smiled. "It is indeed," he said. "Goodbye, Earth! Next stop, Mars!"

—Abraham Beard,
The Burns Family on Mars (1960)

"Dad? You're gone again."

"No, I'm not," I say.

"So," Emma says. "We're moving to California."

"Why?"

She takes a deep breath. "Frank's got a new job. UCLA is offering him a tenured position. Full professor."

"UCLA. *Hmm.* California." I try to sound as noncommittal as possible, although Emma must know how much this news hurts me.

"Yes, California."

"From what I hear, California is a nice place."

She frowns and looks puzzled. "Aren't you going to object?"

"Are you asking me to?"

"Don't you even want to know why we're moving?"

"You told me – Frank's got a job offer." I pause. "What about you?"

"What about me?"

"I don't think you'll be able to keep working at the New-York Historical Society if you're living in L.A. Have you found a job at a museum there?"

Now *she* pauses before speaking. "I'm not planning to get another job, at least not right away."

"Oh?"

"I want to be there full time for the kids."

I stare into her eyes, seeing the six-year-old girl who wanted nothing more than to be the first astronaut to walk on Jupiter. "Is that really what you want?"

She glares at me. "I think at least one parent should be devoted full time to raising the kids."

I feel the sting of her words. I consider once again telling her what I've told her before: that times were tough, that money was tight, and that Sheila and I both had to work to support Emma properly. But then I recall the many times I shut the door of my home office on Emma to meet a deadline, and I realize that the chance for apologies and explanations has passed far into the mists of time.

Allen Davidoff walked around the floating cube of mist, careful not to let any of the tendrils touch him. There was nothing else on this planet for miles around.

The Keeper, still covered entirely in her white garment, walked three paces behind him until he finally came to a stop.

He turned to face her. "Impressive," he said. "An atmospheric phenomenon?"

She laughed and her hazel eyes twinkled. "You are pretending to be the fool," she said. "You know better than that."

Allen nodded; she was right. He did know better, but he had previously allowed his hopes to be raised during his quixotic quest only to have them dashed time and time again.

"Then I've really found it?" he asked.

She nodded. "You have indeed."

Allen looked back into the white mist. "It's the Gateway of Time," he said. "I can go anywhen into the time stream I want."

"It's the Gateway of Time," the Keeper echoed. "You can go to any time period and any location in the universe you want. But there is one problem."

Allen waited. The Keeper remained silent as Allen's watch ticked off the seconds, and so finally he asked, "What's the problem?"

The Keeper grinned evilly. "The only problem is, once you've made your choice and entered the past, you can never return. The trip is one way and final."

"So—"

"So choose wisely."

—Abraham Beard,
Amidst the Mists (1991)

"I hope it works out for you," I say. "You know that I only want what's best for you and the kids."

If she notices that I don't mention Frank, she doesn't say anything about it. Instead, she nods and says, "You said before that you had news as well."

I open my mouth to tell her about my diagnosis, as I had planned to do when she first called to tell me that she and the family wanted to see me, but then I hold back. I'm not dying yet, but I am old. My doctors say that my mind is not as sharp as it once was and my years are drawing to a close. If I tell her, maybe she and Frank will postpone the move, or at least stay closer to New York City, so I can keep seeing them in my dwindling, final days.

The last man on Earth said farewell to the spaceship carrying the rest of humanity to the stars. As the ship became a tiny dot in the sky, he took a deep breath of the fresh air and smiled. Someone had to watch over the planet as it was dying, and it was only right, he felt, that it should be he, and only he.

—Abraham Beard,
The Final Days of Planet Earth (1970)

I decide not to tell Emma about the diagnosis. It wouldn't be fair to her or the kids to add that factor into the equation. But she's waiting for me to tell her my news, and I only have one other piece of news to share. It's extremely private, and possibly just the first symptom of my oncoming dementia, but I've felt the need to tell someone. And Emma is here, and Sheila is no longer here.

"Emma, may I confide in you?"

She tilts her head. "You never have before."

I open my mouth to object, and then realize that she has a point.

"Well, I want to confide in you now. You know all those stories, all those novels that I wrote?"

"Yes," she says flatly. "What about them?"

"My entire life, I never felt like I was coming up with anything on my own." I stare over her shoulder. "Sometimes, when I was lying awake at two or three in the morning, I would get the feeling that the images in my mind weren't just things I was making up myself. I felt as if I was a conduit, as if I had lifted an antenna into some sort of cosmic fog and that I was receiving messages, real messages, from the future in my dreams."

Emma sits stoically as I tell her this. I don't know what reaction I am hoping for, but Emma rolling her eyes is definitely not it. Still, it's what she gives me.

"So what's the news?"

"I'm not really sure," I say. "You know how I haven't written anything new for five years now? That's because the messages stopped. Except . . ."

"Except what?"

"The dreams have started up again. I've been waking up again in the middle of most nights, feeling as if the future is trying to reach me one more time. But as soon as I wake up, the images the future is trying to send me recede into the distance."

She sighs and stands up; I can't tell if she's angry or just frustrated. "You're bouncing story ideas off of me again, aren't you?"

"No," I say, shaking my head. "No, I'm not. This is really happening to me."

Emma's expression is pitiful. "So that's your excuse," she says softly. "The future was really trying to contact you, and that's why you always had your head lost in the clouds."

I try to protest, but, ironically, I have no words. Emma picks up the bowls and used spoons and takes them into the kitchen. I hear her wash them quickly and leave them on the drainer while I sit at the table, unsure of what to say to her to make it all better.

She emerges from the kitchen and dashes through to the hall closet. I hear her put on her coat, and then she is back in the dining room, standing over me.

"Dad, you were always so busy living in the future that you never enjoyed your present. And now you don't even live in the future anymore. You're living in the past."

With that, she walks out of the room and out of the house.

Over the next few days, Emma uses my spare set of keys to let herself into the house. She barely nods hello to me as she climbs to the attic and sifts through the boxes, packing away those few remnants that she wants from her childhood.

I want Emma to leave the photographs, but I've come to realize that she's going to have to take them with her anyway if I want my grandsons to continue to remember what their grandfather and grandmother looked like. Emma tells me that she will scan the photos into her computer and send me back the originals, and I just nod.

The days pass far too quickly. Finally, the last morning arrives in which Emma will be coming over to take the last few boxes of possessions. What she doesn't know as she is driving over is that this morning is also the morning of my final moments on this Earth. And in my final moments on this Earth, I am redeemed.

I am lying in my bed, wearing my favorite blue pajamas and peering through my glasses at the small print of a digest magazine. A half-eaten orange on a plate sits on my end table; I can still taste the juice on my tongue and feel a strand of pulp between two right molars.

And then it begins.

A slight breeze wafts toward me from the foot of my bed. I move my magazine aside and look, but I see nothing there but the wall and the closed bathroom door.

As I begin to read again, another breeze flutters my pages. Then the breeze builds, until a gust of wind flows past.

A tiny crack appears in midair, hovering about six and a half feet above the red-carpeted floor. The crack expands into a circular hole. White light emanates from the hole, which gets wider and wider, until it becomes a sphere about six feet in diameter, crackling softly with electricity. A human figure in a silver spacesuit, its face obscured by a helmet, emerges from the sphere with a loud popping sound.

I know this is no illusion, that whatever is happening in front of me is real. I manage to keep my composure and ask, "Who are you?"

The figure grabs hold of its helmet, breaks the seals, and pulls it off.

The astronaut is a woman. She shakes her long blonde hair out of her face and smiles. "You know who I am, Abe. Take a good look."

I do, and I feel a chill. "It can't be."

She nods. "It is."

"You're Sandra McAllister. But you're fictional. You don't exist. I made you up."

"Yes, you did make me up. But I do exist."

"I don't understand."

"We figured you might not, but we don't have a lot of time, so listen carefully. As far as our scientists have been able to determine, every time you wrote a story, you created a parallel universe, a place where the people you thought of really existed. Apparently, your brain has some connection on a quantum level with the zero-point energy field that exists in the multiverse. You've managed to bend reality, our reality, so that we ended up existing for real."

"That's not possible," I say.

"You're a rational man, Abe, I understand that. So explain my presence some other way."

I know in my heart and soul that I am not hallucinating. And with the impossible eliminated, I am left with the improbable.

"So you're real?"

"Not just me," Sandra says.

I start thinking of all the characters I created throughout my career. "Jackson Smith and Angela Jones? Larry Garner? Jackie Burns? Allen Davidoff? They're all real?"

Sandra nods after I recite each name. "They're all real. We're all real."

"Even if so, how did you break through the barrier between universes? It's not possible."

"It is if you harness the energy of a black hole using the Doorway Device."

I am puzzled for just a moment, and then light dawns. I recall the details of the story cycle from which Sandra comes. "The *HaTikvah* spaceship," I say.

"And the Nichashim," she adds.

I goggle. "You're mortal enemies," I say. "I wrote you that way. How can you be working together?"

"The Nichashim understand that you created them, too. We've got the two ships tethered together in orbit around New Black Hole Omega."

I can't help it; I flip the sheet off of my frail body and swing my legs around so I can stand up and face Sandra. "That's far too dangerous, Sandra. You could lose both ships in a blink."

"Which is why you must hurry."

"I don't understand."

"Why do you think I came here?"

"Um, to say hello? To let me know that I didn't live my life in vain?"

She rolls her eyes. "To rescue you. To cure you of your oncoming sickness, and to impart to you the same immortality you generously granted to all of us."

"Rescue me? You're using all that energy just to rescue me?"

She shrugged. "You're our father. Why wouldn't we?"

I feel tears starting in my eyes, and I move forward and hug Sandra as tightly as I can. She holds me as I cry.

"It's all right, Father," she says. "We've come for you. Welcome home."

The last bit I can only guess at, as I was already gone by then. But the way I see it, as Emma was turning her keys in the lock, the house rumbled, and she heard a loud pop and whoosh coming from upstairs.

"Dad? Dad?" she called out, but I wasn't there to answer her.

She dashed up the stairs and turned right, toward her father's bedroom. She pushed the door open to discover her father already gone, amidst a trace of ozone.

I remembered the future.

And in turn, the future remembered me.

Michael A. Burstein was born in New York City, where he attended Hunter College High School in Manhattan. He has physics degrees from Harvard College and Boston University, and he attended the Clarion Workshop in 1994. His short fiction has been nominated for ten Hugos and four Nebulas; in 1997 he won the John W. Campbell Award for Best New Writer. From 1998 to 2000 he served as secretary of SFWA. He and his wife, Nomi, live with their twin daughters in Brookline, Massachusetts, where he is an elected Library Trustee and Town Meeting Member.

NON-ZERO PROBABILITIES

N. K. Jemisin

FROM THE AUTHOR: It should be pretty obvious that the bulk of the story is a pastiche of my perfectly ordinary daily life in Brooklyn – riding the shuttle to work, traipsing to the farmers' market, thinking scornful thoughts about tourists as if I didn't just move here a few years ago myself, and so on. But there's an understated sort of magic in Brooklyn which I can feel throughout these perfectly ordinary walks and encounters. It rides my skin like humidity, thrums underneath every conversation. The awareness of this is what marks a true New Yorker, I think. You move here, feel out of place for awhile, and then suddenly snap! There's this moment where you feel it. You can look at another person who belongs here, who feels that same magic, and you *know*. It's like a secret handshake, except New Yorkers would never be so gauche. They'd just glance at each other. That would be enough.

So with "Non-Zero Probabilities," all I did was make that undercurrent of perpetual strangeness explicit. I'm thrilled with the response this story has gotten, but I completely didn't expect it, because as the story itself notes – what does it matter whether a city reacts to one improbable disaster (say, 9/11) or another (probability gone haywire)? The city remains, and reacts, the same. That's where the real magic lies.

IN THE MORNINGS, Adele girds herself for the trip to work as a warrior for battle. First she prays, both to the Christian god of her Irish ancestors and to the orishas of her African ancestors – the latter she is less familiar with, but getting to know. Then she takes a bath with herbs, including dried chickory and allspice, from a mixture given to her by the woman at the local botanica. (She doesn't know Spanish well, but she's getting to know that, too. Today's word is *suerte*.) Then, smelling vaguely of coffee and pumpkin pie, she layers on armor: the Saint Christopher medal her mother sent her, for protection on journeys. The hair-clasp she was wearing when she broke up with Larry, which she regards as the best decision of her life. On especially dangerous days, she wears the panties in which she experienced her first self-induced orgasm post-Larry; they're a bit ragged after too many commercial laundromat washings, but still more or less sound. (She washes them by hand now, with Woolite, and lays them flat to dry.)

Then she starts the trip to work. She doesn't bike, though she owns one. A next-door neighbor broke an arm when her bike's front wheel came off in mid-pedal. Could've been anything. Just an accident. But still.

So Adele sets out, swinging her arms, enjoying the day if it's sunny, wrestling with her shitty umbrella if it's rainy. (She no longer opens the umbrella indoors.) Keeping a careful eye out for those who may not be as well-protected. It takes two to tango, but only one to seriously fuck up some shit, as they say in her 'hood. And lo and behold, just three blocks into her trip there is a horrible crash and the ground shakes and car alarms go off and there are screams and people start running. Smoke billows, full of acrid ozone and a taste like dirty blood. When Adele reaches the corner, tensed and ready to flee, she beholds the Franklin Avenue shuttle train, a tiny thing that runs on an elevated track for some portions of its brief run, lying sprawled over Atlantic Avenue like a beached aluminum whale. It has jumped its track, fallen thirty feet to the ground below, and probably killed everyone inside or under or near it.

Adele goes to help, of course, but even as she and other good Samaritans pull bodies and screaming wounded from the wreckage, she cannot help but feel a measure of contempt. It is a cover, her anger; easier to feel that than horror at the shattered limbs, the truncated lives. She feels a bit ashamed, too, but holds onto the anger because it makes a better shield.

They should have known better. The probability of a train derailment was infinitesimal. That meant it was only a matter of time.

Her neighbor – the other one, across the hall – helped her figure it out, long before the math geeks finished crunching their numbers.

"Watch," he'd said, and laid a deck of cards facedown on her coffee table. (There was coffee in the cups, with a generous dollop of Baileys. He was a nice-enough guy that Adele felt comfortable offering this.)

He shuffled it with the blurring speed of an expert, cut the deck, shuffled again, then picked up the whole deck and spread it, still facedown. "Pick a card."

Adele picked. The Joker.

"Only two of those in the deck," he said, then shuffled and spread again. "Pick another."

She did, and got the other Joker.

"Coincidence," she said. (This had been months ago, when she was still skeptical.)

He shook his head and set the deck of cards aside. From his pocket he took a pair of dice. (He was nice enough to invite inside, but he was still *that* kind of guy.) "Check it," he said, and tossed them onto her table. Snake eyes. He scooped them up, shook them, tossed again. Two more ones. A third toss brought up double sixes; at this, Adele had pointed in triumph. But the fourth toss was snake eyes again.

"These aren't weighted, if you're wondering," he said. "Nobody filed the edges or anything. I got these from the bodega up the street, from a pile of shit the old man was tossing out to make more room for food shelves. Brand new, straight out of the package."

"Might be a bad set," Adele said.

"Might be. But the cards ain't bad, nor your fingers." He leaned forward, his eyes intent despite the pleasant haze that the Baileys had brought on. "Snake eyes three tosses out of four? And the fourth a double six. That ain't supposed to happen even in a rigged game. Now check *this* out."

Carefully he crossed the fingers of his free hand. Then he tossed the dice again, six throws this time. The snakes still came up twice, but so did other numbers. Fours and threes and twos and fives. Only one double six.

"That's batshit, man," said Adele.

"Yeah. But it works."

He was right. And so Adele had resolved to read up on gods of luck and to avoid breaking mirrors. And to see if she could find a four-leafed clover in the weed patch down the block. (They sell some in Chinatown, but she's heard they're knockoffs.) She's hunted through the patch several times in the past few months, once for several hours. Nothing so far, but she remains optimistic.

It's only New York, that's the really crazy thing. Yonkers? Fine. Jersey? Ditto. Long Island? Well, that's still Long Island. But past East New York everything is fine.

The news channels had been the first to figure out that particular wrinkle, but the religions really went to town with it. Some of them have been waiting for the End Times for the last thousand years; Adele can't really blame them for getting all excited. She does blame them for their spin on it, though. There have to be bigger "dens of iniquity" in the world. Delhi has poor people coming out of its ears, Moscow's mobbed up, Bangkok is pedophile heaven. She's heard there are still some sundown towns in the Pacific Northwest. Everybody hates on New York.

And it's not like the signs are all bad. The state had to suspend its lottery program; too many winners in one week bankrupted it. The Knicks made it to the Finals and the Mets won the Series. A lot of people with cancer went into spontaneous remission, and some folks with full-blown AIDS stopped showing any viral load at all. (There are new tours now. Double-decker buses full of the sick and disabled. Adele tries to tell herself they're just more tourists.)

The missionaries from out of town are the worst. On any given day they step in front of her, shoving tracts under her nose and wanting to know if she's saved yet. She's getting better at spotting them from a distance, yappy islands interrupting the sidewalk river's flow, their faces alight with an inner glow that no self-respecting local would display without three beers and a fat payday check. There's one now, standing practically underneath a scaffolding ladder. Idiot; two steps back and he'll double his chances for getting hit by a bus. (And then the bus will catch fire.)

In the same instant that she spots him, he spots her, and a grin stretches wide across his freckled face. She is reminded of blind newts that have light-sensitive spots on their skin. This one is *unsaved*-sensitive. She veers right, intending to go around the scaffold, and he takes a wide step into her path again. She veers left; he breaks that way.

She stops, sighing. "What."

"Have you accepted—"

"I'm Catholic. They do us at birth, remember?"

His smile is forgiving. "That doesn't mean we can't talk, does it?"

"I'm busy." She attempts a feint, hoping to catch him off-guard. He moves with her, nimble as a linebacker.

"Then I'll just give you this," he says, tucking something into her hand. Not a tract, bigger. A flyer. "The day to remember is August 8th."

This, finally, catches Adele's attention. August 8th: 8/8 – a lucky day according to the Chinese. She has it marked on her calendar as a good day to do things like rent a Zipcar and go to Ikea.

"Yankee Stadium," he says. "Come join us. We're going to pray the city back into shape."

"Sure, whatever," she says, and finally manages to slip around him. (He lets her go, really. He knows she's hooked.)

She waits until she's out of downtown before she reads the flyer, because downtown streets are narrow and close and she has to keep an eye out. It's a hot day; everybody's using their air conditioners. Most people don't bolt the things in the way they're supposed to.

"A PRAYER FOR THE SOUL OF THE CITY," the flyer proclaims, and in spite of herself, Adele is intrigued. The flyer says that over 500,000 New Yorkers have committed to gathering on that day and concentrating their prayers. *That kind of thing has power now,* she thinks. There's some lab at Princeton – dusted off and given new funding lately – that's been able to prove it. Whether that means Someone's listening or just that human thoughtwaves are affecting events as the scientists say, she doesn't know. She doesn't care.

She thinks, *I could ride the train again.*

She could laugh at the next Friday the 13th.

She could – and here her thoughts pause, because there's something she's been trying not to think about, but it's been awhile and she's never been a very good Catholic girl anyway. But she could, maybe, just maybe, try dating again.

As she thinks this, she is walking through the park. She passes the vast lawn, which is covered in fast-darting black children and lazily sunning white adults and a few roving brown elders with Italian ice carts. Though she is usually on watch for things like this, the flyer has distracted her, so she does not notice the nearby cart-man stopping, cursing in Spanish because one of his wheels has gotten mired in the soft turf.

This puts him directly in the path of a child who is running, his eyes trained on a descending Frisbee; with the innate arrogance of a city child he has assumed that the cart will have moved out of the way by the time he gets there. Instead the child hits the cart at full speed, which catches Adele's attention at last, so that too late she realizes she is at the epicenter of one of those devastating chains of events that only ever happen in comedy films and the transformed city. In a Rube Goldberg string of utter improbabilities, the cart tips over, spilling tubs of brightly colored ices onto the grass. The boy flips over it with acrobatic precision, completely by accident, and lands with both feet on the tub of ices. The sheer force of this blow causes the tub to eject its contents with projectile force. A blast of blueberry-coconut-red hurtles toward Adele's face, so fast that she has no time to scream. It will taste delicious. It will also likely knock her into oncoming bicycle traffic.

At the last instant the Frisbee hits the flying mass, altering its trajectory. Freezing fruit flavors splatter the naked backs of a row of sunbathers nearby, much to their dismay.

Adele's knees buckle at the close call. She sits down hard on the grass, her heart pounding, while the sunbathers scream and the cart-man checks to see if the boy is okay and the pigeons converge.

She happens to glance down. A four-leafed clover is growing there, at her fingertips.

Eventually she resumes the journey home. At the corner of her block, she sees a black cat lying atop a garbage can. Its head has been crushed, and someone has attempted to burn it. She hopes it was dead first, and hurries on.

Adele has a garden on the fire escape. In one pot, eggplant and herbs; she has planted the clover in this. In another pot are peppers and flowers. In the big one, tomatoes and a scraggly collard that she's going to kill if she keeps harvesting leaves so quickly. (But she likes greens.) It's luck – good luck – that she'd chosen to grow a garden this year, because since things changed it's been harder for wholesalers to bring food into the city, and prices have shot up. The farmers' market that she attends on Saturdays has become a barterers' market, too, so she plucks a couple of slim, deep-purple eggplants and a handful of angry little peppers. She wants fresh fruit. Berries, maybe.

On her way out, she knocks on the neighbor's door. He looks surprised as he opens it, but pleased to see her. It occurs to her that maybe he's been hoping for a little luck of his own. She gives it a think-over, and hands him an eggplant. He looks at it in consternation. (He's not the kind of guy to eat eggplant.)

"I'll come by later and show you how to cook it," she says. He grins.

At the farmers' market she trades the angry little peppers for sassy little raspberries, and the eggplant for two stalks of late rhubarb. She also wants information, so she hangs out awhile gossiping with whoever sits nearby. Everyone talks more than they used to. It's nice.

And everyone, everyone she speaks to, is planning to attend the prayer.

"I'm on dialysis," says an old lady who sits under a flowering tree. "Every time they hook me up to that thing I'm scared. Dialysis can kill you, you know."

It always could, Adele doesn't say.

"I work on Wall Street," says another woman, who speaks briskly and clutches a bag of fresh fish as if it's gold. Might as well be; fish is expensive now. A tiny Egyptian scarab pendant dangles from a necklace the woman wears. "Quantitative analysis. All the models are fucked now. We were the only ones they didn't fire when the housing market went south, and now this." So she's going to pray, too. "Even though I'm kind of an atheist. Whatever, if it works, right?"

Adele finds others, all tired of performing their own daily rituals, all worried about their likelihood of being outliered to death.

She goes back to her apartment building, picks some sweet basil, and takes it next door. Her neighbor seems a little nervous. His apartment is cleaner than she's ever seen it, with the scent of Pine-Sol still strong in the bathroom. She tries not to laugh, and demonstrates how to peel and slice eggplant, salt it to draw out the toxins ("it's related to nightshade, you know"), and sauté it with basil in olive oil. He tries to look impressed, but she can tell he's not the kind of guy to enjoy eating his vegetables.

Afterward they sit, and she tells him about the prayer thing. He shrugs. "Are you going?" she presses.

"Nope."

"Why not? It could fix things."

"Maybe. Maybe I like the way things are now."

This stuns her. "Man, the *train fell off its track* last week." Twenty people dead. She has woken up in a cold sweat on the nights since, screams ringing in her ears.

"Could've happened anytime," he says, and she blinks in surprise because it's true. The official investigation says someone – track worker, maybe – left a wrench sitting on the track near a power coupling. The chance that the wrench would hit the coupling, causing a short and explosion, was one in a million. But never zero.

"But . . . but . . ." She wants to point out the other horrible things that have occurred. Gas leaks. Floods. A building fell down, in Harlem. A fatal duck attack. Several of the apartments in their building are empty because a lot of people can't cope. Her neighbor – the other one, with the broken arm – is moving out at the end of the month. Seattle. Better bike paths.

"Shit happens," he says. "It happened then, it happens now. A little more shit, a little less shit . . ." He shrugs. "Still shit, right?"

She considers this. She considers it for a long time.

They play cards, and have a little wine, and Adele teases him about the overdone chicken. She likes that he's trying so hard. She likes even more that she's not thinking about how lonely she's been.

So they retire to his bedroom and there's awkwardness and she's shy because it's been awhile and you do lose some skills without practice, and he's clumsy because he's probably been developing bad habits from porn, but eventually they manage. They use a condom. She crosses her fingers while he puts it on. There's a rabbit's foot keychain attached to the bed railing, which he strokes before returning his attention to her. He swears he's clean, and she's on the pill, but . . . well. Shit happens.

She closes her eyes and lets herself forget for awhile.

The prayer thing is all over the news. The following week is the runup. Talking heads on the morning shows speculate that it should have some effect, if enough people go and exert "positive energy." They are careful not to use the language of any particular faith; this is still New York. Alternative events are being planned all over the city for those who don't want to come under the evangelical tent. The sukkah mobiles are rolling – though it's the wrong time of year – just getting the word out about something happening at one of the synagogues. In Flatbush, Adele can't walk a block without being hit up by Jehovah's Witnesses. There's a "constructive visualization" somewhere for the ethical humanists. Not everybody believes God, or gods, will save them. It's just that this is the way the world works now, and everybody gets that. If crossed fingers can temporarily alter a dice throw, then why not something bigger? There's nothing inherently special about crossed fingers. It's only a "lucky" gesture because people believe in it. Get them to believe in something else, and that should work, too.

Except . . .

Adele walks past the Botanical Gardens, where preparations are under way for a big Shinto ritual. She stops to watch workers putting up a graceful red gate.

She's still afraid of the subway. She knows better than to get her hopes up about her neighbor, but still . . . he's kind of nice. She still plans her mornings around her ritual ablutions, and her walks to work around danger-spots – but how is that different, really, from what she did before? Back then it was makeup and hair, and fear of muggers. Now she walks more than she used to; she's lost ten pounds. Now she knows her neighbors' names.

Looking around, she notices other people standing nearby, also watching the gate go up. They glance at her, some nodding, some smiling, some ignoring her and looking away. She doesn't have to ask if *they* will be attending one of the services; she can see that they won't be. Some people react to fear by seeking security, change, control. The rest accept the change and just go on about their lives.

"Miss?" She glances back, startled, to find a young man there, holding forth a familiar flyer. He's not as pushy as the guy downtown; once she takes it, he moves on. The PRAYER FOR THE SOUL OF THE CITY is tomorrow. Shuttle buses ("Specially blessed!") will be picking up people at sites throughout the city.

WE NEED YOU TO BELIEVE, reads the bottom of the flyer.

Adele smiles. She folds the flyer carefully, her fingers remembering the skills of childhood, and presently it is perfect. They've printed the flyer on good, heavy paper.

She takes out her St. Christopher, kisses it, and tucks it into the rear folds to weight the thing properly.

Then she launches the paper airplane, and it flies and flies and flies, dwindling as it travels an impossible distance, until it finally disappears into the bright blue sky.

N. K. Jemisin is a New York City author. Although she has written novels since childhood (to varying degrees of success), she began writing short stories in 2002 after attending the Viable Paradise writing workshop. Thereafter she joined the Boston-Area SF Writers Group (now BRAWLers), until 2007 when she moved to New York. She is currently a member of the Altered Fluid writing group.

Jemisin's short fiction has been published in a variety of print, online, and audio markets, including *Clarkesworld*, *Strange Horizons*, *Postscripts*, and *Jim Baen's Universe*. She was the first recipient of the Speculative Literature Foundation's Gulliver Travel Research Grant, which was awarded for her short story sample "L'Alchimista." This story and "Cloud Dragon Skies" received Honorable Mentions in two editions of *The Year's Best Fantasy and Horror*, and her short story "Playing Nice With God's Bowling Ball" received an Honorable Mention in *The Year's Best Science Fiction*. Her short story "Cloud Dragon Skies" was also on the Carl Brandon Society's "Recommended" shortlist for the Parallax Award. This story, "Non-Zero Probabilities," also appeared on the 2010 Hugo Awards Ballot. Her first novel, *The Hundred Thousand Kingdoms*, was published by Orbit Books. It is the first of a trilogy, and has received starred reviews from *Publishers Weekly* and *Library Journal*. A full bibliography of her work can be found at nkjemisin.com.

GOING DEEP

James Patrick Kelly

FROM THE AUTHOR: "Going Deep" marked my twenty-fifth appearance in the June issue of *Asimov's Science Fiction Magazine*. Although this streak started entirely by chance, in time it became a centerpiece of my career: most of my Nebula nominees were children of June. I am eternally grateful to the three editors who published these stories, Shawna McCarthy, Gardner Dozois, and Sheila Williams. However, all things must pass, and "Going Deep" is my last June story – for now, at least. Thanks much to my friends and colleagues for the honor of ending my run with a nomination.

MARISKA SHIVERED WHEN she realized that her room had been tapping at the dreamfeed for several minutes. "The Earth is up," it murmured in its gentle singing accent. "Daddy Al is up and I am always up. Now Mariska gets up."

Mariska groaned, determined not to allow her room in. Recently she had been dreaming her own dreams of Jak and his long fingers and the fuzz on his chin and the way her throat tightened when she brushed up against him. But this was one of her room's feeds, one of the best ones, one she had been having as long as she could remember. In it, she was in space, but she wasn't on the moon and she wasn't wearing her hardsuit. There were stars every way she turned. Of course, she'd seen stars through the visor of her helmet but these were always different. Not a scatter of light but a swarm. And they all were singing their names, calling to her to come to them. She could just make out the closest ones: *Alpha Centauri. Barnard's. Wolf. Lalande. Luyten. Sirius.*

"The Earth is up, Daddy Al is up, and I am always up," her room insisted. "Now Mariska gets up." If she didn't wake soon, it would have to sound the gong.

"Slag it." She rolled over, awake and grumpy. Her room had been getting on her last nerve recently When she had been a little girl, she had roused at its whisper, but in the last few weeks it had begun nagging her to wake up. She knew it loved her and was only worried about her going deep, but she was breathing regularly and her heartbeat was probably in the high sixties. It monitored her, so it had to know she was just sleeping.

She thought this was all about Al. He was getting nervous; so her room was nervous.

"*Dobroye utro,*" said Feodor Bear. "Good morn-ing Mar-i-ska." The ancient toy robot stood up on its shelf, wobbled, and then sat down abruptly. It was over a century old and, in Mariska's opinion, needed to be put out of its misery.

"Good morning, dear Mariska," said her room. "Today is Friday, June 15, 2159. You are expected today in Hydroponics and at the Muoi swimming pool. This Sunday is Father's Day."

"I know, I *know*." She stuck her foot out from underneath the covers and wiggled her toes in the cool air. Her room began to bring the temperature up from sleeping to waking levels.

"I could help you find something for Daddy Al, if you'd like." Her room painted Buycenter icons on the wall. "We haven't shopped together in a while."

"Maybe later." Sometimes she felt guilty that she wasn't spending enough time with her room, but its persona kept treating her like a baby. Still calling him *Daddy Al*, for example; it was embarrassing. And she would get to all her expectations eventually. What choice did she have?

The door slid aside a hand's width and Al peered through the opening.

"Rise and shine, Mariska." His smile was a crack on a worried face. "Pancakes for breakfast," he said. "But only if you get up now." He blew a kiss that she ducked away from.

"I'm shining already," she grumbled. "Your own little star."

As she stepped through the cleanser, she wondered what to do about him. She knew exactly what was going on. The *Gorshkov* had just returned from exploring the *Delta Pavonis* system, which meant they'd probably be hearing soon from Natalya Volochkova. And Mariska had just turned thirteen; in another year she'd be able to vote, sign contracts, get married. This was the way the world worked: now that she was almost an adult, it was time for Al to go crazy. All her friends' parents had. The symptoms were hard to ignore: embarrassing questions like *where was she going?* and *who was she going with?* and *who else would be there?* He said he trusted her but she knew he'd slap a trace on her if he thought he could get away with it. But what was the point? This was the moon. There were security cams over every safety hatch. How much trouble could she get into? Walk out an airlock without a suit? She wasn't suicidal – or dumb. Have sex and get pregnant? She was *patched* – when she finally jumped a boy, pregnancy wouldn't be an issue. Crash from some toxic feed? She was young – she'd get over it.

The fact that she loved Al's strawberry pancakes did nothing to improve her mood at breakfast. He was unusually quiet, which meant he was working his courage up for some stupid fathering talk. Something in the news? She brought her gossip feed up on the tabletop to see what was going on. The scrape of his knife on the plate as she scanned headlines made her want to shriek. Why did he have to use her favorite food as a bribe so that he could pester her?

"You heard about that boy from Penrose High?" he said at last. "The one in that band you used to like . . . No Exit? Final Exit?"

"You're talking about Last Exit to Nowhere?" That gossip was so old it had curled around the edges and blown away. "Deltron Cleen?"

"That's him." He stabbed one last pancake scrap and pushed it into a pool of syrup. "They say he was at a party a couple of weeks ago and opened his head to everyone there; I forget how many mindfeeds he accepted."

"So?" She couldn't believe he was pushing Deltron Cleen at her.

"You knew him?"

"I've met him, sure."

"You weren't there, were you?" He actually squirmed, like he had ants crawling up his leg. "When it happened?"

"Oh sure. And when he keeled over, I was the one who gave him CPR." Mariska pinched her nose closed and puffed air at him. "Saved his life – the board of supers is giving me a medal next Thursday."

"This is serious, Mariska. Taking feeds from people you don't know is dangerous."

"Unless they're schoolfeeds. Or newsfeeds. Or dreamfeeds."

"Those are datafeeds. And they're screened."

"God feeds, then."

He sank back against his chair. "You're not joining a church, are you?"

"No." She laughed and patted his hand. "I'm okay, Al. Trust me. I love you and everything is okay."

"I know that." He was so flustered he slipped his fork in his pants pocket. "I know," he repeated, as if trying to convince himself.

"Poor Del is pretty stupid, even for a singer in a shoutcast band," she said. "What I heard was he accepted maybe a dozen feeds, but I guess there wasn't room in his head for more than him and a couple of really shallow friends. But he just crashed is all; they'll reboot him. Might even be an improvement." She reached across the table, picked up Al's empty plate, and slid it onto hers. "You never did anything like that, did you?" She carried them to the kitchen counter and pushed them through the processor door. "Accept mindfeeds from perfect strangers?"

"Not strangers, no."

"But you *were* young once, right? I mean, you weren't born a parent?"

"I'm a father, Mariska." He swiped his napkin across his lips and then folded it up absently. "You're a minor and still my responsibility. This is just me, trying to stay in touch."

"Extra credit to you, then." She check-marked the air. "But being a father is complicated. Maybe we should work on your technique?"

The door announced, "Jak is here."

"Got to go." Mariska grabbed her kit, kissed Al, and spun toward the door in relief. She felt bad for him sometimes. It wasn't his fault he took all the slag in the *Talking to Your Teen* feed so seriously.

Of course, the other reason why Al was acting up was because Mariska's genetic mother was about to swoop down on them. The *Gorshkov* had finally returned after a fifteen-year mission and was now docked at Sweetspot Station. Rumor was that humankind had a terrestrial world to colonize that was only three years away from the new *Delta Pavonis* wormhole. Natalya Volochkova was on the starship's roster as chief medical officer.

Mariska didn't hate her mother, exactly. How could she? They had never met. She knew very little about Volochkova and had no interest in finding out more. Ever, never. All she had from her were a couple of fossil toys: Feodor Bear and that stupid Little Mermaid aquarium. Collector's items from the twenty-first century, which was why Mariska had never been allowed to play with them.

What she did hate was the idea that decisions this stranger had made a decade and a half ago now ruled her life. She was Volochkova's clone and had been carried to term in a plastic womb, then placed in the care of one Alfred DeFord, a licensed father, under a term adoption contract. Her genetic mother had hired Al the way that some people hired secretaries; three fifths of Volochkova's salary paid for their comfortable, if unspectacular, lifestyle. Mariska knew that Al had come to love her over the years, but growing up with an intelligent room and a hired father for parents wouldn't have been her choice, had she been given one.

As if parking her with a hired father wasn't bad enough, Volochkova had cursed Mariska with spacer genes. Which was why she had to suffer though all those boring pre-space feeds from the Ed supers and why everyone was so worried that she might go deep into hibernation before her time and why she'd been matched with her one true love when she had been in diapers.

Actually, having Jak as a boyfriend wasn't all that much of a problem. She just wished that it didn't have to be so damn inevitable. She wanted to be the one to decide that a curly black mop was sexier than a blonde crewcut or that thin lips were more kissable than thick or that loyal was more attractive than smart. He was fifteen, already an adult, but still lived with his parents. Even though he was two years older than she was, they were in the same semester in the spacer program.

Jak listened as Mariska whined, first about Volochkova and then about Al's breakfast interrogation, as they skated to the hydroponics lab. He knew when to squeeze her hand, when to emit understanding moans and concerned grunts. This was what he called taking the weight, and she was gratified by his capacity to bear her up when she needed it. They were good together, in the 57th percentile on the Hammergeld Scale, according to their Soc super. Although she wondered if there might be some other boy for her somewhere, Mariska was resigned to the idea that, unless she was struck by a meteor or kidnapped by aliens, she would drag him into bed one of these days and marry him when she turned fourteen and then they would hibernate happily ever after on their way to Lalande 21185 or Barnard's Star or wherever.

"But we were there, 'Ska," Jak said, as the safety hatch to the lab slid aside. "Del asked *you* to open your head." He bent over to crank the rollers into the soles of his shoes.

"Which is why we left." She pulled a disposable green clingy from the dispenser next to the safety door and shrugged into it. "Which is why we were already in Chim Zone when the EMTs went by, which means we *weren't* really there. How many times do I have to go over this?" She gave him a friendly push toward his bench and headed toward her own, which was on the opposite side of the lab.

Mariska checked the chemistry of her nutrient solution. Phosphorus was down 50ppm so she added a pinch of ammonium dihydrogen phosphate. She was raising tomatoes in rockwool spun from lunar regolith. Sixteen new blossoms had opened since Tuesday and needed to be pollinated; she used one of the battery operated toothbrushes that Mr. Holmgren, the Ag super, favored. Mariska needed an average yield of 4.2 kilograms per plant in order to complete this unit; her tomatoes wouldn't be ripe for another eight weeks. Jak was on tomatoes, too; his spring crop had had an outbreak of mosaic virus and so he was repeating the unit.

Other kids straggled into the lab as she worked. Grieg, who had the bench next to hers, offered one of his lima beans, which she turned down, and a hit from his sniffer, which she took. Megawatt waved hello and Fung stopped by to tell her that their *Gorshkov* tour had been rescheduled for Tuesday, which she already knew.

After a while, Random ambled in, using a vacpac to clean up the nutrient spills and leaf litter. He had just washed out of the spacer program but his mother was a Med super so he was hanging around as a janitor until she decided what to do with him. Everyone knew why he had failed. He was a feed demon; his head was like a digital traffic jam. However, unlike Del Cleen, Random had never once crashed. They said that if you ever opened yourself wide to him, even just for an instant, you would be so filled with other people's thoughts that you would never think your own again.

He noticed her staring and saluted her with the wand of his vacuum cleaner. It was funny, he didn't look all that destroyed to Mariska. Sleepy maybe, or bored, or a little high, but not as if he had had his individuality crushed. Besides, even though he was too skinny, she thought he was kind of cute. Not for the first time, she wondered what their Hammergeld compatibility score might be.

Mariska felt the tingle of Jak offering a mindfeed. She opened her head a crack and accepted.

=giving up for today= She was relieved that Jak just wanted to chat. =you?=

=ten minutes= Mariska was still getting used to chatting in public. She and Jak had been more intimate, of course, had even opened wide for full mental convergence a couple of times, but that had been when they were by themselves, sitting next to each other in a dark room. Swapping thoughts was all the mindfeed she could handle without losing track of where she was. After all, she was still a kid.

=how's your fruit set?= Jak's feed always felt like a fizzing behind her eyes.

=fifty, maybe sixty= She noticed Random drifting toward her side of the lab. =this sucks=

=tomatoes?=

=hydroponics=

=spacers got to eat=

=spacers suck=

Jak's pleasant fizz gave way to a bubble of annoyance. =you're a spacer=

Mariska had begun to have her doubts about that, but this didn't seem like the right time to bring them up, because Random had shut his vacuum off and slouched beside her bench in silence. His presence was a kind of absence. He seemed to have parked his body in front of her and then forgotten where he had left it.

"What?" She poked his shoulder. "Say something."

Jak bumped her feed. =problem?=

=just random=

All kids of spacer stock were thin but, with his spindly limbs and teacup waist and translucent skin, Random seemed more a rumor than a boy. His eyelids fluttered and he touched his tongue to his bottom lip, as if he were trying to remember something. "Your mother," he said.

Mariska could feel a ribbon of dread weave into her feed with Jak. She wasn't sure her feet were still on the floor.

='Ska what?=

=nothing= Mariska clamped her head closed, then gave Jak a feeble wave to show everything was all right. He didn't look reassured.

"What about my mother?" She hissed at Random. "You don't even know her."

He opened his hand and showed her a small, brown disk. At first she thought it was a button but then she recognized the profile of Abraham Lincoln and realized that it was some old coin from Earth. What was it called? A penalty? No, a *penny*.

"I know this," said Random. "Check the date."

She shrank from him. "No."

Then Jak came to her rescue. He rested a hand on Random's shoulder. "Be smooth now." It didn't take much effort to turn the skinny kid away from her. "What's happening?"

Random tried to shrug from Jak's grip, but he was caught. "Isn't about you."

"Fair enough." Jak always acted polite when he was getting angry. "But here I am. You're not telling me to go away, are you?"

"He says it's about Natalya Volochkova," said Mariska.

Random placed the penny on Mariska's bench. "Check the date."

Jak picked the penny up and held it to the light. "2018," he read. "They used to use this stuff for money."

"I know that," Mariska snapped. She snatched the penny out of his hand and shoved it into the front pouch of her tugshirt.

Random seemed to have lost interest in her now that Jak had arrived. He switched on the vacpac, bent over, and touched the wand to a tomato leaf on the deck. It caught crossways for a moment, singing in the suction, and was gone. Then he sauntered off.

"What's this got to do with your mother?" asked Jak.

Mariska had been mad at Random, but since he no longer presented a target, she decided to be mad at Jak instead. "Don't be stupid. She's not my mother." She saw that Grieg was hunched over his beans, pretending to check the leaves for white flies. From the way his shoulders were shaking, she was certain that he was laughing at her. "Let's get out of here."

Jak looked doubtfully at the chemical dispensers and gardening tools scattered across her bench. "You want to clean up first?"

"No." She peeled off her clingy and threw it at the bench.

Jak tried to cheer her up by doing a flip-scrape in the corridor immediately in front of the hydroponics safety hatch. He leapt upwards in the Moon's one-sixth gravity, flipped in midair and scraped the rollers on the bottom of his shoes across the white ceiling, *skritch, skritch*, leaving skid marks. He didn't quite stick the landing and had to catch himself on the bulkhead. "Let Random clean that." His face flushed with the effort. "That slaghead."

"You're so busted," said Mariska, nodding at the security cam. "They're probably calling your parents even as we speak."

"Not," said Jak. "Megawatt and I smeared the cams with agar last night." He smiled and swiped a lock of curly hair from his forehead. "From Holmgren's own petri dishes. All they've got is blur and closeups of bacteria."

He looked so proud of himself that she couldn't help but grin back at him. "Smooth." Her Jak was the master of the grand and useless gesture.

He reached for her hand. "So where are we going?"

"Away."

They skated in silence through the long corridors of Hai Zone; Jak let her lead. He was much better on rollers than she was – a two-time sugarfoot finalist – and matched her stroke-for-stroke without loosening or tightening his feathery grip.

"You were mad back there," said Jak.

"Yes."

"Have you heard from your mother yet?"

"I told you, she's not my mother."

"Sure. Your clone, then."

Technically, Mariska was Natalya Volochkova's clone, but she didn't bother to correct him. "Not yet. Probably soon." He gave her hand a squeeze. "Unless I get lucky and she lets me alone."

"I don't see why you care. If she comes to visit, just freeze her out. She'll leave eventually."

"I don't want to see them together. Her and Al." She could just picture Volochkova in their flat. The heroic explorer would sneer at the way her hired father had spent the money she had given them. Then she would order Al around and turn off her room's persona and tell Mariska to grow up. As if she wasn't trying.

"Move out for a while. Stay with Geetha."

Mariska made a vinegar face. "Her little brother is a brat."

"Come stay with us then. You could sleep in Memaw's room." Jak's grandmother had been a fossil spacer, one of the first generation to go to the stars; she had died back in February.

"Sure, let's try that one on Al. It'll be fun watching the top of his head blow off."

"But my parents would be there."

Being Jak's girlfriend meant having to tolerate his parents. The mom wasn't so bad. A little boring, but then what grownup wasn't? But the dad was a mess. He had washed out of the spacer program when he was Jak's age and his mother – Memaw – had never let him forget it. The dad put his nose in a sniffer more than was good for anyone and when he was high, he had a tongue on him that could cut steel.

"Weren't your parents there when you and Megawatt set off that smoke bomb in your room?"

Jak blushed. "It was a science experiment."

"That cleared all of Tam Zone." She pulled him to a stop and gave him a brush kiss on the cheek. "Besides, your parents aren't going to be patrolling the hall at all hours. What if I get an overpowering urge in the middle of the night? Who'll protect you?"

"Urge?" He dashed ahead, launched a jump 180, and landed it, skating backwards, wiggling his cute ass. "Overpowering?" His stare was at once playful and hungry.

"Show off." Mariska looked away, embarrassed for both of them. Jak was so pathetically eager; it wasn't right to tease him about sex. It had seemed like a grownup thing to say, but just now she wasn't feeling much like an adult. She needed to get away from Jak. Everybody. Be by herself.

She decided to cue a fake call. When her fingernail flashed, she studied it briefly then brought it to her ear. "It's Al," she said. "Sorry, Jak, I've got to go."

The swimming pool in Muoi Zone was one of the biggest in the Moon's reservoir system, but Mariska liked it because it didn't have a sky projected on its ceiling. Somehow images of stars and clouds made the water seem colder, even though all the Moon's pools were kept at a uniform 27°

Celsius. And she felt less exposed looking up at raw rock. The diving plat-forms at the deep end were always crowded with acrobats; in the shallows little kids stood on their hands and wiggled their toes and heaved huge, quivering balls of water high into the air. Their shouts of glee echoed off the low ceiling and drowned in the blue expanse of the pool.

The twenty-five lanes were busy as usual with lap swimmers meeting their daily exercise expectation. Mariska owed the Med supers an hour in the pool four times a week. She sat at the edge in lane twelve and waited for an opening. She was wearing the aquablade bodysuit that Al had bought for her birthday. Jak had wanted her to get a tank suit or a two-piece, but she had chosen the neck-to-knee style because her chest was still flat as the lunar plains. That was why she didn't like to swim with Jak – when they stood next to each other in swimsuits, she looked like his baby sister.

She eased into the cool water just behind an old guy in a blue Speedo and cued up the datafeed she was supposed to review on ground squirrels.

=The hibernating *Spermophilus tridecemlineatus* can spend six months without food. During this period its temperature drops to as low as $0°$ Celsius. With a heart rate at one percent of its active state and oxygen consumption at two percent, the squirrel can survive solely on the combustion of its lipid reserves, especially unsaturated and polyun-saturated fatty acids.=

As Mariska's heart rate climbed to its target of 179 beats per minute, her deep and regular breathing and the quiet slap of water against her body brought on her usual swimming trance. For a brief, blue moment doing the right thing was easy: just bounce off the two walls connected by the black lane line.

Then her thoughts began to tumble over one another. Everything was stuck together, just like in the Love Gravy song. Al and Jak and Volochkova and her life on the moon and her future in space and sex and going deep and the way her room wouldn't let her grow up and Feodor Bear and pancakes and tomatoes and what did Random want with her anyway?

=The gene regulating the enzyme PDK4 (pyruvate dehydrogenase kinase isoenzyme 4) switches the squirrel's metabolism from the active to the hibernating state by inhibiting carbohydrate oxidation.=

She tried to remember exactly when she had decided to block out everything about Natalya Volochkova, but she couldn't. She had a vague memory that it had been her room's idea. She had asked it why her mother had abandoned her and her room had said that maybe grownups didn't always have choices but that had only made her upset. So her room had told Mariska that she was a special girl who didn't need a mother and that she should never ask about her again. *Ever. Never.* Or had that been in a dreamfeed?

= . . . mitochondrial functions are drastically reduced . . . =

Mariska felt as if she were swimming through the data in the feed. She was certain that she would never remember any of it. And Mr. Holmgren was going to have a meltdown when he saw how she had left her bench in the lab and she'd probably flunk tomatoes just like Jak had.

=In 2014 the first recombinant ground squirrel and human genes resulted in activity of PTL – pancreatic triacylglycerol lipase – in both heart and white adipose tissue under supercooling conditions.=

What had happened in 2018? She had never much cared for history. The Oil Crash must have started around that time. And Google 3.0. The founding of Moonbase Zhong? A bunch of extinctions. Datafeeds, sure, but mindfeeds didn't come until the eighties. When did the fossil spacers launch the first starship?

As she touched the wall a foot tapped her on the shoulder. She twisted out of her flip turn and broke the surface of the water, sputtering. Random was standing at the edge of the pool, staring at her. His bathing suit had slid down his bony hips. "My penny," he said. "Can I have it back now?" His pale skin had just a tinge of blue and he was shivering.

Random spilled his bundle of clothes onto the floor in front of her locker; he had the handle of a lunch box clamped between his teeth. Mariska slithered into her tube top as he set the lunch box on the bench between them. It had a picture of an apple on it; the apple was wearing a space helmet.

"This isn't funny, Random." Mariska slipped an arm into the sleeve of her tugshirt. "Are you stalking me?"

"No." He punched the print button on the processor and an oversized pool towel rolled from the output slot above the lockers. "Not funny at all."

She sealed the front placket of the tug and plunged both hands into its pouch. There it was. She must have taken the penny without realizing it. She extended the coin to him on her palm.

"First we talk, then you get the penny." She closed her fist around it. "What's this about?"

"I said already." Random stripped off his wet bathing suit. "Your mother." He crammed it into the input slot and began to dry himself with the towel.

Mariska set her jaw but didn't correct him. "What about her?"

"She's a fossil. The penny could have been hers."

"Okay." She wasn't sure she believed this, but she didn't want him to think that she didn't know if it were true. The heroic fossils had been the first humans to go to the stars. They had volunteered to be genetically altered so that they could hibernate through the three-year voyage to the wormhole at the far edge of Oort Cloud and then hibernate again as their ships cruised at sublight speeds through distant solar systems. Most of the fossils were dead, many from side effects of the crude genetic surgery of the twenty-first century. "So?"

"She probably has stuff. Or maybe you have her stuff?"

"Stuff?"

"To trade." He wrapped the towel around his waist and opened his lunch box. It was crammed with what looked to Mariska like junk wrapped in clear guardgoo. "Like my goods." Random pulled each item out as if it were a treasure.

"Vanilla Girl." He showed her the head of a doll with a patch over one eye. "Pencil," he said. "Never sharpened." He arranged an empty Coke bubble, a paper book with the cover ripped off, a key, a purple eyelight, a pepper shaker in the shape of a robot, and a thumb teaser on the bench. At the bottom of the lunch box was a tiny red plastic purse. He snapped it open and shook it so that she could hear coins clinking. "Please?"

Mariska dropped the penny into the purse. "How did you find out she's a fossil?"

"It's complicated." He tapped his forehead and she felt a tingle as he offered her a feed. "Want to open up?"

"No." Mariska folded her arms over her chest. "I don't think I do." She was chilled at the thought of losing herself in the chaos of feeds everyone claimed were churning inside Random's head. "You'll just have to say it."

Random dropped the towel on the floor and pulled on his janitor's greens. She was disgusted to see that he didn't bother with underwear. "When the *Gorshkov* came back," he said, "everyone was happy." He furrowed his brow, trying to remember how to string consecutive sentences together. "Happy people talk and make feeds and party all over. That's how I know." He nodded as if that explained everything.

Mariska tried not to sound impatient. "Know what?"

"It's a beautiful planet." Random made a circle with his hands, as if to present the new world to her. "Check the feeds, you'll see. It's the best ever. Even better than Earth, at least the way it is now, all crispy and crowded."

"Okay, so it's the Garden of slagging Eden. So what does that have to do with all this crap?"

"Crap?" He drew himself up, and then waved the pepper shaker at her. "My goods aren't crap." He set it carefully back in the lunch box and began to gather up the rest of his odd collection.

"Sorry, sorry, sorry." Mariska didn't want to chase him away – at least not yet. "So it's a beautiful planet. And your goods are great. Tell me what's going on?"

He stacked the Coke bubble and the eyelight on top of the book but then paused, considering her apology. "Most of the crew of the *Gorshkov* are going back." He packed the pile away. "It's their reward, to live on a planet with all that water and all that sky and friendly weather. Going back . . ." he tapped the bench next to her leg ". . . with their families."

Mariska's throat was so tight that she could barely croak. "I'm not her family."

"Okay." He shrugged. "But anything you want to trade before you go – either of you . . ."

Mariska flung herself at the security door.

"Just asking," Random called after her.

When she burst into the kitchen, Al was arranging a layer of lasagna noodles in a casserole. Yet another of her favorite dishes; Mariska should have known something was wrong. She gasped when he looked over his shoulder at her. His eyes were shiny and his cheeks were wet.

"You *knew*." She could actually hear herself panicking. "She wants to drag me off to some stinking rock twenty light years away and you knew."

"I didn't. But I guessed." The weight of his sadness knocked her back onto one of the dining room chairs. "She stopped by right after you left. She's looking for you."

"I'm not here."

"Okay." He picked up a cup of shredded mozzarella and sprinkled it listlessly over the noodles.

"You can't let her do this, Al. You're my daddy. You're supposed to protect me."

"It's a term contract, Mariska. I'm already in the option year."

"Slag the contract. And slag you for signing it. I don't want to go."

"Then don't. I don't think she'll make you. But you need to think about it." He kept his head down and spooned sauce onto the lasagna. "It's space, Mariska. You're a spacer."

"Not yet. I haven't even passed tomatoes. I could wash out. I *will* wash out."

He sniffed and wiped his eyes with his sleeve.

"I don't understand," she said. "Why are you taking her side?"

"Because you're a child and she's your legal parent. Because you can't live here forever." His voice climbed unsteadily to a shout. Al had never shouted at her before. "Because all of this is over." He shook the spoon at their kitchen.

"What do you mean, over?" She thought that it wasn't very professional of him to be showing his feelings like this. "Answer me! And what about Jak?"

"I don't know, Mariska." He jiggled another lasagna noodle out of the colander. "I don't know what I'm going to do."

She stared at his back. The kitchen seemed to warp and twist; all the ties that bound her to Al were coming undone. She scraped her chair from the table and spun down the hall to her room, bouncing off the walls.

"Hello Mariska," said her room as the door slid shut. "You seem upset. Is there anything I can . . . ?

"Shut up, shut up, *shut up*."

She didn't care if she hurt her room's feelings; it was just a stupid persona anyway. She needed quiet to think, sort through all the lies that had been her life. It must have been some other girl who had drawn funny aliens on the walls or listened to the room tell stories – lies! – about a space captain named Mariska or who had built planets inhabited by unicorns and fairies and princesses in her room's simspace. She didn't belong here. Not in this goddamn room, not on the moon, not anywhere.

Then it came to her. She knew what she had to do. Only she wasn't sure exactly how to do it. But how hard could going deep be? It was in her genes – her mother's genes. Slag her. Everyone so worried that she would go deep without really meaning to. So that must mean that she could. That's how the fossils had done it, before there were hibernation pods and proper euthermic arousal protocols.

She didn't know what good going deep would do her. It was probably stupid. Something a kid would do. But that was the point, wasn't it? She was just a kid. What other choice did she have?

She lay back on her bed and thought about space, about stepping out of the airlock without anything on. Naked and alone, just like she had always been. The air would freeze in her lungs and they would burst. Her eyes would freeze and it would be dark. She would be as cold as she had ever been. As cold as Natalya Volochkova, that bitch.

The Earth is up," the room murmured. "And I am always up. Is Mariska ready to get up yet?"

Mariska shivered from the cold. That wasn't right. Her room was supposed to monitor both its temperature and hers.

"The Earth is up, and I am always up," cooed her room. It wasn't usually so patient.

Mariska stretched. She felt stiff, as if she had overdone a swim. She opened her eyes and then shut them immediately. Her room had already brought the lights up to full intensity. It was acting strangely this morning. Usually it would interrupt one of her dreams, but all that she had in her head was a vast and frigid darkness. Space without the stars.

Mariska yawned and slitted her eyes against the light. She was facing the shelf where Feodor Bear sat. "*Dobroye utro*," it said. The antique robot bumped against the shelf twice in a vain attempt to stand. "Good morn-ing Mar-i-ska." There was something wrong with its speech chip; it sounded as if it were talking through a bowl of soup.

"Good morning, dear Mariska," said her room. "Today is Wednesday, November 23, 2163. You have no bookings scheduled for today."

That couldn't be right. The date was way off. Then she remembered.

The door slid open. She blinked several times before she could focus on the woman standing there.

"Mariska?"

Mariska knew that voice. Even though it had a crack to it that her room had never had, she recognized its singing accent.

"Where's Al?" When she sat up the room seemed to spin.

"He doesn't live here anymore." The woman sat beside her on the bed. She had silver hair and a spacer's sallow complexion. Her skin was wrinkled around the eyes and the mouth. "I can send for him, if you like. He's just in Muoi Zone." She seemed to be trying on a smile, to see if it would fit. "It's been three years, Mariska. We couldn't rouse you. It was too dangerous."

She considered this. "Jak?"

"Three years is a long time."

She turned her face to the wall. "The room's voice – that's you. And the persona?"

"I didn't want to go to *Delta Pavonis*, but I didn't have a choice. I'm a spacer, dear, dear Mariska. Just like you. When they need us, we go." She sighed. "I knew you would hate me – *I* would have hated me. So I found another way to be with you; I spent the two months before we left uploading feeds. I put as much of myself into this room as I could." She gestured at Mariska's room.

"You treated me like a kid. Or the room did."

"I'm sorry. I didn't think I'd be gone this long."

"I'm not going to that place with you."

"All right," she said. "But I'd like to go with you, if you'll let me."

"I'm not going anywhere." Mariska shook her head; she still felt groggy. "Where would I go?"

"To the stars," said Natalya Volochkova. "They've been calling you. *Alpha Centauri. Barnard's. Wolf. Lalande. Luyten. Sirius.*"

Mariska propped herself on a elbow and stared at her. "How do you know that?"

She reached out and brushed a strand of hair from Mariska's forehead. "Because," she said, "I'm your mother."

James Patrick Kelly has had an eclectic writing career. He has written novels, short stories, essays, reviews, poetry, plays, and planetarium shows. His most recent book, a collection of stories, was *The Wreck of the Godspeed*. His novella *Burn* was awarded the Nebula in 2007, his only win in twelve nominations – but who's counting? He has won the Hugo Award twice and his fiction has been translated into eighteen languages. With John Kessel he is coeditor of *Feeling Very Strange: The Slipstream Anthology, Rewired: The Post-Cyberpunk Anthology*, and the *The Secret History of Science Fiction*. He writes a column on the Internet for *Asimov's Science Fiction* magazine and is on the faculty of the Stonecoast Creative Writing MFA Program at the University of Southern Maine and the Board of Directors of the Clarion Foundation. Hear him read "Going Deep" and many other stories on his podcasts: James Patrick Kelly's *Story-Pod* on Audible.com and the *Free Reads Podcast*. His website is www.jimkelly.net.

BRIDESICLE

Will McIntosh

FROM THE AUTHOR: One of my writing friends once described my writing process as thinking up a bunch of hopefully cool ideas, throwing them up against the wall, and seeing what stuck. I hope that's not completely accurate, but I do tend to be driven by overt ideas and interesting characters, and underlying themes or resonance tends to develop outside my awareness. In other words, as a writer I'm not terribly self-aware, so writing about my writing can be a struggle.

This same writing friend pointed out that almost all of my fiction to date explores romantic love. It astonished me that I had never noticed. I write love stories – who'd have thought?

"Bridesicle" is a love story. It didn't start out that way, though. I originally wrote "Bridesicle" from the perspective of Lycan, a man visiting a cryogenic dating center who, unbeknownst to his potential mates, can't afford to save any of them. In the original story Mira, who is the protagonist in the final version, was one of a number of women Lycan "dated" at the center. I posted the original story for my online writing group to critique, and they politely panned it. Mary Robinette Kowal suggested the story would work better from the perspective of one of the women trapped at the center and, after a few weeks of acclimating to the idea that I should toss the original story in its entirety and start over, I tossed the original story in its entirety and started over. So I have Mary to thank for guiding me toward the story as it was published in *Asimov's*.

While I'm not exactly suffering from imposter syndrome, to say I was stunned to learn that "Bridesicle" had been nominated for a Nebula Award would be an understatement. When I began writing at age thirty-nine it never occurred to me that I might turn out to be any good at it. I wrote because I discovered I loved it more than anything I had ever done, and eighty-eight straight rejections to begin my career didn't deter me, because I just flat-out love to write. I fully expect the day of the Nebula Awards to be the second-best day of my life. The best was my wedding day. Originally I ranked the birth of my twins, Miles and Hannah, second, and the Nebulas third, but my wife Alison reminded me that the day of their birth actually sucked pretty badly.

THE WORDS WERE gentle strokes, drawing her awake.
"Hello. Hello there."
She felt the light on her eyelids, and knew that if she opened her eyes they would sting, and she would have to shade them with her palm and let the light bleed through a crack.
"Feel like talking?" A man's soft voice.
And then her mind cleared enough to wonder: where was her mom? She called into the corners of her mind, but there was no answer, and that could not be. Once she'd let mom in, there was no tossing her out. It was not like letting Mom move into her apartment; there was no going back once mom was in her mind, because there was no body for mom to return to.
So where was she?
"Aw, I know you're awake by *now*. Come on, sleeping beauty. Talk to me." The last was a whisper, a lover's words, and Mira felt that she had to come awake and open her eyes. She tried to sigh, but no breath came. Her eyes flew open in alarm.
An old man was leaning over her, smiling, but Mira barely saw him, because when she opened her mouth to inhale, her jaw squealed like a sea bird's cry, and no breath came, and she wanted to press her hands to the sides of her face, but her hands wouldn't come either. Nothing would move except her face.
"Hello, hello. And how are you?" The old man was smiling gently, as if Mira might break if he set his whole smile loose. He was not that old, she saw now. Maybe sixty. The furrows in his forehead and the ones framing his nose only seemed deep because his face was so close to hers, almost close enough for a kiss. "Are you having trouble?" He reached out and stroked her hair. "You have to press down with your back teeth to control the air flow. Didn't they show you?"
There *was* an air flow – a gentle breeze, whooshing up her throat and out her mouth and nose. It tickled the tiny hairs in her nostrils. She bit

down, and the breeze became a hiss – an exhale strong enough that her chest should drop, but it didn't, or maybe it did and she just couldn't tell, because she couldn't lift her head to look.

"Where—" Mira said, and then she howled in terror, because her voice sounded horrible – deep and hoarse and hollow, the voice of something that had pulled itself from a swamp.

"It takes some getting used to. Am I your first? No one has revived you before? Not even for an orientation?" The notion seemed to please him, that he was her first, whatever that meant. Mira studied him, wondering if she should recognize him. He preened at her attention, as if expecting Mira to be glad to see him. He was not an attractive man – his nose was thick and bumpy, and not in an aristocratic way. His nostrils were like a bull's; his brow Neanderthal, but his mouth dainty. She didn't recognize him.

"I can't move. Why can't I move?" Mira finally managed. She looked around as best she could.

"It's okay. Try to relax. Only your face is working."

"What happened?" Mira finally managed.

"You were in a car accident," he said, his brow now flexed with concern. He consulted a readout on his palm. "Fairly major damage. Ruptured aorta. Right leg gone."

Right leg *gone*? *Her* right leg? She couldn't see anything except the man hanging over her and a gold-colored ceiling, high, high above. "This is a hospital?" she asked.

"No, no. A dating center."

"What?" For the first time she noticed that there were other voices in the room, speaking in low, earnest, confidential tones. She caught snippets close by:

". . . *neutral colors. How could anyone choose violet?*"

". . . *last time I was at a Day-Glows concert I was seventeen . . .*"

"I shouldn't be the one doing this." The man turned, looked over his shoulder. "There's usually an orientation." He raised his voice. "Hello?" He turned back around to face her, shrugged, looking bemused. "I guess we're on our own." He clasped his hands, leaned in toward Mira. "The truth is, you see, you died in the accident . . ."

Mira didn't hear the next few things he said. She felt as if she were floating. It was an absurd idea, that she might be dead yet hear someone tell her she was dead. But somehow it rang true. She didn't remember dying, but she sensed some hard, fast line – some demarcation between now and before. The idea made her want to flee, escape her body, which was a dead body. Her teeth were corpse's teeth.

". . . your insurance covered the deep-freeze preservation, but full revival, especially when it involves extensive injury, is terribly costly. That's where the dating service comes in—"

"Where is my mother?" Mira interrupted.

The man consulted his palm again. He nodded. "You had a hitcher. Your mother." He glanced around again, raised his hand as if to wave at someone, then dropped it.

A hitcher. What an apropos term. "Is she gone?" Mira wanted to say, "Is she dead?" but that had become an ambiguous concept.

"Yes. You need consistent brain activity to maintain a hitcher. Once you die, the hitcher is gone."

Like a phone number you're trying to remember, Mira thought. You have to hold it with thought, and if you lose it, you never get it back. Mira felt hugely relieved. From the moment she waked, she kept expecting to hear her mother's voice. Now she knew it wouldn't come, and she could relax. She felt guilty for feeling relieved that her mother was dead, but who would blame her? Certainly not anyone who'd known her mother. Certainly not Lynn.

"I have a sister," she said. "Lynn." Her jaw moved so stiffly.

"Yes, a twin sister. Now that would be interesting." The man grinned, his eyebrows raised.

"Is she still alive?"

"No," he said in a tone that suggested she was a silly girl. "You've been gone for over eighty years, sleeping beauty." He made a sweeping gesture, as if all of that was trivial. "But let's focus on the present. The way this works is, we get acquainted. We have dates. If we find we're compatible," he raised his shoulders toward his ears, smiled his dainty smile, "then I might be enticed to pay for you to be revived, so that we can be together."

Dates.

"So. My name is Red, and I know from your readout that your name is Mira. Nice to meet you, Mira."

"Nice to meet you," Mira murmured. He'd said she died in a car accident. She tried to remember, but nothing came. Nothing about the accident, anyway. The memories that raced up at her were arguments – arguments with her mother. An argument at a shopping mall. Mom hating everything Mira liked, trying to get Mira to go to the Seniors section and buy cheap, drab housedresses. Mom had had no control of Mira's body (she was only a hitcher, after all), but there are lots of ways to control.

"So. Mira." Red clapped his hands together. "Do you want to bullshit, or do you want to get intimate?"

The raised eyebrows again, the same as when he made the twins comment. "I don't understand," Mira said.

"Weeeell. For example, here's a question." He leaned in close, his breath puffing in her ear. "If I revived you, what sorts of things would you do to me?"

Mira was sure that this man's name was not Red, and she doubted he was here to revive anyone. "I don't know. That's an awfully intimate question. Why don't we get to know each other first?" She needed time to think. Even just a few minutes of quiet, to make sense of this.

Red frowned theatrically. "Come on. Tease me a little."

Should she tell Red she was gay? Surely not. He would lose interest, and maybe report it to whoever owned the facility. But why hadn't whoever owned the facility known she was gay? Maybe that was to be part of the orientation she'd missed. Whatever the reason, did she want to risk being taken out of circulation, or unplugged and buried?

Would that be the worst thing?

The thought jangled something long-forgotten. Or more like deeply forgotten; everything in her life was long-forgotten. She'd thought something along those lines once, and there had been *so much* pain that the pain still echoed, even without the memory. She reached for the memory, but it was sunk deep in a turgid goo that she encountered whenever she tried to remember something. Had she really been able to effortlessly pull up memories when she was alive, or was that just how she remembered it?

"I'm just—" she wanted to say "not in the mood," but that was not only a cliché, but a vast understatement. She was dead. She couldn't move anything but her face, and that made her feel untethered, as if she were floating, drifting. Hands and feet grounded you. Mira had never realized. "I'm just not very good at this sort of thing."

"Well." Red put his hands on his thighs, made a production of standing. "This costs quite a bit, and they charge by the minute. So I'll say goodbye now, and you can go back to being dead."

Go back? "Wait!" Mira said. They could bring her back, and then let her die again? She imagined her body, sealed up somewhere, maybe for years, maybe forever. The idea terrified her. Red paused, waiting. "Okay. I would . . ." She tried to think of something, but there were so many things running through her mind, so many trains of thought she wanted to follow, none of them involving the pervert leaning over her.

Were there other ways to get permanently "revived"? Did she have any living relatives she might contact, or maybe a savings account that had been accruing interest for the past eighty years? Had she had any savings when she died? She'd had a house – she remembered that. Lynn would have inherited it.

"Fine, if you're not going to talk, I'll just say goodbye," Red snapped. "But don't think anyone else is coming. Your injuries would make you a costly revival, and there are tens of thousands of women here. Plus men don't want the women who'd been frozen sixty years before the facility opened, because they have nothing in common with those women."

"Please," Mira said.

He reached for something over her head, out of sight.

Mira dreamed that she was running on a trail in the woods. The trail sloped upward, growing steeper and steeper until she was running up big steps. Then the steps entered a flimsy plywood tower and wound up, up. It was dark, and she could barely see, but it felt so good to run; it had been such a long time that she didn't care how steep it was. She climbed higher, considered turning back, but she wanted to make it to the top after having gone so far. Finally she reached the top, and there was a window where she could see a vast river, and a lovely college campus set along it. She hurried over to the window for a better view, and as she did, the tower leaned under her shifting weight, and began to fall forward. The tower built speed, hurtled toward the buildings. *This is it*, she thought, her stomach flip-flopping. *This is the moment of my death.*

Mira jolted awake before she hit the ground.

An old man – likely in his seventies – squinted down at her. "You're not my type," he grumbled, reaching over her head.

"Hi." It came out phlegmy; the man cleared his throat. "I've never done this before." He was a fat man, maybe forty.

"What's the date?" Mira asked, still groggy.

"January third, twenty-three fifty-two," the man said. Nearly thirty years had passed. The man wiped his mouth with the back of his wrist. "I feel a little sick for being here, like I'm a child molester or something." He frowned. "But there are so many stories out there of people finding true love in the drawers. My cousin Ansel met his second wife Floren at a revival center. Lovely woman."

The man gave her a big, sloppy smile. "I'm Lycan, by the way."

"I'm Mira. Nice to meet you."

"Your smile is a little wavery, in a cute way. I can tell you're honest. You wouldn't use me to get revived and then divorce me. You have to watch out for that." Lycan sat at an angle, perhaps trying to appear thinner.

"I can see how that would be a concern," Mira said.

Lycan heaved a big sigh. "Maybe meeting women at a bridesicle place is pathetic, but it's not as pathetic as showing up at every company party alone, with your hands in your pockets instead of holding someone else's, or else coming with a woman who not only has a loud laugh and a lousy sense of humor, but is ten years older than you and not very attractive. *That's* pathetic. Let people suspect my beautiful young wife was revived. They'll still be jealous, and I'll still be walking tall, holding her hand as everybody checked her out."

Lycan fell silent for a moment. "My grandmother says I'm talking too much. Sorry."

So Lycan had a hitcher. At least one. It was so difficult to tell – you got so good at carrying on two conversations at once when you had a hitcher.

"No, I like it," Mira said. It allowed her precious time to think. When she was alive, there had been times in Mira's life when she had little free time, but she had always had time to think. She could think while commuting to work, while standing in lines, and during all of the other in-between times. Suddenly it was the most precious thing.

Lycan wiped his palms. "First dates are not my best moments."

"You're doing great." Mira smiled as best she could, although she knew the smile did not reach her eyes. She had to get out of here, had to convince one of these guys to revive her. One of these guys? This was only the third person to revive her in the fifty years that the place had been open, and if the first guy, the pervert, was to be believed, she'd become less desirable the longer she was here.

Mira wished she could see where she was. Was she in a coffin? On a bed? She wished she could move her neck. "What's it like in here?" she asked. "Are we in a room?"

"You want to see? Here." Lycan held his palm a foot or so over her face; a screen embedded there flashing words and images in three dimensions transformed into a mirror.

Mira recoiled. Her own dead face looked down at her, her skin grey, her lips bordering on blue. Her face was flaccid – she looked slightly unbalanced, or mentally retarded, rather than peaceful. A glittering silver mesh concealed her to the neck.

Lycan angled the mirror, giving her a view of the room. It was a vast, open space, like the atrium of an enormous hotel. A lift was descending through the center of the atrium. People hurried across beautifully designed bridges as crystal blue water traced twisting paths through huge transparent tubes suspended in the open space, giving the impression of flying streams. Nearby, Mira saw a man sitting beside an open drawer, his mouth moving, head nodding, hands set a little self-consciously in his lap.

Lycan took the mirror away. His eyes had grown big and round.

"What is it?" Mira asked.

He opened his mouth to speak, then changed his mind, shook his head. "Nothing."

"Please, tell me."

There was a long pause. Mira guessed it was an internal dispute. Finally, Lycan answered. "It's just that it's finally hitting me at a gut level: I'm talking to a dead person. If I could hold your hand, your fingers would be cold and stiff."

Mira looked away, toward the ceiling. She felt ashamed. Ashamed of the dead body that housed her.

"What's it like?" he whispered, as if he were asking something obscene.

Mira didn't want to answer, but she also didn't want to go back to being dead. "It's hard. It's hard to have no control over anything, not when I can be awake, or who I talk to. And to be honest, it's scary. When you end this date I'm going to be gone – no thoughts, no dreaming, just nothingness. It terrifies me. I dread those few minutes before the date ends."

Lycan looked sorry he'd asked, so Mira changed the subject, asking about Lycan's hitchers. He had two: his father and his grandmother.

"I don't get it," Mira said. "Why are there still hitchers if they've figured out how to revive people?" In her day, medical science had progressed enough that there was hope of a breakthrough, and preservation was common, but the dead stayed dead.

"Bodies wear out," Lycan said, matter-of-factly. "If you revive a lady who's ninety-nine, she'll just keep dying. So, tell me about yourself. I see you had a hitcher?"

Mira told Lycan about her mother, and Lycan uttered the requisite condolences, and she pretended they were appropriate. She held no illusions about why she had agreed to host her mother. It was, in a sense, a purely selfish motive: she knew she couldn't live with the guilt if she said no. It was emotional blackmail, what her mother did, but it was flawlessly executed.

But I'm dying. Mira, I'm scared. Please. Even across eighty years and death, Mira could still hear her mother's voice, its perpetually aggrieved tone.

An awful darkness filled her when she thought of her mother. She felt guilty and ashamed. But what did she have to feel ashamed of? What do you owe your mother if the only kindness she had ever offered was giving birth to you? Do you owe her a room in your mind? What if you loved a woman instead of a "nice man," and your mother barely spoke to you? How about if your soulmate died, painfully, and your mother's attempt to console you was to say, "Maybe next time you should try a man." As if Jeanette's death justified her mother's disapproval.

"What if I actually find someone here, and she agrees to marry me in exchange for being revived?" Lycan was saying. "Would people sense she was too good-looking to be with me, and guess that I'd met her at a bridesicle place? We'd have to come up with a convincing story about how and where we met – something that doesn't sound made-up."

"Bridesicle?"

Lycan shrugged. "That's what some people call this sort of place."

Then even if someone revived her, she would be a pariah. People would want nothing to do with her. Her mother's voice rang in her mind, almost harmonizing the line.

I want nothing to do with you. You and your girlfriend.

"I'm afraid it's time for me to say goodbye. I should circulate. But maybe we can talk again?" Lycan said.

She didn't want to die again, didn't want to be thrown into that abyss. She had so much to think about, to remember. "I'd like that," was all she said, resisting the urge to scream, to beg this man not to kill her. If Mira did that, he'd never come back. As he reached over to turn her off, Mira used her last few seconds to try to reach for the memory of her accident. It sat like a splinter under her skin.

Lycan came back. He told her it had been a week since his first visit. Mira had no sense of how much time had passed, the way you do when you've been asleep. A week felt the same as thirty years.

"I've talked to eleven women, and none of them were half as interesting as you. Especially the women who died recently. Modern women can be so shallow, so unwilling to seek a common ground. I don't want a relationship that's a struggle – I want to care about my wife's needs, to be able to say, 'no, honey, let's go see the movie you want to see,' and count on her saying, 'no, that's okay, I know how much you want to see that other one.' And sometimes we would see her movie, and sometimes mine."

"I know just what you mean," Mira said, in what she hoped was an intimate tone. As intimate as her graveyard voice could manage.

"That's why I came to the bottom floor, to the women who died one hundred, one hundred and twenty-five years ago. I thought, why not a woman from a more innocent time? She would probably be more appreciative. The woman at the orientation told me that choosing a bridesicle instead of a live woman was a generous thing to do – you were giving a life to someone who'd been cheated out of hers. I don't kid myself, though – I'm not doing this out of some nobility, but it's nice to think I'm doing something good for someone, and the girls at the bottom need it more than the girls at the top. You've been in line longer."

Mira had been in line a long time. It didn't seem that way, though. It had only been, what, about an hour of life since she died? It was difficult to gauge, because she didn't remember dying. Mira tried to think back. Had her car accident been in the city, or on a highway? Had she been at fault? Nothing came, except memories of what must have been the weeks leading up to it, of her mother driving her crazy.

Once she took in her mother, she could never love again. How could she make love to someone with her mother watching? Even a man would have been out of the question, although a man was out of the question in any case.

"It's awkward, though," Lycan was saying. "There aren't any nice ways to tell someone that you aren't interested. I'm not in practice rejecting women. I'm much more familiar with the other end of the equation. If you weren't in that drawer, you probably wouldn't give me a second glance."

Mira could see that he was fishing, that he wanted her to tell him he was wrong, that she would give him a second glance. It was difficult – it wasn't in her nature to pretend that she felt something she didn't. But she didn't have the luxury of honoring her nature.

"Of course I would. You're a wonderful man, and good looking."

Lycan beamed. What is it about us, Mira wondered, that we will believe any lie, no matter how outrageous, if it's flattering?

"Some people just spark something in you, make you breathe fast, you know?" Lycan said. "Others don't. It's hard to say why, but in those first seconds of seeing someone," he snapped his fingers, "you can always tell." He held her gaze for a moment, something that was clearly uncomfortable for him, then looked at his lap, blushing.

"I know what you mean," Mira said. She tried to smile warmly, knowingly. It made her feel like shit.

There was constant murmur of background chatter this time.

. . . *through life and revival, to have and to hold* . . .

"What is that I'm hearing? Is that a marriage ceremony?" Mira asked.

Lycan glanced over his shoulder, nodded. "They happen all the time here. It's kind of risky to revive someone otherwise."

"Of course," Mira said. She'd been here for decades, yet she knew nothing about this place.

There's something I have to tell you," Lycan said. It was their sixth or seventh date. Mira had grown fond of Lycan, which was a good thing, because the only thing she ever saw was Lycan's doughy jowls, the little bump of chin poking out of them. He was her life, such as it was.

"What is it?" Mira asked.

He looked off into the room, sighed heavily. "I've never enjoyed a woman's company as much as yours. I have to be honest with you, but I'm afraid if I am I'll lose you."

Mira tried to imagine what this man could possibly say that would lead her to choose being dead over his company. "I'm sure that won't happen, whatever it is. You can trust me."

Lycan put his hand over his eyes. His chest hitched. Mira made gentle shushing sounds, the sort of sounds her mother had never made, not even when Jeanette died.

"It's okay," she cooed. "Whatever it is, it's okay."

Lycan finally looked at her, his eyes red. "I really like you, Mira. I think I even love you. But I'm not a rich man. I can't afford to revive you, and I never will. Not even if I sold everything I owned."

She hadn't even realized how much hope she was harboring until it was dashed. "Well, that's not your fault, I guess." She tried to sound chipper, though inside she felt black despair.

Lycan nodded. "I'm sorry I lied to you."

Mira didn't have to ask why he came here pretending to be looking for a wife if he couldn't afford to revive anyone. The women here must all be kind to him, must hang on his every word in the hope that he'd choose them and free them from their long sleep. Where else would a man like Lycan get that sort of attention?

"Can you forgive me?" Lycan asked, looking like a scolded bulldog. "Can I still visit you?"

"Of course. I'd miss you terribly if you didn't." The truth was, if Lycan didn't visit Mira would be incapable of missing anyone. No one else was visiting, or likely to stumble upon her among the army of bridesicles lined shoulder-to-shoulder in boxes in this endless mausoleum.

That was the end of it. Lycan changed the subject, struck up a conversation about his collection of vintage gaming code, and Mira listened, and made "mm-hm" sounds in the pauses, and thought her private thoughts.

She found herself thinking about her mom more than Jeanette. Perhaps it was because she'd already learned to accept that Jeanette was gone, and mom's death was still fresh, despite being not nearly as heart-breaking. After Jeanette died, Mira had worked through her death until there were no new thoughts she could possibly think. And then she had finally been able to let Jeanette rest. . . .

She had the most astonishing thought. She couldn't believe it hadn't occurred to her until now. Mira had worked for Capital Lifekey, just like Jeanette. Preservation had been part of Jeanette's benefits package, just like Mira's.

"Lycan, would you do something for me?" It felt as if an eternity rode on the question she was about to ask.

"Sure. Anything."

"Would you run a search on a friend of mine who died?"

"What's her name?"

"Jeanette Zierk. Born twenty-two twenty-four."

Mira was not as anxious as she thought she should be as Lycan checked, probably because her heart could not race, and her palms could not sweat. It was surprising how much emotion was housed in the body instead of the mind.

Lycan checked. "Yes. She's here."

"She's *here*? In this place?"

"Yes." He consulted the readout, pulling his palm close to his nose, then he pointed across the massive atrium, lower down than they were. "Over there. I don't know why you're surprised, if she was stored she'd be here – it's a felony to renege on a storage contract."

Mira wished she could lift her head and look where he was pointing. She had spent the last few years of her life accepting that Jeanette was really gone, and would never come back. "Can you wake her, and give her a message from me? Please?"

Lycan was rendered momentarily speechless.

"Please?" Mira said. "It would mean so much to me."

"Okay. I guess. Sure. Hold on." Lycan stood tenuously, looked confused for a moment, and then headed off.

He returned a moment later. "What message should I give her?"

Mira wanted to ask Lycan to tell Jeanette she loved her, but that might be a bad idea. "Just tell her I'm here. Thank you so much."

Maybe it was someone else, or Mira's imagination, but she felt sure she heard a distant caw of surprise. Jeanette, reacting to the news.

Soon Lycan's smiling face poked into view above her. "She was very excited by the news. I mean, out of her head excited. I thought she'd leap out of her crèche and hug me."

"What did she say?" Mira tried to sound calm. Jeanette was here. Suddenly, everything had changed. Mira had a reason to live. She had to figure out how to get out of there.

"She said to tell you she loved you."

Mira sobbed. He had really talked to Jeanette. What a strange and wonderful and utterly incomprehensible thing.

"She also said she hoped you didn't suffer much in the accident."

"It wasn't an accident," Mira said.

It just came out. She said it without having thought it first, which was a strange experience, as if someone had taken control of her dead mouth and formed the words, rode them out of her on the hiss of air coursing through her throat.

There was a long, awkward silence.

"What do you mean?" Lycan said, frowning.

Mira remembered now. Not the moment itself, but planning it, intending it. She had put on her best tan suit. Mother kept asking what the occasion was. She wanted to know why Mira was making such a fuss when they were only going to Pan Pietro for dinner. She said that Mira wasn't as beautiful as she thought she was and should get off her high horse. Mira had barely heard her. For once, she had not been bothered by her mother's words.

"I mean it wasn't an accident," she repeated. "You were honest with me, I want to be honest with you." She did not want to be honest with him, actually, but it had come out, and now that it was out she didn't have the strength to draw it back in.

"Oh. Well, thank you." Lycan scratched his scalp with one finger, pondering. Mira wasn't sure if he got what she was saying. After all their conversation, she still had little sense of whether Lycan was intelligent or not. "You know, if I figure out a way to revive you, you could come with me to my company's annual picnic. Last year I announced to my whole table that I was going to win the door prize, and then I did!"

Lycan went on about his company picnic while Mira thought about Jeanette, who had just told Mira she loved her, even though they were both dead.

Far too soon, Lycan said goodbye. He told Mira he would see her on Tuesday, and killed her.

*   *   *

The man hovering over her was wearing a suit and tie, only the suit was sleeveless and the tie rounded, and the man's skin was bright orange.

"What year is it, please?" Mira said.

"Twenty-four seventy-seven," he said, not unkindly.

Mira couldn't remember the date Lycan had last come. Twenty-four? It had been twenty-three something, hadn't it? It was a hundred years later. Lycan had never come back. He was gone – dead, or hitching with some relative.

The orange man's name was Neas. Mira didn't think it would be polite to ask why he was orange, so instead she asked what he did for a living. He was an attorney. It suggested to Mira that the world had not changed all that much since she'd been alive, that there were still attorneys, even if they had orange skin.

"My grandfather Lycan says to tell you hello," Neas said.

Mira grinned. It was hard to hold the grin with her stiff lips, but it felt good. Lycan had come back after all. "Tell him he's late, but that's okay."

"He insisted we talk to you."

Neas chatted amiably about Lycan. Lycan had met a woman at a Weight Watchers meeting, and his wife didn't think it was appropriate that he visit Mira anymore. They had divorced twenty years later. He died of a heart attack at sixty-six, was revived, then hitched with his son when he reached his nineties. Lycan's son had hitched with Neas a few years ago, taking Lycan with him.

"I'm glad Lycan's all right," Mira said when Neas had finished. "I'd grown very fond of him."

"And he of you." Neas crossed his legs, cleared his throat. "So tell me Mira, did you want to have children when you were alive?" His tone had shifted to that of a supervisor interviewing a potential employee.

The question caught Mira off guard. She'd assumed this was a social call, especially after Neas said that Lycan had insisted they visit her.

"Yes, actually. I had hoped to. Things don't always work out the way you plan." Mira pictured Jeanette, a stone's throw away, dead in a box. Neas's question raised a flicker of hope. "Is this a date, then?" she asked.

"No." He nodded, perhaps to some suggestion from one of his hitchers. "Actually we're looking for someone to bear a child and help raise her. You see, my wife was dying of Dietz Syndrome, which is an unrevivable illness, so she hitched with me. We want to have a child. We need a host, and a caregiver, for the child."

"I see." Mira's head was spinning. Should she blurt out that she'd love the opportunity to raise their child, or would that signal that she was taking the issue too lightly? She settled on a thoughtful expression that hopefully conveyed her understanding of the seriousness of the situation.

"We would marry for legal reasons, of course, but the arrangement would be completely platonic."

"Yes, of course."

Neas sighed, looking suddenly annoyed. "I'm sorry Mira, my wife says you're not right." Neas was very upset. He stood, reached over Mira's head. "We've interviewed forty or fifty women, but none are good enough," he added testily.

"No, wait!" Mira said.

Neas paused.

Mira thought fast. What had she done to make the wife suddenly rule her out? The wife must feel terribly threatened at the idea of having a woman in the house, raising her child. Tempting her husband. If Mira could allay the wife's fears . . .

"I'm gay," she said.

Neas looked beyond surprised. Evidently Lycan hadn't realized who Jeanette was, even after carrying the verbal love note. Friends could say they loved each other. Neas said nothing, and Mira knew they were having a powwow. She prayed she'd read the situation correctly.

"So, you *couldn't* fall in love with me?" Neas finally asked. It was such a bizarre question. Neas was not only a man, he was an orange man, and not particularly attractive.

"No. I'm in love with a woman named Jeanette. Lycan met her."

There was another long silence.

"There's also this business about your auto accident not being an accident."

Mira had forgotten. How could she so easily forget that she killed herself and her own mother? Maybe because it had been so long ago. Everything from before her death seemed so long ago now. Like another lifetime.

"It was so long ago," Mira murmured. "But yes, it's true."

"You took your mother's life?"

"No, that's not what I intended." It wasn't. Mira hadn't wanted her mother dead, she just wanted to escape her. "I fled from her. Just because someone is your mother doesn't mean she can't be impossible to live with."

Neas nodded slowly. "It's difficult for us to imagine that. Hitching has been a very powerful experience for us. Oona and I never dreamed we could be this close, and we're happy to have dad and grandfather and great-grandmother as companions. I know I wouldn't trade it for anything."

"I can see how it could be beautiful," Mira said. "It's like a marriage, I think, but more so. It magnifies the relationship – good ones get closer and deeper; bad ones become intolerable."

Neas's eyes teared up. "Lycan said we can trust you. We need someone we can trust." He kept on nodding for a moment, lost in thought. Then he waved his hand; a long line of written text materialized in the air. "Do you believe in spanking children?" he asked, reading the first line.

"Absolutely not," Mira answered, knowing her very existence depended on her answers.

Mira's heart was racing so fast it felt as if there were wings flapping in her chest. Lucia was sleeping, her soft little head pressed to Mira's racing heart. The lift swept them up; the vast atrium opened below as people on the ground shrank to dots.

She wanted to run, but kept her pace even, her transparent shoes thwocking on the marble floor.

She cried when Jeanette opened her eyes, swept her fingers behind Jeanette's bluish-white ear, lightly brushed her blue lips.

Jeanette sobbed. To her, it would have been only a moment since Lycan had spoken to her.

"You made it," Jeanette croaked in that awful dead voice. She noticed the baby, smiled. "Good for you." So like Jeanette, to ask for nothing, not even life. If Jeanette had come to Mira's crèche alive and whole, the first words out of Mira's stiff mouth would have been "Get me out of here."

Vows from a wedding ceremony drifted from a few levels above, the husband's voice strong and sure, the wife's toneless and froggy.

"I can't afford to revive you, love," Mira said, "but I've saved enough to absorb you. Is that good enough? Will you stay with me, for the rest of our lives?"

You can't cry when you're dead, but Jeanette tried, and only the tears were missing. "Yes," she said. "That's a thousand times better than good enough."

Mira nodded, grinning. "It will take a few days to arrange." She touched Jeanette's cold cheek. "I'll be back in an eyeblink. This is the last time you have to die."

"Promise?"

"I promise."

Mira reached up, and Jeanette died, for the last time.

Will McIntosh's work has appeared in *Asimov's Science Fiction: Best of the Year,* the acclaimed anthology *The Living Dead, Strange Horizons, Interzone,* and many other venues. A New Yorker transplanted to the rural South, Will is a psychology professor at Georgia Southern University, where he studies Internet dating, and how people's TV, music, and movie choices are affected by recession and terrorist threat. Last December he became the father of twins.

NEBULA AWARD WINNER »»»

SPAR

Kij Johnson

From the author: Science fiction and fantasy are the literature of the edge. We have resources that other genres don't because we are not restricted by naturalistic (or realistic) conventions. We can create outrageous thought experiments and explore human nature through situations that just can't exist in the real world. Sometimes our medium for exploring human nature isn't even human.

A lot of SF and fantasy explores concepts and worlds that are out there on the edge, but there are limits to how close to the edge we like to go when we're discussing human experience. There's a reason: they're not very pleasant to read, for me anyway. Stories like Richard Matheson's "Born of Man and Woman" leave me a little soul-sick. They are horrific, and they are also asking disturbing questions about what makes us loving, or keeps us alive. Or human. They're not very pleasant, but they are saying and doing something fiction that is pulled back from the edge does not. Hearing it – saying it – is worth it. When I wrote "Spar," I was trying to see how close to the edge I could bear to get, as both reader and writer. As it happened, it was far enough out that I didn't know whether I could get it published, even in SF and fantasy markets. I am so glad that *Clarkesworld* did so, and to know that people are reading past the horror to the heart of it.

I N THE TINY lifeboat, she and the alien fuck endlessly, relentlessly.

They each have Ins and Outs. Her Ins are the usual: eyes, ears, nostrils, mouth, cunt, ass. Her Outs are also the common ones: fingers and hands and feet and tongue. Arms. Legs. Things that can be thrust into other things.

The alien is not humanoid. It is not bipedal. It has cilia. It has no bones, or perhaps it does and she cannot feel them. Its muscles, or what might be muscles, are rings and not strands. Its skin is the color of dusk and covered with a clear thin slime that tastes of snot. It makes no sounds. She thinks it smells like wet leaves in winter, but after a time she cannot remember that smell, or leaves, or winter.

Its Ins and Outs change. There are dark slashes and permanent knobs that sometimes distend, but it is always growing new Outs, hollowing new Ins. It cleaves easily in both senses.

It penetrates her a thousand ways. She penetrates it, as well.

The lifeboat is not for humans. The air is too warm, the light too dim. It is too small. There are no screens, no books, no warning labels, no voices, no bed or chair or table or control board or toilet or telltale lights or clocks. The ship's hum is steady. Nothing changes.

There is no room. They cannot help but touch. They breathe each other's breath – if it breathes; she cannot tell. There is always an Out in an In, something wrapped around another thing, flesh coiling and uncoiling inside, outside. Making spaces. Making space.

She is always wet. She cannot tell whether this is the slime from its skin, the oil and sweat from hers, her exhaled breath, the lifeboat's air. Or come.

Her body seeps. When she can, she pulls her mind away. But there is nothing else, and when her mind is disengaged she thinks too much. Which is: at all. Fucking the alien is less horrible.

She does not remember the first time. It is safest to think it forced her.

The wreck was random: a mid-space collision between their ship and the alien's, simultaneously a statistical impossibility and a fact. She and Gary just had time to start the emergency beacon and claw into their suits before their ship was cut in half. Their lifeboat spun out of reach. Her magnetic boots clung to part of the wreck. His did not. The two of them fell apart.

A piece of debris slashed through the leg of Gary's suit to the bone, through the bone. She screamed. He did not. Blood and fat and muscle swelled from his suit into vacuum. An Out.

The alien's vessel also broke into pieces, its lifeboat kicking free and the waldos reaching out, pulling her through the airlock. In.

Why did it save her? The mariner's code? She does not think it knows she is alive. If it did it would try to establish communications. It is quite possible that she is not a rescued castaway. She is salvage, or flotsam.

She sucks her nourishment from one of the two hard intrusions into the featureless lifeboat, a rigid tube. She uses the other, a second tube, for whatever comes from her, her shit and piss and vomit. Not her come, which slicks her thighs to her knees.

She gags a lot. It has no sense of the depth of her throat. Ins and Outs. There is a time when she screams so hard that her throat bleeds.

She tries to teach it words. "Breast," she says. "Finger. Cunt." Her vocabulary options are limited here.

"Listen to me," she says. "Listen. To. Me." Does it even have ears?

The fucking never gets better or worse. It learns no lessons about pleasing her. She does not learn anything about pleasing it either; would not if she could. And why? How do you please grass and why should you? She suddenly remembers grass, the bright smell of it and its perfect green, its cool clean soft feel beneath her bare hands.

She finds herself aroused by the thought of grass against her hands, because it is the only thing that she has thought of for a long time that is not the alien or Gary or the Ins and Outs. But perhaps its soft blades against her fingers would feel like the alien's cilia. Her ability to compare anything with anything else is slipping from her, because there is nothing to compare.

She feels it inside everywhere, tendrils moving in her nostrils, thrusting against her eardrums, coiled beside the corners of her eyes. And she sheathes herself in it.

When an Out crawls inside her and touches her in certain places, she tips her head back and moans and pretends it is more than accident. It is Gary, he loves me, it loves me, it is a He. It is not.

Communication is key, she thinks.

She cannot communicate, but she tries to make sense of its actions.

What is she to it? Is she a sex toy, a houseplant? A shipwrecked Norwegian sharing a spar with a monolingual Portuguese? A companion? A habit, like nailbiting or compulsive masturbation? Perhaps the sex is communication, and she just doesn't understand the language yet.

Or perhaps there is no It. It is not that they cannot communicate, that she is incapable; it is that the alien has no consciousness to communicate with. It is a sex toy, a houseplant, a habit.

On the starship with the name she cannot recall, Gary would read aloud to her. Science fiction, Melville, poetry. Her mind cannot access the plots, the words. All she can remember is a few lines from a sonnet, "Let me not to the marriage of true minds admit impediments" – something something something – "an ever-fixèd mark that looks on tempests and is never shaken; it is the star to every wand'ring bark. . . ."

She recites the words, an anodyne that numbs her for a time until they lose their meaning. She has worn them treadless, and they no longer gain any traction in her mind. Eventually she cannot even remember the sounds of them.

If she ever remembers another line, she promises herself she will not wear it out. She will hoard it. She may have promised this before, and forgotten.

She cannot remember Gary's voice. Fuck Gary, anyway. He is dead and she is here with an alien pressed against her cervix.

It is covered with slime. She thinks that, as with toads, the slime may be a mild psychotropic drug. How would she know if she were hallucinating? In this world, what would that look like? Like sunflowers on a desk, like Gary leaning across a picnic basket to place fresh bread in her mouth. The bread is the first thing she has tasted that feels clean in her mouth, and it's not even real.

Gary feeding her bread and laughing. After a time, the taste of bread becomes "the taste of bread" and then the words become mere sounds and stop meaning anything.

On the off-chance that this will change things, she drives her tongue through its cilia, pulls them into her mouth, and sucks them clean. She has no idea whether it makes a difference. She has lived forever in the endless reeking fucking now.

Was there someone else on the alien's ship? Was there a Gary, lost now to space? Is it grieving? Does it fuck her to forget, or because it has forgotten? Or to punish itself for surviving? Or the other, for not?

Or is this her?

When she does not have enough Ins for its Outs, it makes new ones. She bleeds for a time and then heals. She pretends that this is a rape. Rape at least she could understand. Rape is an interaction. It requires intention. It would imply that it hates or fears or wants. Rape would mean she is more than a wine glass it fills.

This goes both ways. She forces it sometimes. Her hands are blades that tear new Ins. Her anger pounds at it until she feels its depths grow soft under her fist, as though bones or muscle or cartilage have disassembled and turned to something else.

And when she forces her hands into the alien? If intent counts, then what she does, at least, is a rape – or would be if the alien felt anything, responded in any fashion. Mostly it's like punching a wall.

She puts her fingers in herself, because she at least knows what her intentions are.

Sometimes she watches it fuck her, the strange coiling of its Outs like a shockwave thrusting into her body, and this excites her and horrifies her; but at least it is not Gary. Gary, who left her here with this, who left her here, who left.

One time she feels something break loose inside the alien, but it is immediately drawn out of reach. When she reaches farther in to grasp the broken piece, a sphincter snaps shut on her wrist. Her arm is forced out. There is a bruise like a bracelet around her wrist for what might be a week or two.

She cannot stop touching the bruise. The alien has had the ability to stop her fist inside it, at any time. Which means it has made a choice not to stop her, even when she batters things inside it until they grow soft.

This is the only time she has ever gotten a reaction she understands. Stimulus: response. She tries many times to get another. She rams her hands into it, kicks it, tries to tears its cilia free with her teeth, claws its skin with her ragged, filthy fingernails. But there is never again the broken thing inside, and never the bracelet.

For a while, she measures time by bruises she gives herself. She slams her shin against the feeding tube, and when the bruise is gone she does it again. She estimates it takes twelve days for a bruise to heal. She stops after a time because she cannot remember how many bruises there have been.

She dreams of rescue, but doesn't know what that looks like. Gary, miraculously alive pulling her free, eyes bright with tears, I love you he says, his lips on her eyelids and his kiss his tongue in her mouth inside her hands inside him. But that's the alien. Gary is dead. He got Out.

Sometimes she thinks that rescue looks like her opening the lifeboat to the deep vacuum, but she cannot figure out the airlock.

Her anger is endless, relentless.

Gary brought her here, and then he went away and left her with this thing that will not speak, or cannot, or does not care enough to, or does not see her as something to talk to.

On their third date, she and Gary went to an empty park: wine, cheese, fresh bread in a basket. Bright sun and cool air, grass and a cloth to lie on. He brought Shakespeare. "You'll love this," he said, and read to her.

She stopped him with a kiss. "Let's talk," she said, "about anything."

"But we are talking," he said.

"No, you're reading," she said. "I'm sorry, I don't really like poetry."

"That's because you've never had it read to you," he said.

She stopped him at last by taking the book from his hands and push-ing him back, her palms in the grass; and he entered her. Later, he read to her anyway.

If it had just been that.

They were not even his words, and now they mean nothing, are not even sounds in her mind. And now there is this thing that cannot hear her or does not choose to listen, until she gives up trying to reach it and only reaches into it, and bludgeons it and herself, seeking a reaction, any reaction.

"I fucking hate you," she says. "I hate fucking you."

The lifeboat decelerates. Metal clashes on metal. Gaskets seal.

The airlock opens overhead. There is light. Her eyes water helplessly and everything becomes glare and indistinct dark shapes. The air is dry and cold. She recoils.

The alien does not react to the light, the hard air. It remains inside her and around her. They are wrapped. They penetrate one another a thousand ways. She is warm here, or at any rate not cold: half-lost in its flesh, wet from her Ins, its Outs. In here it is not too bright.

A dark something stands outlined in the portal. It is bipedal. It makes sounds that are words. Is it human? Is she? Does she still have bones, a voice? She has not used them for so long.

The alien is hers; she is its. Nothing changes.

No. She pulls herself free of its tendrils and climbs. Out.

Kij Johnson is the author of several novels and more than thirty fantasy, science fiction, and slipstream stories; winner of the 2009 World Fantasy Award; and a finalist for the Hugo, Nebula, and World Fantasy Awards. She is also the winner of the Theodore Sturgeon Award for best short story of the year, and the IAFA's Crawford Award, for best new fantasist of the year. She is the vice chairman for the Clarion West Writers Workshop, and an associate director for the Center for the Study of Science Fiction at the University of Kansas, where she teaches an annual summer workshop on the novel. She lives in Seattle.

SFWA AUTHOR EMERITUS

– Neal Barrett, Jr.

AUTHOR EMERITUS
– NEAL BARRETT, JR.

SFWA inaugurated the Author Emeritus program in 1995 to recognize and appreciate senior writers in the genres of science fiction and fantasy who have made significant contributions to our field but who are no longer active or whose excellent work is no longer as well known as it once was. SFWA is proud to name Neal Barrett, Jr. this year's Author Emeritus.

Within the past fifty years, Neal Barrett, Jr. has penned such lauded works as *Prince of Christler-Coke* (2004), *Dawn's Uncertain Light* (1989), *Through Darkest America* (1987), and over 50 other novels in the fields of science fiction, fantasy, western, and mystery. His short works, which number more than 70, have appeared in such major magazines such as *Amazing*, *Galaxy*, *Omni*, *The Magazine of Fantasy & Science Fiction*, and *Isaac Asimov's Science Fiction Magazine*.

His early inspirations included the Barsoom books of Edgar Rice Burroughs, as well as the science fiction of such well-known magazines as *Planet Stories*, *Startling Stories*, *Astounding*, and *If*. Neal has also lent his enormous talent to the world of juveniles writing Hardy Boys adventures as Franklin W. Dixon and Tom Swift stories as Victor Applegate. He's also produced novelizations of Judge Dredd and Dungeons & Dragons, and put some time in writing comic scripts for *Batman*, *Predator*, *Dark Horse Presents*, and others. He continues to write and publish. His most recent stories appear at Subterranean Press, and collected in *Perpetuity Blues and Other Stories* from Golden Gryphon Press.

NEAL BARRETT, JR.: WRITER OF EXCELLENCE, AND MY BROTHER

Joe R. Lansdale

First off, don't misspell his name.

It's Neal, not Neil.

His first name, as well as his last, has been misspelled as much as my last name, and he hates that. I know. Just to get him going I used to write him letters with his name misspelled, and he in turn would write me letters with Lansdale spelled Landsdale, with two Ds. He always told me that the first D was silent.

But back to my purpose for being here with you on the printed page.

It's hard to express how honored, how excited I am that my good friend, and great writer, Neal Barrett, Jr., is receiving this award.

For years, Neal has been a favorite writer of mine, and I have actually been amazed at the lack of attention his work has received, compared to that of some others.

Don't misunderstand me. I wish all those others the best. I am not saying they are not deserving of their recognitions.

But Neal Barrett, Jr. is an amazing stylist and creator of some of the most original fiction ever consigned to paper, or computer screen. And to be honest, he has been taken for granted. He has not been without respect or influence. He has taught many a new writer a thing or two with his smooth prose, humorous point of view, and brilliant ideas.

I am one of those influenced by him, and maybe, considering that admission, I should apologize to him and readers everywhere. I may have learned a thing or two from the master, but Neal, he's still the man.

I met Neal . . . Oh, my God! I met Neal in the mid-seventies, though he may not remember it. Met him in Houston, Texas, at a science-fiction convention. I brought a few things of his I had, asked him to sign, and he did. I was there not only because I was a fan of his, knew he was going to be there, but because I, too, wanted to write, and my wife insisted I go because she knew how deeply I loved his work and wanted to meet him.

I had already sold a few nonfiction articles, and maybe even a piece of fiction or two, but what I remember was, when I first met him and told him I badly wanted to write full time. He told me "Good luck."

Seemed he hadn't figured that whole full time thing out himself. At least not then. That was to come later.

I also remember that there were some young writers there, my age, a little older in some cases, or a little younger, who wouldn't give me the time of day. They treated my like a leper. I've never forgotten that. I don't hate them for it, but somewhere in the back of my mind I made a little mark in a mental book, and that mark is still as darkly blood red and clear in my brain as the first day I made it. They knew not what they did. But I damn sure did.

Neal was different. I've never forgotten how kindly he treated a stranger who desperately wanted to make a career as a writer.

Bless you for that, Neal. You have no idea how encouraging that was then.

Neal gave me advice. Most of it simple and direct.

Keep doing it, and keep trying to do it better. This is really the only advice that matters.

It may not sound profound, but it was exactly what I needed at the time. It was nice to meet one of your heroes and find out they were as special as you hoped they would be.

A few years later I met Neal again, at AggieCon, and this time we really hit it off. Maybe it's because I complimented his work again. Neal enjoys that sort of thing, and, he should.

His work is worth complimenting.

After that meeting, we not only became fast friends, I soon had the privilege of reading some of his works as they came out of his typewriter, via Xerox and mail. That's how we did it in the old days.

It was a real treat to read stories and books by Neal before they were printed. It was great to spend time on the phone talking. We talked about everything under the sun, but mostly we talked about writing. Of course we met in person as often as possible, but we certainly burned those phone wires down, and faxed each other back and forth. In fact, one time Neal sent me a fax sheet with only a spot on it. It said, "Smell. Indian Food."

He, who had introduced me to it, knew how much I loved Indian food, so he sent me the fax, called me a few minutes later.

He said, "Did you smell?"

"Yep," I said. "Even though I knew better."

"Knew you would," he said, and hung up.

But the thing that is more important to me, even than the writing, good as it is, is Neal himself. We have been close friends for over thirty years. We've had ups and downs over this and that, but never any ups and downs where one of us fell off the seesaw. In the end, we were always there to balance each other out. We love each other as family.

Me and Neal, we've had some odd adventures together. We attract weirdness alone, but together, we seem to pull it out of the woodwork.

I adore Neal's wit. I adore his honesty and loyalty. I adore that he sees curiosity in things other people take for granted, or think of as everyday. He is like a small child when it comes to that. And in many other ways. I think his wife will stand by that statement as well.

Like me, he loves animals. I adore that. I also adore that he adores his wife.

Hell, I love the guy. My whole family does.

And because of that, along with the fact I think he is a worthy recipient of this honor, I write this from the heart: I love you, Neal. I'm glad you are being honored in this way, and I've yet to forgive you for giving me a gift of a dollar bill torn in half.

GETTING DARK

Neal Barrett, Jr.

FROM THE AUTHOR: I chose this story for the collection because it came to me in one of those pleasant moments when a writer feels he's truly done it right this time – that he's pierced that barrier between the world that seems real, and that other state of being, the one we've feared all along.

I was a child growing up where "John-William's mother" grew up, and during the very same years. I listened to the radio, read the funnies, and was deathly afraid of the dark. For me, that awesome, timeless moment between daylight and dark was, as John-William's mother recalls, "like sorrow come to stay." I also heard the same grandmother tales that frightened John-William's mother, and carried many nightmare memories for years. I can't say what was real and what wasn't in John-William's mother's life, and very possibly she couldn't either. But that's the point here, isn't it? I sincerely hope you enjoy the story, and thank you for the privilege of having it appear in this volume.

JOHN-WILLIAM'S MOTHER TURNS the water on low and peels carrots in the sink. Wet skins slick-slick quick off the cutter and stick in a huddle where they fall. This is what skins like to do. They like to huddle up, stick with their own kind. Peel a potato and a carrot in the sink, they won't speak at all, they'll bunch up with someone they know. Like nigger-folks and whites, thinks John-William's mother. That's what Jack used to say. One's dark and one's not. One's that snake in the Garden, would've stuck it in Eve, but couldn't figure how.

John-William's mother drops carrots in a pot, puts the pot on the stove. Leaves the skins alone, leaves them where they fell. They look like bird tongues to John-William's mother, cut-cut dagger tongues, curled up at the end. She thinks about birds, big old black birds, hare-lipped fat birds without any tongues. " 'weet! 'weet!" go the birds, poor little birds without any tongues. Poke in a peel now, that'd be fine, stick a little tongue in a pointy yellow bill.

John-William's mother peers out the screen door. The birds have black ruffle necks and glitter-green eyes. They perch on phone wires just behind the house. Birds in twos now, birds in threes, birds like notes on the music at Mama Sarah's house. Note birds hop from one wire to the next. Hop down, hop up, up and down again. The birds play "Summit Ridge Drive," play "Chatanooga Choo Choo," and "Puttin' on the Ritz." When she hears those songs, John-William's mother gets a tingle where a tingle shouldn't ought to be.

"Not if you're a lady," giggles John-William's mother, "not 'less you come from the Wilcher branch of the tree."

The fan on the counter hum-hums to the left, hum-hums to the right, gives a little jerk and starts back again. John-William's mother smells Camay soap and Lipton iced tea. Smells meatloaf and pepper and water on the stove. Flour and catsup and old coffee grounds. Summer sucks Oklahoma heat through the open screen door, mingles with the smells from inside. John-William's mother draws damp hair off her neck, pins it up back. Her dress is stuck to her skin. She pulls at her collar, lets the breeze in. Lord God, too hot for underwear in August. Grandmas and aunts in Shawnee and Maud can keep their corsets and their buttons and their snaps. This is Oke City, and a girl can jiggle what she likes down here.

John-William's mother peeks down for a look. They're still down there, and still looking fine. You can say what you like about your big old melons, sagging on the vine when you're still eighteen. There's not a man living doesn't have a liking for a grown-up woman's got a pair of thirty-fours poking right up like happy puppy dogs.

John-William's mother looks past her pretties, down past her tummy, feels a little shudder, feels a little warm start to grow, thinks, for an instant, why not leave the pot a'bubble, run back to bed and have a little tingle, who's going to know? Blushes at the image like a movie show flicking in her head, raises the lid off the carrots, which don't need checking at all . . .

. . . stops right there, holds the steamy lid in her hand, stops there and listens, hears it coming, hears it on the way, long before it gets there at all. Sets down the lid, drops her apron on a chair, kicks off her flats, and walks out the screen door. The steps are still warm. She pulls up her skirt, leans back against the door. If some old man gets a peek, well maybe she'll let him have two.

There's no wind at all, but it's better out back than inside.

Still a little light, but the sky's turning dull pewter-gray, turning dish-water blue, like the bottom of a worn-out pan. John-William's mother doesn't like this time of day, doesn't now and never did. When she was little on the farm she'd sit on the back porch steps past Mama's kitchen door. The wood was dull gray, worn by lye soap and long dead years. Sit real still and look past the gravel back yard, past the henhouse and the barn, past the smokehouse and the dirt storm cellar with its tin door in the ground. Out past the pile where Papa put things he meant to fix, and never did. A plow with no handles, busted wagon wheels, the carcass of a Ford, its rusty hide now a 12-gauge target, fine as Irish lace. Broken shovels, dull washtubs with the bottoms burned out.

And, past the orchard and the fence and the fields full of rattle-paper corn, to the land that stretched forever to the sky.

That's when John-William's mother sat still as mice and held her breath. Held it, and waited for the last pallid whisper of the light to disappear, waited for the day to give a final sigh and slide away.

You had to watch close. It happened, just like that, and it was gone. It wasn't day and it wasn't night; it was something in between. Every color died and the faraway fields began to smudge against the sky. The barn, the henhouse, the rusted-out Ford began to blur, grow faint and indistinct, dull and undefined. The dark descended and sucked the day dry.

And it was then when John-William's mother, Betty Ann, heard the great stone clock, felt it strike deep, deep within the earth, felt it beat against her heart. When the time was just right, at the moment in between, she listened, and heard what the clock had come to say . . .

Not just before, Betty Ann
And not just after, Betty Ann.
Not quite day
And not quite night,
What it is, Betty Ann,
Is getting dark again . . .

That's when the big clock stopped for a beat, and the world grew silent and still. It seemed to Betty Ann like sorrow had come to stay, as if all the lonely had spilled out from the day. Grandmaw Wilcher said this was the moment dark came to snatch life away. "You can see it if you look real close," Grandmaw Wilcher said. "You might see a dead bird out in the yard, claw feet stickin' right up, bill wide open, sucking for a last breath of air. You might see a rock or a stick you was lookin' right at, and now it's not there. For a blink, for a wink, you're seeing things gone, things that were there a minute or so before. It might be a toad, it might be a stone, it *might* be someone you know."

Mama told Betty Ann not to listen to Grandmaw's trash, said she wasn't right in the head. And maybe that was so, but every night after, Betty Ann ran back in, safe inside before the night caught her, caught her right between the light and dark, fled to the good smell of cornbread and jelly, to the oilcloth mustard-yellow bright, to the table set with cold ham and beans, the cloth still sticky from the noon summer meal. The kerosene lamp warmed her soul, and her mother brought cool cream butter in a bowl and said, "Time you came in, Betty Ann, it's getting dark again . . ."

In spite of the prickly sullen heat, Betty Ann, John-William's mother, feels a chill. She knows what's happened. She's waited just a beat, just a breath too long and the dark has caught her there, standing outside her kitchen door. Caught her as the night swept in and drew its cape across the yard and the trees and the house next door, and nearly got Betty Ann, John-William's mother, too. John-William's mother doesn't even look back. Looking back's like Grandmaw said, when you saw, from the corner of your eye, things that were missing, things that had been there just a blink before.

Betty Ann, John-William's mother, moves quickly inside, shuts the screen door, snaps the latch, stops, pauses just a minute, listens, almost certain she can hear that great stone clock beat down-down-down, deep in the earth and far away.

Betty Ann checks the meatloaf and the carrots, pulls an Old Gold from the pack on the counter, leans in, and lights it from the stove.

John-William's mother, Jack's wife, Betty Ann, gets a jelly glass of water, reaches past the Sunbeam mixer and flips on the Philco radio, watches the dial begin to glow, settles in a breakfast room chair. Old familiar voices make her smile. The Kingfish tries to talk Andy into some fool scheme. Betty Ann knows exactly what'll happen next. Andy falls for it, like Andy always does. Amos has to come in and straighten the whole mess out.

Lord, they were funny. Better than Benny or Fred Allen, either one. Jack wouldn't listen, wouldn't stay in the room if they were on. Said they weren't even coloreds on the show, said niggers weren't like that at all. Said they stole stuff fast as you could blink, didn't matter what it was.

The very next time Betty Ann looks up, the dark has creeped in from outside, hid the catsup and the flour in shadow. All she can see is the dim blue flame below the pot.

If I had any sense, thinks Betty Ann, I'd've opened a can of tuna fish instead of heating up the kitchen on a hot summer night. John-William didn't care, long as there were cookies or pies or something sweet in the house.

John-William's mother thinks he ought to be home right now. She doesn't like him out at night, but boys didn't know about the dark, didn't know what happens out there when the sun goes down and the day hides out of sight.

Amos 'n' Andy were gone. The radio plays a song she likes a lot.

It must have been moonglow,

Way out to the sea . . .

She and Jack used to hear it all the time when they'd take his daddy's big LaSalle out and park. That was when they first began to date, before they even thought about getting married or anything else besides parking, feeling up, and having fun. And even after that, sometimes, before Jack pumped her up like a tub with John-William inside, they'd hear that song and everything would be fine. Betty Ann's father didn't trust Jack at all. He knew what they were doing in the back of that LaSalle. Jack didn't wear overalls, wore a Searsucker suit and a snappy bow tie. He came from Paul's Valley, which didn't say much, even for an Oklahoma town. Still, like Betty Ann's mother Sarah said, anyone don't have shit on his shoes is worth looking at twice. Well that was a lie, considering Mr. Searsucker suit didn't hang around all that long after John-William's mother, Betty Ann, brought two more babies in the world who curled up and died.

John-William's mother walks from one shadow room to the next. The furniture is dim, like chairs and tables and beds all covered in a ghosty kind of light, the pale green glow like the fireflies John-William's mother used to capture in a jar.

It was the first brick house she'd ever lived in in her life. The first time she'd lived in town except once. Betty Ann and her mother had moved to Atoka from the farm when Mama Steck took sick and they had to live there till she died. When it happened, Betty Ann was right there, Betty Ann saw it, watched the night come until the room was inky black, watched while it hovered over Mama Steck a while, then plunged down into that dry and withered mouth and sucked her life away. Betty Ann peed her britches right then, and never, ever, told Mother what she saw.

Jack's wife, John-William's mother, walks through the dark, walks from one room to the next. To the living room, the big bedroom where she sleeps alone now, through the bathroom and John-William's room, even in the closets, out through the doorway that leads to the shed that sags against the house. Light from a half-moon slants through the holes that Jack never fixed. Truth to tell, Jack never fixed shit, never put a nail in a wall, never fixed a leak.

Lord, what a mess, thinks John-William's mother, Betty Ann. It's like your whole life's stacked up in there, gathering dust, soaking up time, hours used up and tossed away, moments dead and gone, rusted and frozen where they lay. Jack's hammers and his nails and his saws and his files and his broken axe, waiting to finish some goddamn thing he never even started at all. John-William's bike, broken and twisted, one wheel missing and one wheel bent. Wasn't anyone going to fix it. Why in heaven's name was she hanging onto that?

Just too much to bother about, thinks John-William's mother, and not enough time, not any time at all. . . .

Betty Ann, John-William's mother, perches on the edge of the tub and turns on the hot water tap. John-William's clothes are wadded in a pile. He'd ridden out for crawdads with bacon on a string, down by the creek behind the park. He'd gotten all soaked, peeled everything off, left it on the floor. John-William's mother gave him a proper scolding, the boy knew better than that. She'd scrubbed him good, tossed socks and under-pants into the bin. Picked up his shirt and shook her head. His brand new Ferdinand the Bull shirt and already ruined for good.

In John-William's pockets she found a Krazy Kat button and a string from a top, a cap from a Nehi Orange and a broken lead soldier with his legs cut off above the knees. When Betty Ann was fifteen, she stayed with her cousin Helen for a while. One night they drove into Lawton for a picture show and ice cream. Helen took her daddy's new Packard. They were supposed to be back before dark. They told Helen's daddy they had a flat. What happened was they met two soldiers in town from Fort Sill. The soldiers were both nineteen. They had a pint of gin and a carton of Wings cigarettes. Helen made Betty Ann drive while she and the best-looking boy sat and giggled in the back. Betty Ann knew they were doing more than that.

Betty Ann and the other soldier spread a blanket on the grass. Helen and her friend never left the back seat. Betty Ann couldn't stand the taste of gin. She drank a little all the same and smoked a lot of cigarettes. She let the boy kiss her, and he kissed real fine. After a while she let him reach in and touch her breasts. Just on the tops and not any lower than that. She hadn't meant to but the boy was real nice and he came from out of state. He said he'd like to see her naked. Betty Ann said absolutely not. They kissed a lot more. Betty Ann was flattered he was getting so hot. The cigarettes made her too dizzy to stop. She let him get on top and rub against her through his clothes. His hardness touched her once and that was that. The boy made a noise and walked off in the grass for some time. On the way home, when they'd let the soldiers off, Helen made Betty Ann tell her everything that happened in the grass. Then Helen told Betty Ann things she hadn't even thought about before.

John-William's mother lets the water run in the tub. Back in the bedroom she peels the sticky dress up over her head, drops it on the floor. Just like John-William, she thinks. Doesn't get all his bad habits from Jack. On the way back she stops, stands there in the hall. Something seems to move, something in the almost not quite corner in the dark. Something nearly there, something nearly out of sight. John-William's mother turns around fast. Gives a *little* jump, a little start. And there's Betty Ann looking back, just as surprised, just as naked as Betty Ann herself. Betty Ann knows she ought to look away, knows she shouldn't stand there staring in her birthday suit. Still, the sight in the mirror holds her fixed, holds her still, like a doe caught frightened in the light.

My lord, who's that, thinks John-William's mother. *It sure isn't me, isn't anyone that I ever knew!* It looks like her. But it can't be John-William's mother, can't be Jack's wife. Betty Ann feels sticky from the heat, from the sweat between her breasts, from the tingle in her nipples, from the heat between her knees. The woman in the mirror has beaded points of light in the dark between her thighs, has slick-silver flesh, has an opalescent glow like she's just stepped out of a moonlit sea. The woman in the mirror doesn't think about meatloaf at all, doesn't think about carrots on the stove. She thinks about the soldier and the need in his eyes and the hard thing pressed against her belly that night.

The woman in the mirror remembers every feeling, every moment with the soldier in the grass, later with a boy named Freddie and one named Alex, and Bob after that, and every single night, every morning with Jack, even the moments when he hit her too hard, when her face swelled up and she went out back to cry. . . .

Goodness sake, thinks John-William's mother, uneasy with the thoughts in her head, and the warm spots farther down than that. "Well that's what you get," she thinks out loud, "gawking at yourself like a Fort Worth floozie struttin' down Third Avenue."

John-William's mother remembers the water in the tub. Lord, she'd gone and left it on. There'd be water running out the door, into the hall and onto the carpet, and Jack's wife, Betty Ann, running naked 'round the house with a mop and John-William's supper in the stove.

Betty Ann stops right there and frowns at the tub. She's real sure she turned the water on, but there isn't a drip or a drop, and the tub's dry as a bone. Betty Ann shakes her head, says "Well, I declare," pads in her bare feet back down the hall, back to the kitchen, back to the stove, back to the counter and the peels in the sink, back to the meatloaf in the stove. Walks to the screen to check the latch. Stops, looks out the back. Remembers where she is and has to laugh. No one walks around naked in the kitchen, bare ass naked, not a stitch at all, even in the dark. If Jack came in right then he'd think she was crazy as a loon. Which doesn't much matter, she remembers, Jack's not coming back at all.

Betty Ann stands at the screen and looks out. Doesn't seem that long ago she was watching the light slink away, waiting for the dark to slide in. She looks past the drive to the Hooper's back yard. The walls are black, the roof has faded into night. She can see the Prewitts' fence, but the Kamps are out of sight. John-William's mother looks up as something flutters in the night. Just for an instant, it hangs there, a smudge against the inky sky. Maybe it has red eyes, she thinks. Maybe its tongue is colored orange.

A wind hot as syrup fills the night. Betty Ann's heart skips a beat. Skips two, hesitates, decides to try again. Betty Ann catches her breath, backs away from the door, leans against the sink. Lets her eyes touch the room. The garbage can, the broom, the chair, and the stove. She opens the pot, peers inside. The carrots are limp, dry as brittle leaves. The pale blue flame has gone out. She opens the oven door. The meatloaf is cold, pink, with little eyes of fat. The radio is dead, the refrigerator, too. The lights, the gas.

Turn on the faucet. A sputter and a cough. Betty Ann tries the phone. "Hello? Hello?" Just like in the movies. Nobody's there.

Betty Ann walks naked through the gray heavy gauze of her first brick house. She'd been real scared once before, when she and John-William were alone and Jack was in Tulsa overnight. Something had scratched on the window and made wet steps on the lawn. In the morning, there was nothing there to see. The next night Jack was snoring by her side, but Betty Ann didn't sleep for a week.

"It's all right," she says, "everything's fine. Everything's *off* right now, but it'll all go on again." Her voice sounds funny in the still and empty house. She feels her way back to the kitchen, finds her Old Golds, a box of matches on the sink. Paws through the junk drawer, finds a wad of string, pencil stubs, and dry fountain pens. No candles at all.

John-William's mother moves back down the hall. Looks in the mirror. Can't hardly see herself at all. Lights a kitchen match. Betty Ann naked, skin white as tallow in the flare of sudden light. The living room carpet's black as tar. The easy chairs are blurs against the greater dark. Feels for the sofa. Can't find it anywhere at all. The match doesn't work. She tries another and another after that. Tosses the box on the floor.

Moving real slow, doesn't want to bump her toes. Opens the front door a crack. Can't see much better than she did in the back.

The houses across the street are just like hers. Stubby brick, living room, bedrooms, kitchen in the back. Arch across the porch. Now all the houses are solemn and gray, all the color drained out, the life washed away. No lights in the windows, no lights at all.

Betty Ann opens the door a little wider, a little wider still. One bare foot outside and then the next. John-William's mother, Jack's wife, Betty Ann, stands naked on the hot front porch. Night wind brushes her flesh, tickles her breasts, whispers naughties in her ear.

Betty Ann stands very, very still. She can't remember when she last stood out in the night. Didn't flee, didn't run when the big clock deep in the earth warned everyone the light was dying and the dark was sweeping in, told everyone to hurry, get safe inside.

Still, it isn't so bad if you stand real still, if you don't think hard – *if you don't let the dark know you're there. It can't see everything, can it? A whole world of night out there, it can't watch every leaf, every stone, every time a dog does his business on the lawn. . . .*

It comes to her then, like the secret was there all the time, like she knew it in her head. Grandmaw didn't know it all – she knew the scary part, knew about the bad, but she didn't know the rest. All you have to do is stand very, very still, listen, listen, to the great stone clock down deep-deep within the earth, listen to it tick-tick-tick away the quiet moments, the hours, the long years of the night. Don't move, don't breathe, feel the silence and the wind, feel the whisper of the dark against your skin. . . .

John-William's mother, Jack's wife, Betty Ann, peers into the dark, looks into the inky night for a very long time, and after a while she wonders if she might not *be* Betty Ann standing naked on the porch, she might be Betty Ann dreaming somewhere, Betty Ann back at Mama's on the farm, looking at the rusty old Ford. She might be Betty Ann having ice cream with Johnny Two Horse, who said he was pure Cherokee. She liked Johnny Two Horse a whole lot, kissed him twice till Mama found out he wasn't white, washed her mouth with soap and put a stop to that.

Johnny Two Horse kissed her again, or maybe it was only the hot breeze sliding in upon the night to sweep the dream away. And, when she peered once more into the dark, Betty Ann could see things she hadn't seen before. The houses and the lawns and the trees looked different now, like the shiny things you get when they send your pictures back. Everything that used to be black was murky gray, and everything white went just the other way. It didn't seem *wrong*, turned inside out, it seemed, to Betty Ann, the way things ought to be. Maybe the way things had been all along and were getting right again.

Up past the Harpers and the Smiths and the Roers, where the street lamp stood on the corner, something seemed to shimmer, seemed to tremble, seemed to hide behind a veil, like looking through Grandmaw's glasses where the world was all a blur. Betty Ann blinked and the blur went away.

Then, for an instant, something was there and something not, something just beyond the corner, something coming, something waiting, something maybe in-between, something not quite ready, something not really there.

Betty Ann feels her mouth go dry, feels her legs go weak, backs up against the cold brick wall, backs up, finds the wall isn't there, knows, for sure, that isn't right at all. Walls stay where they are, where a wall's supposed to be. Betty Ann tries again, staggers, very nearly falls, slips through the wall, through the wires, through the wood, through the pipes and the nails, through the cobwebs and little dead spiders and bugs that huddle there.

John-William's mother, Sarah's daughter, Betty Ann, walks through the curtains that trickle like powder, like snow, like ash, before her eyes, walks through the sofa that crumbles into dust, into the hall where the walls begin to vanish, into the kitchen where the stove, the mixer, and the radio sigh and fall away.

Betty Ann stands naked, looks through the screen door, where it used to be, looks for the black birds singing on the wire, black birds white now, sees them on the ground, lying on their backs with their little beaks open, claws up in the air.

"Well my goodness," says Betty Ann, "now isn't that a sight to see. Why, it's like Andy always says, 'You neber do knows what gon' be happ'nin' but you kin bets it will.'"

John-William's mother laughs at the thought, walks back through where her first brick home used to be. Stops, for a moment, glances at the mirror in the hall. The mirror's not there but someone is, someone Betty Ann thinks she ought to know. Just for an instant, just for a blink, then just as quickly gone.

Betty Ann stands outside where the porch used to be, stands there naked and watches the corner past the Smiths and the Harpers and the Roers, looks at the lamp that's black instead of white, at the murky light on the street down below. Now, the thing on the corner, the thing that seemed to shimmer, seemed to tremble, seemed to hide behind a veil, isn't something maybe there anymore, isn't something maybe not, isn't waiting in-between anymore. . . .

John-William's mother can feel her heart pound, feel the big clock down far-far below begin to chime. Whatever wasn't there is coming on slow, dark and heavy, faint and distant, closer, closer still, hardly even there, turning, turning, past the Roers and the Smiths and the Harpers, coming right up to where John-William's mother stands naked where her first brick house used to be. . . .

They glide down the street now, slide on in without a sound, slip on in without a hum from their engines, a whisper from their tires. One before the other, one behind the next, hazy Buicks, Franklins, and Cords. Cloudy Chryslers, Lincolns, and Fords. Plymouths, Packards, Porsches, and Rolls, dusty and obscure. Duesenbergs, Dodges, Ramblers, and Olds, scarcely present, hardly there at all. Studebakers, Chevys, Rovers, and nearly invisible Saabs. Bentleys, Austins, Minors, and – goodness sakes, cars Betty Ann never heard about before.

They keep on coming, gliding down the street in a motion so slight they hardly stir the air. Each one black where they ought to be white, white where the black ought to be. Everything backwards, inside out. Just the way the big stone clock down, down, way below likes to see.

Betty Ann knows she shouldn't ought to move, shouldn't do anything at all. Ought to just mind her own business, shouldn't ought to pry. Still, she feels she's got to know, got to see what it's all about, got to know why these peculiar cars are driving by. Ought to see who, ought to see what's inside.

Betty Ann walks naked in the street, gets close to the windows, peers inside an old Franklin, looks inside a Saab. Can't see anything at all. The glass in each and every window is cold, cold, icy to the touch, covered with frost, dark and river deep.

John-William's mother wipes a little hole free and peers inside a 1930 Cadillac. And, to Betty Ann's surprise, there's Grandmaw Wilcher sitting up straight, straight as you please, hand-bones clutching the wheel, shriveled, shrunk, stiff as a board, hair hanging this way and that.

"Grandmaw Wilcher," Betty Ann says, "why, you can't even drive!" Driving she is, though, nothing you can do about that.

There's no one she knows in the Lincoln or the Cord. No one in the Nash. Helen, though, is there in the back seat of the Packard, caught in what seems intimate, dark coagulation with the soldier boy from Fort Sill. Ruin and rot have set in and a coat of fuzzy green. Still, Helen looks happy as a clam and, as Betty Ann's mother Sarah always said, happy's better than not.

Mama Steck looks not much worse than the night Betty Ann watched the dark slide in and slide out again, and suck her life away. Betty Ann can't recall anyone drove a Studebaker back then, but there's lots she can't recall.

"Jack, Jack, Jack," thinks John-William's mother, as she peeks into the LaSalle, "I got to say you do look a sight." Except for the blight and the ruin and the dent where she'd hit him with the axe. Except for that and the gross degeneration – well, time is going to take a toll, that and ancient ulceration of the soul – "Told you to stop," says Betty Ann. "Told you hit me one more time, that's it, and by God it's just what you did, you got nothing to complain about that."

Papa is in the rusted-out Ford, not looking all that good, something like tar and tallow dried on his overalls down into his shoes and some distortion of the bones.

Betty Ann thinks she might cry when she gets to the Chevy, she knew she'd find him there. That truck had hit him head on, wrapping the brand new Schwinn around him twice, penetrating bodily parts, leaving limbs twisted, badly out of whack.

Still, he did the best he could, God bless him, holding the wheel real steady, one hand sort of going this way, the other going that.

"You were my pride," says Betty Ann, "and I never forgot you, not for a minute, John-William, not for all the years that passed. I kept that Krazy Kat button and the Nehi cap as well. You tore that Ferdinand shirt real bad, but I don't guess you care about that."

Betty Ann opens the door, and slides real quiet inside. Looks at John-William, pictures in her head that he's looking back.

Just for a moment, no more than that, Betty Ann glances behind her, sees the two she lost sitting quiet, sitting still, looks there once and doesn't look back.

Nobody said it was time to drive on, but real soon everybody did. Rolling down the window, she listened to the music playing on the car radios: "Moonlight Cocktail," "Twilight Time," "One for My Baby," "Laura," "Willow Weep for Me."

And, coming from somewhere, out of the hot and inky night, just before the clock deep-deep in the earth strikes again, a whisper in the hot night air:

Not just before, Betty Ann,
And not just after,
It's not getting dark, Betty Ann,
The dark's already here. . . .

NOVELETTE

THE GAMBLER

Paolo Bacigalupi

FROM THE AUTHOR: "The Gambler" was conceived while I was still working at *High Country News*, an environmental news magazine that covers the Western United States. As the online editor, one of my jobs was to find ways to increase hits and web traffic, and it quickly became apparent that a simple blog post and an in-depth piece of investigative journalism had exactly the same value in terms of hits and traffic revenue. "The Gambler" was an attempt to follow the implications of this to its logical conclusion. One of the great kicks for me about "The Gambler" was later hearing that it found its way to the offices of Gawker Media and was circulated amongst the people who are actively building the new media future. As a science fiction writer, that's pretty much the best reward I could ever ask for.

MY FATHER WAS a gambler. He believed in the workings of karma and luck. He hunted for lucky numbers on license plates and bet on lotteries and fighting roosters. Looking back, I think perhaps he was not a large man, but when he took me to the muy thai fights, I thought him so. He would bet and he would win and laugh and drink laolao with his friends, and they all seemed so large. In the heat drip of Vientiane, he was a lucky ghost, walking the mirror-sheen streets in the darkness.

Everything for my father was a gamble: roulette and blackjack, new rice variants and the arrival of the monsoons. When the pretender monarch Khamsing announced his New Lao Kingdom, my father gambled on civil disobedience. He bet on the teachings of Mr. Henry David Thoreau and on whisper sheets posted on lampposts. He bet on saffron-robed monks marching in protest and on the hidden humanity of the soldiers with their well-oiled AK-47s and their mirrored helmets.

My father was a gambler, but my mother was not. While he wrote letters to the editor that brought the secret police to our door, she made plans for escape. The old Lao Democratic Republic collapsed, and the

New Lao Kingdom blossomed with tanks on the avenues and tuk-tuks burning on the street corners. Pha That Luang's shining gold chedi collapsed under shelling, and I rode away on a UN evacuation helicopter under the care of kind Mrs. Yamaguchi.

From the open doors of the helicopter, we watched smoke columns rise over the city like nagas coiling. We crossed the brown ribbon of the Mekong with its jeweled belt of burning cars on the Friendship Bridge. I remember a Mercedes floating in the water like a paper boat on Loi Kratong, burning despite the water all around.

Afterward, there was silence from the land of a million elephants, a void into which light and Skype calls and email disappeared. The roads were blocked. The telecoms died. A black hole opened where my country had once stood.

Sometimes, when I wake in the night to the swish and honk of Los Angeles traffic, the confusing polyglot of dozens of countries and cultures all pressed together in this American melting pot, I stand at my window and look down a boulevard full of red lights, where it is not safe to walk alone at night, and yet everyone obeys the traffic signals. I look down on the brash and noisy Americans in their many hues, and remember my parents: my father who cared too much to let me live under the self-declared monarchy, and my mother who would not let me die as a consequence. I lean against the window and cry with relief and loss.

Every week I go to temple and pray for them, light incense and make a triple bow to Buddha, Damma, and Sangha, and pray that they may have a good rebirth, and then I step into the light and noise and vibrancy of America.

My colleagues' faces flicker gray and pale in the light of their computers and tablets. The tap of their keyboards fills the newsroom as they pass content down the workflow chain and then, with a final keystroke and an obeisance to the "publish" button, they hurl it onto the net.

In the maelstrom, their work flares, tagged with site location, content tags, and social poke data. Blooms of color, codes for media conglomerates: shades of blue and Mickey Mouse ears for Disney-Bertelsmann. A red-rimmed pair of rainbow Os for Google's AOL News. Fox News Corp. in pinstripes gray and white. Green for us: Milestone Media – a combination of NTT DoCoMo, the Korean gaming consortium Hyundai-Kubu, and the smoking remains of the New York Times Company. There are others, smaller stars, Crayola shades flaring and brightening, but we are the most important. The monarchs of this universe of light and color.

New content blossoms on the screen, bathing us all in the bloody glow of a Google News content flare, off their WhisperTech feed. They've scooped us. The posting says that new earbud devices will be released by Frontal Lobe before Christmas: terabyte storage with Pin-Line connectivity for the Oakley microresponse glasses. The technology is next-gen, allowing personal data control via Pin-Line scans of a user's iris. Analysts predict that everything from cell phones to digital cameras will become obsolete as the full range of Oakley features becomes available. The news flare brightens and migrates toward the center of the maelstrom as visitors flock to Google and view stolen photos of the iris-scanning glasses.

Janice Mbutu, our managing editor, stands at the door to her office, watching with a frown. The maelstrom's red bath dominates the newsroom, a pressing reminder that Google is beating us, sucking away traffic. Behind glass walls, Bob and Casey, the heads of the Burning Wire, our own consumer technology feed, are screaming at their reporters, demanding they do better. Bob's face has turned almost as red as the maelstrom.

The maelstrom's true name is LiveTrack IV. If you were to go downstairs to the fifth floor and pry open the server racks, you would find a sniper sight logo and the words SCRY GLASS – KNOWLEDGE IS POWER stamped on their chips in metallic orange, which would tell you that even though Bloomberg rents us the machines, it is a Google-Nielsen partnership that provides the proprietary algorithms for analyzing the net flows – which means we pay a competitor to tell us what is happening with our own content.

LiveTrack IV tracks media user data – Web site, feed, VOD, audio-stream, TV broadcast – with Google's own net statistics gathering programs, aided by Nielsen hardware in personal data devices ranging from TVs to tablets to ear buds to handsets to car radios. To say that the maelstrom keeps a finger on the pulse of media is an understatement. Like calling the monsoon a little wet. The maelstrom is the pulse, the pressure, the blood-oxygen mix; the count of red cells and white, of T-cells and BAC, the screening for AIDS and hepatitis G . . . It is reality.

Our service version of the maelstrom displays the performance of our own content and compares it to the top one hundred user-traffic events in real-time. My own latest news story is up in the maelstrom, glittering near the edge of the screen, a tale of government incompetence: the harvested DNA of the checkerspot butterfly, already extinct, has been destroyed through mismanagement at the California Federal Biological Preserve Facility. The butterfly – along with sixty-two other species – was subjected to improper storage protocols, and now there is nothing except a little dust in vials. The samples literally blew away. My coverage of the story opens with federal workers down on their knees in a $2 billion, climate-controlled vault, with a dozen crime scene vacuums that they've borrowed from LAPD, trying to suck up a speck of butterfly that they might be able to reconstitute at some future time.

In the maelstrom, the story is a pinprick beside the suns and pulsing moons of traffic that represent other reporters' content. It doesn't compete well with news of Frontal Lobe devices, or reviews of Armored Total Combat, or live feeds of the Binge-Purge Championships. It seems that the only people who are reading my story are the biologists I interviewed. This is not surprising. When I wrote about bribes for subdivision approvals, the only people who read the story were county planners. When I wrote about cronyism in the selection of city water recycling technologies, the only people who read were water engineers. Still, even though no one seems to care about these stories, I am drawn to them, as though poking at the tiger of the American government will somehow make up for not being able to poke at the little cub of New Divine Monarch Khamsing. It is a foolish thing, a sort of Don Quixote crusade. As a consequence, my salary is the smallest in the office.

"Whoooo!"

Heads swivel from terminals, look for the noise: Marty Mackley, grinning.

"You can thank me . . ." He leans down and taps a button on his keyboard. "Now."

A new post appears in the maelstrom, a small green orb announcing itself on the "Glamour Report," *Scandal Monkey* blog, and *Marty's* byline feeds. As we watch, the post absorbs pings from software clients around the world, notifying the millions of people who follow his byline that he has launched a new story.

I flick my tablet open, check the tags:

Double DP,
Redneck HipHop,
Music News,
Schadenfreude,
underage,
pedophilia . . .

According to Mackley's story, Double DP the Russian mafia cowboy rapper – who, in my opinion, is not as good as the Asian pop sensation

Kulaap, but whom half the planet likes very much – is accused of impregnating the fourteen-year-old daughter of his face sculptor. Readers are starting to notice, and with their attention Marty's green-glowing news story begins to muscle for space in the maelstrom. The content star pulses, expands, and then, as though someone has thrown gasoline on it, it explodes. Double DP hits the social sites, starts getting recommended, sucks in more readers, more links, more clicks . . . and more ad dollars.

Marty does a pelvic grind of victory, then waves at everyone for their attention. "And that's not all, folks." He hits his keyboard again, and another story posts: live feeds of Double's house, where . . . it looks as though the man who popularized Redneck Russians is heading out the door in a hurry. It is a surprise to see video of the house, streaming live. Most freelance paparazzi are not patient enough to sit and hope that maybe, perhaps, something interesting will happen. This looks as though Marty has stationed his own exclusive papcams at the house, to watch for something like this.

We all watch as Double DP locks the door behind himself. Marty says, "I thought DP deserved the courtesy of notification that the story was going live."

"Is he fleeing?" Mikela Plaa asks.

Marty shrugs. "We'll see."

And indeed, it does look as if Double is about to do what Americans have popularized as an "OJ." He gets into his red Hummer. Pulling out.

Under the green glow of his growing story, Marty smiles. The story is getting bigger, and Marty has stationed himself perfectly for the development. Other news agencies and blogs are playing catch-up. Follow-on posts wink into existence in the maelstrom, gathering a momentum of their own as newsrooms scramble to hook our traffic.

"Do we have a helicopter?" Janice asks. She has come out of her glass office to watch the show.

Marty nods. "We're moving it into position. I just bought exclusive angel view with the cops, too, so everyone's going to have to license our footage."

"Did you let Long Arm of the Law know about the cross-content?"

"Yeah. They're kicking in from their budget for the helicopter."

Marty sits down again, begins tapping at his keyboard, a machinegun of data entry. A low murmur comes from the tech pit, Cindy C. calling our telecom providers, locking down trunklines to handle an anticipated data surge. She knows something that we don't, something that Marty has prepared her for. She's bringing up mirrored server farms. Marty seems unaware of the audience around him. He stops typing. Stares up at the maelstrom, watching his glowing ball of content. He is the maestro of a symphony.

The cluster of competing stories are growing as *Gawker* and *Newsweek* and *Throb* all organize themselves and respond. Our readers are clicking away from us, trying to see if there's anything new in our competitor's coverage. Marty smiles, hits his "publish" key, and dumps a new bucket of meat into the shark tank of public interest: a video interview with the fourteen-year-old. On-screen, she looks very young, shockingly so. She has a teddy bear.

"I swear I didn't plant the bear," Marty comments. "She had it on her own."

The girl's accusations are being mixed over Double's run for the border, a kind of synth loop of accusations:

"And then he . . ."

"And I said . . ."

"He's the only one I've ever . . ."

It sounds as if Marty has licensed some of Double's own beats for the coverage of his fleeing Humvee. The video outtakes are already bouncing around YouTube and MotionSwallow like Ping-Pong balls. The maelstrom has moved Double DP to the center of the display as more and more feeds and sites point to the content. Not only is traffic up, but the post is gaining in social rank as the numbers of links and social pokes increase.

"How's the stock?" someone calls out.

Marty shakes his head. "They locked me out from showing the display."

This, because whenever he drops an important story, we all beg him to show us the big picture. We all turn to Janice. She rolls her eyes, but she gives the nod. When Cindy finishes buying bandwidth, she unlocks the view. The maelstrom slides aside as a second window opens, all bar graphs and financial landscape: our stock price as affected by the story's expanding traffic – and expanding ad revenue.

The stock bots have their own version of the maelstrom; they've picked up the reader traffic shift. Buy and sell decisions roll across the screen, responding to the popularity of Mackley's byline. As he feeds the story, the beast grows. More feeds pick us up, more people recommend the story to their friends, and every one of them is being subjected to our advertisers' messages, which means more revenue for us and less for everyone else. At this point, Mackley is bigger than the Super Bowl. Given that the story is tagged with Double DP, it will have a targetable demographic: thirteen- to twenty-four-year-olds who buy lifestyle gadgets, new music, edge clothes, first-run games, boxed hairstyles, tablet skins, and ringtones: not only a large demographic, a valuable one.

Our stock ticks up a point. Holds. Ticks up another. We've got four different screens running now. The papcam of Double DP, chase cycles with views of the cops streaking after him, the chopper lifting off, and the window with the fourteen-year-old interviewing. The girl is saying, "I really feel for him. We have a connection. We're going to get married," and there's his Hummer screaming down Santa Monica Boulevard with his song "Cowboy Banger" on the audio overlay.

A new wave of social pokes hits the story. Our stock price ticks up again. Daily bonus territory. The clicks are pouring in. It's got the right combination of content, what Mackley calls the "Three Ss": sex, stupidity, and schadenfreude. The stock ticks up again. Everyone cheers. Mackley takes a bow. We all love him. He is half the reason I can pay my rent. Even a small newsroom bonus from his work is enough for me to live. I'm not sure how much he makes for himself when he creates an event like this. Cindy tells me that it is "solid seven, baby." His byline feed is so big he could probably go independent, but then he would not have the resources to scramble a helicopter for a chase toward Mexico. It is a symbiotic relationship. He does what he does best, and Milestone pays him like a celebrity.

Janice claps her hands. "All right, everyone. You've got your bonus. Now back to work."

A general groan rises. Cindy cuts the big monitor away from stocks and bonuses and back to the work at hand: generating more content to light the maelstrom, to keep the newsroom glowing green with flares of Milestone coverage – everything from reviews of Mitsubishi's 100 mpg Road Cruiser to how to choose a perfect turkey for Thanksgiving. Mackley's story pulses over us as we work. He spins off smaller additional stories, updates, interactivity features, encouraging his vast audience to ping back just one more time.

Marty will spend the entire day in conversation with this elephant of a story that he has created. Encouraging his visitors to return for just one more click. He'll give them chances to poll each other, discuss how they'd like to see DP punished, ask whether you can actually fall in love with a fourteen-year-old. This one will have a long life, and he will raise it like a proud father, feeding and nurturing it, helping it make its way in the rough world of the maelstrom.

My own little green speck of content has disappeared. It seems that even government biologists feel for Double DP.

*   *   *

When my father was not placing foolish bets on revolution, he taught agronomy at the National Lao University. Perhaps our lives would have been different if he had been a rice farmer in the paddies of the capital's suburbs, instead of surrounded by intellectuals and ideas. But his karma was to be a teacher and a researcher, and so while he was increasing Lao rice production by 30 percent, he was also filling himself with gambler's fancies: Thoreau, Gandhi, Martin Luther King, Sakharov, Mandela, Aung San Suu Kyi. True gamblers, all. He would say that if white South Africans could be made to feel shame, then the pretender monarch must right his ways. He claimed that Thoreau must have been Lao, the way he protested so politely.

In my father's description, Thoreau was a forest monk, gone into the jungle for enlightenment. To live amongst the banyan and the climbing vines of Massachusetts and to meditate on the nature of suffering. My father believed he was undoubtedly some arhat reborn. He often talked of Mr. Henry David, and in my imagination this falang, too, was a large man like my father.

When my father's friends visited in the dark – after the coup and the countercoup, and after the march of Khamsing's Chinese-supported insurgency – they would often speak of Mr. Henry David. My father would sit with his friends and students and drink black Lao coffee and smoke cigarettes, and then he would write carefully worded complaints against the government that his students would then copy and leave in public places, distribute into gutters, and stick onto walls in the dead of night.

His guerrilla complaints would ask where his friends had gone, and why their families were so alone. He would ask why monks were beaten on their heads by Chinese soldiers when they sat in hunger strike before the palace. Sometimes, when he was drunk and when these small gambles did not satisfy his risk-taking nature, he would send editorials to the newspapers.

None of these were ever printed, but he was possessed with some spirit that made him think that perhaps the papers would change. That his stature as a father of Lao agriculture might somehow sway the editors to commit suicide and print his complaints.

It ended with my mother serving coffee to a secret police captain while two more policemen waited outside our door. The captain was very polite: he offered my father a 555 cigarette – a brand that already had become rare and contraband – and lit it for him. Then he spread the whisper sheet onto the coffee table, gently pushing aside the coffee cups and their saucers to make room for it. It was rumpled and torn, stained with mud. Full of accusations against Khamsing. Unmistakable as one of my father's.

My father and the policeman both sat and smoked, studying the paper silently.

Finally, the captain asked, "Will you stop?"

My father drew on his cigarette and let the smoke out slowly as he studied the whisper sheet between them. The captain said, "We all respect what you have done for the Lao Kingdom. I myself have family who would have starved if not for your work in the villages." He leaned forward. "If you promise to stop writing these whispers and complaints, everything can be forgotten. Everything."

Still, my father didn't say anything. He finished his cigarette. Stubbed it out. "It would be difficult to make that sort of promise," he said.

The captain was surprised. "You have friends who have spoken on your behalf. Perhaps you would reconsider. For their sake."

My father made a little shrug. The captain spread the rumpled whisper sheet, flattening it out more completely. Read it over. "These sheets do nothing," he said. "Khamsing's dynasty will not collapse because you print a few complaints. Most of these are torn down before anyone reads them. They do nothing. They are pointless." He was almost begging. He looked over and saw me watching at the door. "Give this up. For your family, if not your friends."

I would like to say that my father said something grand. Something honorable about speaking against tyranny. Perhaps invoked one of his idols. Aung San Suu Kyi or Sakharov, or Mr. Henry David and his penchant for polite protest. But he didn't say anything. He just sat with his hands on his knees, looking down at the torn whisper sheet. I think now that he must have been very afraid. Words always came easily to him, before. Instead, all he did was repeat himself. "It would be difficult."

The captain waited. When it became apparent that my father had nothing else to say, he put down his coffee cup and motioned for his men to come inside. They were all very polite. I think the captain even apologized to my mother as they led him out the door.

We are into day three of the Double DP bonanza, and the green sun glows brightly over all of us, bathing us in its soothing, profitable glow. I am working on my newest story with my Frontal Lobe ear buds in, shutting out everything except the work at hand. It is always a little difficult to write in one's third language, but I have my favorite singer and fellow countryperson Kulaap whispering in my ear that "Love Is a Bird," and the work is going well. With Kulaap singing to me in our childhood language, I feel very much at home.

A tap on my shoulder interrupts me. I pull out my ear buds and look around. Janice, standing over me. "Ong, I need to talk to you." She motions me to follow.

In her office, she closes the door behind me and goes to her desk. "Sit down, Ong." She keys her tablet, scrolls through data. "How are things going for you?"

"Very well. Thank you." I'm not sure if there is more that she wants me to say, but it is likely that she will tell me. Americans do not leave much to guesswork.

"What are you working on for your next story?" she asks.

I smile. I like this story; it reminds me of my father. And with Kulaap's soothing voice in my ears I have finished almost all of my research. The bluet, a flower made famous in Mr. Henry David Thoreau's journals, is blooming too early to be pollinated. Bees do not seem to find it when it blooms in March. The scientists I interviewed blame global warming, and now the flower is in danger of extinction. I have interviewed biologists and local naturalists, and now I would like to go to Walden Pond on a pilgrimage for this bluet that may soon also be bottled in a federal reserve laboratory with its techs in clean suits and their crime scene vacuums.

When I finish describing the story, Janice looks at me as if I am crazy. I can tell that she thinks I am crazy, because I can see it on her face. And also because she tells me.

"You're fucking crazy!"

Americans are very direct. It's difficult to keep face when they yell at you. Sometimes, I think that I have adapted to America. I have been here for five years now, ever since I came from Thailand on a scholarship, but at times like this, all I can do is smile and try not to cringe as they lose their face and yell and rant. My father was once struck in the face with an official's shoe, and he did not show his anger. But Janice is American, and she is very angry.

"There's no way I'm going to authorize a junket like that!"

I try to smile past her anger, and then remember that the Americans don't see an apologetic smile in the same way that a Lao would. I stop smiling and make my face look . . . something. Earnest, I hope.

"The story is very important," I say. "The ecosystem isn't adapting correctly to the changing climate. Instead, it has lost . . ." I grope for the word. "Synchronicity. These scientists think that the flower can be saved, but only if they import a bee that is available in Turkey. They think it can replace the function of the native bee population, and they think that it will not be too disruptive."

"Flowers and Turkish bees."

"Yes. It is an important story. Do they let the flower go extinct? Or try to keep the famous flower, but alter the environment of Walden Pond? I think your readers will think it is very interesting."

"More interesting than that?" She points through her glass wall at the maelstrom, at the throbbing green sun of Double DP, who has now barricaded himself in a Mexican hotel and has taken a pair of fans hostage.

"You know how many clicks we're getting?" she asks. "We're exclusive. Marty's got Double's trust and is going in for an interview tomorrow, assuming the Mexicans don't just raid it with commandos. We've got people clicking back every couple minutes just to look at Marty's blog about his preparations to go in."

The glowing globe not only dominates the maelstrom's screen, it washes everything else out. If we look at the stock bots, everyone who doesn't have protection under our corporate umbrella has been hurt by the loss of eyeballs. Even the Frontal Lobe/Oakley story has been swallowed. Three days of completely dominating the maelstrom has been very profitable for us. Now Marty's showing his viewers how he will wear a flak jacket in case the Mexican commandos attack while he is discussing the nature of true love with DP. And he has another exclusive interview with the mother ready to post as well. Cindy has been editing the footage and telling us all how disgusted she is with the whole thing. The woman apparently drove her daughter to DP's mansion for a midnight pool party, alone.

"Perhaps some people are tired of DP and wish to see something else," I suggest.

"Don't shoot yourself in the foot with a flower story, Ong. Even Pradeep's cooking journey through Ladakh gets more viewers than this stuff you're writing."

She looks as though she will say more, but then she simply stops. It seems as if she is considering her words. It is uncharacteristic. She normally speaks before her thoughts are arranged.

"Ong, I like you," she says. I make myself smile at this, but she continues. "I hired you because I had a good feeling about you. I didn't have a problem with clearing the visas to let you stay in the country. You're a good person. You write well. But you're averaging less than a thousand pings on your byline feed." She looks down at her tablet, then back up at me. "You need to up your average. You've got almost no readers selecting you for Page One. And even when they do subscribe to your feed, they're putting it in the third tier."

"Spinach reading," I supply.

"What?"

"Mr. Mackley calls it spinach reading. When people feel like they should do something with virtue, like eat their spinach, they click to me. Or else read Shakespeare."

I blush, suddenly embarrassed. I do not mean to imply that my work is of the same caliber as a great poet. I want to correct myself, but I'm too embarrassed. So instead I shut up, and sit in front of her, blushing.

She regards me. "Yes. Well, that's a problem. Look, I respect what you do. You're obviously very smart." Her eyes scan her tablet. "The butterfly thing you wrote was actually pretty interesting."

"Yes?" I make myself smile again.

"It's just that no one wants to read these stories."

I try to protest. "But you hired me to write the important stories. The stories about politics and the government, to continue the traditions of the old newspapers. I remember what you said when you hired me."

"Yeah, well." She looks away. "I was thinking more about a good scandal."

"The checkerspot is a scandal. That butterfly is now gone."

She sighs. "No, it's not a scandal. It's just a depressing story. No one reads a depressing story, at least, not more than once. And no one subscribes to a depressing byline feed."

"A thousand people do."

"A thousand people." She laughs. "We aren't some Laotian community weblog, we're Milestone, and we're competing for clicks with them." She waves outside, indicating the maelstrom. "Your stories don't last longer than half a day; they never get social-poked by anyone except a fringe." She shakes her head. "Christ, I don't even know who your demographic is. Centenarian hippies? Some federal bureaucrats? The numbers just don't justify the amount of time you spend on stories."

"What stories do you wish me to write?"

"I don't know. Anything. Product reviews. News you can use. Just not any more of this 'we regret to inform you of bad news' stuff. If there isn't something a reader can do about the damn butterfly, then there's no point in telling them about it. It just depresses people, and it depresses your numbers."

"We don't have enough numbers from Marty?"

She laughs at that. "You remind me of my mother. Look, I don't want to cut you, but if you can't start pulling at least a fifty thousand daily average, I won't have any choice. Our group median is way down in comparison to other teams, and when evaluations come around, we look bad. I'm up against Nguyen in the Tech and Toys pool, and Penn in Yoga and Spirituality, and no one wants to read about how the world's going to shit. Go find me some stories that people want to read."

She says a few more things, words that I think are meant to make me feel inspired and eager, and then I am standing outside the door, once again facing the maelstrom.

The truth is that I have never written popular stories. I am not a popular story writer. I am earnest. I am slow. I do not move at the speed these Americans seem to love. Find a story that people want to read. I can write some follow-up to Mackley, to Double DP, perhaps assist with sidebars to his main piece, but somehow, I suspect that the readers will know that I am faking it.

Marty sees me standing outside of Janice's office. He comes over.

"She giving you a hard time about your numbers?"

"I do not write the correct sort of stories."

"Yeah. You're an idealist."

We both stand there for a moment, meditating on the nature of idealism. Even though he is very American, I like him because he is sensitive to people's hearts. People trust him. Even Double DP trusts him, though Marty blew his name over every news tablet's front page. Marty has a good heart. Jai dee. I like him. I think that he is genuine.

"Look, Ong," he says. "I like what you do." He puts his hand around my shoulder. For a moment, I think he's about to try to rub my head with affection and I have to force myself not to wince, but he's sensitive and instead takes his hand away. "Look, Ong. We both know you're terrible at this kind of work. We're in the news business, here. And you're just not cut out for it."

"My visa says I have to remain employed."

"Yeah. Janice is a bitch for that. Look." He pauses. "I've got this thing with Double DP going down in Mexico. But I've got another story brewing. An exclusive. I've already got my bonus, anyway. And it should push up your average."

"I do not think that I can write Double DP sidebars."

He grins. "It's not that. And it's not charity; you're actually a perfect match."

"Is it about government mismanagement?"

He laughs, but I think he's not really laughing at me. "No." He pauses, smiles. "It's Kulaap. An interview."

I suck in my breath. My fellow countryperson, here in America. She came out during the purge as well. She was doing a movie in Singapore when the tanks moved, and so she was not trapped. She was already very

popular all over Asia, and when Khamsing turned our country into a
black hole, the world took note. Now she is popular here in America as
well. Very beautiful. And she remembers our country before it went into
darkness. My heart is pounding.

Marty goes on. "She's agreed to do an exclusive with me. But you
even speak her language, so I think she'd agree to switch off." He pauses,
looks serious. "I've got a good history with Kulaap. She doesn't give interviews to just anyone. I did a lot of exposure stories about her when Laos
was going to hell. Got her a lot of good press. This is a special favor
already, so don't fuck it up."

I shake my head. "No. I will not." I press my palms together and touch
them to my forehead in a nop of appreciation. "I will not fuck it up." I
make another nop.

He laughs. "Don't bother with that polite stuff. Janice will cut off your
balls to increase the stock price, but we're the guys in the trenches. We
stick together, right?"

In the morning, I make a pot of strong coffee with condensed milk; I boil
rice noodle soup and add bean sprouts and chiles and vinegar, and warm
a loaf of French bread that I buy from a Vietnamese bakery a few blocks
away. With a new mix of Kulaap's music from DJ Dao streaming in over
my stereo, I sit down at my little kitchen table, pour my coffee from its
press pot, and open my tablet.

The tablet is a wondrous creation. In Laos, the paper was still a paper:
physical, static, and empty of anything except the official news. Real
news in our New Divine Kingdom did not come from newspapers, or
from television, or from handsets or ear buds. It did not come from the
net or feeds unless you trusted your neighbor not to look over your shoulder at an Internet café and if you knew that there were no secret police
sitting beside you, or an owner who would be able to identify you when
they came around asking about the person who used that workstation
over there to communicate with the outside world.

Real news came from whispered rumor, rated according to the trust
you accorded the whisperer. Were they family? Did they have long
history with you? Did they have anything to gain by the sharing? My
father and his old classmates trusted one another. He trusted some of his
students, as well. I think this is why the security police came for him in
the end. One of his trusted friends or students also whispered news to
official friends. Perhaps Mr. Inthachak, or Som Vang. Perhaps another.
It is impossible to peer into the blackness of that history and guess at who
told true stories and in which direction.

In any case, it was my father's karma to be taken, so perhaps it does not matter who did the whispering. But before then – before the news of my father flowed up to official ears – none of the real news flowed toward Lao TV or the *Vientiane Times*. Which meant that when the protests happened and my father came through the door with blood on his face from baton blows, we could read as much as we wanted about the three thousand schoolchildren who had sung the national anthem to our new divine monarch. While my father lay in bed, delirious with pain, the papers told us that China had signed a rubber contract that would triple revenue for Luang Namtha Province and that Nam Theun Dam was now earning BT 22.5 billion per year in electricity fees to Thailand. But there were no bloody batons, and there were no dead monks, and there was no Mercedes-Benz burning in the river as it floated toward Cambodia.

Real news came on the wings of rumor, stole into our house at midnight, sat with us and sipped coffee and fled before the call of roosters could break the stillness. It was in the dark, over a burning cigarette that you learned Vilaphon had disappeared or that Mr. Saeng's wife had been beaten as a warning. Real news was too valuable to risk in public.

Here in America, my page glows with many news feeds, flickers at me in video windows, pours in at me over broadband. It is a waterfall of information. As my personal news page opens, my feeds arrange themselves, sorting according to the priorities and tag categories that I've set, a mix of Muang Lao news, Lao refugee blogs, and the chatting of a few close friends from Thailand and the American college where I attended on a human relief scholarship.

On my second page and my third, I keep the general news, the arrangements of *Milestone*, the *Bangkok Post*, the *Phnom Penh Express* – the news chosen by editors. But by the time I've finished with my own selections, I don't often have time to click through the headlines that these earnest news editors select for the mythical general reader.

In any case, I know far better than they what I want to read, and with my keyword and tag scans, I can unearth stories and discussions that a news agency would never think to provide. Even if I cannot see into the black hole itself, I can slip along its edges, divine news from its fringe.

I search for tags like Vientiane, Laos, Lao, Khamsing, China-Lao friendship, Korat, Golden Triangle, Hmong independence, Lao PDR, my father's name . . . Only those of us who are Lao exiles from the March Purge really read these blogs. It is much as when we lived in the capital. The blogs are the rumors that we used to whisper to one another.

Now we publish our whispers over the net and join mailing lists instead of secret coffee groups, but it is the same. It is family, as much as any of us now have.

On the maelstrom, the tags for Laos don't even register. Our tags bloomed brightly for a little while, while there were still guerrilla students uploading content from their handsets, and the images were lurid and shocking. But then the phone lines went down and the country fell into its black hole and now it is just us, this small network that functions outside the country.

A headline from *Jumbo Blog* catches my eye. I open the site, and my tablet fills with the colorful image of the three-wheeled taxi of my childhood. I often come here. It is a node of comfort.

Laofriend posts that some people, maybe a whole family, have swum the Mekong and made it into Thailand. He isn't sure if they were accepted as refugees or if they were sent back.

It is not an official news piece. More, the idea of a news piece. SomPaBoy doesn't believe it, but Khamchanh contends that the rumor is true, heard from someone who has a sister married to an Isaan border guard in the Thai army. So we cling to it. Wonder about it. Guess where these people came from, wonder if, against all odds, it could be one of ours: a brother, a sister, a cousin, a father. . . .

After an hour, I close the tablet. It's foolish to read any more. It only brings up memories. Worrying about the past is foolish. Lao PDR is gone. To wish otherwise is suffering.

The clerk at Novotel's front desk is expecting me. A hotel staffer with a key guides me to a private elevator bank that whisks us up into the smog and heights. The elevator doors open to a small entryway with a thick mahogany door. The staffer steps back into the elevator and disappears, leaving me standing in this strange airlock. Presumably, I am being examined by Kulaap's security.

The mahogany door opens and a smiling black man who is forty centimeters taller than I and who has muscles that ripple like snakes, smiles and motions me inside. He guides me through Kulaap's sanctuary. She keeps the heat high, almost tropical, and fountains rush everywhere around. The flat is musical with water. I unbutton my collar in the humidity. I was expecting air-conditioning, and instead I am sweltering. It's almost like home. And then she's in front of me, and I can hardly speak. She is beautiful, and more. It is intimidating to stand before someone who exists in film and in music but has never existed before you in the flesh. She's not as stunning as she is in the movies, but there's more life, more presence;

the movies lose that quality about her. I make a nop of greeting, pressing my hands together, touching my forehead.

She laughs at this, takes my hand, and shakes it American-style. "You're lucky Marty likes you so much," she says. "I don't like interviews."

I can barely find my voice. "Yes. I only have a few questions."

"Oh no. Don't be shy." She laughs again, and doesn't release my hand, pulls me toward her living room. "Marty told me about you. You need help with your ratings. He helped me once, too."

She's frightening. She is of my people, but she has adapted better to this place than I have. She seems comfortable here. She walks differently, smiles differently; she is an American, with perhaps some flavor of our country, but nothing of our roots. It's obvious. And strangely disappointing. In her movies, she holds herself so well, and now she sits down on her couch and sprawls with her feet kicked out in front of her. Not caring at all. I'm embarrassed for her, and I'm glad I don't have my camera set up yet. She kicks her feet up on the couch. I can't help but be shocked. She catches my expression and smiles.

"You're worse than my parents. Fresh off the boat."

"I am sorry."

She shrugs. "Don't worry about it. I spent half my life here, growing up; different country, different rules."

I'm embarrassed. I try not to laugh with the tension I feel. "I just have some interview questions," I say.

"Go ahead." She sits up and arranges herself for the video stand that I set up.

I begin. "When the March Purge happened, you were in Singapore."

She nods. "That's right. We were finishing *The Tiger and the Ghost*."

"What was your first thought when it happened? Did you want to go back? Were you surprised?"

She frowns. "Turn off the camera."

When it's off she looks at me with pity. "This isn't the way to get clicks. No one cares about an old revolution. Not even my fans." She stands abruptly and calls through the green jungle of her flat. "Terrell?"

The big black man appears. Smiling and lethal. Looming over me. He is very frightening. The movies I grew up with had falang like him. Terrifying large black men whom our heroes had to overcome. Later, when I arrived in America, it was different, and I found out that the falang and the black people don't like the way we show them in our movies. Much like when I watch their Vietnam movies, and see the ugly way the Lao freedom fighters behave. Not real at all, portrayed like animals. But still, I cannot help but cringe when Terrell looks at me.

Kulaap says, "We're going out, Terrell. Make sure you tip off some of the papcams. We're going to give them a show."

"I don't understand," I say.

"You want clicks, don't you?"

"Yes, but—"

She smiles. "You don't need an interview. You need an event." She looks me over. "And better clothes." She nods to her security man. "Terrell, dress him up."

A flashbulb frenzy greets us as we come out of the tower. Papcams everywhere. Chase cycles revving, and Terrell and three others of his people guiding us through the press to the limousine, shoving cameras aside with a violence and power that are utterly unlike the careful pity he showed when he selected a Gucci suit for me to wear.

Kulaap looks properly surprised at the crowd and the shouting reporters, but not nearly as surprised as I am, and then we're in the limo, speeding out of the tower's roundabout as papcams follow us.

Kulaap crouches before the car's onboard tablet, keying in pass codes. She is very pretty, wearing a black dress that brushes her thighs and thin straps that caress her smooth bare shoulders. I feel as if I am in a movie. She taps more keys. A screen glows, showing the taillights of our car: the view from pursuing papcams.

"You know I haven't dated anyone in three years?" she asks.

"Yes. I know from your Web site biography."

She grins. "And now it looks like I've found one of my countrymen."

"But we're not on a date," I protest.

"Of course we are." She smiles again. "I'm going out on a supposedly secret date with a cute and mysterious Lao boy. And look at all those papcams chasing after us, wondering where we're going and what we're going to do." She keys in another code, and now we can see live footage of the paparazzi, as viewed from the tail of her limo. She grins. "My fans like to see what life is like for me."

I can almost imagine what the maelstrom looks like right now: there will still be Marty's story, but now a dozen other sites will be lighting up, and in the center of that, Kulaap's own view of the excitement, pulling in her fans, who will want to know, direct from her, what's going on. She holds up a mirror, checks herself, and then she smiles into her smartphone's camera.

"Hi everyone. It looks like my cover's blown. Just thought I should let you know that I'm on a lovely date with a lovely man. I'll let you all know how it goes. Promise." She points the camera at me. I stare at it stupidly. She laughs. "Say hi and good-bye, Ong."

"Hi and good-bye."

She laughs again, waves into the camera. "Love you all. Hope you have as good a night as I'm going to have." And then she cuts the clip and punches a code to launch the video to her Web site.

It is a bit of nothing. Not a news story, not a scoop even, and yet, when she opens another window on her tablet, showing her own miniversion of the maelstrom, I can see her site lighting up with traffic. Her version of the maelstrom isn't as powerful as what we have at Milestone, but still, it is an impressive window into the data that is relevant to Kulaap's tags.

"What's your feed's byline?" she asks. "Let's see if we can get your traffic bumped up."

"Are you serious?"

"Marty Mackley did more than this for me. I told him I'd help." She laughs. "Besides, we wouldn't want you to get sent back to the black hole, would we?"

"You know about the black hole?" I can't help doing a double-take.

Her smile is almost sad. "You think just because I put my feet up on the furniture that I don't care about my aunts and uncles back home? That I don't worry about what's happening?"

"I—"

She shakes her head. "You're so fresh off the boat."

"Do you use the Jumbo Café—" I break off. It seems too unlikely.

She leans close. "My handle is Laofriend. What's yours?"

"Littlexang. I thought Laofriend was a boy—"

She just laughs.

I lean forward. "Is it true that the family made it out?"

She nods. "For certain. A general in the Thai army is a fan. He tells me everything. They have a listening post. And sometimes they send scouts across."

It's almost as if I am home.

We go to a tiny Laotian restaurant where everyone recognizes her and falls over her and the owners simply lock out the paparazzi when they become too intrusive. We spend the evening unearthing memories of Vientiane. We discover that we both favored the same rice noodle cart on Kaem Khong. That she used to sit on the banks of the Mekong and wish that she were a fisherman. That we went to the same waterfalls outside the city on the weekends. That it is impossible to find good dum mak hoong anywhere outside of the country. She is a good companion, very alive. Strange in her American ways, but still, with a good heart. Periodically, we click photos of one another and post them to her site, feeding the voyeurs. And then we are in the limo again and the paparazzi are all around us. I have the strange feeling of fame. Flashbulbs everywhere. Shouted questions. I feel proud to be beside this beautiful intelligent woman who knows so much more than any of us about the situation inside our homeland.

Back in the car, she has me open a bottle of champagne and pour two glasses while she opens the maelstrom and studies the results of our date. She has reprogrammed it to watch my byline feed ranking as well.

"You've got twenty thousand more readers than you did yesterday," she says.

I beam. She keeps reading the results. "Someone already did a scan on your face." She toasts me with her glass. "You're famous."

We clink glasses. I am flushed with wine and happiness. I will have Janice's average clicks. It's as though a bodhisattva has come down from heaven to save my job. In my mind, I offer thanks to Marty for arranging this, for his generous nature. Kulaap leans close to her screen, watching the flaring content. She opens another window, starts to read. She frowns.

"What the fuck do you write about?"

I draw back, surprised. "Government stories, mostly." I shrug. "Sometimes environment stories."

"Like what?"

"I am working on a story right now about global warming and Henry David Thoreau."

"Aren't we done with that?"

I'm confused. "Done with what?"

The limo jostles us as it makes a turn, moves down Hollywood Boulevard, letting the cycles rev around us like schools of fish. They're snapping pictures at the side of the limo, snapping at us. Through the tinting, they're like fireflies, smaller flares than even my stories in the maelstrom.

"I mean, isn't that an old story?" She sips her champagne. "Even America is reducing emissions now. Everyone knows it's a problem." She taps her couch's armrest. "The carbon tax on my limo has tripled, even with the hybrid engine. Everyone agrees it's a problem. We're going to fix it. What's there to write about?"

She is an American. Everything that is good about them: their optimism, their willingness to charge ahead, to make their own future. And everything that is bad about them: their strange ignorance, their unwillingness to believe that they must behave as other than children.

"No. It's not done," I say. "It is worse. Worse every day. And the changes we make seem to have little effect. Maybe too little, or maybe too late. It is getting worse."

She shrugs. "That's not what I read."

I try not to show my exasperation. "Of course it's not what you read." I wave at the screen. "Look at the clicks on my feed. People want happy stories. Want fun stories. Not stories like I write. So instead, we all write what you will read, which is nothing."

"Still—"

"No." I make a chopping motion with my hand. "We newspeople are very smart monkeys. If you will give us your so lovely eyeballs and your click-throughs we will do whatever you like. We will write good news, and news you can use, news you can shop to, news with the 'Three Ss.' We will tell you how to have better sex or eat better or look more beautiful or feel happier or how to meditate – yes, so enlightened." I make a face. "If you want a walking meditation and Double DP, we will give it to you."

She starts to laugh.

"Why are you laughing at me?" I snap. "I am not joking!"

She waves a hand. "I know, I know, but what you just said 'double'—" She shakes her head, still laughing. "Never mind."

I lapse into silence. I want to go on, to tell her of my frustrations. But now I am embarrassed at my loss of composure. I have no face. I didn't used to be like this. I used to control my emotions, but now I am an American, as childish and unruly as Janice. And Kulaap laughs at me.

I control my anger. "I think I want to go home," I say. "I don't wish to be on a date anymore."

She smiles and reaches over to touch my shoulder. "Don't be that way."

A part of me is telling me that I am a fool. That I am reckless and foolish for walking away from this opportunity. But there is something else, something about this frenzied hunt for page views and click-throughs and ad revenue that suddenly feels unclean. As if my father is with us in the car, disapproving. Asking if he posted his complaints about his missing friends for the sake of clicks.

"I want to get out," I hear myself say. "I do not wish to have your clicks."

"But—"

I look up at her. "I want to get out. Now."

"Here?" She makes a face of exasperation, then shrugs. "It's your choice."

"Yes. Thank you."

She tells her driver to pull over. We sit in stiff silence.

"I will send your suit back to you," I say.

She gives me a sad smile. "It's all right. It's a gift."

This makes me feel worse, even more humiliated for refusing her generosity, but still, I get out of the limo. Cameras are clicking at me from all around. This is my fifteen minutes of fame, this moment when all of Kulaap's fans focus on me for a few seconds, their flashbulbs popping.

I begin to walk home as paparazzi shout questions.

Fifteen minutes later I am indeed alone. I consider calling a cab, but then decide I prefer the night. Prefer to walk by myself through this city that never walks anywhere. On a street corner, I buy a pupusa and gamble on the Mexican Lottery because I like the tickets' laser images of their Day of the Dead. It seems an echo of the Buddha's urging to remember that we all become corpses.

I buy three tickets, and one of them is a winner: one hundred dollars that I can redeem at any TelMex kiosk. I take this as a good sign. Even if my luck is obviously gone with my work, and even if the girl Kulaap was not the bodhisattva that I thought, still, I feel lucky. As though my father is walking with me down this cool Los Angeles street in the middle of the night, the two of us together again, me with a pupusa and a winning lottery ticket, him with an Ah Daeng cigarette and his quiet gambler's smile. In a strange way, I feel that he is blessing me.

And so instead of going home, I go back to the newsroom.

My hits are up when I arrive. Even now, in the middle of the night, a tiny slice of Kulaap's fan base is reading about checkerspot butterflies and American government incompetence. In my country, this story would not exist. A censor would kill it instantly. Here, it glows green; increasing and decreasing in size as people click. A lonely thing, flickering amongst the much larger content flares of Intel processor releases, guides to low-fat recipes, photos of lol-cats, and episodes of *Survivor! Antarctica*. The wash of light and color is very beautiful.

In the center of the maelstrom, the green sun of the Double DP story glows – surges larger. DP is doing something. Maybe he's surrendering, maybe he's murdering his hostages, maybe his fans have thrown up a human wall to protect him. My story snuffs out as reader attention shifts.

I watch the maelstrom a little longer, then go to my desk and make a phone call. A rumpled hairy man answers, rubbing at a sleep-puffy face. I apologize for the late hour, and then pepper him with questions while I record the interview.

He is silly looking and wild-eyed. He has spent his life living as if he were Thoreau, thinking deeply on the forest monk and following the man's careful paths through what woods remain, walking amongst birch and maple and bluets. He is a fool, but an earnest one.

"I can't find a single one," he tells me. "Thoreau could find thousands at this time of year; there were so many he didn't even have to look for them."

He says, "I'm so glad you called. I tried sending out press releases, but . . ." He shrugs. "I'm glad you'll cover it. Otherwise, it's just us hobbyists talking to each other."

I smile and nod and take notes of his sincerity, this strange wild creature, the sort that everyone will dismiss. His image is bad for video; his words are not good for text. He has no quotes that encapsulate what he sees. It is all couched in the jargon of naturalists and biology. With time, I could find another, someone who looks attractive or who can speak well, but all I have is this one hairy man, disheveled and foolish, senile with passion over a flower that no longer exists.

I work through the night, polishing the story. When my colleagues pour through the door at 8 A.M. it is almost done. Before I can even tell Janice about it, she comes to me. She fingers my clothing and grins. "Nice suit." She pulls up a chair and sits beside me. "We all saw you with Kulaap. Your hits went way up." She nods at my screen. "Writing up what happened?"

"No. It was a private conversation."

"But everyone wants to know why you got out of the car. I had someone from the *Financial Times* call me about splitting the hits for a tell-all, if you'll be interviewed. You wouldn't even need to write up the piece."

It's a tempting thought. Easy hits. Many click-throughs. Ad-revenue bonuses. Still, I shake my head. "We did not talk about things that are important for others to hear."

Janice stares at me as if I am crazy. "You're not in the position to bargain, Ong. Something happened between the two of you. Something people want to know about. And you need the clicks. Just tell us what happened on your date."

"I was not on a date. It was an interview."

"Well then publish the fucking interview and get your average up!"

"No. That is for Kulaap to post, if she wishes. I have something else."

I show Janice my screen. She leans forward. Her mouth tightens as she reads. For once, her anger is cold. Not the explosion of noise and rage that I expect. "Bluets." She looks at me. "You need hits and you give them flowers and Walden Pond."

"I would like to publish this story."

"No! Hell, no! This is just another story like your butterfly story, and your road contracts story, and your congressional budget story. You won't get a damn click. It's pointless. No one will even read it."

"This is news."

"Marty went out on a limb for you—" She presses her lips together, reining in her anger. "Fine. It's up to you, Ong. If you want to destroy your life over Thoreau and flowers, it's your funeral. We can't help you if you won't help yourself. Bottom line, you need fifty thousand readers or I'm sending you back to the Third World."

We look at each other. Two gamblers evaluating one another. Deciding who is betting, and who is bluffing.

I click the "publish" button.

The story launches itself onto the net, announcing itself to the feeds. A minute later a tiny new sun glows in the maelstrom.

Together, Janice and I watch the green spark as it flickers on the screen. Readers turn to the story. Start to ping it and share it amongst themselves, start to register hits on the page. The post grows slightly.

My father gambled on Thoreau. I am my father's son.

Paolo Bacigalupi's writing has appeared in the *Magazine of Fantasy & Science Fiction, Asimov's Science Fiction* magazine, *High Country News,* and *Salon.com.* It has been anthologized in various Year's Best collections, nominated for three Nebula and four Hugo Awards, and won the Theodore Sturgeon Memorial Award for best SF short story of the year. His short story collection, *Pump Six and Other Stories,* was a 2008 *Locus* Award winner for Best Collection, and his debut novel, *The Windup Girl,* was named by *Time* magazine as one of the ten best novels of 2009. *Ship Breaker,* his first young adult novel, was released in May 2010 from Little, Brown.

VINEGAR PEACE

(or, The Wrong-Way, Used-Adult Orphanage)

Michael Bishop

FROM THE AUTHOR: I wrote "Vinegar Peace" – in August
of 2007 – because I had to. Our thirty-five-year-old son, Jamie,
died on the morning of April 16, 2007, as one of thirty-two
victims of a disturbed shooter on the campus of Virginia Tech in
Blacksburg, Virginia. Jamie, an accomplished digital artist who
did lovely covers for four or five of my books, was holding forth
in Room 2007 of Norris Hall in his German class more than
two hours after his eventual murderer had slain two students
in a dormitory on another part of campus. The administration
failed to issue a warning – a warning that might well have saved
many lives – in a timely fashion. However, some of its members
secured their own offices and notified family members of this
initial event; and so the worst school shooting in the history of
the United States claimed our son, four other faculty members
(including a man, Dr. Librescu, who had survived the Holocaust
and who held a table against his classroom door until all his
own students could escape), four of Jamie's students, and twenty-
one other young people in Norris Hall, not to mention the first
two victims in West Ambler-Johnston dorm. Another twenty-
eight students were wounded by bullets or injured leaping from
upper-story windows. Some of them will live with their injuries
the rest of their lives.

"Vinegar Peace" grew from this disaster and from a grief that
I cannot imagine ever laying totally aside. Jeri and I mourn
Jamie's loss every day in some private way, and we think contin-
ually of all the other parents and loved ones of the slain and
injured who will carry a similar burden with them until they
die. We think, too, of the parents and loved ones of the dead
and wounded from the United States' optional war in Iraq,
who long for their dead and who pray for their injured with

an intensity not a whit different from our own. How ironic that our son died on American soil. How sad the wasted potential and the disfigured lives resulting from violence everywhere. And forgive me the inadequacy of these remarks. Clearly, I wrote this story because I could not address either my outrage or my grief in any other way. Finally, allow me to thank Sheila Williams for accepting the story for *Asimov's*, Tony Smith for featuring it both on a podcast on *StarShipSofa* and in an anthology of *StarShipSofa* stories, and Diane Severson for a moving, heartfelt reading of the piece.

ON THURSDAY EVENING, your doorbell rings. Two small men in off-white shirts and black trousers, like missionaries of a dubious religious sect, stand outside your threshold giving you scary pitying looks.

Are you Ms. K—? they ask.

When you assent, they say they've come to transport you to the Vinegar Peace Wrong-Way, Used-Adult Orphanage thirty minutes north of your current residence in a life-help cottage of the Sour Thicket Sanatorium, where your father died seven years ago. But *you* don't wish to be transported anywhere.

The smaller of the two small men, seizing your arm above the elbow, says that an *order* has come down and that they must establish you, before 8:30 P.M., in a used-adult orphanage – upon penalty of demotion for them and unappealable eviction for you. If you don't cooperate, they will ransack your cottage and throw you out on the street with your musty belongings.

Why now? you ask. Neither stooge manifests a glimmer of humanity. After all, you've been an *orphan* – as they insist on terming your condition – since you were a vigorous fifty-nine. They should show some respect.

The man holding your bicep smirks. That's why they call it a *Wrong-Way, Used-Adult Orphanage*, he says. You get into one not because you've lost a parent. Your last living child has to die.

Jesus! blurts the other man. That goes against all our training.

You say nothing. You feel as if someone has opened a trap in your stomach and shoved in a package of wet cement. You sink to your knees, but not all the way because the smaller small man refuses to release your arm.

You feel you've just climbed twelve sets of stairs. Someone has injected stale helium into your head, inflating it to beach-ball size.

O God, you cry. *O God, O God.*

Even to yourself you sound like a scared puppy, not a woman. Your only living offspring, one of only two who bore your genes, has just died in the interminable War on Worldwide Wickedness, probably in a snowy province of R—.

Because Elise and her earlier-lost brother died childless years after Mick, your husband, passed away, *you* have passed from a state of natural, late-life orphanhood to the sad, wrong-way orphancy of the issue-shorn. Only someone similarly bereft can know your devastation.

Put your stuff in two plastic duffels, the cruel stooge says: Only two.

Please don't make me leave my home, you beg of him. Just give me a knock-me-out so I can die.

Your lightheadedness persists: your dead daughter swims before your eyes like a lovely human swan, but the rock in your stomach keeps you from taking pleasure in her shock-generated image.

Against your will, you must say goodbye to Elise forever, as you once did to Mick and later to your darling son Brice.

Eventually, despite your protests, you cram clothing and toiletries into a duffel bag, and some file discs and image cubes into another. Then the cruel stooge and his only slightly kinder partner escort you out to the van for *transport* to Vinegar Peace.

Mr. Weevil, director of this Wrong-Way, Used-Adult Orphanage, looks maybe twenty-six, with slicked-back hair you've seen before on leading men in old motion pictures, but he greets you personally in the rotunda-like foyer, points you to a chair, and triggers a video introduction to the place. His head, projected on a colossal screen at gallery level, spiels in a monotone:

The death of your last surviving child (good riddance) *in the War on Worldwide Wickedness makes you too valuable* (unfit) *to continue residing among the elder denizens* (constipated old fools) *of your life-help cottage* (costly codger dump). *So we've brought you here to shelter* (warehouse) *you until our Creator calls you to an even more glorious transcendent residency above* (blah-blah, blah-blah).

The talking head of Mr. Weevil – whose living self watches *with* you, his hands clasped above his coccyx – remarks that you can stroll inside the orphanage anywhere, but that you can *never leave* – on pain of solo confinement (for a first violation) or instant annihilation (for any later misstep).

The building has many mansions (rooms), *viz.*, 1) Cold Room, 2) Arboretum, 3) Mail Room, 4) Guest Suite, 5) Chantry, 6) Sleep Bay,

7) Refectory, 8) Furnace Room, and 9) Melancholarium. Orphans will, and *should*, visit all nine rooms at some point, for every room will disclose its significance to its visitors, and these elucidations will charge any resident's stay with meaning.

Don't be alarmed, the director's talking head concludes, *if I haven't mentioned a room you view as necessary. The existence of restrooms, closets, offices, kitchens, servant quarters, attics, basements, secret nooks, and so forth, goes without saying.*

A young woman dressed like the men who snatched you from your lodgings takes your elbow – gently – and escorts you from the rotunda. And as Mr. Weevil's body glides smoothly away, his face fades from the gallery-level screen.

Where are we going? you ask the woman.

She smiles as she might at an infant mouthing a milk bubble.

Where are the other residents? Will I have my own room?

That the director included a dormitory in his list of mansions suggests otherwise, but you have to ask. Still, you have begun to think you're in a reeducation camp of some sort. Your stomach tightens even as you tighten your hold on the duffels, which now feel as heavy as old lead sash weights.

Miss, you plead. Why am I here? Where are we going?

She stops, stares you in the eye, and says, Oldsters who've lost children in the war often make trouble. Hush. It isn't personal. We're sheltering all orphaned adults in places like this, for everybody's benefit. You'll meet other orphans soon, but now Mr. Weevil'd like you to visit the refrigitorium.

What?

The Cold Room. Relax, Ms. K—. It's nice. It's a surprise, sort of.

It's a surprise, all right, and no *sort of* about it. Your escort has abandoned you inside the Cold Room, which drones like a refrigerator but sparkles all about you as if you were its moving hub. Ice coats the walls in ripples and scales, each its own faintly glowing color.

Effigies of frozen liquid occupy shallow niches about the walls, and you soon find that three of these, interleaved with simulacra of unfamiliar persons, commemorate your dead: Mick, Brice, and Elise.

As if over a skin of crushed ping-pong balls, you totter gingerly to each beloved ice figure in turn.

Tears spontaneously flow, only to harden on the planes of your face. You clutch your gut and bend in agony before each image of loss. You sob into the chamber's dull hum, stupidly hopeful that no one's wired it for video or sound, and that your pain has no commiserating spies.

You've done this before. Must you indulge again? Have you no shame?

Over time your tears reliquefy, and the ice effigies glisten *more* wetly. The Cold Room has grown imperceptibly warmer. The ice on its walls stays solid, but the statues – by design or accident, but more likely the former – begin to shimmer and melt. Do they stand on hotplates or coil about intricate helices of invisible heating wires? Whatever the case, they dissolve. They go. And there's no reversing the process.

So much water collects – from your tear ducts and the desolidifying statues – that puddles gather in the floor. Even the ceiling drips.

If you stay here out of a misbegotten desire to honor your treasured dead, you'll wind up drenched, ill, and soul-sick.

Freezing, sweating, weeping, you back away. You must.

You have a slick card in hand: a floor diagram of the Vinegar Peace Wrong-Way, Used-Adult Orphanage. YOU ARE HERE, it asserts in a box next to the blueprint image of the Cold Room, BUT YOU COULD BE HERE.

An arrow points to Room 2, the *Arboretum*. Well, you could use a sylvan glade about now – an orchard or a grove – and because you walk purposefully, the room pops up just where the arrow indicates.

Like the Cold Room, the Arboretum is unlocked. Unlike the Cold Room, it soars skyward four or more floors, although its dome has an ebony opaqueness that hides the stars. You gape. Willows stretch up next to sycamores, oaks shelter infant firs and pines, disease-free elms wave in the interior breeze like sea anemones in a gnarl of current, and maples drop whirling seeds, in windfalls lit like coins by the high fluorescents.

Twilight grips the Arboretum.

Out of this twilight, from among the pillars of the trees, figures in cloaks of pale lemon, lime, lavender, ivory, blue, pink, orange, and other soft hues emerge at intervals. They amble forward only a little way, find a not-too-nearby tree, and halt: they decline to impose themselves.

None of these persons qualifies as a wrong-way orphan because all are too young: between thirty and forty. All stand on the neat margins of this wood like passengers with tickets to bleak destinations. Although none seems fierce or hostile – just the opposite, in fact – you prepare yourself to flee, if your nerve fails you. Your heart bangs like an old jalopy engine.

Pick one of us, a woman in a lavender cape tells you. She speaks conversationally from under a willow in the middle distance, but you hear her just fine. The acoustics here are excellent: maybe she's been miked.

Pick one of you for what?

Condolence and consolation: as a sounding board for whatever feeds your angst. The woman advances one tree nearer.

You snort. You've had more sounding boards than a cork-lined recording room. Why take on another?

The people in coats and capes approach in increments, picking new trees much nearer you. They appear devoid of menace, but you think again about fleeing. Even in this twilight, their pastel garments are tinged by the shade thrown by overarching foliage: a disquieting phenomenon.

Pastel shades, you think. These people are *pastel shades*.

Soon your gaze picks up a man approaching steadily through a sycamore copse, a figure in gray twill pants and a jacket the pale ash of pipe dottle. He has boyish features, but crow's feet at his eyes and a salt-and-pepper beard lift him out of the crib of callow naïfs. He wears a mild don't-patronize-me smile and doesn't stop coming until he stands less than an arm's length away.

Ah, Ms. K—, I'm delighted to see you, despite the inauspicious circumstances that bring you here. His elevated vocabulary satirizes itself, deliberately. Call me Father H—. He gives his hand, which you clasp, aware now the pastel holograms beneath the trees have retreated. Their withdrawal has proceeded without your either ignoring or fully remarking it.

You're not wearing colors, you tell Father H—.

Tilting his head, he says, *Colors?*

A host of pastel shades besieged me just now, but you, well, you wear heartsick gray. To illustrate, you pinch his sleeve.

Father H— laughs. Gray's the pastel of black, and I'm a child of the cloth who *always* wears this declension.

If you say so, you reply skeptically.

He chuckles and draws you – by his steps rather than his hand – into the nearest glimmering copse. Tell me about Elise, he says. Tell me all about Elise.

Later, drained again, you return to the entry clearing still in the father's company, unsure of the amount of time that has passed but grateful for the alacrity with which it has sped. Twilight still reigns in the Arboretum, but the clock-ticks in your heart hint that you have talked with Father H— forever. You touch his shoulders and yank him to you in an irrepressible hug.

Thank you, you tell him. Thank you. I may be able to sleep now.

The gray-clad pastor separates from you and smiles through his beard. I've done nothing, Ms. K—.

You've done everything.

His smile turns inward, but you *feel* like a little boy who makes mud pies and carries them to the hungry.

Padre H— takes your plastic card, which he calls a crib sheet, and accompanies you to the mailroom.

If you use this thing – he fans himself with the card, like some dowager aunt in an airless August sanctuary – you'll look like a clueless newbie. He chuckles and shakes his head.

Am I the only one?

Hardly. Soldiers die every hour. But try to look self-assured – as if you belong.

The corridor now contains a few used-adult orphans, some walking in wind suits, some pushing mobile IVs, some hobbling on canes or breathing through plastic masks as they enter lifts or try the stairs. None looks self-assured, but all appear to know their way about. None wears an institutional gown, but beiges, browns, and sandy hues characterize the garments they do wear.

Raw depression returns to knot your stomach and redden your eyes. One or two residents glance toward you, but no one speaks.

Friendly bunch, you mumble.

They just don't trust anyone they haven't met, says Father H—. And who can blame them? You could be a security creep or an insurance snoop.

Carrying these bags?

What better way to insinuate yourself among them?

You enter the Mail Room by a door near the screen on the second gallery. This shadowy chamber teems with ranks of rainbow-colored monitors, not with persons, and Father H— bids you goodbye. (Where is he going? Maybe to hear the confession of a sinful yew?)

A young person in a milky-orange vest approaches. You can't really tell if she's male or female, but you decide to think of her as a woman.

May I help you?

I don't know. I've just come. You hoist your duffels, aware now that they prove absolutely nothing.

Tell me your name, ma'am.

You do, and she takes you to a monitor, keyboards briefly, and summons a face-on portrait of Elise in her battle regalia. Several other people sit in this room (you realize now) before pixel images of *their* dead, trying to talk with them, or their spirits, through arthritic fingertips. You touch the liquid shimmer of the screen with an index finger, and

Elise's skin blurs and reshapes after each gentle prod. Your guide asks if you would like to access any family messages in her unit file, for often soldiers leave private farewells in their unclassified e-folders.

You murmur a supplicating Please.

A message glows on the monitor: either Elise's last message or the message that she *arranged* to appear last.

Dear Mama,

    Do you remember when Brice died? (Well, of course you do.) I recall you telling somebody after they'd shipped Brice's body home, Elise was Mick's and Brice was mine; now I'm forever bereft. You didn't see me in the corner, you had no idea I'd heard.

    From that day on, Mama, I began thinking, *What can I do to become yours, if I'm not yours now?*

    Then it hit me: I had to change myself into the one you claimed – without betraying Dad or Brice or my own scared soul. So I tried to *become* Brice without pushing away Dad or undoing myself.

    As soon as I could, I enlisted. I trained. I went where they sent me. I did everything you and they said, just like Brice, and *you* sent *me* messages about how proud you were – but also how scared.

    If you're reading this, your fears have come true, and so has my wish to do everything just like Brice, even if someone else had to undo me for me to *become* just what you loved. With all my heart, I wish you pleasant mourning, Mama, and a long bright day.

    Love,
    Elise

You read this message repeatedly. You must wipe your eyes to do so, also using the linen tail of your blouse to towel the keyboard and your hands.

Upsettingly, you have something else to tell Father H— about Elise, and indeed about yourself.

The young woman, or young man, from the Mail Room gives you directions to your next stop. You ride a slow glass-faced elevator up two gallery levels to the Guest Suite, which has this legend in tight gold script across its smoky door:

Grief is a species of prestige. – Wm. Matthews

A bellhop – or an abrupt young man in the *getup* of a bellhop – takes your duffels. I'll carry these to the Sleep Bay, ma'am, he says. Stow them there later, under your cot or whatever. And he swings away.

Old people in brown evening clothes stand at the bar sipping whiskey or imported dusky beer. A gaunt pretty woman detaches herself from the bar and moves insouciantly into your space. Her nose tip halts only inches from your own.

It's terrible when a child dies, she declares, but people *treat* you so well, at least for a while.

You take a step back. Is that right?

Didn't you find that to be true after your son was killed?

I suppose. I didn't know much of anything then. I just sort of— You stop, stymied by the task of saying *exactly* what you found to be true.

An IED transformed *our* son into rain. It fell red, you understand, but he scarcely suffered. And afterward – afterward, everyone was very sweet. For as long as they could stand to be, of course.

You gape at the woman.

To save him from an IED, I could have used an IUD – but that occasion was so long ago I never imagined *a* child of mine facing such danger. You just don't think.

That's true, you reply, because *You just don't think* rings with more truth than any other utterance out of her mouth.

(And, by the way, has she just equated an Improvised Explosive Device with an intrauterine contraceptive?)

And, she continues, people's kindness toward the bereaved merits our notice and gratitude. She waves at the bar – at the banks of flowers, an alcove of evening clothes, the teeming buffet, a table of architecturally elaborate desserts.

You say: I'd prefer people rude and my children still alive.

Come now, the woman counters. Bereavement bestows glamour. Pick out a gown, have a dry martini.

No, you say. You plant a dismissive kiss on the woman's papery brow and weave your way back to the door.

The nearby glass-faced elevator drops you into the mazelike basement of the Wrong-Way, Used-Adult Orphanage, where you sashay, as if by instinct, to the Chantry. The Chantry now accommodates Father H— and several old-looking women, virtual babushkas, so unlike the denizens of the Guest Suite that they appear to belong to a different species.

These women groan on kneelers before the altar at which Father H— stands, his arms spread like those of the military effigy impaled on an olivewood cross hanging overhead. They wear widows' weeds, which strain at the seams about their arms, waists, and hips. Maybe the father has shrived them. Now, though, he blesses a monstrance of tiny spoiled rice cakes and a syringe of red-wine vinegar, and moves along the altar rail to dispense these elements.

Ms. K—, he says upon noticing you. 'S great to see you again.

You stand inside the door, appalled and humbled by the warrior Christ floating in shadow above the altar. It wears Brice's face, but also Elise's, and surely the faces of all the babushkas' lost children. You see that two or three of these wrong-way orphans have stuffed their smocks with tissues or rags, and that a few, whatever their burdens of flesh, look barely old enough to have *babies*, although they wouldn't be kneeling here – would they? – if that were true. They gaze up raptly, not at the padre but at the suspended effigy: Sacrificer and Sacrificed.

The father nods a welcome. Care to join these communicants?

I'm not of your creedal persuasion, Father.

Oh, but you are, Ms K—. He gestures welcomingly again. The Church of the Forever Bereft. Come. I've got something better than mud pies. He lifts the chalice and nods at the monstrance: A *little* better, anyway.

You walk to the front and kneel beside a woman with a heart-shaped face and the eyes of a pregnant doe. She lays her hand on your wrist.

Our kids didn't deserve to die, she says. Them dying before us turns everything upside-down. And when our high and mighty mucky-mucks aren't having whole towns blown up, they spew bunkum to keep us quiet.

Bunk cum? you ask yourself, too confused to take offense. But maybe you should tell the father how you slew Elise.

Says Father H—: The more the words the less they mean.

—Yeah, say several women. —We know *that*'s scriptural. —You said a throat's worth. —Selah to that, Padre. And so on.

Let me give you vinegar peace, he interrupts their outburst. Take, eat; take, drink: the flesh and blood of your offspring in remembrance of a joy you no longer possess; in honor of a sacrifice too terrible to share.

He lays a rice cake on each tongue and follows it with a ruby squirt of vinegar.

You can hardly keep your head or your eyelids up. The evening – the devastating news – your exile from your life-help cottage – have exhausted you beyond mere fatigue, and you collapse over the altar rail. Father H— lifts your chin and pulls your lip to give you the elements.

The babushka with the heart-shaped face braces you to prevent your rolling to the floor. You behold her from one bloodshot eye, knowing you must seem to her a decrepit old soul: a fish with fading scales and a faint unpleasant smell.

The Eucharist *clicks* in: You see Brice and Elise as preschool children. In stained shorts and jerseys, they dangle a plump Siamese kitten between them and grin like happy little jack-o-lanterns. *Click.* In some adolescent year they are videotaping each other with recorders long since obsolete. Then – *click* – you're gaping at a ticket stub, drawn months later from a jacket pocket, from a ballgame you attended the day before you got word of Brice's death. *Click.* Elise poses saucily in an ice-green gown with a long-stemmed rose between her teeth. *Click.* Much too soon: Elise in khaki.

O God, you say under the floating soldier Christ. Forgive, my children, my failure to march ahead of you. . . .

Who helps you to the Sleep Bay on an upper gallery you cannot, in your febrile state, tell. But when you arrive, you find this space larger than the fenced-in confines of a refugee camp, with so many *used adults* milling about that it seems, also, a vast carnival lot. TVs on poles rest at intersections amidst the ranks and files of cots and pallets, most of these showing black-and-white military sitcoms from your girlhood, with a smattering in color from more recent years:

There's *Rin Tin Tin*. There's *F Troop*. There's *Hogan's Heroes*. There's *Sergeant Bilko*. There's *McHale's Navy*. There's *Gomer Pyle, U.S.M.C.* There's *M*A*S*H*. There's *China Beach Follies*. There's *My Mama, the Tank*. There's *I Got Mine at Gitmo*. There's *Top Gun, 2022*. There's . . . but they just go on and on, the noise of gunshots, choppers *thwup-thwuping*, IEDs exploding, and combatants crying out in frustration, anger, or pain punctuating almost every soundtrack.

The young woman – anyway, the young *person* – from the Mail Room waves at you across an archipelago of pallets.

Ms. K—! she shouts. Over here, over *here!*

And you stagger toward her through the crowds, past heaped and denuded cots, past old folks and younger folks: some blessedly zonked, some playing card games like Uno, Old Maid, pinochle, or CutThroat, and some gazing ceiling-ward as if awaiting the Voice of God the Freshly Merciful. One bearded old guy chunks invisible missiles at the actors in *I Got Mine at Gitmo*.

Barely upright, you make it to the person who called to you.

These are your duffels, she says. This is your pallet – unless you'd like to look for something nearer a wall.

Where are the restrooms?

She points. Through there, Ms. K—. You peer down a crooked aisle of
bedding at a wall of wrong-way, used-adult orphans obstructing any view
of the lavatories she has tried to point out. I know, I know: Just walk that
way and ask again.

No, you say. No. You crawl onto the raised pallet – it's resting on
a pair of empty ammo crates – and curl up in a fetal hunch between
your duffels. The woman, the *person*, touches your shoulder gently, and
departs.

Before you can fall asleep, a line of people forms in the aisle. Your
pallet rests at its head while its tail snakes back into the depths of the bay
like a queue from Depression Era newsreels.

Everybody has photographs or image cubes of their slain warrior children, and as the line advances the people in it squat, kneel, or sit to show
them to you, even though you see in each face either Brice's or Elise's,
no matter how minimal the resemblance or how weary your vision.

—Very pretty. —Very handsome. —A smart-looking fella. —What a
shame you've lost her. —How can he be gone? —Golly, what a smile! . . .

You compliment ten or twelve orphaned parents in this way until your
tiredness and the faces of Brice and Elise, rising through the images of
these other dead children, make it impossible to go on. Still horizon-
tal, you press your palms to your eyes and shake like a storm-buffeted
scarecrow.

Leave her alone, somebody says. For Pete's sake, let the woman rest.

A hand shoves your head down into your rough olive-green blanket,
but the voice that you attach to the hand's body roars, *Heal, O Lord,
heal! Take her hurt away tonight, and torment her no more!*

But you don't want that. You don't. All you want is sleep and the
honest-to-God resurrection of three particular persons, but sleep is all
you're likely to get. Somebody big perches on the pallet edge and lulla-
bies in a guttural whisper *All the Pretty Little Horses;* he kneads your
spine with fingers that feel more like metal bolts than flesh and bone.
And despite the Sleep Bay's din and stench (and despite the hole in the
middle of your chest), you drift down into a Lost Sea of Consciousness
and let go of all pain but a last acrid fuse of heartbreak. . . .

A twin rumble ghosts through the Sleep Bay, an outer one from the old
orphans waking to face their pain afresh and an inner one from your
complaining gut. You sit up and peer about at this new Reality.

The lavatories have to be packed – so, casting about for a solution, you
find a wide-mouthed jar inside one of the crates supporting your pallet.
After shaping a tent with your blanket, you relieve your bladder – no easy

task – into the jar and stand there amidst the chaos wondering how to proceed.

Slops! Slops! cries an electronic voice, and a simulacrum of a person, smaller than the small cruel man who helped transport you from your life-help cottage, rolls through the crowd with a slotted tray hooked to its midsection.

It takes jars, bottles, beakers, and suchlike from other bleary residents and rattles them into the partitioned tray going before it like an antique cowcatcher. You hand over yours uncertainly.

The simulacrum – a *dormitron* or a *refectorian*, depending on its duty du jour – asks what you'd like for breakfast. You recoil at taking anything edible from this rolling slops collector, but say, Some toast, I guess, it really doesn't matter, to keep from stalling it by saying nothing. It rolls on.

Another *refectorian* – for at mealtimes the Sleep Bay becomes the Refectory – cruises up behind a serving cart, the cart a part of its own fabricated anatomy, and lets you fumble at its topmost shelf for a cup of tea and a slice of toast and persimmon jam. Other such simulacra tend to others there in the bay, sometimes dropping plastic crockery or spilling sticky liquids. From a few pallets away, a woman as thin as a spaghetti strap sidles into your space.

What did your children like to eat? she asks.

Ma'am?

Your dead kids – what'd they like to eat? You can get it here, whatever it was. I always do – what mine ate, I mean. I eat it for them and feel connected to them the rest of the hideous day.

Our son liked cold pizza; our daughter even colder fresh fruit.

Want me to get you tidbits of those things?

You hesitate.

The strap-thin woman mumbles into a diamond of perforations on her inner wrist. They're on their way, she tells you afterward.

And so you wind up with two slices of cold garbage-can pizza and a bowl of even colder cantaloupe, pineapple, muskmelon, and kiwi wedges, which you down between bites of pizza. Your benefactor watches in approval, then asks you to tell a breakfast story about Brice and Elise.

A breakfast story!

You think first of a morning on which teenager Brice sat slumped at the table, his eyes lazing in their sockets like gravid guinea pigs. Mick directed him to have some juice and cereal, to clean up afterward, and to take his sister to school, but Brice dawdled. Stop dicking around, Mick cried. Then, infuriated, he wrestled Brice from his chair, apparently to frog-march him to the cupboard, but Brice flopped deadweight to the floor; and though Mick twisted, prodded, and even tried to *snatch* him erect, neither his body nor his smirk budged, and he remarked, dryly, that Mick's parenting skills had gone so far south that he'd just resorted to all-out *child abuse*. Stunned, Mick let Brice go and stormed outside. You and Elise exchanged stunned looks of your own.

Come on, the woman prompts again: Every mama has a breakfast story.

So you tell about the time when Brice and Elise, then nine and five, got up early one morning and made Mick and you breakfast in bed: mounds of toast, two eggs each, orange juice, and so on. But thinking it olive oil, they had scrambled the eggs in rancid tuna juice, and despite their hard work and the eggs' lovely sunrise yellowness, you had to throw them out.

The eggs, you say, *not* the kids. Mick and I felt like total Eggs Benedict Arnolds. Just like I feel now.

The woman laughs and then purses her lips in sympathy. Good story, Ms. K—. Just remember: You'll *always* feel like that. She grimaces grotesquely, as much for her sake as yours, and places a call via her wrist perforations to somebody in another part of the Refectory.

Meanwhile, the servitors roll on.

Feeling each of your years as a blood-borne needle of sleet, you ride a glass-faced lift to the Chantry level and follow the wives of two sick old men to the Furnace Room, which turns out to be an intensive care unit (ICU) for last-leggers and a crematorium for those who don't make it. Indeed, when you arrive, an orderly slouches past pushing a sheeted figure on a gurney toward an oven down a claustrophobia-inducing tributary corridor. You think about following this gurney but instead continue to tag along behind the ICU widows and at length reach the care unit's hub.

The arc of the hub's perimeter is lined with windowed rooms in which you can see the orphans in extremis. They lie here in weirdly tilted beds, attended by dormitrons and tightlipped RNs. Tubes and electrodes sprout from their bodies like odd mechanical fungi. All of them seem to be equipped with oxygen masks, tracheotomies, or respirators. Even over the machines laboring to sustain them, you can hear them breathing from fifty or sixty feet away.

Father H—, a gray silhouette against a luminous white backdrop, stands at the bedside of one such person. His posture tells you he is listening to the patient's whispers or measuring his or her laggard unassisted breaths. The TV set in this room, muted, runs through a succession of familiar

images from the War on Worldwide Wickedness: statues toppling, buildings dropping in cascades of dust and smoke, warriors on patrol through
rubble-strewn courtyards or past iced-over stone fountains.

The patient couldn't care less. Neither could you, if this enterprise had
not also devoured Brice and Elise, many thousands of their contemporar-
ies, and so many civilian *slammies* – as the media now insists on calling
civilian natives of foreign war zones – that not even the Pan Imperium
can number them.

Mr. Weevil, the director, enters from an outer corridor with several
cronies, five or six small men and women, wearing ivory smocks and
sneakers. They float past you to a treatment unit. Mr. Weevil slides the
glass door open and calls the doctor and his team to the portal to report
on the patient's condition.

Dr. S—, a cadaverous Dravidian with lemur eyes, flatly and loudly
says that his patient is a near goner whose lungs need help, whose liver
has badly deteriorated, whose kidneys have failed, and whose blood,
despite a full course of antibiotics, still teems with pernicious microbes.

None of this person's organs retains its original life-sustaining function, says Dr. S—, and he must soon die. I say *must* in the sense of an
eminent inevitability, not as a Hippocratic recommendation.

The doctor might just as well have spoken over a PA system. His words
echo through the hub like the pronouncement of a god.

Helplessly, you step forward. I'll bet he can still *hear*, you say.

Everybody turns to look. You bear their gazes as the Incredible He-She
at an old-time freak show would bear those of a paying crowd.

What? Mr. Weevil says. What did you say?

I said I'll bet he can still *hear*. Hearing is the last of the senses to go, so
even this patient may still be able to hear you.

Dr. S—'s mouth quirks sourly. And what good does *that* do him?
None. No good at all.

The director and his cronies agree, as do the RNs and the promoted
dormitrons at the doctor's back. You dwindle before them like a melting ice statue in a time-lapse video. Amazingly, not one of these obtuse
brains gets the poignant underlying import of your observation.

Mr. Weevil turns to address the doctor: Every life has huge merit, of
course, but we *really* need that bed. *Carry on!* He and his smock-clad
retinue exit the intensive care hub while Dr. S— and *his* team fall back
into the treatment unit to await the convenient inevitable.

Appalled, you walk about the hub in rings of increasing size until
Father H— comes out and hails you as he might a lost friend. Ah, Ms.
K—, what a surprise and a treat to see you!

Michael Bishop

What day is it, Padre?

Friday – another *good* Friday – why do you ask?

You hear the stress on *good*, but not the Easter-designating capital G that would turn your fugue into an enacted allegory. You note that it's been little more than twelve hours since two cruel stooges informed you of Elise's death.

And a little over two years since you learned of Brice's, he says gently.

You smile and ask after the women who journeyed to the Furnace Room to visit their spouses.

Their hearts will grow heavier soon, Father H— says. Given their ages, how could they not?

They'll die without seeing the war's end.

'*War Is Peace*,' Orwell said. Besides, who will? Who sees anything well finished, even one's own life? It's little different from those medieval stonemasons who worked on cathedrals.

I don't like your analogy, you tell him.

Father H— laughs heartily. Of course you don't: it stinks.

Moments later, he leads you to the mouth of a nearby tunnel.

Care to visit the ovens, Ms. K—?

You like this question less than you did his cathedral analogy because it suggests an analogy even more distasteful. But what else do you have to do?

Okay.

As you walk, the father offers you a rice cake and an ampoule of red-wine vinegar from a communion kit sewn into his jacket lining. For your spiritual sustenance, he says, but you bemusedly shake your head.

Two gurneys trundle up behind you, one pushed by a dormitron, the other by a young woman in uniform. To let them pass in tandem, you press your backs to opposite walls of the tunnel. The first gurney takes a corridor to the left; the second, bearing not only a body but a casket draped in a flag of the nation's newly adopted colors, swings right. You raise an eyebrow at the father.

Vinegar Peace cremates our war dead as well as wrong-way orphans, he explains. Which way would you like to go?

You answer by angling right. Far down this corridor you see a wide brick apron before double crematory doors and ranks of scarlet-draped caskets before these doors. An honor guard in full dress stands at formal ease to one side of the tunnel; a military choir on crepe-decorated risers, to the other.

Both contingents await you in this incarnadine cul-de-sac; in fact, when you have almost drawn close enough to read the soldiers' name-tags, they crack to attention and a pitch pipe sounds. They then begin to sing, the expanded honor guard and the choir, as if triggered by your arrival as auditors. You recognize the melody as a halt-footed variation on an old hymn's tune:

> *If we were ever sorry,*
> > *Oh, we would never tell –*
> *We're gravely in a hurry*
> > *To sleep at last in hell.*

> **'Pro patria mori'**
> > *Is our true warrior's cry.*
> *We never, ever worry;*
> > *We boldly spit and die.*

> *Out for patriot glory,*
> > *Brave maid and gallant stud,*
> *We all revere Bold Gory –*
> > *Its **Red**, its **Wine**, its **Blood**!*

The choristers conclude fortissimo and stand at ease again. The Red, Wine, and Blood – Bold Gory – has recently replaced the Red, White, and Blue – Old Glory – , and these soldiers gladly hymn the new banner's praises.

Two members of the honor guard open the double doors of the oven, and Father H— nods you forward, as if accustomed to this ritual.

Go in? you ask him. Really?

Just for a look-see. You might not think so, but it's an honor, their approving you for an impromptu tour.

Why me?

Most young enlistees have living parents. You're a proxy.

A soldier yanks the scarlet banner from a coffin and brings it to you as if to throw it over your shoulders. Its stars and stripes are mutedly visible as different shades of red. You lift a hand, palm outward. No thank you.

Our dead would wish us to robe you in it, the soldier says.

You count sixteen coffins – one of them minus its patriotic drapery. Who *are* your dead today? you wonder aloud.

Sixteen trainees in a reconstructed Osprey vertical takeoff/landing aircraft, he says. It crashed a half-mile from camp, the third bird this year. He again offers the scarlet flag.

No, I can't. I'm partial to the old version, even at its foulest.

The soldier courteously withdraws, to redrape the naked coffin.

Father H— takes your arm and leads you straightaway into the oven.

The Cold Room had ice effigies. The Furnace Room – or this part of its crematory extension – has a cindery floor and dunes of ash. When its doors close behind you, you stand in the gray hemisphere like snow-globe figures, lit by thin skylights. Black scales etch continents and islands on the walls, and the sooty dunes, when you move, suck at you like whirlpools. The furnace scares you. It seems both an execution chamber and a tomb, full of drifting human fallout.

I thought the ash and bone fragments were collected to give to the families, and that everything else went up the smokestack.

Some ovens work more efficiently than others, the father replies.

You walk deeper into this peculiar space and kneel before an ashen dune. You run your hands into it and let its motes sift through your fingers like desiccated rain. You rub your wrists and arms with it. You pour its grayness over your head in a sort of baptism, a dry baptism befitting your age and orphanhood. You scrub it into your clothes and run your tongue around your mouth to taste its grit.

Father H— breaks a dozen ampoules of red-wine vinegar over the ashes before you and stirs the bitter into the bleak. He shapes a pie from this mixture and urges you to follow suit. You obey. After a while, you've made a dozen or so together, but still must make a dozen more for the unfed soldiers in the tunnel. Kneeling, you work side by side to accomplish that task.

Weeks go by before you visit the Melancholarium.

Father H— has told you that it's a memory room that only two people at a time may enter: an orphaned couple, or the only surviving orphan and a person of his or her choice. No one may enter alone, or in a party of three or more. None of these rules makes much sense, but little about Vinegar Peace ever does, even if it sometimes seems to have a coherent underlying principle of organization that you can't fathom owing to an innate personal failing.

Meanwhile, you've grown used to the noisy Sleep Bay, learned when to visit the crowded jakes, perfected the art of getting servitors to do your bidding, and made enough *friends* to feel – well, if not *connected*, at least not entirely estranged from the protocols of what passes for normal life here. You no longer bolt up when bombs go off at Fort Pugnicose (where many of the recruits for the War on Worldwide Wickedness train), or when air-raid sirens wail in the galleries, or when some of the older orphans sidle up to your cot at night and plead, *Take me home, take me home*. Even the twilight influx of dispossessed oldsters, addle-wits with confusion writ large in their pupils, has ceased to faze you. After all, they'll adjust . . . maybe.

Then a dormitron sporting Henry Kissinger glasses and nose gives you a pass to visit the Melancholarium.

The name itself sabotages the place. Just hearing it, who'd want to go there? You, indeed, would rather return to your life-help cottage in Sour Thicket. Vinegar Peace isn't a concentration camp, but neither is it a Sun City spa. It's a training facility for people with little time to make use of that training in the Real World, which in your opinion no longer exists.

Choose somebody to go with you, the dormitron says.

You pick Ms. B—, the strap-thin woman who asked you to tell her a breakfast story, and one morning in your second month of residency, the two of you ride a lift to the fifth level and walk together to a tall cylindrical kiosk where a familiar-looking young person, probably female, seats you next to each other at a console and fits you both with pullover goggles.

You walk side by side into the Melancholarium. Now, though, Ms. B— is no longer Ms. B— but your late husband Mick, whose hand you hold as you approach the gurney on which Elise lies in a pair of jeans and a blue chambray shirt open at the collar. Her clothing is so blatantly neither a gown nor a full dress uniform that the simplicity of her look – her sweet girlishness – briefly stops your breath, as hers is stopped. You reach to touch her. Mick seizes your wrist, not to prevent you but instead to guide your fingers to Elise's arm, which you both clutch for as long as you have now endured in this grand human depository. Or so it oddly seems.

Elise's red-tinged hair, which the military cut short, now hangs behind her off the gurney. It sparkles like a sequined veil. The expression on her face suggests neither terror nor pain, but serenity; and if you addressed her, saying, *Elise, it's time to get up, come out to the porch to see the sun shining on the spider webs in the grass,* you believe with the same soft ferocity that you once believed in God that she will obey – that she'll open her eyes, sit up, and embrace you briefly before striding out of the Melancholarium into the stolen remainder of her life.

You kiss Elise's brow. Leaning across her, you give her the hug that she'd give you if only the same green power seethed there. Her body has a knobby hardness that would estrange you from her if you didn't love her so much. All your pity re-collects and flows from your bent frame into her unyielding one. She has the frail perdurability of Cold Room effigies – but none of their alienness – and so she has finally become yours, although neither you nor anybody else can own her now. When her smoke rises through the crematory flue, it won't dissipate until your smoke also rises and clasps her last white particles to yours. Then both clouds will drift away together.

You step back. Mick gives you room. You want to freeze this tableau and visit it like a window decorator, keeping its centerpiece – Elise – intact but endlessly rearranging the furniture and flowers. You kiss her brow again, hold her hands, and finger the runnels in her jeans.

You undo the buttons next to her heart to confirm a report that three high-caliber rounds inflicted her *nonsustainable* injuries. You find and examine them with a clinical tenderness. You must know *everything*, even the worst, and you rejoice in the tameness of her fatal mutilation.

Joyce, Mick says, the first time anyone has spoken your given name in so long that it jars like a stranger's. *Are you okay?*

You embrace, leaning into each other. Of course, it isn't really Mick holding you upright in the vivid deceit of the Melancholarium, but so what, so what?

You pull back from his image and murmur, *Mick, her hands . . .*

What about them?

They're so cold, colder than I thought possible.

Yes, Mick says, smiling, *but if you rub them, they warm up.*

On your journey back to the Sleep Bay, you tell Ms. B—, Mick would never have said that. That was you.

Ms. B— says, Well, I've never seen such a pretty kid.

You should have seen Brice.

Stop it. I was just being polite. *You* should've seen *mine*: absolute love-lies fed into the chipper by tin-men with no guts or gadgets.

You don't reply because you notice a short tunnel to a door with a red neon sign flashing over it: EXIT and then the same word inside a circle with a slash through it. You think about detouring down this tunnel and even try to pull Ms. B— along with you. She resists.

Stop it, she says. You can check out whenever you feel like it. Just don't try to leave. Don't you know that by now?

I've heard there's an escape, you say. A way to get out alive.

That's not it, Ms. B— says, nodding at the flashing EXIT/DON'T EXIT sign.

Don't you even want to hear?

Enlist? Is that it? Sign up to wage war on the wicked? Well, that's a crock, too.

I'm sure it is.

Okay, then – what is it, your secret way to get out?

Adoption, you tell her. The padre says that if a soldier with six tours adopts you, you're no longer a wrong-way orphan and you can leave.

Ms B— regards you as if you've proposed sticking nasturtiums down the barrel of an enemy soldier's rifle. Oh, I've heard that, too, it's a fat load of bunkum.

You don't reply, but you also don't go down the tunnel to try the door with the contradictory flashing messages. You return with your *friend* to the Sleep Bay without raising the subject again.

But it makes sense, doesn't it? A decent orphanage adopts out its charges. If you believe, just *believe*, somewhere there's a compassionate Brice or Elise, a person who's survived six tours and wants nothing more than to rescue some poor wrong-way orphan from terminal warehousing. Such people do exist. They exist to lead you from Vinegar Peace to a place of unmerited Milk and Honey.

That night, huddled on your cot amid the hubbub in the Sleep Bay, you envision a woman very like Elise sitting with you on a porch in late autumn or early winter. You sit shivering under scarlet lap robes, while this person whispers a soothing tale and tirelessly rubs your age-freckled hands.

Michael Bishop published his first story, "Piñon Fall," in *Galaxy* over forty years ago. Since that time, living in Pine Mountain, Georgia, with his wife, Jeri, an elementary school counselor, he has published seven story collections and many novels, including the Nebula Award–winning *No Enemy But Time*, the Mythopoeic Fantasy Award–winning *Unicorn Mountain*, and the Locus Award–winning *Brittle Innings*, which Twentieth Century Fox optioned for a film in 1993 and bought outright in 1995. (To date, no film has been made.) The Bishops have a daughter, Stephanie Loftin (a fitness trainer), and two grand-children, Annabel and Joel.

In 1996, LaGrange College in LaGrange, Georgia, secured Bishop as its writer-in-residence. He teaches creative-writing courses and January interim-term courses (including "Art & Story: Graphic Literature in Contemporary World Culture"), and has assisted other department members in organizing three art-and-literature conferences called Slipstreaming in the Arts. In April 2007, Bishop's anthology *A Cross of Centuries: Twenty-five Imaginative Tales About the Christ* appeared from Thunder's Mouth Press. Currently, he is compiling a collection of his Georgia-based stories, *Other Arms Reach Out to Me*; marketing a mainstream novel, *An Owl at the Crucifixion*; and slowly working on a novel about Jonathan Swift visiting many of the invented lands in his classic satire, *Gulliver's Travels*. In the fall of 2009, PS Publishing in England released a reprint anthology that Bishop coedited with Steven Utley, *Passing for Human*, with an original digital-collage cover by Jamie Bishop.

I NEEDS MUST PART, THE POLICEMAN SAID

Richard Bowes

FROM THE AUTHOR: In his generous essay/review of my novelette, Richard Larson refers to the story as a "speculative memoir," a blend of speculative fiction with memoir. It's the story of a narrator with the same name as the author who gets sick, nearly dies, goes into a hospital, is operated on, and released. The story involves memory and hallucination. I wanted among other things to make the reader feel the ways that dream and memory overlap and the way Time carries the world we once knew away from us. Over the years, friends and lovers and family members, sick and sometimes dying lay in hospital beds and spoke of their dreams and hallucinations. I'd seen more than one while still alive go off to another kingdom and look back on this world as a semi-stranger. I was afraid of this, kept a pen and notebook with me at all times and wrote down what I saw while conscious or remembered when I woke up.

Before I got sick I'd been listening to a John Dowland song, "Now, Oh Now, I Needs Must Part." The aptness of the lyrics and the way they tied into hallucinations of my own evoked the Philip K. Dick title, *Flow My Tears the Policeman Said*, for which he also used a John Dowland lyric.

Shortly after I got out of the hospital the National Public Radio show RadioLab broadcast an episode titled "Memory and Forgetting," about how memory is created and implanted, manipulated and lost. They also did a show on sleep and explored the fringes of that land in which we spend so much of our time.

As I write this essay, the place in which my story is mainly set, the legendary Greenwich Village institution Saint Vincent's Hospital, harbor for the Village poor in the late nineteenth and early twentieth centuries, beacon in the nightmare landscape of AIDS in the 1980s, is in the process of closing its doors. It's being described as a casualty of the changing urban demographics, of modern medical practice. I think of it as having been carried away in the stream of time which moves ceaselessly as we sleep or are distracted or lie sick in bed and leaves only our flawed and distorted memories.

1.

In the predawn one morning last April, I woke up from a violent and disturbing dream. In it, I was somewhere that I realized was the Southwest with three other guys whom I knew in the dream but didn't quite recognize when I thought about them later.

All of us were engaged in smuggling something – drugs as it turned out. We were tough. Or they were anyway, big guys with long hair and mustaches. There was, I knew, another bunch of guys much tougher than us with whom we didn't get along and there were cops.

The end of the dream was that I heard police sirens and was scared but relieved because they weren't as bad as the other guys. The last image in the dream, however, was the cops smashing two of the big guys' faces right into the adobe wall of the building we stayed in. And I knew, in the way one does in dreams, that the other guy and I were in for something as bad or worse. Then I woke up before dawn in my apartment on MacDougal Street in Greenwich Village.

From the time I was a small boy I've been afraid of the long marches of the night, the time in the dark when the lights inside me went out. The fear that would hit me as my head was on the pillow was that I, the one falling asleep, would not be the one who woke up.

Imagining the fragility of my identity chilled me. I did fall asleep again though and dreamed once more.

This time, I saw the main cop with his short white hair and gray suit sitting in his car, smoking a cigarette, staring blue eyed and expressionless at me. I was much younger than I am now, maybe in my mid-twenties instead of my sixties.

In my dream, I realized that I had been looking at a computer and had viewed all this on some kind of a website.

When I awoke this time, the sun was up. Except for my having seen it as a website, the dream seemed like a fragment of the past, a time when I might, in fact, have found myself in places almost as bad as the dream.

I felt sick, my stomach was upset, every bone and muscle ached, and each move I made took an effort.

Nothing seemed to have led up to this illness. I'd been to the theater the night before with my friend Ellen. We'd seen a show with music about eighteenth century boy sopranos (played by women) and abducted orphans.

A few hours before that, an affair I'd been having for some time with a guy named Andre was broken off very suddenly. The man with whom Andre lived had called me up and said that Andre had told him everything. They both wanted me to stay away from him from now on. It was a once-a-week thing that had become routine and boring, as I told the man, and I asked him to say good-bye to Andre for me.

I'm a veteran of more than forty years in Manhattan and normally neither big, melodramatic Broadway shows nor sudden disruptions in love cause the kind of distress I felt that morning.

Even as I wondered if I should call my doctor, I was aware of a kind of web stream that ran constantly in a corner of my brain. The fever dream took the form of a constant Google search complete with web pages and blogs I couldn't remember looking for.

Pictures and stories with elusive contexts appeared. At one point, I found myself looking at the profiles of the members of a tough cop unit somewhere in the Southwest. It had short bios, photos of them with mustaches and holsters and masklike sunglasses.

As I wondered why and how I had looked this up, I saw a familiar face with a white crewcut and expressionless cop eyes.

I remembered I wanted to call my doctor. As I dialed the number, I thought of the tune and lyrics of a song I'd been listening to recently. It was by John Dowland, a poet and composer who was kind of the Kurt Cobain of Elizabethan England. Something in the melancholy grace of the tune, the resignation of the song's lyrics had caught me.

> *Now, oh now I needs must part,*
> *Parting though I absent mourn.*
> *Absence can no joy impart:*
> *Joy once fled cannot return.*

Maybe this attachment had been a kind of harbinger, some part of my consciousness telling me I had started dying. I wondered how Dowland's song "Flow My Tears," had affected Philip K. Dick when he'd used it in a title.

Somehow the call to the doctor never got made. I couldn't remember what day it was. People who phoned me – friends, the godchildren who in sentimental moments I thought of as my kids, the woman who had been my work-wife before I retired from the university – seemed concerned.

Many things ran on the screen inside my head. The Macabres when I found myself looking at their site seemed like many a New York late seventies punk group. The photos showed the musicians – emaciated, decked in bondage accessories, with their hair hacked off at odd angles. A bit of one of their songs played. Then police sirens wailed just like they had when my friends and I had gotten caught.

I realized that the sirens were my phone ringing. A friend who had once been a nurse wanted the telephone number of my medical group and the number of someone who could take me there next morning.

2.

That night was especially awful: a long confusion of dreams. Chris, my speculative fiction godchild who lives in Ohio, seemed almost frantic. He kept calling me but I was too sick to talk to him for more than a minute or two.

When I looked at my inner computer screen it showed me palm trees and bright sun and elephants. The Macabres now worked nearly naked in a prison chain gang. A woman with the face of a peacock seemed very familiar. I thought I spotted the policeman with the blue eyes that gave away nothing. He looked right at me and was about to speak

Then my doorbell sounded and it was my friend Bruce who was there to take me to the doctor's. With his help I walked the few blocks to my medical group office on Washington Square. A very concerned doctor ordered me into Saint Vincent's hospital. Shortly afterward Bruce escorted me to the emergency room admittance desk. Then he hugged me and was off to another job and I was in the power of the hospital.

There was no waiting. I identified myself, was given a form to fill out, and was shown right into the middle of the beds and gurneys, patients, and orderlies. Numbers flashed on computer screens, and machines beeped.

Nurses and doctors clustered around an enormously fat, comatose woman then dispersed. A social worker took the life history of an elderly black man who very patiently explained to her how he had lost everything he had ever had and lived now in a shelter. A moaning patient rolled by on a gurney hung with IV bags. Two cops wheeled in a shooting victim.

Then an orderly threw back the curtains around a bed and told me to come inside. My clothes were taken away. I was dressed in two gowns, one worn forward, the other backward, and socks with skid-proof soles. I was bled and examined and hauled through cold corridors and x-rayed.

Tubes got attached to me. A catheter was stuck up my urinary tract; at one point a very new intern tried to stick a tube down my throat and I choked and gagged. A horrible brown goop came up my guts and into my mouth and nose. My hospital gowns got soaked and there was commotion. People talked about me as if I was dead or not there.

It reminded me of an accident scene. I heard police radios, saw flares illuminating a nighttime car crash. I saw a familiar picture on a computer screen. It was in black and white, a 1950s newspaper shot.

A kid in his late teens had been thrown onto the branch of a tree by the force of a collision. He hung there bent at the waist over the branch of the tree, his loafers gone, his legs still in jeans, his upper body bare. The cool striped shirt he wore now hung down over his head. That was probably for the best: the face and eyes under those circumstances are not something you'd want to see.

That image haunted me at fourteen. I had imagined myself dramatically dead in just that manner, if only I could drive and had a car.

"That photograph was his own private version of the old primitive painting, 'Death On A Pale Horse,' " I read on a screen in front of me and realized I was looking at a website about me.

Then the screen was gone and I was back in the tumult of the emergency room. "Intestinal blockage – massive fluid build-up," said a female resident. "It's critical."

"Rejected the drain," said the intern who had failed to get it in.

A male nurse spoke quietly to me like I was a frightened animal, put his hand on my chest to calm me, and stuck the tube into my nose and down my throat in a single gesture. A tall, wheeled IV pole with hooks that held my drains, feeding bag, urine bag, and various meters was attached to me.

Doctors examined me further. I felt like my insides were grinding themselves apart. A bag hanging next to my head rapidly filled with brown goop that had been inside me.

It was very late at night when I was wheeled onto elevators and off them, then down silent corridors. I was still dirty and wearing the damp hospital gowns when I was brought into a ward on the twelfth floor.

A young Asian nurse named Margaret Yang took over. Before I was placed on a bed, she called and four orderlies appeared. Women talking in the accents of Puerto Rico, Ukraine, and Jamaica, brought me into a bathroom, sponged me off, put me under shower water, and turned me around under it saying, as I tried to cover myself, "It's okay. You are as God made you."

3.

Only when I was clean, in clean clothes and on a bed looking out at the night did I remember that I had been in this hospital forty-two years before.

When I was a kid first coming into the city from Long Island, I woke one night with no idea who I was or where I was. The place I was in seemed vast, chilly, and sterile. The lighted windows in the brownstones across the street revealed stylish apartments and I knew it looked like a magazine cover without knowing what that was or how I knew this.

A nurse told me I'd been found facedown in a hallway, bleeding from a cut on my forehead and without any wallet or ID. I had lots of alcohol and a couple of drugs in my bloodstream.

A very old nun, thin and stiff, her face almost unlined, came around late in that night. She inspected the bandage on my forehead and talked about Dylan Thomas. I was still enough of a Catholic kid to feel embarrassed talking to a nun while sitting on a bed in just a hospital gown.

"He was brought here not ten or twelve years ago after a hard night's drinking. He died from that and pneumonia on the floor just below this one.

"I thought of him when I saw you," she said, looking at me calmly. "I wonder if you, too, are a young man who has an uneasy relationship with death."

I said I didn't know if I was or even who I was.

"Time will reveal those things," she said. "You're still very young."

Then I found myself looking at that long-ago night on a computer screen. It was all conveyed in images: a *New Yorker* cover of figures silhouetted against the lighted windows of their brownstones, a figure of a nun that seemed almost translucent.

What appeared at first to be the famous drawing of the young Rimbaud unconscious in a bed after being shot by his lover Verlaine turned out to be a photo of Dylan Thomas dead in Saint Vincent's Hospital – and became me at twenty-one with my poet's hair and empty, blue amnesiac eyes.

I pulled back from the screen and saw all around me a vast dark space with green globes rotating through it. Then I squinted and saw that the globes were the glowing screens that monitored each patient in this hospital. Beyond us, further out in the endless dark, were other screens in other hospitals, stretching on into infinity.

4.

Apparently I called out, because then Nurse Yang was speaking to me, asking if I was okay. The universe and the globes disappeared. Saint Vincent's, as I saw it all these years later, seemed a small, slightly shabby, and intensely human place.

"I'm so glad," I told her. "You people have saved my life."

She was amused and said that this was what they tried to do for everyone brought in here but that it was always nice to be appreciated. When she started to leave, I got upset and she showed me how to ring for help if I needed it.

After she was gone I lay in the cool quiet with the distant sound of hospital bells and the voices of the women at the nurses' station. But I didn't sleep.

My fear that all trace of me would be lost while I slept was out and active that night. Lying there, it seemed likely that this person with a search engine installed in his head was not the me who had existed a few days ago.

Drugs and the tubes siphoning the liquid out of my guts and into plastic bags had eased my pain and I did drift off every once in a while. But nurses and orderlies came and woke me quite regularly to take my signs and measure my temperature.

At one moment I would be awake in the chill quiet of that hospital with a view out the window of the Con Edison building and the Zeckendorf Towers at Union Square visible over the low buildings of Greenwich Village.

In the next, I'd be looking at a computer screen that showed a map of the old Village – a vivid 1950s touristy affair with cartoon painters in berets and naked models, beatnik kids playing guitars in Washington Square and Dylan Thomas with drinks in both hands at the bar of the White Horse Inn.

Awake again in the dark, I waited, listened, half expecting the old nun to reappear. Instead what I got was a moment's glimpse of the white-haired cop who had watched me get beaten. He looked at me now with the same deadpan.

5.

I came out of a doze, awakened by a gaggle of bright-eyed young residents. "Mr. Bowes," one of them, a woman with an Indian accent, said, "we were all amazed by the x-rays of your intestines. It was the talk of the morning rounds."

"Why?" I asked.

"Because of the blockage they were extremely distended. You came very close to having a rupture which would have been very bad. You could easily have died." All of them, a small Asian woman, a tall rather dizzy-looking blond American boy, and a laid-back black man nodded their agreement and stared at me fascinated.

"How did this happen?" I wanted to know.

"We believe it was from twenty-three years ago when you had cancer and they removed part of your colon," she said. "After all this time, the stitching began to unravel and adhered to the other side of your intestines."

Other doctors appeared: the gastroenterological resident spoke to me, my own internist popped in. They told me that I was out of immediate danger. Sometimes the blockage eased all by itself. Sometimes it required surgery. The surgeon would see me the next day.

My bedside phone had now been connected. I made some calls. People came by, friends and family, old flames and godchildren. They brought flowers and disposable razors, my CD player, a notebook, they gave me backrubs and went out and asked questions at the nurse's station. They established my presence, showed the world that I was someone who was loved and cared for.

Margaret Yang came and sat for a while, talked to my sister Lee who was visiting, about this unique old hospital and how they were all devoted to it. I wanted to hang on to everyone, nurses, friends, family who was there in the bright daylight.

They had brought me the Dowland CD. The countertenor sang:

> *Part we must though now I die,*
> *Die I do to part with you.*

Gradually on that lovely spring day with the sun pouring down on the old bricks of the Village, twilight gave way to night. Lights in the hospital dimmed, the halls got quiet.

When I was operated on for cancer it was uptown at Mt. Sinai. The ward I was in overlooked Central Park and at night in the intensity of my illness and fear and the drugs inside me, I saw lights passing amid the leafless winter trees.

And I imagined an alternate world called Capricorn where people dying of cancer in this world appeared to the population as glowing apparitions.

The night before that operation, I awoke with the feeling I was falling through the furniture, through the floor, and into Capricorn.

Remembering that, I saw a picture of myself, ethereal and floating amid a stand of winter trees in a hospital bed. The white-haired cop was showing it to me on a screen.

"When we spotted that we knew you were in no way run-of-the-mill," he said. "Our seeing you like this confirmed an initial report from when you were in this place as a kid with a busted head and no memory. Someone spoke to you and said you had an uneasy relationship with death and the potential to see more than the world around you."

6.

Some people have the gift of being perfect hospital visitors. The flowers my friend Mark brought the next morning looked like a Flemish still life, his conversation was amusing and aimless.

He sat beside my bed that morning and I told him about a book I'd once written.

"The first things I wrote after I had cancer was a fantasy novel called *Feral Cell*. In it, people dying of cancer in this world are worshipped in an adjacent world named Capricorn. They call our world 'Cancer' and call themselves the 'Capri.'

"The faithful among them find ways of bringing a few people who are doomed on our world over to theirs. To prevent us from drifting back here, we are dressed in the skins of deceased Capri, drink their blood, which is called the Blood of the Goat, and are objects of awe.

"But there are others on that world – decadent aristocrats, of course – who hunt us. They throw silver nets over us and drag us down. They skin us and drain our blood and use those things to cross into this world."

"That must almost have made getting sick worthwhile," he said.

"The future New York City I depicted in the book – turn of the third millennium Manhattan – was all open-air drug markets and rival gangs of roller skaters and skateboarders clashing in the streets. What we got, of course, was gentrification and Disneyland.

"A lot of being sick is like one long nightmare. In my Capricorn everything was terror and magic. At night, patients in a children's cancer ward could be seen floating amid the trees of a sacred grove."

Mark walked with me as I pushed my IV stand around the floor. One of the hall windows overlooked Seventh Avenue. Outside on a glorious day in spring, traffic flowed south past the Village Vanguard jazz club.

"The low buildings make it look like the 1950s," Mark said.

"Time travel," I said.

It was a quiet Sunday. Later that afternoon, my godchild Antonia was giving me a backrub. Suddenly a dark-haired woman, not tall but with great presence and wearing a red dress suit, appeared. She introduced herself as the one who would be my surgeon if the intestinal blockage didn't ease. And I knew that it hadn't and wouldn't and that she would operate on me.

As night came and friends and family had departed, I thought of Jimmy when he was a patient at this hospital. Jimmy had been a friend of mine in the years of AIDS terror. He designed and constructed department store window displays.

Since I'd first known him he talked about the little people inside his head, the ones he relied on for his ideas.

"Last night they put on this show with fireflies and ice floes. Perfect for Christmas in July," he'd say. "Sadly, what I'm looking for is ideas for Father's Day which is, as always, a wilderness of sports shirts and fishing tackle."

Just before Jimmy died in this very hospital, I came into his room and found him in tears.

"They're all sprawled on the stage dead," he told me.

7.

Without being aware of a transition to sleep, somewhere in the night I became part of a Milky Way of bodies lying hooked up to lighted screens. I saw all of us, patients here and across the world, floating in a vast majestic orbit.

Then the cop, tough, his blue eyes giving away nothing, watched as I looked at the photo he'd handed me.

It showed me in my dream of the Southwest along with my companions who would later get arrested and beaten into pulp.

"How did you know these guys?" he asked.

"I was a friend of one of them. Louis."

"Friend, you mean like a boyfriend?" He displayed no attitude but past experience with cops made me wary. I shook my head.

Then he told me, "It must be tough for someone like you. Kind of comfortable, retired, having something like this from his past brought up after all these years."

"Nothing like that happened to me. It's just a dream."

"A dream, maybe, but made up of bits of your past."

Then I heard voices and he was gone. Lights went on in my room and curtains got drawn around the other bed. Since my arrival I had been the only patient in the room. That ended.

"In here."

"Easy."

The new patient cried out as they moved him. Through an opening in the curtain, I saw nurses and orderlies transfer him to the bed. Then they stood back and two young surgeons from the emergency room approached. From their talk, I learned that the patient had been in some kind of an incident that had damaged his scrotum.

The doctors spoke to him. "We saved one testicle and your penis," they said. "But we couldn't save the other."

The patient asked a question too mumbled for me to hear and a doctor said, "Yes, you'll have full function."

Then they were gone and almost immediately the kid slept and snored. His name, I found out later, was Jamine Wilson and he was nineteen.

8.

Dawn was just about to break. I opened the notebook and wrote out a will, divided my possessions among my siblings and friends. Making out a will was a way of trying to hold onto my self, to indicate that I still knew who I was and what was mine.

That afternoon my sister Lee visited me. I had named her my executor. I dreaded the thought of living in a coma and said I didn't want extreme measures to be taken to keep me alive if I couldn't be revived. She went out to the desk and informed them of this.

Then we talked and listened to Jamine Wilson in the next bed on his phone. He talked about buying hot iPods. He called a woman and told her to bring him burgers and fries from McDonald's.

He lived in a halfway house to which he didn't want to return. A social worker came by and informed him that he would have to be out of the hospital the next morning. He ignored her.

"Where are you now," he asked the woman on the phone. "Can't you get on the subway?"

My sister left when they came to take me downstairs for x-rays. They gave me barium and recorded its progress through my digestive tract. I was there for hours, lying flat on a cold metal slab while they took each series of shots, resting, sleeping sometimes on the metal slab, until it was time for the next pictures.

It reminded me of the esoteric forms of modeling. Hand models, foot models; unprepossessing people with one exquisite feature. "Intestine model, that's me," I told the technician who smiled and didn't understand.

I dozed and saw a screen that read, "An example of his early modeling work." And there I was, very young, in Frye boots and jeans and leather jacket, a kerchief tied around my neck but with my hands cuffed behind me. It looked like some S&M scenario I might once have posed for. But the setting was the Southwest of that dream.

Then they woke me up and took some more x-rays.

When I got back to the room, Jamine's hospital lunch was untouched beside his bed. I had taken nothing by mouth for days. He looked up at me dark and angry. Our eyes met and for a moment I saw a bit of myself: the kid in the nightmare, the one who'd ended up in this hospital with his memory gone. And I think, maybe, he saw something similar.

"Where are you now?" he asked someone on the phone then said, "You were there five minutes ago."

Some time later, his caller finally arrived whizzing down the hall on a motorized wheelchair, the McDonald's bag on her lap. She was Hispanic with eyes that looked hurt or afraid.

She maneuvered her chair next to the bed. The two of them ate. He chewed noisily, talked while he did. "I was so scared," he said, "when I saw all the blood. And it took so long for them to call for help."

The cell phone rang and he talked to someone. Shortly afterward a girl and a guy in their late teens came down the hall on their chairs. These were his friends from the halfway house. They seemed oddly impressed by whatever had happened to him.

Before the evening was over there were five wheelchairs in the room and I realized that Jamine, too, must have one. I was surprised by how quiet and lost everyone but Jamine seemed. At some point they were told they had to leave. My roommate turned off his phone and went back to sleep.

9.

The room, the ward, the floor, the hospital grew silent.

"The place ran with ghosts," Randall, an old queen I knew from when I was first in the city had said about the very classy hospital uptown where he had been for major heart surgery.

"They came and talked to me at night, taunted me. An awful man I lived with when I was young and stupid and new to New York, was cruising the halls like it was still 1925. He was a cruel bastard, physically abusive, and I'd walked out on him. He told me he was waiting for me, that sooner or later he'd have me again."

Randall liked to have me stay at his place once or twice a week. It was an easy gig. He really got off on having a young guy around. Give him a chance encounter in his own apartment with a twenty-two-year-old in jockey shorts and he was happy.

"I know when I pop off that awful sadist will be waiting for me, and I'm afraid," he said.

I smiled like he had made a joke and he shook his head and looked sad. He died at that hospital a year later and I felt bad. He'd been good to me, generous, kind. I liked him well enough then but I really understood him now.

Deep in the night the cop and I stood at the window and looked at the very late traffic flowing south on Seventh Avenue. I could tell by the car models that it was the late 1960s. The constant flow of traffic downtown was like the passage of time.

"We can do it, you know," he said. "Bring you back forty years to face trial."

"For what?" I asked. "What crimes did I ever commit that were worth that kind of attention?"

"Look at yourself." Again the screen came up and it was the three guys whose faces I could almost remember and myself all in boots and jeans and leather vests and kerchiefs around our necks. Like musicians on an album cover imitating desperados.

The one farthest away from me handed a cloth bag to the next guy who handed a smaller brown paper package to the guy next to me who handed me a white packet and I turned and handed a glassine envelope to someone not in the picture: like a high school textbook illustration of a drug distribution system.

"A kid died from something you sold," the cop said. The screen showed a girl, maybe eighteen, sprawled on the floor of a suburban bedroom with a needle in her arm and a Jim Morrison poster on the wall.

"None of that ever happened," I said. "I never did anything like that."

"We don't plant this stuff. It was inside you. Back in 1969 a family wants vengeance," he replied.

I saw myself from behind kneeling with my hands tied at my back. All around on the sand, my clothes lay in strips where they'd been cut off me. My belt and my boots were tossed aside; the kerchief I'd worn around my neck was now tied over my eyes. Behind me the three other guys all hung by their necks from the branches of a tree.

The cop said, "You'll wish they'd hanged you, too. What the family wants to do will make what happened to that black kid in your room a joke."

Then I saw myself frontally. Mutilated and bleeding to death into the sand, my mouth open in a silent scream.

That woke me and I lay in my hospital bed in the first dawn light. But I had trouble shaking the dream.

10.

Greenwich Village was partly an Irish neighborhood in the days gone by and Saint Vincent's still reflected that. My nurse that morning was Mary Collins, an old woman originally from Kerry with a round unlined face, the last of the breed. I'd established my credentials, told her about my grandparents from Aran.

After the policeman had mentioned that initial report, I'd asked Mary Collins about the nun I'd talked to. She looked at me and said, "You saw Sister Immaculata. I haven't thought about her in years. They said she roamed the halls and talked to the patients. Some of them she comforted, others she frightened."

"But she was real."

She shrugged. "Well, when I first worked here, they told stories about catching glimpses of her. But I never did."

Behind the curtains around the other bed, Nurse Yang spoke quietly to Jamine. "No matter what our health issues, we need to eat healthy food. Try this orange juice."

"I'm not hungry."

"Try it for me." And we heard him slurp some orange juice.

"She has the patience of Job," murmured Mary Collins and turned to leave.

I said, "There's this guy I keep seeing in my dreams. He looks like a cop, shows me all kinds of things, threatens to drag me back to face punishment for crimes I never committed."

Nurse Collins paused. In the silence, I heard Margaret Yang say, "Would you try this cereal?"

"His name wouldn't be McGittrick would it?" Mary Collins asked.

"I don't know."

"Immaculata and McGittrick both – ah, you are a rare one! If that's how it is, tell him to back away. While you're a patient in this hospital, you're ours not his." She winked and nodded at me and I guessed she was doing for me what Nurse Yang was doing for my roommate.

Word came that my surgery was scheduled for that night. The exact time was not set. Jamine was on his cell phone. He was due to be released from the hospital that afternoon and sent back to his halfway house. I wondered about the pain he didn't seem to be feeling and the desperate moment that had left him partially castrated.

Lying there, I thought of people I knew who had come out of surgery with hallucinations attached to their brain like parasites.

A few years before, an old professor of mine was not doing well after heart surgery. He was incoherent. Things hung in the balance and then with his eyes shut and seemingly unconscious, he said quite clearly, "Surgeon Major Herzog of the Israeli Air Medical Brigade orders you to get off your asses and get me cured."

"Herzog straightened things out," my professor told me a few days later when he had rallied and begun recovery. "The first time I saw him was shortly after the operation. I came to and he was standing in full uniform at the end of my bed reading the computer screen. He told me I was someone they needed to have alive and he was going to save me. Then he changed some of the instructions on the screen."

No one on the staff had ever heard of Surgeon Major Marvin Herzog. The doctors attributed the now rapid recovery not to a series of crisp orders and clandestine changes in the patient's treatment but to the body's wonderful will to live.

A week or two later when I visited him at home, my professor told me, "Doctor Herzog said last night that usually they don't let people like me see him. But he thinks I can handle it. He explained how his unit oversees everybody who's under anesthesia . . ."

As he went on, I had realized he was still talking to his imaginary Doctor and maybe always would.

Finally I was wheeled out for more x-rays. When I came back hours later, doctors, nurses, and Jamine's social worker were in attendance. His motorized chair, a shabby, beat-up item, had been brought into the room. When he was helped into it, he screamed with pain. A hurried conference took place out in the hall. The patient was helped back into bed.

Late that night, he was still there, talking quietly into his cell phone. It had been arranged that he was to be sent, not to his halfway house, but to a rehab facility. He seemed pleased. Was it for this that he or someone else had used the knife?

McGittrick had noticed him. Was that a first sighting, like Immaculata observing me all those years ago?

11.

That night I waited at the window feeling very small and lonely and watched the taillights of the cars as they rushed into the past.

A woman I know underwent a long and intense operation for cancer. During the hospitalization that followed she was well taken care of by the hospital nurses and orderlies and seemed to love them.

She walked with help immediately after the operation as you're supposed to. Everyone was amazed at how quickly she moved, looking around impatiently, fascinated by the other rooms on the floor – the vacant ones with their empty beds, the locked doors that led to conference rooms and doctors' hideaways.

Later, when reminded of this, she remembered nothing of her treatment. All she could recall was a movie being made night after night in which her body was used to portray a corpse. The ones making the film were criminals, threatening and intimidating her. The hospital workers were helping them. This went on all during her time in recovery.

She wanted to walk as quickly as possible, she said, so she could escape. Her fascination with the rest of the floor was because those were places that figured in the dreams. She pretended to love the staff because she was terrified of them.

By daylight she found them drab and ordinary, devoid of the desperate drama they held during her nights.

Then someone calling my name interrupted me. Word had come that the surgical team was ready and the gurney was on its way.

I went back to my room and the gurney was there. As I was loaded aboard and my IV pole was strapped to its side like a flag, I saw my godchild Antonia, twenty years old, but tiny as a child, come down the hall. Somehow she had gotten into the hospital at that late hour.

In that wonderful place, it was quite alright with everyone that she accompany me down to surgery. "You'll have to leave before they begin the procedure," one of the nurses told her.

Off we went and the attendant sang as we rolled along and told me that I was going to be fine. Then deep in the hospital, far into the night, we were in the surgical anteroom. One of the young doctors who had operated on Jamine was part of the team.

He and the others seemed like college students as they joked with Antonia and me while we awaited the surgeon who was late. Then she was there in her red jacket and dress and greeted us all.

I thanked Antonia for being with me as they hooked me up. I held onto the image of her, as everyone smiled at me and I was gone while wondering if I was ever coming back.

12.

When I awoke a young man with a shaved head said, "Good morning, Richard, you're in surgical recovery. My name is Scott Horton and I'm a nurse. How do you feel?"

"Like I've just been hit by a truck but haven't felt the pain yet," I said and he grinned, nodded with approval, pleased I was coherent enough to attempt a joke.

Just before I had awakened, in the moment between darkness and light, I had been in the vast space with only the light of the hospital patients' computer screens revolving around me like suns in galaxies.

In the way it happens in dreams, I knew these were all the unconscious patients in all the hospitals in the world. Together we formed an anima, an intelligence. Most of us were part of this for a few hours, for a day sometimes. For a few it was for months and even years.

The policeman looked up from the computer with his white crewcut, his battered nose, his cigarette.

"Someone told me your name is McGittrick," I said.

"If that name pleases you . . ." he shrugged.

"In other words I'm making you up as I go along."

"Somewhere inside you knew someone oversaw the intersection of one world and the next. First you put a face on that one. Now you've found a name for me. Mostly I don't deal personally with people in your situation. I don't have to because they aren't aware of me.

had begun to gnaw at my guts. I hit the button, waited a few minutes, and then hit it again.

Scott walked by and I called him. He had just come on duty. He had other patients but he stopped for me. "How are you?"

"Bad night." I wanted to tell him about the men endlessly cleaning the floor and the smell of ammonia but I didn't.

"Did McGittrick talk to you again?"

"Sorry I bothered you about that. I feel stupid." What I was sorry about was having brought him to McGittrick's attention.

"It's why I'm here. We're going to get you ready to return to your ward. I want you to walk before then."

Later when he was watching me push my IV stand around Recovery, I asked him, "Does everybody in this hospital know about McGittrick?"

He grinned. "If they worked with Mary Collins they do. I started out with her."

When they came to take me back upstairs Scott said good-bye and I knew it was unlikely I'd ever see him again. Unless, of course, I took McGittrick up on his offer.

When I returned to the twelfth floor, I was in a new room all by myself. Jamine was gone. Even Nurse Yang, busy with her current patients, barely remembered him. That's how it would be with me.

I hit the painkiller button, got up, and walked. I needed the pole to lean on a little. Nurses and orderlies nodded their approval. I was a model patient, a teacher's pet.

When my phone rang it was my godchild Chris planning to come in from Ohio and stay with me after I got out of the hospital. Friends came by. Flowers got delivered. I fell asleep, exhausted.

It was getting dark when I awoke and there was commotion and a gigantic man was wheeled in. "Purple," he said. "Don't go far from me, girl." My new roommate had a private healthcare worker. He called her Purple which wasn't her name and which made her quite angry.

He sang Prince songs. He called people by names he'd given them. He told me he was an architect who had stepped through a door in a half-finished building he'd designed and fallen two floors because there was no floor on the other side. All the bones in his feet had been shattered. It took the healthcare worker and all the orderlies on the floor to help him change his position in the bed.

At one point I dozed off but awoke to hear a Jamaican orderly whom he called Tangerine, saying, "I do not have to take this. I will be treated with respect. My name to you is Mrs. Jackson."

"Oh Tangerine!" he cried in a despairing voice.

I hit the pain button, got up, and walked to the window overlooking Seventh Avenue. In the night, the streetlights turned from red to green.

McGittrick's face danced on the window in front of me. A computer screen on a nearby station counter faced the window and was reflected on the dark glass.

When I turned to look the computer screen was blank. I turned back and the face was there. It might have been the drugs or I may have been asleep on my feet. But as hard as I looked McGittrick remained.

Then Jamine's face appeared on the screen. McGittrick said, "He stands out kind of the way you did, flirting with death but afraid of it. Bear in mind that if you don't work for us someone else will – maybe him."

"What exactly would I do?"

"Be around; make sure all is running as it should. Be a cop," he said. "Think it over."

"Okay. But when I sleep from now on, you have to stay out of my dreams."

"You're not dreaming. It's just easier to reach you when you're asleep. But we'll give you a little time to consider."

When I came back to my own ward, the nurses at the desk, as if they sensed something about me, looked up as I passed by. When I went into my room the architect was crooning a song to his caregiver who was telling him to shut up.

They stopped when they saw me and I wondered if I was marked somehow.

"Look," I said, "I'm recovering from major surgery. I need to sleep." They stared at me, nodded and were quiet. I hit the painkiller button and hit it again every few minutes until I drifted away.

14.

I awoke and it was morning. The architect, quite deferentially, asked if I had slept well. "I made sure all these ladies kept very quiet so you could rest and get better."

This guy was a harmless lunatic with none of Jamine's vibes. I thanked him.

Then Mrs. Jackson helped me wash up and I was taken for x-rays. When I returned the architect was gone, brought to another ward for physical therapy, Nurse Collins said.

She was on duty and had come in to check on me. "You're doing well," she said. "They didn't get you this time."

"Who was Immaculata? Who is McGittrick?"

"I don't think she was any kind of angel and I don't think he's a banshee because I don't believe in them. Ones like that lurk in the cracks of every hospital there ever was. Most places they don't even know about it anymore. But they still have them. Give them the back of your hand."

I'd begun feeling that if I performed certain tasks – walked rapidly three times around the floor, say, then I was practically recovered.

That night I paused on my rounds and looked out the window. The Greenwich Village crowds on a Friday night in spring reminded me of the rush of being twenty and in the city. I thought of Andre and how I'd lost him just before I got sick.

McGittrick was reflected in the window "You know," he said. "That guy that got away might still be with you if you'd been well when his friend called. We can let you replay that scene." Cops offer candy when they believe you're beginning to soften and cooperate. But they still can't be trusted.

"I enjoy the sweet melancholy of affairs gone by," I said. "I'd like to be with Andre as if nothing ever happened. But I'd know that wasn't true and wouldn't be able to stand it." As I headed back to my room, I said, "Thanks, though."

As I hit the pain button, a young guy who'd had an emergency appendectomy was brought into the room. He lay quietly, breathing deep unconscious breaths. I passed into sleep remembering moments when someone with whom I'd made love fell into slumber like this just before I did.

15.

The next morning was a Saturday. A resident and a nurse came in and drew a curtain around my bed. They detached me from the catheter, pulled the feeding tube out of my throat and out through my nose.

That morning I ate liquids for the first time since I'd been there. Everything tasted awful. I forced myself to eat a little JELL-O, drink clear soup and apple juice because that was the way to get better.

Dale, my roommate, cast no aura, had no vibes that I could feel. He was twenty-seven, a film editor who had collapsed in horrible pain on Friday night. He was getting out later that day. His insurance paid for no more than that.

After ten days in the hospital, I was a veteran and showed him how to push his IV rack, how to ring for a nurse.

Mark came by. I told him, "When I wrote *Feral Cell*, I had the narrator drink blood. Blood of the Goat binds him to the alternate world, Capricorn. Blood of the Crab binds him here. As one world fades the other gets clearer. What I was writing about was being sick. It's like this other country. You get pulled in there without wanting to and have to haul your ass out."

He said, "Remember first coming to the city and how hard it was to stick here? Like at any moment the job, the apartment you were sharing, the best friend, the lover would all come loose and you'd be sucked back to Metuchen or Doylestown or Portsmouth. Kind of the same thing."

The roommate was on the phone. "It felt like a bad movie, waking up and finding all these people staring down at me. The guy in here with me is this amazing Village character."

He was still on the phone when his lovely Korean girlfriend came in with his clothes. She took his gown off him as he stood talking and dressed him from his skin out. It bothered me that he was getting out and I was still inside. As they left, he turned, waved good-bye, and grinned because he was young and this was all an adventure. I had more in common with Jamine than with this kid.

That evening, I was served a horrible dish of pasta and chicken but it was a test of my recovery and I ate a bit of it.

That night McGittrick said, "If it's not love that interests you, how about revenge? Ones who screwed you around when you were a kid? You wrote a story about that. We can go deep into the past. You could go back and make sure they never did that to anyone else."

I shook my head. "The one I most wanted to kill was myself. It took a long time to untangle that. This is who I am," I told him. "I'm turning down your offer."

He smiled and shook his head like my stupidity amused him. On the screen, I knelt blindfolded in the desert. "Did you forget about that?" he asked as I walked away.

16.

Sunday morning, as I tried to choke down tasteless jelly on dry toast, a guy named John was brought in to have kidney stones removed. He was tall, thin, and long-haired, almost my age. "I was born on Bank Street, lived in the Village my whole life," he told me.

There was something in the face with its five o'clock shadow and hawk nose that looked familiar. He was an archetype: the guy who held the dope, the guy who hid the gun, the guy who knew how to get in the back way. He was like Jamine. Like me.

It was confirmed that I was going home the next day. At one point that afternoon my niece walked with me around the floor. When we came to the window on Seventh Avenue, I looked around and realized there's no way that a computer screen could be reflected from the desk onto the glass.

"Thank you," I told Margaret Yang later. "You people gave me a life transfusion."

"We just did our job. You are an interesting patient," she said. That night when I stopped and looked out, the traffic was a Sunday night dribble without any magic at all.

17.

The next morning, I awoke with the memory of a visitor. The night before I had opened my eyes and seen Sister Immaculata. "I'm disappointed," she told me. "That you aren't willing to give others the same chance that was given to you."

"What chance was that?" I asked.

"You were a stumbling wayfarer," she said. "We helped you survive in the hope you would eventually help us."

"What is it that you do?"

"Hope and Easeful Death," she said with a radiant smile and I realized that I trusted cops more than nuns.

That morning they disconnected me from the last of my attachments. The IV pole was wheeled away.

John was about to go down to the operating room. He would spend this day in the hospital and then be released the next.

"You ever go to Washington Square Park?" he asked. "Look for me around the chess tables in the southwest corner."

Then my friend Bruce was there, pulling my stuff together, helping me get my pants on, tying my shoes for me. I was in my own clothes and feeling kind of lost.

Nurse Collins was on duty. "Good luck," she said as I passed the desk for the last time. She looked at me for a long moment. "And let's hope we see no more of you in here."

The taxi ride home took only a few minutes. The flight of stairs to my apartment was the first I had climbed in almost two weeks and I had to stop and rest halfway up.

I'd thought that when I got out of the hospital I would magically be well, and had a hundred errands to do. Bruce insisted I get undressed again and helped me into bed.

"When what they gave you in there wears off," he said. "You will feel like you've been hit by a fist the size of a horse."

He filled my prescriptions for Oxycontin and antibiotics, bought me food we thought I could eat, lay on my couch and looked at a book of Paul Cadmus's art he'd found on my shelves. I dozed and awoke and dozed some more. People called and asked how I was. A friend brought by a huge basket of fruit.

Bruce taped the phone extension cord to the floor so that I wouldn't trip on it: more than any other single thing that spelled old age and sickness to me. It struck me as I fell asleep that Bruce was HIV positive and taking a cocktail of drugs to stay alive, yet I was so feeble he was taking care of me.

The second day Bruce came by in the morning, watched to make sure I didn't fall down in the shower, helped me get dressed, and went with me for a little walk. The third day I got myself dressed.

Late that night, I looked at myself in the mirror. It was a stranger's face, thin with huge eyes. This was a taste of what very old age would be like. I missed the large ever-present organization devoted to making me better. My life felt flat without the spice of hallucination and paranoia.

The next day my godson Chris came to stay with me. That year we both had works in nomination for a major speculative fiction award. The ceremonies were to be held in New York City.

We were in different categories, fortunately. It was on my mind that if I could attend the ceremonies and all the related events, it would mean I had passed a critical test and was well.

Chris was shocked at first seeing me, though he tried to hide it. When one person is in his sixties and sick and the other less than half his age and well their pace of life differs.

He adapted to mine, walked slowly around the neighborhood with me, sat in the park on the long sunny afternoons, ate in my favorite restaurants where to me the food all tasted like chalk now, read me stories.

The awards that weekend were in a hotel in Lower Manhattan. All the magic of speculative fiction is on the pages and in the cover art. The physical reality is dowdy. Internet photos of the book signing and reception show Chris happy and mugging and me fading out of the picture. Like those sketches Renaissance artists did of youth and old age.

As the awards ceremony dragged on I realized I'd be unable to walk to the dais if I won. I needn't have worried. A luminary of the field, quite remarkably drunk, after complaining bitterly that he for once hadn't been nominated, mangled all names and titles beyond recognition, then presented the award to the excellent writer who won. When it was over I rode home in a cab and went to bed.

Chris was nice enough to stay on and keep me company. One day as we walked into the park I saw John, my last roommate at the hospital. Looking as gray and thin as I did, he sat at a chess table in the southwest corner of Washington Square. The chess players share that space with drug dealers and hustlers.

I said hello. He nodded very slightly and I realized he was at work and that he was a spotter.

The spotters are paid to warn dealers if the heat is on the prowl or tip them off that a customer is at hand. I glanced back and saw John watching me.

One evening I took Chris to see a play that was running at a theater around the corner from my place. As we walked down narrow, old Minetta Lane, kids on motorized wheelchairs rolled past the Sixth Avenue end of the lane.

For a moment I saw Jamine. Then I wasn't sure and then they were gone.

One day on the street we found a guy selling candid black and white photos that his father had taken fifty, forty, thirty years ago on the streets of Greenwich Village. One shot taken from an upstairs window on West Tenth Street and dated 1968 showed the Ninth Circle Bar with young guys in tight jeans and leather jackets standing on the front stairs. I felt a rush of déjà vu.

That night on a website I saw that scene again, the street, the stairs, the figures. But this time there was a close-up. The kid in the center of the group was me. The other guys were my partners in crime from the dream.

I clicked the mouse and the next picture came up. It was a figure in a motorized wheelchair rolling up Minetta Lane toward the camera. My face was a twisted mask. My hands were claws. I was ancient and partially paralyzed: the ultimate nightmare.

"You see how long we've been keeping an eye on you. And how long we'll keep it up," McGittrick said and I awoke in the dawn light.

That evening when Chris and I kissed good-bye at Penn Station and he went off on the airport train, I felt the most incredible loneliness and loss. He'd been sharing his energy and youth with me and now I was on my own again.

Back downtown, I sat on a bench in Washington Square in the May twilight. Dogs yapped in the runs. As the light went away a jazz quintet played "These Foolish Things."

McGittrick stood studying me. "Why," I asked, "was it necessary to screw my head around as you've been doing?"

"Think of it as boot camp. Break you down, rebuild you. Would the you who went to sleep the night before you got sick have sat in a public park having this conversation?"

"How did you get into this racket?"

He smiled, "Immaculata recruited me. Said I was a restless soul that wouldn't be happy unless I got to see a little more of life and death than others did."

"And now?"

"I'm ready to move on. You'll understand when you're in my place."

My guts, where they had been cut open and stapled back together, still hurt a little. I'd pretty much tapered off the medication but I needed to go home and take half an oxycontin tablet.

I arose and he asked, "Would you rather talk to Sister Immaculata?"

"That's okay. You're less scary than a nun."

"You've got a while to decide," he said. "But not, you know, for ever."

I nodded and continued on my way. But we both knew how I'd decided.

Dowland wrote:

> Sad despair doth drive me hence
> This despair unkindness sends
> If that parting be offence
> It is I which then offends

I had seen death and didn't want to die. Maybe I was a restless soul or maybe I was too big a coward to face death all at once and forever.

From a little reading I'd done, some research on the Internet, I knew that injury or illness actually can change a personality. What I'd always feared had happened. The one who had gone to sleep that night a few weeks before had awakened as someone else.

And I now was different enough from the one I had been that I didn't much care about that person who now was lost and gone.

Richard Bowes has lived in Manhattan for most of his adult life. He has published five novels, two collections of stories, and over forty short stories. Bowes has won two World Fantasy Awards, as well as Lambda, International Horror Guild, and Million Writers awards. This is his sixth Nebula Award nomination. Recent and forthcoming stories will appear in *The Magazine of Fantasy & Science Fiction*, and in the *Digital Domains, Wilde Stories, The Beastly Bride, Haunted Legends, Year's Best Gay Stories*, and *Naked City* anthologies.

Most of these, like this year's Nebula nominated novelette, "I Needs Must Part, the Policeman Said," are part of his novel in stories: *Dust Devil: My Life In Speculative Fiction*.

DIVINING LIGHT

Ted Kosmatka

FROM THE AUTHOR: The idea for "Divining Light" was in my head for a couple of years before I finally figured out how to write it. There were a lot of false starts that ended up in the wastebasket, and I eventually realized that before I could write the story in a way that held together as a narrative, there were several problems I'd first need to overcome – not the least of which being that the science behind the story was so impenetrable.

In "Divining Light," the whole premise hinges on the reader understanding a twist extrapolated from a loophole in the logic of quantum mechanics. For the story to succeed, the reader had to understand not just the basics of QM, but also my particular spin on it – which in turn would require me to dump about a metric ton of physics into the story.

I knew it would never work.

You can't say, *hey, read this chapter on physics, and then the real story will start on page sixteen.* So the big problem became, how do I get the reader to slog through pages and pages of raw physics without realizing it? I'd need to perform an act of prestidigitation, and I really had no idea how to pull it off. It was almost like a math problem. When I looked at it that way, I decided to move my variables around like algebra, throwing in different characters, different conflicts, trying to find a narrative that best tolerated the necessary info-dumps while at the same time serving the themes that grew naturally from the premise. Still, nothing I tried really clicked. At the time, I had a day job in a research lab, so I'd work eight to ten hours in this analytical environment, and then I'd come home and hammer away at a story that was beginning to look more like some dense, technical treatise than any kind of fiction worth reading. It was pretty discouraging.

I ended up shaking the Etch A Sketch one last time and started over. I asked myself what story I wanted to tell from the perspective of the characters, rather than the science. When I focused on that and only that, the writing finally opened up, and I managed to tell the story.

It is impossible that God should ever deceive me, since in all fraud and deceit is to be found a certain imperfection.

—Descartes

I CROUCHED IN THE rain with a gun.

A wave climbed the pebbly beach, washing over my foot, filling my pants with grit and sand. Around me, the rocks loomed black and big as houses.

I shivered as I came back to myself and for the first time realized my suit jacket was missing. Also my left shoe, brown leather, size twelve. I looked for the shoe, scanning the rocky shoreline, but saw only stone and frothy, sliding water.

I took another pull from the bottle and tried to loosen my tie. Since I had a gun in one hand and a bottle in the other – and since I was unwilling to surrender either – loosening my tie was difficult. I used the gun hand, working the knot with a finger looped through the trigger guard, cold steel brushing my throat. I felt the muzzle under my chin – fingers numb and awkward, curling past the trigger.

It would be so easy.

I wondered if people have died this way – drunk, armed, loosening their ties. I imagined it was common among certain occupations.

Then the tie opened, and I hadn't shot myself. I took a drink from the bottle as reward.

The waves rumbled in. This place was nothing like the dunes of Indiana, where Lake Michigan makes love to the shoreline. Here in Gloucester, the water hates the land.

As a child, I'd come to this beach and wondered where all the boulders came from. Did the tides carry them in? Now I knew better. The boulders, of course, were here all along – buried in soft soils. They are left-behind things. They are what remains when the ocean subtracts everything else.

Behind me, near the road, there is a monument – a list of names. Fishermen. Gloucestermen. The ones who did not come back.

This is Gloucester, a place with a history of losing itself to the ocean.

I told myself I'd brought the gun for protection, but sitting here in the dark sand, I no longer believed it. I was beyond fooling myself. It was my father's gun, a .357. It had not been fired for sixteen years, seven months, four days. Even drunk, the math came quickly.

My sister Mary had called it a good thing, this new place that was also an old place. *A new start,* she'd said. *You can do your work again. You can continue your research.*

Yeah, I'd said. A lie she believed.

You won't call me, will you?

Of course I'll call. A lie she didn't.

I turned my face away from the wind and took another burning swig. I drank until I couldn't remember which hand held the gun and which the bottle. I drank until they were the same.

During the second week, we unpacked the microscopes. Satish used a crowbar while I used a claw hammer. The crates were heavy, wooden, hermetically sealed – shipped in from some now-defunct research laboratory in Pennsylvania.

The sun beat down on the lab's loading dock, and it was nearly as hot today as it was cold the week before.

I swung my arm, and the claw hammer bit into the pale wood. I swung again. It was satisfying work. Satish saw me wipe the perspiration from my forehead, and he smiled, straight white teeth in a straight dark face.

"In India," he said, "this is sweater weather."

Satish slid the crowbar into the gash I made, and pressed. I'd known him for three days, and already I was his friend. Together we committed violence on the crates until they yielded.

The industry was consolidating, the Pennsylvania lab the latest victim. Their equipment came cheap. Here at Hansen, it was like Christmas for scientists. We opened our boxes. We ogled our new toys. We wondered, vaguely, how we had come to deserve this. For some, like Satish, the answer was complicated and rooted in achievement. Hansen was more than just another Massachusetts think tank after all, and Satish had beaten out a dozen other scientists to work here. He'd given presentations and written up projects that important people liked. For me it was simpler.

For me this was a second chance given by a friend. A last chance.

We cracked open the final wooden crate, and Satish peered inside. He peeled out layer after layer of foam packing material. It was a big crate, but inside we found only a small assortment of Nalgene volumetric flasks, maybe three pounds weight. It was somebody's idea of a joke – somebody at the now-defunct lab making a statement of opinion about their now-defunct job.

"The frog is in the well," Satish said, one of his many opaque expressions.

"It certainly is," I said.

There were reasons for moving here. There were reasons not to. They were the same reasons. Both had everything, and nothing, to do with the gun.

The lab gates are the first thing a person sees when driving up on the property. From the gates, you can't see the building at all, which in the real estate sector surrounding Boston, speaks not just of money, but *money*. Everything out here is expensive, elbow room most of all.

The lab is tucked into a stony hillside about an hour upcoast of the city. It is a private, quiet place, shaded by trees. The building itself is beautiful – two stories of reflective glass spread over the approximate dimensions of a football field. What isn't glass is matte black steel. It looks like art. A small, brick-paved turnaround curves up to the main entrance, but the front parking lot there is merely a decorative ornament – a small asphalt pad for visitors and the uninitiated. The driveway continues around the building where the real parking, the parking for the researchers, is in the back.

That first morning, I parked in front and walked inside.

A pretty blonde receptionist smiled at me. "Take a seat."

Two minutes later, James rounded the corner and shook my hand. He walked me back to his office. And then came the offer, like this was just business – like we were just two men in suits. But I could see it in his eyes, that sad way he looked at me, my old friend.

He slid a folded sheet of paper across the desk. I unfolded it. Forced myself to make sense of the numbers.

"It's too generous," I said.

"We're getting you cheap at that price."

"No," I said. "You're not."

"Considering your patents and your past work—"

I cut him off. "I can't do that anymore."

"I'd heard that. I'd hoped it wasn't true."

"If you feel I came here under false pretenses—" I began climbing to my feet.

"No, no." He held his hand up to stop me. "The offer stands. We can carry you for four months." He leaned back in his leather chair. "Probationary researchers get four months to produce. We pride ourselves on our independence; so you can choose whatever research you like, but after four months, it's not up to me anymore. I have bosses, too; so you have to have something to show for it. Something publishable, or on its way to it. Do you understand?"

I nodded.

"This can be a new start for you," he said, and I knew then that he'd already talked to Mary. "You did some great work at QSR. I followed your publications; hell, we all did. But considering the circumstances under which you left . . ."

I nodded again. The inevitable moment.

He was silent, looking at me. "I'm going out on a limb for you," he said. "But you've got to promise me."

That was the closest he'd come to mentioning it.

I looked away. His office suited him, I decided. Not too large, but bright and comfortable. A Notre Dame engineering diploma graced one wall. Only his desk was pretentious – a teak monstrosity large enough to land aircraft on – but I knew it was inherited. His father's old desk. I'd seen it once when we were still in college a dozen years ago. A lifetime ago.

"Can you promise me?" he asked.

I knew what he was asking. I met his eyes. Silence. And he was quiet for a long time after that, looking at me, waiting for me to say something. Weighing our friendship against the odds this would come back to bite him.

"All right," he said finally. "You start tomorrow."

There are days I don't drink at all. Here is how those days start: I pull the gun from its holster and set it on the desk in my hotel room. The gun is heavy and black. It says *Ruger* along the side in small, raised letters. It tastes like pennies and ashes. I look into the mirror across from the bed and tell myself, *If you drink today, you're going to kill yourself.* I look into my own gray eyes and see that I mean it.

Those are the days I don't drink.

There is a rhythm to working in a research laboratory. Through the glass doors by 7:30, nodding to the other early arrivals, then sit in your office until 8:00, pondering this fundamental truth: even shit coffee – even mud-thick, brackish, walkin'-out-the-pot shit coffee is better than no coffee at all.

I like to be the one who makes the first pot in the morning. Swing open the cabinet doors in the coffee room, pop the tin cylinder and take a deep breath, letting the smell of grounds fill my lungs. It is better than drinking the coffee, that smell.

There are days when I feel everything is an imposition – eating, speaking, walking out of the hotel room in the morning. Everything is effort. I exist mostly in my head. It comes and goes, this crushing depression, and I work hard not to let it show, because the truth is that it's not how you feel that matters. It's how you act. It's your behavior. As long as your intelligence is intact, you can make cognitive evaluations of what is appropriate. You can force the day to day.

And I want to keep this job; so I do force it. I want to get along. I want to be productive again. I want to make Mary proud of me.

Working at a research lab isn't like a normal job. There are peculiar rhythms, strange hours – special allowances are made for the creatives.

Two Chinese guys are the ringleaders of lunchtime basketball. They pulled me into a game my first week. "You look like you can play," was what they said.

One is tall, one is short. The tall one was raised in Ohio and has no accent. He is called Point Machine. The short one has no real idea of the rules of basketball, and for this reason, is the best defensive player. His fouls leave marks, and that becomes another game – a game within a game – to see how much abuse you can take without calling it. This is the real reason I play. I drive to the hoop and get hacked down. I drive again.

One player, a Norwegian named Umlauf, is six feet eight inches. I marvel at the sheer size of him. He can't run or jump or move at all, really, but his big body clogs up the lane, huge arms swatting down any jump shot made within reach of his personal zone of asphalt real estate. We play four-on-four, or five-on-five, depending on who is free for lunch. At thirty-one, I'm a few years younger than most of them, a few inches taller – except for Umlauf, who is a head taller than everyone. Trash is talked in an assortment of accents.

Some researchers go to restaurants on lunch hour. Others play computer games in their offices. Still others work through lunch – forget to eat for days. Satish is one of those. I play basketball because it feels like punishment.

The atmosphere in the lab is relaxed; you can take naps if you want. There is no outside pressure to work. It is a strictly Darwinian system – you compete for your right to be there. The only pressure is the pressure you put on yourself, because everyone knows that the evaluations come every four months, and you've got to have something to show. The turnover rate for probationary researchers hovers around 25 percent.

Satish works in circuits. He told me about it during my second week when I found him sitting at the SEM. "It is microscopic work," he said.

A scanning electron microscope is a window. Put a sample in the chamber, pump to vacuum, and it's like looking at another world. What had been flat, smooth sample surface now takes on another character, becomes topographically complex. Using the SEM is like looking at satellite photography – you're up in space, looking down at this elaborate landscape, looking down at Earth, and then you turn the little black dial and zoom toward the surface. Zooming in is like falling. Like you've been dropped from orbit, and the ground is rushing up to meet you, but you're falling faster than you ever could in real life, faster than terminal velocity, falling impossibly fast, impossibly far, and the landscape keeps getting bigger, and you think you're going to hit, but you never do, because everything keeps getting closer and sharper, and you never do hit the ground – like that old riddle where the frog jumps half the distance of a log, then half again, and again, and again, and never reaches the other side, not ever. That's an electron microscope. Falling forever down into the picture. And you never do hit bottom.

I zoomed in to 14,000X once. Like God's eyes focusing. Looking for that ultimate, indivisible truth. I learned this: there is no bottom to see.

Satish and I both had offices on the second floor.

Satish was short and thin. His skin was a deep, rich brown. He had an almost boyish face, but the first hints of gray salted his mustache. His features were balanced in such a way that he could have been the fine, prodigal son of any number of nations: Mexico, or Libya, or Greece, or Sicily – until he opened his mouth. When he opened his mouth and spoke, all those possible identities vanished, and he was suddenly Indian, solidly Indian, completely, like a magic trick; and you could not imagine him being anything else.

The first time I met Satish, he clamped both hands over mine, shook, then clapped me on the shoulder and said, "How are you doing, my friend? Welcome to research." He smiled so wide it was impossible not to like him.

It was Satish who explained that you never wore gloves when working with liquid nitrogen. "Make a point of it," Satish said. "Because the gloves will get you burned."

I watched him work. He filled the SEM's reservoir – icy smoke spilling out over the lip, cascading down to the tile floor.

Liquid nitrogen doesn't have the same surface tension as water; spill a few drops across your hand and they'll tend to bounce off harmlessly and run down your skin without truly wetting you – like little balls of mercury. The drops will evaporate in moments, sizzling, steaming, gone.

But if you're wearing gloves when you fill the reservoir, the nitrogen could spill down inside and be trapped against your skin. "And if that happens," Satish said while he poured. "It will hurt you bad."

Satish was the first to ask my area of research.

"I'm not sure," I told him.

"How can you not be sure?"

I shrugged. "I'm just not."

"You are here. It must be something."

"I'm still working on it."

He stared at me, taking this in, and I saw his eyes change – his understanding of me shifting, like the first time I heard him speak. And just like that, I'd become something different to him.

"Ah," he said. "I know who you are now. You are the one from Stanford."

"That was eight years ago."

"You wrote that famous paper on de-coherence. You are the one who had the breakdown."

Satish was blunt, apparently.

"I wouldn't call it a breakdown."

He nodded, perhaps accepting this; perhaps not. "So you still are working in quantum theory?"

"No, I stopped."

"Why stop?"

"Quantum mechanics starts to affect your worldview after a while."

"What do you mean?" he asked.

"The more research I did, the less I believed."

"In quantum mechanics?"

"No. In the world."

There are days when I don't drink at all. On those days, I pick up my father's .357 and look in the mirror. I convince myself what it will cost me, today, if I take the first sip. It will cost me what it cost him.

But there are also days I *do* drink. Those are the days I wake up sick. I walk into the bathroom and puke into the toilet, needing a drink so bad my hands are shaking. I look in the bathroom mirror and splash water in my face. I say nothing to myself. There is nothing I would believe.

It is Vodka in the morning. Vodka because vodka has no smell. A sip to calm the shakes. A sip to get me moving. If Satish knows, he says nothing.

*   *   *

Divining Light 187

Satish studied circuits. He bred them, in little ones and zeroes, in a Thomlin's Field Programmable Gate Array. The array's internal logic was malleable, and he allowed selective pressure to direct chip design. Genetic algorithms manipulated the best codes for the task. "Nothing is ideal," he said. "There's lots of modeling."

I didn't have the slightest idea how it all worked.

Satish was a genius who had been a farmer in India until he came to America at the age of twenty-eight. He earned an electrical engineering degree from MIT. After that, Harvard, and patents, and job offers. "I am just a simple farmer," he liked to say. "I like to challenge the dirt."

Satish had endless expressions. When relaxed, he let himself lapse into broken English. Sometimes, after spending the morning with him, I'd fall into the pattern of his speech, talking his broken English back at him, an efficient pidgin that I came to respect for its streamlined efficiency and ability to convey nuance.

"I went to dentist yesterday," Satish told me. "He says I have good teeth. I tell him 'Forty-two years old, and it is my first time at dentist.' And he could not believe."

"You've never been to the dentist?" I said.

"No, never. Until I am in twelfth grade in my village back home, I did not know there was special doctor for teeth. I never went because I had no need. The dentist says I have good teeth, no cavities, but I have stain on my back molars on the left side where I chew tobacco."

"I didn't know you chewed."

"I am ashamed. None of my brothers chew tobacco. Out of my family, I am the only one. I try to stop." Satish spread his hands in exasperation. "But I cannot. I told my wife I stopped two months ago, but I started again, and I have not told her." His eyes grew sad. "I am a bad person."

Satish stared at me. "You are laughing," he said. "Why are you laughing?"

Hansen was a gravity well in the tech industry – a constantly expanding force of nature, always buying out other labs, buying equipment, absorbing the competition.

Hansen labs only hired the best, without regard to national origin. It was the kind of place where you'd walk into the coffee room and find a Nigerian speaking German to an Iranian. Speaking German because they both spoke it better than English, the other language they had in common. Most of the engineers were Asian, though. It wasn't because the best engineers were Asian – well, it wasn't *only* because the best engineers were Asian. There were also simply more of them. America graduated four thousand engineers in 2008. China graduated more than three hundred thousand. And Hansen was always hungry for talent.

The Boston lab was just one of Hansen's locations, but we had the largest storage facility, which meant that much of the surplus lab equipment ended up shipped to us. We opened boxes. We sorted through supplies. If we needed anything for our research, we signed for it, and it was ours. It was the opposite of academia, where every piece of equipment had to be expensed and justified and begged for.

Most mornings I spent with Satish. I helped him with his gate arrays. He talked of his children while he worked. Lunch I spent on basketball. Sometimes after basketball, I'd drop by Point Machine's lab to see what he was up to. He worked with organics, searching for chemical alternatives that wouldn't cause birth defects in amphibians. He tested water samples for cadmium, mercury, arsenic. Point Machine was a kind of shaman. He studied the gene expression patterns of amphioxus; he read the future in deformities.

"Unless something is done," he said. "A generation from now, most amphibians will be extinct." He had aquariums filled with frogs – frogs with too many legs, with tails, with no arms. Monsters.

Next to his lab was the office of a woman named Joy. Sometimes Joy would hear us talking and stop by, hand sliding along the wall – tall, and beautiful, and blind. Did acoustical research of some kind. She had long hair and high cheekbones – eyes so clear and blue and perfect that I didn't even realize at first.

"It's okay," she said. "I get that a lot." She never wore dark glasses, never used a white cane. "Detached retinas," she explained. "I was three."

In the afternoons, I tried to work.

Alone in my office, I stared at the marker board. The great white expanse of it. I picked up the marker, closed my eyes, wrote from memory.

When I looked at what I'd written, I threw the marker across the room.

James came by later that night. He stood in the doorway, cup of coffee in his hand. He saw the papers scattered across the floor. "It's good to see you working on something," he said.

"It's not work."

"It'll come," he said.

"No, I don't think it will."

"It just takes time."

"Time is what I'm wasting here. Your time. This lab's time." Honesty welled up. "I shouldn't be here."

"It's fine, Eric," he said. "We have researchers on staff who don't have a third of your citings. You belong here."

"It's not like before. I'm not like before."

James looked at me. That sad look back again. His voice was soft when he spoke. "R&D is a tax writeoff. At least finish out your contract. That gives you another two months. After that, we can write you up a letter of recommendation."

That night in my hotel room, I stared at the phone, sipped the vodka. I imagined calling Mary, dialing the number. My sister, so like me, yet not like me. I imagined her voice on the other end.

Hello? Hello?

This numbness inside of me, strange gravity, the slow accretion of things I could have said, not to worry, things are fine; but instead I say nothing, letting the phone slide away, and hours later find myself at the railing outside, coming out of another stupor, soaked to the skin, watching the rain. Thunder advances from the east, from across the water, and I stand in the dark, waiting for life to be good again.

There is this: the slow dissolution of perspective. I see myself outside myself, an angular shape cast in sodium lights – eyes gray like storm clouds, gray like gunmetal. Because once you've learned something, you can't unlearn it. Darwin once said that the serious study of math endows you with an extra sense, but what do you do when that sense contradicts your other senses?

My arm flexes and the vodka bottle flies end over end into the darkness – the glimmer of it, the shatter of it, glass and asphalt and shards of rain. There is nothing else until there is nothing else.

The lab.

Satish said, "Yesterday in my car I was talking to my daughter, five years old, and she says, 'Daddy, please don't talk.' I asked her why, and she said, 'Because I am praying. I need you to be quiet.' So I asked her what she is praying about, and she said, 'My friend borrowed my glitter ChapStick and I am praying she remembers to bring it back.' "

Satish was trying not to smile. We were in his office, eating lunch across his desk.

He continued. "I told her, well, maybe she is like me and she forgets. But my daughter says, 'No, it has been more than one week now.' "

This amused Satish greatly – the talk of ChapStick, and the prayers of children. We finished our lunches.

"You eat the same thing every day," I observed.

"I like rice," he said.

"But every day?"

"You insult me. I am a simple man trying to save for my daughter's college." Satish spread his hands in mock outrage. "Do you think I am born with golden spoon?"

In the fourth week, I told him I wasn't going to be hired after my probationary period.

"How do you know?"

"I just know."

His face grew serious. "You are certain?"

"Yeah."

"In that case, do not worry." He clapped me on the shoulder. "Sometimes the boat just gets sink, my friend."

I thought about this for a moment. "Did you just tell me that you win some and you lose some?"

Satish considered this. "Yes," he said. "That is correct, except I did not mention the win part."

During my fifth week at the lab, I found the box from Docent. It started as an e-mail from Bob, the shipping guy, saying there were some crates I might be interested in. Crates labeled "Physics," sitting in the loading dock.

I went down to receiving and looked at the boxes. Got out the crowbar and opened them.

Three of the boxes were of no interest; they held only weights, scales, and glassware. But the fourth box was different. I stared into the fourth box for a long time.

I closed the box again and hammered the lid down with the edge of the crowbar. I went to Bob's office and tracked down the shipping information. A company called Ingram had been bought by Docent a few years ago – and now Docent had been bought by Hansen. The box had been in storage the whole time.

I had the box taken to my office. Later that day, I signed for lab space, Room 271.

I was drawing on my marker board when Satish walked into my office.

"What is that?" he said, gesturing to what I'd written.

"It is my project."

"You have a project now?"

"Yes."

"That is good." He smiled and shook my hand. "Congratulations, my friend. How did this wonderful thing happen?"

"It's not going to change anything. Just busywork to give me something to do."

"What is it?"

"You ever hear of the Feynman double-slit?" I asked.

"Physics? That is not my area, but I have heard of Young's double-slit."

"It's the same thing, almost; only instead of light, they used a stream of electrons." I patted the box on the table. "And a detector. The detector is key. The detector makes all the difference."

Satish looked at the box. "The detector is in there?"

"Yeah, I found it in a crate today, along with a thermionic gun."

"A gun?"

"A thermionic gun. An electron gun. Obviously part of a replication trial."

"You are going to use this gun?"

I nodded. "Feynman once said, 'Any other situation in quantum mechanics, it turns out, can be explained by saying, You remember the case of the experiment with two holes? It's the same thing.' "

"Why are you going to do this project?"

"I want to see what Feynman saw."

Autumn comes quick to the East Coast. It is a different animal out here, where the trees take on every color of the spectrum, and the wind has teeth. As a boy, before the moves and the special schools, I'd spent an autumn evening camped out in the woods behind my grandparents' house. Lying on my back, staring up at the leaves as they drifted past my field of vision.

It was the smell that brought it back so strong – the smell of fall, as I walked to the parking lot. Joy stood near the roadway, waiting for her cab.

The wind gusted, making the trees dance. She turned her collar against the wind, oblivious to the autumn beauty around her. For a moment, I felt pity for that. To live in New England and not see the leaves.

I climbed into my rental. I idled. No cab passed through the gates. No cab followed the winding drive. I was about to pull away, but at the last second spun the wheel and pulled up to the turnaround.

"Is there a problem with your ride?" I asked her.

"I'm not sure. I think there might be."

"Do you need a lift home?"

"I'll be okay." She paused. Then, "You don't mind?"

"It's fine, seriously."

She climbed in and shut the door. "Thank you," she said. "It's a bit of a drive."

"I wasn't doing much anyway."

"Left at the gate," she said.

She guided me by stops. She didn't know the street names, but she counted the intersections, guiding me to the highway, blind leading the blind. The miles rolled by.

Boston. A city that hasn't forgotten itself. A city outside of time. Crumbling cobblestones and modern concrete. Road names that existed before the Redcoats invaded. It is easy to lose yourself, to imagine yourself lost, while winding through the hilly streets.

Outside the city proper, there is stone everywhere, and trees – soft pine and colorful deciduous. I saw a map in my head, Cape Cod jutting into the Atlantic. The cape is a curl of land positioned so perfectly to protect Boston that it seems a thing designed. If not by man, then by God. God wanted a city where Boston sits.

The houses, I know, are expensive beyond all reason. It is a place that defies farming. Scratch the earth, and a rock will leap out and hit you. People build stone walls around their properties so they'll have some-place to put the stones.

At her apartment, I pulled to a stop, walked her to her door, like this was a date. Standing next to her, she was almost as tall as me – maybe 5'11", too thin, and we were at the door, her empty blue eyes focused on something far away until she looked at me, *looked*, and I could swear for a moment that she saw me.

Then her eyes glided past my shoulder, focused again on some dim horizon.

"I'm renting now," she said. "Once my probationary period is over, I'll probably buy a condo closer to work."

"I didn't realize you were new to Hansen, too."

"I actually hired in the week after you. I'm hoping to stay on."

"Then I'm sure you will."

"Perhaps," she said. "At least my research is cheap. It is only me and my ears. Can I entice you in for coffee?"

"I should be going, but another time perhaps."

"I understand." She extended her hand. "Another time then. Thank you for the ride."

I turned to go, but her voice stopped me. "James said you were brilliant."

I turned. "He told you that?"

"Not me. I talk with his secretary, and James has spoken about you a lot, apparently – your days in college. But I have a question before you go. Something I was wondering."

"Okay."

She brought her hand up to my cheek. "Why are the brilliant ones always so screwed-up?"

I said nothing, looking into those eyes.

"You need to be careful," she said. "The alcohol. I can smell it on you some mornings. If I can smell it, so can others."

"I'll be fine."

"No. Somehow I don't think you will."

The lab.

Satish stood in front of the diagram I'd drawn on my white board.

I watched him studying it. "What is this?" he asked.

"The wave-particle duality of light."

"And these lines?"

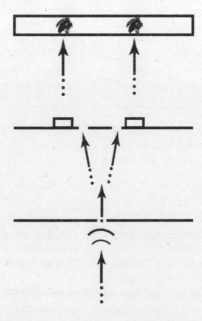

"This is the wave part," I said, pointing at the diagram. "Fire a photon stream through two adjacent slits, and the waves create an image on the phosphorescent screen behind the slits. The frequencies of the waves zero-sum each other at certain intervals, and a characteristic interference pattern is captured on the screen. Do you see?"

"Yes, I think so."

"But if you put a detector at the two slits . . ." I began drawing another picture under the first. "Then it changes everything. When the detectors are in place, light stops behaving like a wave and starts acting like a particle series."

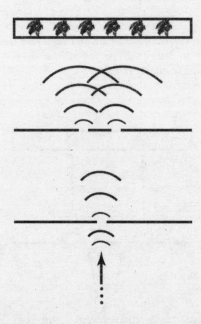

I continued. "So instead of an interference pattern, you get two distinct clusters of phosphorescence where the particles pass through the slits and contact the screen."

"Yes, I remember now," Satish said. "This is familiar. I believe there was a chapter on this in grad school."

"In grad school, I *taught* this. And I watched the students' faces. The ones who understood what it meant – who truly understood – always looked troubled by it. I could see it in their expressions, the pain of believing something which can't be true."

"This is a famous experiment. You are planning to replicate?"

"Yeah."

"Why? It has already been replicated many times; no journal will publish."

"I know. I've read papers on the phenomena; I've given class lectures on the details; I understand it mathematically. Hell, most of my earlier research is based on the assumptions that came out of this experiment. But I've never actually *seen* it with my eyes. That's why."

"It is science." Satish shrugged. "You don't need to see it."

"I think I do," I said. "Need to. Just once."

The next few weeks passed in a blur. Satish helped me with my project, and I helped him with his. We worked mornings in his lab. Evenings we spent in Room 271, setting up. The phosphorescent plate was a problem – then the alignment of the thermionic gun. In a way, it felt like we were partners, almost, Satish and I. And it was a good feeling. After working so long by myself, it was good to be able to talk to someone.

We traded stories to pass the time. Satish talked of his problems. They were the problems good men sometimes have when they've lived good lives. He talked about helping his daughter with her homework, and worrying about paying for her college. He talked of his family *backhome* – saying it fast that way, *backhome*, so you heard the proper noun; and he talked of the fields, and the bugs, and the monsoon, and the ruined crops. "It is going to be a bad year for sugar cane," he told me, as if we were farmers instead of researchers. He talked about his mother's advancing years. He talked of his brothers, and his sisters, and his nieces and nephews; and I came to understand the weight of responsibility he felt.

Bending over the gate arrays, soldering tool in hand, he told me, "I talk too much, you must be sick of my voice."

"Not at all."

"You have been a big help me with my work. How can I ever repay you, my friend?"

"Money is fine," I told him. "I prefer large bills."

I wanted to tell him of my life. I wanted to tell him of my work at QSR, and that some things you learn, you wish you could unlearn. I wanted to tell him that memory has gravity, and madness a color; that all guns have names, and it is the same name. I wanted to tell him I understood about his tobacco; that I'd been married once, and it hadn't worked out; that I used to talk softly to my father's grave; that it was a long time since I'd really been okay.

Instead of telling him these things, I talked about the experiment. That I could do. Always could do.

"It started a half-century ago as a thought experiment," I told him. "To prove the incompleteness of quantum mechanics. Physicists felt quantum mechanics couldn't be the whole story, because the math takes too many liberties with reality. There was still that impossible contradiction: the photoelectric effect required light be particulate; Young's results showed it to be a wave. Only later, of course, when the technology finally caught up to the theory, it turned out the experimental results followed the math. The math says you can either know the position of an electron, or the momentum, but never both. The math, it turned out, wasn't metaphor at all. The math was dead serious. The math wasn't screwing around."

Satish nodded like he understood.

Later, working on his gate arrays, he traded his story for mine.

"There once was a guru who brought four princes into the forest," he told me. "They were hunting birds."

"Birds," I said.

"Yes, and up in the trees, they see one, a beautiful bird with bright feathers. The first prince said, 'I will shoot the bird,' and he pulled back on his arrow and shot into the trees. But the arrow missed. Then the second prince tried to shoot, and he, too, missed. Then the third prince. Finally the fourth prince shot high into the trees, and this time the arrow struck and the beautiful bird fell dead. The guru looked at the first three princes and said, 'Where were you aiming?'

" 'At the bird.'

" 'At the bird.'

" 'At the bird.'

" 'The guru looked at the fourth prince, 'And you?'

" 'At the bird's eye.' "

Once the equipment was set up, the alignment was the last hurdle to be cleared. The electron gun had to be aimed so the electron was just as likely to go through either slit. The equipment filled most of the room – an assortment of electronics and screens and wires.

In the mornings, in the hotel room, I talked to the mirror, made promises to gunmetal eyes. And by some miracle did not drink.

One day became two. Two became three. Three became five. Then I hadn't had a drink in a week.

At the lab, the work continued. When the last piece of equipment was positioned, I stood back and surveyed the whole setup, heart beating in my chest, standing at the edge of some great universal truth. I was about to be witness to something few people in the history of the world had ever seen.

When the first satellite was launched toward the deep space in 1977, it carried a special golden record of coded messages. The record held diagrams and mathematical formulas. It carried the image of a fetus, the calibration of a circle, and a single page from Newton's *System of the World*. It carried the units of our mathematical system, because mathematics, we're told, is the universal language. I've always felt that golden record should have carried a diagram of this experiment, the Feynman double-slit.

Because this experiment is more fundamental than math. It is what lives under the math. It tells of reality itself.

Richard Feynman said this about the slit experiment: "It has in it the heart of quantum mechanics. In truth, it contains only mystery."

Room 271 held two chairs, a marker board, a long lab bench, and several large tables. I'd hung dark canvas over the windows to block out the light. The setup sprawled across the length of the room.

Slits had been cut into sheets of steel that served to divide the areas of the setup. The phosphorescent screen was loaded into a small rectangular box behind the second set of slits.

James came by a little after 5:00, just before going home for the evening.

"They told me you signed up for lab space," he said.

"Yeah."

He stepped inside the room. "What is this?" he said, gesturing to the equipment.

"Just old equipment from Docent. No one was using it, so I thought I'd see if I could get it to work."

"What are you planning exactly?"

"Replicating results, nothing new. The Feynman double-slit."

He was quiet for a moment. "It's good to see you working on something, but isn't that a little dated?"

"Good science is never dated."

"But what are you expecting to prove?"

"Nothing," I said. "Nothing at all."

The day we ran the experiment, the weather was freezing. The wind gusted in from the ocean, and the East Coast huddled under a cold front. I got to work early and left a note on Satish's desk.

> Meet me in my lab at 9:00.
> —Eric.

I did not explain it to Satish. I did not explain further.

Satish walked through the door of room 271 a little before 9:00, and I gestured toward the button. "Would you like to do the honors?"

We stood motionless in the near-darkness of the lab. Satish studied the apparatus spread out before him. "Never trust engineer who doesn't walk his own bridge."

I smiled. "Okay then." I hit the button. The machine hummed.

I let it run for a few minutes before walking over to check the screen. I opened the top and looked inside. And then I saw it, what I'd been hoping to see. The experiment had produced a distinctive banded pattern, an interference pattern on the screen. Just like Young, just like the Copenhagen interpretation said it would.

Satish looked over my shoulder. The machine continued to hum, deepening the pattern as we watched.

"Would you like to see a magic trick?" I asked.

He nodded solemnly.

"Light is a wave," I told him.

I reached for the detector and hit the "on" switch – and just like that, the interference pattern disappeared.

"Unless someone is watching."

The Copenhagen interpretation posits this: Observation is a principle requisite of reality. Nothing exists until it is first observed. Until then there are only probability waves. Only possibility.

For purposes of the experiment, these waves describe the probability of a particle being found at any given location between the electron gun and the screen. Until a particle is detected by some consciousness at a specific point along the wave, its location remains theoretical. Therefore, until a particle is observed passing through one slit, it could be equally anticipated to pass through either – and thus will actually propagate through both in the form of probability waves. These wave systems interfere with each other at regular intervals and thereby assemble a visible interference pattern on the capture screen behind the slits. But if a particle is detected by an observer at one slit, then that excludes the possibility of it passing through the other; and if it can't propagate through both, it can't compile an interference pattern.

This would seem self-contradictory, except for one thing. Except that the interference pattern disappears if someone is watching.

We ran the experiment again and again. Satish checked the detector results, being careful to note which slit the electrons passed through.

With the detectors turned on, roughly half the electrons were recorded passing through each slit, and no interference pattern accrued. We turned the detectors off again – and again, instantly, the interference pattern emerged on the screen.

"How does the system know?" Satish asked.

"How does it know what?"

"That the detectors are on. How does it know the electron's position has been recorded?"

"Ah, the big question."

"Are the detectors putting out some kind of electromagnetic interference?"

I shook my head. "You haven't seen the really weird stuff yet."

"What do you mean?"

"The electrons aren't really responding to the detectors at all. They're responding to the fact that you'll eventually read the detectors' results."

Satish looked at me, blank-faced.

"Turn the detectors back on," I said.

Satish hit the button. The detectors hummed softly. We let the experiment run.

"It is just like before," I told him. "The detectors are on, so the electrons should be acting as particles, not waves; and without waves, there's no interference pattern, right?"

Satish nodded.

"Okay, turn it off."

The machine cycled down to silence.

"And now the magic test," I said. "This is the one. This is the one I wanted to see."

I hit the "clear" button on the detector, erasing the results.

"The experiment was the same as before." I said. "With the same detectors turned on both times. The only difference was that I erased the results without looking at them. Now check the screen."

Satish opened the box and pulled out the screen.

And then I saw it. On his face. The pain of believing something which can't be true.

"An interference pattern," he said. "How could that be?"

"It's called *retrocausality*. By erasing the results after the experiment was run, I caused the particle pattern to never have occurred in the first place."

Satish was silent for five full seconds. "Is such a thing possible?"

"Of course not, but there it is. Unless a conscious observer makes an ascertainment of the detector results, the detector itself will remain part of the larger indeterminate system. The detectors don't induce wave function collapse; consciousness observation does. Consciousness is like this giant roving spotlight, collapsing reality wherever it shines – and what isn't observed remains probability. And it's not just photons or electrons. It is everything. All matter. It is a flaw in reality. A testable, repeatable, flaw in reality."

Satish said, "So this is what you wanted to see?"

"Yeah."

"Is it different for you now that you've actually seen it?"

I considered this for a moment, exploring my own mind. "Yes, it is different," I said. "It is much worse."

We ran the slit experiment again and again. The results never changed. They matched perfectly the results that Feynman had documented decades earlier. Over the next two days, Satish hooked the detectors up to a printer. We ran the tests, and I hit print. We listened as the printer buzzed and chirped, printing out the results.

Satish pored over the data sheets as if to make sense of them by sheer force of will. I stared over his shoulder, a voice in his ear. "It's like an unexplored law of nature," I said. "Quantum physics as a form of statistical approximation – a solution to the storage problem of reality. Matter behaves like a frequency domain. Why resolve the data fields nobody is looking at?"

Satish put the sheets down and rubbed his eyes.

"There are schools of mathematical thought which assert that a deeper order lies enfolded just below the surface of our lives. Bohm called it the implicate."

"We have a name for this, too," Satish said. He smiled. "We call it *Brahman*. We've known about it for five thousand years."

"I want to try something," I said.

We ran the test again. I printed up the results, being careful not to look at them. We turned off the equipment.

I folded both pages in half and slid them into manila envelopes. I gave Satish the envelope with the screen results. I kept the detector results. "I haven't looked at the detector results yet," I told him. "So right now the wave function is still a superposition of states. Even though the results are printed, they're still un-observed and so still part of the indeterminate system. Do you understand?"

"Yes."

"Go in the next room. I'm going to open my envelope in exactly twenty seconds. In exactly thirty seconds, I want you to open yours."

Satish walked out. And here it was: the gap where logic bleeds. I fought an irrational burst of fear. I lit the nearby Bunsen burner and held my envelope over the open flame. The smell of burning paper. Black ash. A minute later Satish was back, his envelope open.

"You didn't look," he said. He held out his sheet of paper. "As soon as I opened it, I knew you didn't look."

"I lied," I said, taking the paper from him. "And you caught me. We made the world's first quantum lie detector – a divination tool made of light." I looked at the paper. The interference pattern lay in dark bands across the white surface. "Some mathematicians say there is either no such thing as free will, or the world is a simulation. Which do you think is true?"

"Those are our choices?"

I crushed the paper into a ball. Something slid away inside of me; a subtle change, and I opened my mouth to speak but what came out was different from what I intended.

I told Satish about the breakdown, and the drinking, and the hospital. I told him about the eyes in the mirror, and what I said to myself in the morning.

I told him about the smooth, steel "erase" button I put against my head – a single curl of an index finger to pay for everything.

Satish nodded while he listened, the smile wiped clean from his face. When I finished speaking, Satish put his hand on my shoulder. "So then you are crazy after all, my friend."

"It's been thirteen days now," I told him. "Thirteen days sober."

"Is that good?"

"No, but it's longer than I've gone in two years."

We ran the experiment. We printed the results.

If we looked at the detector results, the screen showed the particle pattern. If we didn't, it showed an interference pattern.

We worked through most of the night. Near morning, sitting in the semidarkness of the lab, Satish spoke. "There once was a frog who lived in a well," he said.

I watched his face as he told the story.

Satish continued. "One day a farmer lowered a bucket into the well, and the frog was pulled up to the surface. The frog blinked in the bright sun, seeing it for the first time. 'Who are you?' the frog asked the farmer.

"The farmer was amazed. He said, 'I am the owner of this farm.'

" 'You call your world *farm*?' the frog asked.

" 'No, this is not a different world,' the farmer said. 'This is the same world.'

"The frog laughed at the farmer. He said, 'I have swum to every corner of my world. North, south, east, west. I am telling you, this is a different world.' "

I looked at Satish and said nothing.

"You and I," Satish said. "We are still in the well." He closed his eyes. "Can I ask you a question?"

"Go ahead."

"You do not want to drink?"

"No."

"I am curious, what you said with the gun, that you'd shoot yourself if you drank . . ."

"Yeah."

"You did not drink on those days you said that?"

"No."

Satish paused as if considering his words carefully. "Then why did you not just say that everyday?"

"That is simple," I said. "Because then I'd be dead now."

Later, after Satish had gone home, I ran the experiment one final time. Hit "print." I put the results in two envelopes without looking at them. On the first envelope, I wrote the words "detector results." On the second, I wrote "screen results."

I drove to the hotel. I took off my clothes. Stood naked in front of the mirror.

I put the enveloped marked "detector results" up to my forehead. "I will never look at this," I said. "Not ever, unless I start drinking again." I stared in the mirror. I stared at my own gray eyes and saw that I meant it.

I glanced down at the other envelope. The one with the screen results. My hands shook.

I laid the envelope on the desk, stared at it. Keats said, *Beauty is truth, truth beauty*. What was the truth? Will I drink again? The envelopes knew.

One day, I would either open the detector results, or I wouldn't.

Inside the other envelope there was either an interference pattern, or there wasn't. A "yes" or a "no." The answer was in there. It was already in there.

I waited in Satish's office until he arrived in the morning. He put his briefcase on his desk. He looked at me, at the clock, then back at me.

"What are you doing?" he asked.

"Waiting for you."

"How long have you been here?"

"Since 4:30."

He glanced around the room. I leaned back in his chair, fingers laced behind my head.

Satish just watched me. Satish was bright. He waited.

"Can you rig the detector to an indicator light?" I asked him.

"How do you mean?"

"Can you set it up so that the light goes off when the detector picks up an electron at the slit?"

"It shouldn't be hard. Why?"

"Let's define, exactly, the indeterminate system."

Point Machine watched the test. He studied the interference pattern. "You're looking at one-half the wave particle duality of light," I said.

"What's the other half look like?"

I turned the detectors on. The banded pattern diverged into two distinct clumps on the screen.

"This."

"Oh," Point Machine said.

Standing in Point Machine's lab. Frogs swimming.

"They're aware of light, right?" I asked.

"They do have eyes."

"But, I mean, they're aware of it?"

"Yeah, they respond to visual stimuli. They're hunters. They have to see to hunt."

"But I mean, aware?"

"What did you do before here?"

"Quantum research."

"I know that," Point Machine said. "But what did you do?"

I tried to shrug him off. "There were a range of projects. Solid state photonic devices, *Fourier transforms*, liquid NMR."

"*Fourier transforms*?"

"They're complex equations that can be used to translate visual imagery into the language of wave forms."

Point Machine looked at me, dark eyes tightening. He said again, very slowly, enunciating each word, "What did you do, *exactly*?"

"Computers," I said. "We were trying to build a computer. Quantum encryption processing extending up to twelve qubits. We used the *Fourier transforms* to remodel information into waves and back again."

"Did it work?"

"Kind of. We reached a twelve-coherence state then used nuclear magnetic resonance to decode."

"Why only 'kind of'? So then it *didn't* work?"

"No, it worked, it definitely worked. Even when it was turned off." I looked at him. "Kind of."

It took Satish two days to rig up the light.

Point Machine brought the frogs in on a Saturday. We separated the healthy from the sick, the healthy from the monsters. "What is wrong with them?" I asked.

"The more complex a system, the more ways it can go wrong."

Joy was next door, working in her lab. She heard our voices and stepped into the hall.

"You work weekends?" Satish asked her.

"It's quieter," Joy said. "I do my more sensitive tests when there's nobody here. What about you? So you're all partners now?"

"Eric has the big hands on this project," Satish said. "My hands are small."

"What are you working on?" she asked. She followed Satish into the lab.

He shot me a look, and I nodded.

So Satish explained it the way only Satish could.

"Oh," she said. She blinked. She stayed.

We used Point Machine as a control. "We're going to do this in real-time," I told him. "No record at the detectors, just the indicator light. When I tell you, stand there and watch for the light. If the light comes on, it means the detectors picked up the electron. Understand?"

"Yeah, I get it," Point Machine said.

Satish hit the button. I watched the screen, an interference pattern materializing before my eyes – a now-familiar pattern of light and dark.

"Okay," I told Point Machine. "Now look in the box. Tell me if you see the light."

Point Machine looked in the box. Before he even spoke, the interference pattern disappeared. "Yeah," he said. "I see the light."

I smiled. Felt that edge between known and unknown. Caressed it.

I nodded at Satish, and he hit the switch to kill the gun. I turned to Point Machine. "You collapsed the probability wave by observing the light, so we've established proof of principle." I looked at the three of them. "Now let's find out if all observers were created equal."

Point Machine put a frog in the box.

And here it was, the stepping-off point – a view into the implicate, where objective and subjective might be experimentally defined.

I nodded to Satish. "Fire the gun."

He hit the switch and the machine hummed. I watched the screen. I closed my eyes, felt my heart beating in my chest. Inside the box, I knew a light had come on for one of the two detectors; I knew the frog had seen it. But when I opened my eyes, the interference pattern still showed on the screen. The frog hadn't changed it at all.

"Again," I told Satish.

Satish fired the gun again. Again. Again.

Point Machine looked at me. "Well?"

"There's still an interference pattern. The probability wave didn't collapse."

"What does that mean?" Joy asked.

"It means we try a different frog."

We tried six. None changed the result.

"They're part of the indeterminate system," Satish said.

I was watching the screen closely, and the interference pattern vanished. I was about to shout, but when I looked up, I saw Point Machine peeking into the box.

"You looked," I said.

"I was just making sure the light worked."

"I could tell."

We tried every frog in his lab. Then we tried the salamanders.

"Maybe it's just amphibians," he said.

"Yeah, maybe."

"How is it that we affect the system, but frogs and salamanders can't?"

"Maybe it's our eyes," Point Machine said. "It has to be the eyes – coherence effects in the retinal rod-rhopsin molecules themselves."

"Why would that matter?"

"Our optic nerve cells can only conduct measured information to the visual cortex; eyes are just another detector."

"Can I try?" Joy interrupted.

I nodded. We ran the experiment again, this time with Joy's empty eyes pointed at the box. Again, nothing.

The next morning, Point Machine met Satish and me in the parking lot before work. We climbed into my car and drove to the mall.

We went to a pet store.

I bought three mice, a canary, a turtle, and a squish-faced Boston terrier puppy. The sales clerk stared at us.

"You pet lovers, huh?" He looked suspiciously at Satish and Point Machine.

"Oh, yes," I said. "Pets."

The drive back was quiet, punctuated only by the occasional whining of the puppy.

Point Machine broke the silence. "Perhaps it takes a more complex nervous system."

"That shouldn't matter," Satish said. "Life is life. Real is real."

I gripped the steering wheel. "What's the difference between mind and brain?"

"Semantics," said Point Machine. "Different names for the same idea."

Satish regarded us. "Brain is hardware," he said. "Mind is software."

The Massachusetts landscape whipped past the car's windows, a wall of ruined hillside on our right – huge, dark stone like the bones of the earth. A compound fracture of the land. We drove the rest of the way in silence.

Back at the lab, we started with the turtle. Then the mice, then the canary, which escaped, and flew to sit atop a filing cabinet. None of them collapsed the wave.

The Boston terrier looked at us, google-eyed.

"Are its eyes supposed to look like that?" Satish said. "In different directions?"

I put the puppy in the box. "It's the breed, I think. But all it has to do is sense the light. Either eye will do." I looked down at man's best friend, our companion through the millennia, and harbored secret hope. This one, I told myself. This species, certainly, of all of them. Because who hasn't looked into the eyes of a dog and not sensed something looking back.

The puppy whined in the box. Satish ran the experiment. I watched the screen.

Nothing. There was no change at all.

That night I drove to Joy's. She answered the door. Waited for me to speak.

"You mentioned coffee?"

She smiled, and there was another moment when I felt sure she saw me.

Hours later, in the darkness, I spoke. "It's time for me to go."

She ran a hand along my bare spine.

"Time," she whispered. "There is no such beast. Only now. And now." She put her lips again on my skin. "And now."

*   *   *

The next day, I had James come by the lab.

"You've made a finding?" he asked.

"We have."

James watched us run the experiment. He looked in the box. He collapsed the wave function himself.

Then we put the puppy in the box and ran the experiment again. We showed him the interference pattern.

"Why didn't it work?" he asked.

"We don't know."

"But what's different?"

"Only one thing. The observer."

"I don't think I understand."

"So far, none of the animals we've tested have been able to alter the quantum system."

He brought his hand to his chin. His brow furrowed. He was silent for a long time, looking at the setup. "Holy shit," he said finally.

"Yeah," Point Machine said.

I stepped forward. "We want to do more tests. Work our way up through every phylum, class, and order. Primates being of particular interest, because of their evolutionary connection to us."

"As much as you want," he said. "As much funding as you want."

It took ten days to arrange. We worked in conjunction with the Boston Zoo.

Transporting large numbers of animals can be a logistical nightmare, so it was decided that it would be easier to bring the lab to the zoo than to bring the zoo to the lab. Vans were hired. Technicians were assigned. Point Machine put his own research on hold and assigned a technician to feed his amphibians in his absence. Satish's research also went on hiatus. "It seems suddenly less interesting," he said.

James attended the experiment on the first day. We set up in one of the new exhibits under construction – a green, high-ceilinged room that would one day house muntjac. For now, though, it would house scientists. Satish worked the electronics. Point Machine liaisoned with the zoo staff. I built a bigger wooden box.

The zoo staff didn't seem particularly inclined to cooperate until the size of Hansen's charitable donation was explained to them by the zoo superintendent. After that, they were very helpful.

The following Monday we started the experiment. We worked our way through representatives of several mammal lineages: Marsupialia, Afrotheria, and the last two evolutionary holdouts of Monotremata – the platypus and the echidna. The next day we tested species from Xenarthra, and Laurasiatheria. The fourth day, we tackled Euarchontoglires. None of them collapsed the wave function; none carried the spotlight. On the fifth day, we started on the primates.

We began with the primates most distantly related to humans.

We tested lemuriforms and New World monkeys. Then Old World monkeys. Finally, we moved to the anthropoid apes. On the sixth day, we did the chimps.

"There are actually two species," Point Machine told us. "Pan paniscus, commonly called the bonobo, and Pan troglodytes, the common chimpanzee. They're congruent species, so similar in appearance that by the time scientists caught on in the 1930s, they'd already been hopelessly mixed in captivity." Zoo staff maneuvered two juveniles into the room, holding them by their hands. "But during World War Two, we found a way to separate them again," Point Machine continued. "It happened at a zoo outside Hellabrunn, Germany. A bombing leveled most of the town but, by some fluke, left the zoo intact. Or most of it, anyway. When the zookeepers returned, they expected to find their chimps alive and well. Instead, they found dozens of them dead, lying in undamaged cages. Only the common chimps had survived. The Bonobos had all died of fright."

We tested both species. The machine hummed. We double-checked the results, then triple-checked, and the interference pattern did not budge. Even chimps didn't cause wave function collapse.

"We're alone," I said. "Totally alone."

Later that night, Point Machine paced the lab. "It's like tracing any characteristic," he said. "You look for homology in sister taxa. You organize clades, catalogue synapomorphies, identify the outgroup."

"And who is the outgroup?"

"Who do you think?" Point Machine stopped pacing. "The ability to cause wave function collapse is apparently a derived characteristic that arose uniquely in our species at some point in the last several million years."

"And before that?" I said.

"What?"

"Before that Earth just stood there as so much un-collapsed reality? What, waiting for us to show up?"

Writing up the paper took several days. I signed Satish and Point Machine as coauthors.

Species and Quantum Wave function Collapse.
Eric Argus, Satish Gupta, Mi Chang. Hansen Labs, Boston MA.

ABSTRACT

Multiple studies have revealed the default state of all quantum systems to be a superposition of both collapsed and un-collapsed probability wave forms. It has long been known that subjective observation is a primary requirement for wave function collapse. The goal of this study was to identify the higher-order taxa capable of inciting wave function collapse by act of observation and to develop a phylogenetic tree to clarify the relationships between these major animal phyla. Species incapable of wave function collapse can be considered part of the larger indeterminate system. The study was carried out at the Boston Zoo on multiple orders of mammalia. Here we report that humans were the only species tested which proved capable of exerting wave function collapse onto the background superposition of states, and indeed, this ability appears to be a uniquely derived human characteristic. This ability most likely arose sometime in the last six million years after the most recent common ancestor of humans and chimpanzees.

James read the abstract. He came to my office.

"But what do the results *mean*?"

"They mean whatever you think they mean."

Things moved fast after that. The paper was published in *The Journal of Quantum Mechanics*, and the phone started ringing. There were requests for interviews, peer review, and a dozen labs started replication trials. It was the interpretations that got crazy though. I stayed away from interpretations. I dealt with the facts. I turned down the interviews.

Satish worked on perfecting the test itself. He worked on downsizing it, minimizing it, digitizing it. Turning it into a product. It became the Hansen double-slit, and when he was done, it was the size of a loaf of bread – with an easy indicator light and small, efficient output. Green for "yes," and red for "no." I wonder if he knew then. I wonder if he already suspected what they'd use it for.

"It doesn't matter what is known," he said. He touched the box. "It's about what is knowable."

He abandoned his gate arrays. Above his work station I found a quote taped to the wall, torn from an old book.

Can animals be just a superior race of marionettes, which eat without pleasure, cry without pain, desire nothing, know nothing, and only simulate intelligence?

—Thomas Henry
Huxley, 1859

In the spring, a medical doctor named Robbins made his interest in the project known through a series of carefully worded letters.

The letters turned into phone calls. The voices on the other end belonged to lawyers, the kind that come from deep pockets. Robbins worked for a consortium with a vested interest in determining, once and for all, exactly when consciousness first arises during human fetal development.

Hansen Labs turned him down flat until the offer grew a seventh figure.

James came to me. "He wants you there."

"I don't care."

"Robbins asked for you specifically."

"I don't give a damn. I don't want any part of it, and you can fire me if you want to."

James grew a weary smile. "Fire you? If I fired you, my bosses would fire me. And then hire you back. Probably with a raise." He sighed. "This guy Robbins is a real prick, do you know that?"

"Yeah, I know. I've seen him on TV."

"But that doesn't mean he's wrong."

"Yeah, I know that, too."

Hansen provided technicians for the testing. The week before the tests were going to occur, I got the call. I'd been expecting it. Robbins himself.

"Are you sure we can't get you to come?"

"No," I said. "I don't think that's possible."

"If the issue is monetary, I can assure you—"

"It's not."

There was a pause on the line. "I understand," he said. "All the same, I wanted to personally thank you. It's a great thing you've accomplished. Your work is going to save a lot of lives."

I was silent. "How did you get the mothers?"

"They're committed volunteers, each one. Special women. We're a large, national congregation, and we were able to find several volunteers from each trimester of pregnancy – though I don't expect we'll need more than the first one to prove the age at which a baby is ensouled. Our earliest mother is only a few weeks along."

I spoke the next words slowly. "You're fine with them taking the risk?"

"We have a whole staff of doctors attending, and medical experts have already determined that the procedure carries no more risk than amniocentesis. The diode inserted into the amniotic fluid will be no larger than a needle."

"One thing I never understood about this . . . a fetus's eyes are closed."

"I prefer the word *baby*," he said, voice gone tight. "A *baby*'s eyelids are very thin, and the diode is very bright. We have no doubt they'll be able to sense it. Then we have merely to note wave function collapse, and we'll finally have the proof we need to change the law and put a stop to the plague of abortions that has swept across this land."

I put the phone down. Looked at it. Plague of abortions.

There were men like him in science, too – ones who had all the answers. Fanaticism, applied to any facet of an issue, has always seemed dangerous to me. I picked up the phone again. "You think it's as simple as that?"

"I do. When is a human life a human life? That is always what this particular argument has been about, has it not? Now we'll finally be able to prove that abortion is murder, and who could argue? I sense that you don't like me very much."

"I like you fine. But there's an old saying, 'Never trust a man with only one book.' "

"One book is all a man needs if it's the right book."

"Have you considered what you'll do if you're proven wrong?"

"What do you mean?"

"What if wave function collapse doesn't occur until the ninth month? Or the magical moment of birth? Will you change your mind?"

"That's not going to happen."

"Maybe," I said. "But I guess now we find out, don't we."

The night before the experiment, I called Point Machine. It was call or drink. And I didn't want to drink. Because I knew if I drank again, even a single sip, I'd never stop. Not ever.

He picked up on the fifth ring. Faraway voice.

"What's going to happen tomorrow?" I asked.

There was a long pause. Long enough that I wondered if he'd heard me. "Not sure," he said. The voice on the other end was coarse and weary. It was a voice that hadn't been sleeping well. "Entogeny reflects phylogeny," he said. "Look early enough in gestation and we've got gills, a tail, the roots of the whole animal kingdom. You climb the phylogenetic tree as the fetus develops, and the newer characteristics, the things that make us human, get tacked on last. What Robbins is testing for is only found in humans, so my gut tells me he's wrong, and wave collapse comes late. Real late."

"You think it works that way?"

"I have no idea how it works."

The day of the experiment came and went.

The first hint that something went wrong came in the form of silence. Silence from the Robbins group. Silence in the media. No press conferences. No TV interviews. Just silence.

The days turned to weeks.

Finally, a terse statement was issued by the group which called their results inconclusive. Robbins came out a few days later, saying bluntly that there had been a failure in the mechanism of the tests.

The truth was something stranger, of course. And of course, that came out later, too.

The truth was that some of the fetuses *did* pass the test. Just like Robbins hoped. Some *did* trigger wave function collapse.

But others didn't.

And gestational age had nothing to do with it.

Two months later, I received the call in the middle of the night. "We found one in New York." It was Satish.

"What?" I rubbed my eyes, trying to make sense of the words.

"A boy. Nine years old. He didn't collapse the wave function."

"What's wrong with him?"

"Nothing. He's normal. Normal vision, normal intelligence. We tested him five times, but the interference pattern didn't budge."

"What happened when you told him?"

"We didn't tell him. He stood there staring at us."

"Staring?"

"It was like he already knew. Like he knew the whole time it wouldn't work."

Summer turned to fall. The testing continued.

Satish traveled the country, searching for that elusive, perfect cross-section and a sample size large enough to prove significance. He collected data points, faxed copies back to the lab for safekeeping.

In the end, it turned out there were others. Others who couldn't collapse the wave function – a certain consistent percentage of the population who looked like us, and acted like us, but lacked this fundamental quality of humanity. Though Satish was careful not to use the term "soul" in his late night phone calls, we heard it in the gaps between the words. We heard it in the things he didn't say.

I pictured him on the other end of the line, sitting in some dark hotel room, fighting a growing insomnia, fighting the terrible loneliness of what he was doing.

Point Machine sought comfort in elaborately constructed phylogenies and retreated into his cladograms. But there was no comfort for him there. "There's no frequency distribution curve," he told me. "No disequilibrium between ethnographic populations, nothing I can get traction on."

He pored over Satish's data, looking for the pattern that would make sense of it all.

"Distribution is random," he said. "It doesn't act like a trait."

"Then maybe it's not," I said.

He shook his head. "Then who are they, some kind of empty-set? Nonplayer characters in the indeterminate system? Part of the game?"

Satish had his own ideas, of course.

"Why none of the scientists?" I asked him one night, phone to my ear. "If it's random, why none of us?"

"If they're part of the indeterminate system, why would they become scientists?"

"What do you mean?"

"It's like a virtual construct," Satish said. "You write the code, a series of response algorithms. Wind them up and let them go."

"This is crazy."

"I didn't make the rules."

"Do they even know what you're testing them for, when they look at your little light? Do they know they're different?"

"One of them," he said. He was silent for a moment. "One of them knew."

And then days later, the final late night call. From Denver. The last time I'd ever speak to him.

"I don't think we're supposed to do this," he said, voice strangely harsh.

I rubbed my eyes, sitting up in bed.

"I don't think we're supposed to build this kind of thing," he said. "The flaw in reality that you talked about . . . I don't think we were expected to take advantage of it this way. To make a test."

"What happened?"

"I saw the boy again."

"Who?"

"The boy from New York," he said. "He came here to see me." And then he hung up.

Ten days later, Satish disappeared, along with his special little box. He got off a plane in Boston, but didn't make it home. I was at the lab when I got the call from his wife.

"No," I said. "Not for days."

She was crying into the phone.

"I'm sure he's fine," I lied.

When I hung up, I grabbed my coat and headed for the door. Bought a fifth of vodka and drove home to the hotel.

Stared in the mirror. Eyes gray like storm clouds, gray like gunmetal.

I spun the cap off the bottle and smelled the burn. Music filtered through the thin walls, a soft melody, a woman's voice. I imagined my life different. I imagined that I could stop here. Not take the first drink.

My hands trembled.

The first sip brought tears to my eyes. Then I upended the bottle and drank deep. I tried to have a vision. I tried to picture Satish happy and healthy in a bar somewhere, working on a three-day binge, but the image wouldn't come. That was me, not Satish. Satish didn't drink. I tried to picture him coming home again. I couldn't see that either.

Do they know they're different, I'd asked him.

One of them, he'd said. *One of them knew.*

When the bottle was half empty, I walked to the desk and picked up the envelope marked "screen results." Then I looked at the gun. I imagined what a .357 round could do to a skull – lay it open wide and deep. Reveal that place where self resides – expose it to the air where it would evaporate like liquid nitrogen, sizzling, steaming, gone. A gun could be many things, including a vehicle to return you to the implicate. The dream within a dream.

I imagined the world like an Escher drawing, part of either of two different scenes, and our brains decide which to see.

The more complex the system, the more ways it can go wrong. Point Machine had said that.

And things go wrong. That spotlight. Little engines of wave function collapse. Humans are blind to the beauty; the truth is beyond us. We can't see reality as it is: only observe it into existence.

But what if you could control that spotlight, dilate it like the pupil of an eye? Stare deep into the implicate order. What would you see? What if you could slide between the sheaths of the subjective and objective?

Maybe there have always been people like that. Mistakes. People who walk among us, but are not us. Only now there was a test. A test to point them out.

And maybe they didn't want to be found.

I pulled the sheet of paper out of the envelope.

I unfolded it and spread it out flat on the desk. I looked at the results – and in so doing, finally collapsed the probability wave of the experiment I'd run all those months ago.

I stared at what was on the paper, a series of shaded semicircles – a now familiar pattern of light and dark.

Though, of course, the results had been there all along.

Over the last five years, Ted Kosmatka has published more than a dozen stories in places like *Asimov's*, *The Magazine of Fantasy & Science Fiction*, and *Subterranean*. His writing has been reprinted in seven Year's Best anthologies, serialized over the radio, performed on stage, and translated into Russian, Hebrew, Polish, and Czech.

Ted was born in Indiana, not far from Lake Michigan. He studied biology at Indiana University and since then has gradually assembled one of those crazy work histories that writers so often seem to have. Among other things, he's been a zookeeper, a chem tech, and a laborer in a steel mill. More recently, he worked in a research laboratory where he ran an electron microscope. He left the lab in 2009 to take a job writing for a video game company. He now lives with his family in the Pacific Northwest.

A MEMORY OF WIND

Rachel Swirsky

FROM THE AUTHOR: In the spring of 2006, I attended a production of Euripedes' *Iphigenia at Aulis* at the San Jose Repertory Theatre. It was the U.S. premiere of Don Taylor's adaptation, featuring the San Francisco Dance Brigade as the Greek chorus. It was an exceptional production, smart and intense and brilliantly acted. I was familiar with the original Greek myth which provides the basis for the play. After Paris abducts Helen, troops mass in the harbor at Aulis under the leadership of King Agamemnon, preparing to make war on Troy. But they can't leave the harbor – there's no wind. A priest named Calchus informs Agamemnon that Artemis will only let them sail if he sacrifices his daughter, Iphigenia. So he does.

I had always been a little peeved with what I felt was the traditional interpretation of the myth, which poses Agamemnon as the tragic figure. Taylor's adaptation of the play moved Clytemnestra into the pivotal role, imagining the tragedy from her perspective, as she is helpless to prevent Agamemnon from killing their daughter (an interpretation which gains emotional freight when you remember that she later kills him in revenge, and then is murdered by their son, Orestes).

While Taylor's shifting the point of view created an interesting, new way of looking at the myth – and allowed him to comment on the politics of war – I found it unsatisfying. The original myth was about Agamemnon. The reinterpretation was about Clytemnestra. What about Iphigenia? Surely the story of her death was her own, not someone else's.

So I tried to imagine it.

From a certain perspective, Iphigenia is an unsuitable main character. She has minimal agency. She is young and trapped and sad and passive and dying. It seems much easier to write about Agamemnon, who could call off the sacrifice, or about Clytemnestra, who will eventually have the power to exact revenge. But sometimes we are the ones who are trapped. Sometimes we are the ones who can't change our fates. Those stories are also important.

After helen and *her lover Paris fled to Troy, her husband King Menelaus called his allies to war. Under the leadership of King Agamemnon, the allies met in the harbor at Aulis. They prepared to sail for Troy, but they could not depart, for there was no wind.*

Kings Agamemnon, Menelaus, and Odysseus consulted with Calchas, a priest of Artemis, who revealed that the angered goddess was balking their departure. The kings asked Calchas how they might convince Artemis to grant them a wind. He answered that she would only relent after King Agamemnon brought his eldest daughter, Iphigenia, to Aulis and sacrificed her to the goddess.

I began turning into wind the moment that you promised me to Artemis.

Before I woke, I lost the flavor of rancid oil and the shade of green that flushes new leaves. They slipped from me, and became gentle breezes that would later weave themselves into the strength of my gale. Between the first and second beats of my lashes, I also lost the grunt of goats being led to slaughter, and the roughness of wool against calloused fingertips, and the scent of figs simmering in honey wine.

Around me, the other palace girls slept fitfully, tossing and grumbling through the dry summer heat. I stumbled to my feet and fled down the corridor, my footsteps falling smooth against the cool, painted clay. As I walked, the sensation of the floor blew away from me, too. It was as if I stood on nothing.

I forgot the way to my mother's rooms. I decided to visit Orestes instead. I also forgot how to find him. I paced bright corridors, searching. A male servant saw me, and woke a male slave, who woke a female slave, who roused herself and approached me, bleary-eyed, mumbling. "What's wrong, Lady Iphigenia? What do you require?"

I had no answers.

I have no answers for you either, father.

I imagine what you did on that night when I paced the palace corridors, my perceptions vanishing like stars winking out of the night sky. You presided over the war council in Aulis. I imagine you standing with the staff of office heavy in your hands – heavy with wood, heavy with burdens.

Calchas, priest of Artemis, bowed before you and the other kings. "I have prayed long and hard," he said. "The goddess is angry with you, Agamemnon. She will not allow the wind to take your ships to Troy until you have made amends."

I imagine that the staff of office began to feel even heavier in your hands. You looked between your brother, Menelaus, and the sly Odysseus. Both watched you with cold, expressionless faces. They wanted war. You had become an obstacle to their desires.

"What have I done?" you asked Calchas. "What does the goddess want?"

The priest smiled.

What would a goddess want? What else but virgin blood on her altar? One daughter's life for the wind that would allow you to launch a fleet that could kill thousands. A child for a war.

Odysseus and Menelaus fixed you with hungry gazes. Their appetite for battle hollowed the souls from their eyes as starvation will hollow a man's cheeks. Implicit threats flickered in the torchlight. Do as the priest says, or we'll take the troops we've gathered to battle Troy and march on Mycenae instead. Sacrifice your daughter or sacrifice your kingdom.

Menelaus took an amphora of rich red wine and poured a measure for each of you. A drink; a vow. Menelaus drank rapidly, red droplets spilling like blood through the thicket of his beard. Odysseus savored slow, languorous sips, his canny eyes intent on your face.

You held your golden rhyton at arm's length, peering into redness as dark as my condemned blood. I can only imagine what you felt. Maybe you began to waver. Maybe you thought of my eyes looking up at you, and of the wedding I would never have, and the children I would never bear. But whatever thoughts I may imagine in your mind, I only know the truth of your actions. You did not dash the staff of office across your knee and hurl away its broken halves. You did not shout to Menelaus that he had no right to ask you to sacrifice your daughter's life when he would not even sacrifice the pleasure of a faithless harlot who fled his marital bed. You did not laugh at Calchas and tell him to demand something else.

You clutched the staff of office, and you swallowed the wine.

I lost so much. Words. Memories. Perceptions. Only now, in this liminality that might as well be death (if indeed it isn't) have I begun recovering myself.

All by your hand, father. All by your will. You and the goddess have dispersed me, but I will not let you forget.

*   *   *

Next I knew, mother's hands were on me, firm and insistent. She held her face near mine, her brows drawn with concern.

She and her slaves had found me hunched beside a mural that showed children playing in a courtyard, my hands extended toward the smallest figure which, in my insensibility, I'd mistaken for Orestes. The slaves eyed me strangely and made signs to ward off madness.

"It must have been a dream," I offered to excuse the strangeness which lay slickly on my skin.

"We'll consult a priest," said Clytemnestra. She put her hand on my elbow. "Can you stand? I have news."

I took a ginger step. My foot fell smoothly on the floor I could no longer feel.

"Good," said mother. "You'll need your health." She stroked my cheek, and looked at me with odd sentimentality, her gaze lingering over the planes of my face as if she were trying to paint me in her memory.

"What is it?" I asked.

"I'm sorry. I just wanted to look at you." She withdrew her fingers. "Your father has summoned us to Aulis. Achilles wants you as his wife!"

The word *wife* I knew, but Aulis? Achilles?

"Who?" I asked.

"Achilles!" Clytemnestra repeated. "We'll leave for Aulis this afternoon."

I looked into the familiar depths of mother's eyes. Her pupils were dark as unlit water, but her irises were gone. They weren't colored; they weren't white. They were nothing.

Green, I remembered briefly, *mother's eyes are like new green leaves.* But when I tried to chase the thought, I could no longer remember what *green* might be.

"Where are we going?" I asked.

"You're going to be married, my heart," said mother. "Everything changes all at once, doesn't it? One day your daughter's a girl, and the next she's a woman. One day your family is all together, and the next there's a war, and everyone's leaving. But that's how life is. There's stasis and then there's change, and then before you even know what the next stasis is, it's gone, and all you can do is try to remember it. You'll understand what I mean. You're so young. Then again, you're going to be a wife. So you're not that young, are you?"

"Who is Achilles?" I repeated.

But mother had already released my hands and begun to pace the room. She was split between high spirits and fretting about the upcoming preparations, with no part of her left for me. She gave orders to her attending slaves. Pack this. Take those. Prepare. Clean. Polish. The slaves chattered like a flock of birds, preening under her attention.

I was not quite forgotten; a lone young girl had been assigned to prepare me for the journey. She approached, her hands filled with wedding adornments. "You're going to marry a hero," she said. "Isn't that wonderful?"

I felt a gentle tugging at my scalp. She began braiding something into my hair. I reached up to feel what. She paused for a moment, and let me take one of the decorations.

I held the red and white thing in my palm. It was delicately put together, with soft, curved rows arrayed around a dark center. A sweet, crushed scent filled the air.

"This smells," I said.

"It smells good," said the slave, taking the thing gently from my hand. I closed my eyes and searched for the name of the sweet scent as she wound red-and-white into my bridal wreath.

Once, when I was still a child with a shaved scalp and a ponytail, you came at night to the room where I slept. Sallow moonlight poured over your face and hands as you bent over my bed, your features wan like shadows beneath the yellowed tint of your boar's tusk helmet. Torchlight glinted off of the boiled leather of your cuirass and skirt.

As a child, I'd watched from time to time from the upper-story balconies as you led your troops, but I'd never before been so close while you wore leather and bronze. Here stood my father the hero, my father the king, the part of you that seemed so distant from the man who sat exhausted at meals eating nothing while mother tried to tempt you with cubes of cheese and mutton, as if you were any hard-worn laborer. Here you stood, transformed into the figure I knew from rumors and daydreams. It seemed impossible that you could be close enough for me to smell olives on your breath and hear the clank of your sword against your thigh.

"I had a sudden desire to see my daughter," you said, not bothering to whisper.

The other girls woke at the sound of your voice, mumbling sleepily as they shifted to watch us. I felt vain. I wanted them to see you, see me, see us together. It reminded me that I was Iphigenia, daughter of Agamemnon and Clytemnestra, niece of Helen, descendent of gods and heroes.

How easy it is to be a thing but not feel it. Greatness slips into the mundanity of weaving, of pitting olives, of sitting cooped up in the megaron during storms and listening to the patter of rain on stone.

"Get up," you said. "I want to show you something."

I belted my garment and followed you out of my chamber and down the echoing stairs to the bottom story. Flickers of firelight rumbled through the doors that led to the megaron. The servants who attended the fire through the night gossiped, their laughter rushing like the hiss and gutter of the flames.

You led the way outside. I hung back at the threshold. I rarely left the palace walls, and I never left at night. Yet you stepped outside without so much as turning back to be certain I'd follow. Did it ever occur to you that a daughter might hesitate to accede to her father's whims? Did you ever think a girl might, from time to time, have desires that outweighed her sense of duty?

But you were right. I followed you onto the portico where you stood, tall and solemn, in your armor.

We descended stone steps and emerged at last beneath the raw sky. A bright, eerie moon hung over the cliff's rocky landscape, painting it in pale light. Fragile dandelion moons blossomed here and there between the limestone juts, reflecting the larger moon above. The air smelled of damp and night-blooming plants. An eagle cried. From elsewhere came a vixen's answering call.

The smell of your sweat drifted on the night breeze, mixing with horsehair and manure. The combined scents were both foul and tantalizing. When you visited the women's quarters, it was always after events had ended, when the sweat was stale or washed away. Suddenly, things were fresh and new. You had brought me into the middle of things.

We reached the place where the river cuts through the rocks. You began running. Ahead of us, voices drifted from a copse of trees, accompanied by the clang of metal on metal. I raced behind you, stumbling over the stones that studded the grass. We veered toward the trees. A low fog gathered over the ground, illuminated from above by shifting white streams of moonlight. Needled cedar branches poked through the veil.

I fell behind, gasping with increasingly ragged breath. Your footsteps crunched onto leaves as you crossed into the copse. I trailed after, one hand pressed against the urgent pain in my side.

You turned when I was mere paces behind you. "If you were out of breath, why didn't you tell me?" you asked while I struggled the last few steps.

I leaned against a cedar to take the weight off of my trembling legs.

Ahead of us, your men stood in the thick foliage, enveloped by the fog. They wore bronze breastplates and thick felt greaves that loomed darkly out of the haze like tree trunks. Their swords emerged from the obscuring whiteness as they swung, metal clanging against metal as blades found each other. The soldiers seemed a ghostly rank of dismembered limbs and armor that appeared with the glint of moonbeams and then vanished into nothing.

The blunt of a sword crashed against a man's breastplate with a sound like thunder. I cringed. Tears of fright welled in my eyes. I felt exposed beneath the vastness of a sky nothing like the ceilings I'd lived below for most of my life.

You were watching me, your eyes focused on my face instead of on the wonder before us. "I told my hequetai to lead the men in exercises. The fog came up, and look! I had to show someone."

I tried to give you what you wanted. "It's marvelous." My voice quivered with fear that sounded like delight.

"I have an idea," you said, a wicked smile nestled in your beard.

You scavenged through the leaf fall with rustle and crunch until you prized out a branch the length of my forearm. You tested its weight against your palm and gave it an experimental swing.

"Try this," you said, presenting me with the branch.

Tentatively, I placed my palm against the bark.

"Go on." You pointed impatiently at your men battling through the fog. "Pretend you're a warrior."

I waved the branch back and forth, the way I thought they wielded their swords. It rattled in my hand.

"Stop," you commanded. You plucked a dandelion from the ground and laid it across a fallen log. "Here, swing at this. One strong, smooth motion."

The dandelion was a fragile silver moon. I swung the branch up and out. Its weight dragged me forward. I stumbled across a stone.

You took the branch away. "No. Like this."

How I loved the smooth motion of your arm as it moved through the air: the strength of your shoulders, the creak of boiled leather moving with your body. I strove to memorize your arcs and footfalls, but when you returned the branch to me, my fingers felt numb and strange around the bark. I flailed at the leaves and your shins until an accidental swing carried me off balance. My foot came down on the tiny moon of the dandelion. It died with a wet noise.

Wounded petals lay crushed against the wood, releasing the scent of moist soil. You took the branch from me and threw it aside.

"It's a good thing you were born a girl," you said, tugging playfully at my ponytail.

It was, you know. I've never been sorry about that. What I regret most is the children I never bore. I imagined them before you promised me to Artemis: strong boys and dark-haired girls with eyes blue enough to make Zeus lustful. One after the other, each thought-born child disappeared into forgetfulness after you bartered me for wind.

Do you remember that? Perhaps you do. My memories are still strange and partial, like a blanket that has been cut into pieces and then sewn up again. Stitches obscure old connections. The sense of continuity is gone. I no longer remember what it is like to have a normal recollection.

But I'm not speaking solely for your benefit. I need this, too. I cannot articulate the joy of reaching for memories and discovering them present to be touched, and brought forth, and described. I need my memories to transcend the ephemera of thought. I need them to be tangible for the brief moment when they exist as gale winds shrieking in your ear.

I remembered that night when you brought me to see your soldiers for a long time. It was one of the last things Artemis took from me. I've pondered it, and polished it, and fretted about it, as if it were a faceted jewel I could turn in my hand and study from many different angles.

Why did you fetch me when you wanted to share that marvel? Why not my mother? Why weren't you content to share the moment with your men, with whom you've shared so many of your days and nights?

Did you really fail to understand why I ran until I staggered rather than ask you to slow down? You seemed confused then, but you've never stopped expecting me to stumble after you. You've never hesitated to see if I will obey your commands, no matter how wild and cruel, any more than you hesitated that night to see if I would follow you past the palace threshold to a place I'd never been.

Maybe it wasn't ignorance that made me fear your men in the fog. Maybe it was prescience: things have never ended well for me when you've led me out of the world of women and into the world of men.

Clytemnestra completed preparations to leave the palace by noon. She packed me in the wagon with the clothing and the yarn and the dried fruit. I was one more item of baggage to bring to Aulis: a bride for Achilles.

Mother placed Orestes in my lap to hold while she supervised the loading. If she noticed my stillness and silence, she must have believed they were part of a bride's normal reticence.

The wagon set off under full day's sun. Our wheels churned dust into the stifling air. It swirled through gaps in our canopy. Choking grains worked their way into our eyes and mouths. I braved more dust to peek through the curtains; beyond our car, the air hung heavy and motionless.

Orestes jounced on my lap as the wagon tumbled over dirt and rocks. He twisted up to look at me, enormous eyes blinking against the dust. He grabbed a lock of my hair in his fists and put it in his mouth, chewing contemplatively.

"Stop that," said mother, tugging my hair out of his mouth. She inspected the ragged, chewed ends and sighed.

I was content to allow Orestes to chew my hair. During his two short years of life, we'd always communicated by gestures. I understood what he meant by taking an expendable part of me into himself.

Oh, Orestes, so steady and sincere. He never rushed into anything, least of all trivial matters like speech. He took his first steps long after his age-mates were already toddling around the palace, getting into mischief. When he did begin to walk, it was with slow, arduous caution, as if he were always gauging whether independence was worth the risk of falling.

Do you know these things about him? You must. And yet, you never knew me. Why should you know your son?

Really, how could you know him? Even when you were at home, you only saw him at feast evenings, during the chilly twilight hours before we women scooped up the babies and took them back to our spaces. I knew Orestes like my own skin. I worried about the day when he would begin the imperfect translation of his thoughts into speech. I worried that words would obliterate the easy understanding of our hands and faces. This is one fear that your betrayal has made moot. I'll never know what words might have passed between me and my brother.

Orestes began to fuss. I rocked him and sang a ditty about a fleet-footed nymph and the god who loved her. Halfway through the second verse, my memory of the song decayed. Orestes fell asleep anyway, tiny fists still clutching my hair.

I began another song. Mother put her hand over my mouth. "He's already asleep, Iphigenia. Give our ears a rest."

She released me, and I turned to regard her. Through the fog of my dissipating mind, I knew there were things I needed her to tell me.

I couldn't ask the questions I didn't remember so I asked the questions I did remember.

"What is it like to be married? Will I have to live with Achilles's family while he fights in Troy? Can I go to live with father in the army camp instead? How long will the fighting last? Is Achilles a good man? When Orestes is grown and becomes king of Mycenae, will you come to live with me so that I can take care of you as you've cared for me?"

Clytemnestra let me ask questions until my words ran out. The wind had spoiled her elaborate braids, and the dust emphasized the lines of her face, making her look weary. Her eyes were wet and red.

"Every marriage is its own," she said. "Achilles will decide where you're to live, and you'll wait for him there, as I wait for your father. Achilles is a hero, which is a good judge of a man, although a good man is not always a hero. I'll visit you when I can, but I'll never be as happy as I was yesterday, with all my children in my house."

Mother worried her hands as she spoke. Her knotted knuckles had grown larger in the past few years as her arthritis worsened in proportion to her worry over the crisis whirling around her sister Helen and the scoundrel who abducted her to Troy. Mother wouldn't have sent a pig into battle for her whore of a sister, but the kings had been called to war by their oaths, and all her men would go. She'd always known she'd be left to raise Orestes without you, but until that morning she'd believed that she would have me with her to share both loneliness and companionship. Now I was supposed to wed a stranger and disappear as completely as if I'd gone to war.

My mother, stern and sentimental, always happiest in that moment after she set things in their designated places: dyes by hue, spices from mild to pungent, children in their proper rooms – easy to assess and admire.

The first thing my mother told me about Helen was, "She is my sister, but not my sister. Zeus fathered her when he was in the shape of a swan. We share the same mother but she was born in an egg. I was born the normal way. Helen distorts the world around her. Never look at her too closely. You'll go blind."

I was young when she told me that, still so young that I stretched up for her hand when I wanted to take an unsteady, toddling step. Nevertheless, I still sensed that she had said something important, even though I didn't understand what it meant.

When Helen came to Mycenae during my ninth summer, I was old enough to walk on my own, but I still didn't understand the things my mother said about my famous aunt. Helen seemed glamorous and mysterious and unfathomable – like you.

I wove through the maze of the servants' feet and legs, trying to catch a glimpse of her. Hushed words of praise drifted down, all uttered in the same awed tones, whether the speaker was a slave, a servant, or a hequetai, a man or a woman. They marveled over Helen's skin like beaten gold; her deep blue eyes the shade of newly fallen night; the smooth swell of her high, brown-tipped breasts.

You were busy with your brother Menelaus, the two of you clapping each other's shoulders as you exchanged information about recent military encounters. You didn't even glance at your beautiful sister-in-law, or at the way your wife paced uncomfortably, barking at the slaves to carry out orders they were already rushing to fulfill.

Your men retreated to the megaron to drink and discuss. We women went out to the courtyard. Slaves erected a canopy to shelter us from the sun, and set up benches for us to sit on. Clytemnestra walked among them, shouting that the canopy was hung too low, the benches were in the wrong places, bring more food, bring thicker blankets, and don't forget to set aside lamps and oil to set out at dusk.

Helen arrayed herself on a bench near the front of the canopy where fresh breezes would reach her first. She arranged her garments fetchingly around her form as she lay down. She brushed her hand through her braids, allowing the breeze to blow through her stray hairs so that she looked tousled and intimate and all the more beautiful. I thought she was very vain to pose like that.

A girl my age nearly collided with me as I stood watching Helen. She gave me a glare, and then turned abruptly away as if I wasn't worth her time. "Put my bench there," she directed a slave, pointing to a spot near Helen. I wanted to ask her who she thought she was, but before I got the chance, my mother caught me by the shoulders.

Her grip was harder than normal, her fingernails digging into my skin. "Come sit down," she said, guiding me to the bench where she sat near Helen.

I sat at Clytemnestra's feet while she ruffled my hair, and looked up at my aunt. From below, Helen was just as beautiful, but her features looked sharper. Braids coiled around her face like snakes, bound back by a beribboned brass headband that caught the gold flecks in her eyes.

Mother kept a firm grip on my shoulders as if she could keep my mind from straying by holding my body in place. She began a monologue about housekeeping, a subject that was impersonal, factual, and utterly under her control. "Next month, we'll begin drying the fruit stores," she said. "It was too cold this year for the figs. We lost nearly half our crop. But we've traded for nuts that will keep us through the winter."

"You're an excellent steward, sister mine," said Helen, not bothering to disguise her boredom.

"Mother," interjected the awkward girl who had collided with me earlier. "I found you a perfect one."

She extended her hand, in which nestled a cube of goat cheese, its corners unbroken. A bemused smile crossed Helen's face as she looked down at the morsel.

"Thank you," she said awkwardly, taking the cheese. She rewarded the girl with an uncertain pat on the head.

The girl lay stretched out on the bench, imitating Helen, but to completely different effect. The languorous pose accentuated her skinny, ungainly limbs. Stray tangles poked out of her braids like thistles.

"You're Hermione? You're my *cousin*?" I blurted.

Hermione bristled. Her mother looked down at me with a slow, appraising gaze. "Why, hello," Helen said. "Are you my niece?"

Clytemnestra's hand tightened protectively on my shoulder. "This is Iphigenia."

Helen's eyes were hot like sunlight on my cheeks. I burned with embarrassment.

"She'll be a beauty someday," Helen said to my mother.

Clytemnestra shrugged. "There's time enough for that."

Hermione pushed a tray of honeyed figs out of a slave's hands. It clattered to the ground. "None of those are good enough for my mother!" she shouted.

Helen looked uncertainly at Clytemnestra, and then over at Hermione, and then up at the sky. She gave a sigh. "I don't know how you do it, Clytemnestra. I was never raised to be a mother. I was only taught to be a wife."

"Children are just small people, Helen," mother said. "Albeit, occasionally stupid ones."

Helen tugged a red ribbon off of her headband and held it out to me. "Here, Iphigenia, would you like this?"

Wordlessly, I accepted. The ribbon was soft and silken and magic with her touch.

"I'd like to talk with you, Iphigenia. Somewhere where other people can't listen in. Just you and me. If your mother will agree?"

Helen lifted her gaze to Clytemnestra's face. Mother's fingers dug into my shoulders.

"Of course," said mother. "She's your niece."

I knew my mother didn't want me to be alone with Helen. I also knew that I wanted to be near that beauty, that glamour, that heat. I pulled the ribbon taut between my fingers.

"All right," I said.

As I rode to Aulis, I forgot the day when I was eight when my mother plucked my embroidery out of my lap and held it up to the light. I waited for her to tear out my stitches and return it to my lap for me to do over again, as she had done every morning since I could first grip a needle. Instead she stared at my work with a thoughtful expression. "Hmm," she said. "You're getting better."

I lost that day, but I remembered Helen in Mycenae, her searing eyes and her haughty pose and her daughter sitting forlornly nearby, trying to earn a moment's attention by finding a perfect bite of food.

The wagon stopped at Aulis with a jolt. Prickling dust settled onto our clothing and skin. I pulled the canopy aside and spat onto the ground to clear my mouth. Mother reached out to stop me, but as her hand touched my shoulder, she changed her mind. She leaned over beside me and spat onto the ground, too.

A slave helped my mother down onto the soil of Aulis. He was old and bent, his right leg dragging behind his left. I felt a tug of recognition, but I couldn't remember who he was. *Iamas*, my mind suggested, but Artemis had stolen everything else I knew about him.

I accepted his hand to help me down. He looked up at me and startled. His hand jerked away. I stumbled, only barely catching my balance. Orestes began to cry.

"What's the matter?" mother demanded.

The slave whimpered.

"Iamas," mother repeated, more softly. "What's the matter?"

Iamas trembled. "King Agamemnon said you might not come."

"Don't be ridiculous," said mother. "How could there be a wedding if we didn't come? Help my daughter down."

Iamas offered his hand again. This time, his grip remained steady as I descended. His gaze lingered on the smelly decorations in my hair that I had forgotten were there. I reached up to touch them, and felt their softness, their fragility.

A shudder ran through Iamas. He looked away from me, and clutched himself as if he were cold, even though the air was hot and stagnant. I knew that he was sad and uncomfortable and lying about something. I couldn't care much. He was a stranger.

"You could still ride back to Mycenae," he suggested, softly.

"Iamas!" Mother's voice grew sharp. "What's wrong with you?"

I remember now what I didn't then: Iamas, the old slave, who had been with my mother since before I was born. I remember him holding me when I was so small that I understood the world in images. He was younger then, his nose crooked from a healed fracture, his smile gap-toothed and ever-wide. When his work was mobile, he came to sit near me while I played, watching me run around and chatter as toddlers will.

When I exhausted myself, he made a place for me to lie beside him, and told me stories through the sleepy afternoon.

He was little more than a shadow to me. I walked past him, toward the harbor where a thousand ships sat motionless on a sea as flat as glass. Wilted sails drooped from their masts, pining for a wind that refused to come. The painted eyes on the ships' prows stared blankly forward, as if trying to make out the shape of Troy in the distance. Ten thousand oars waited.

"Why are all the ships still moored?" I asked.

Iamas spoke from behind me. "They're trapped. There's no wind to send them to Troy."

"They're just sitting there?"

"They have no choice."

I watched the ships bob up and down with the almost imperceptible motion of the water. Seabirds circled silently beneath the brazen sun. Even they seemed to be waiting.

I turned my back to the water and surveyed the camp. It was larger than I'd thought a camp could be, an immense array of men and equipment. Regiments formed restless circles around banked fires, their strength turned to games of chance played with stones and carved figures.

The soldiers who had grown bored with sitting rubbed wax into their armor with strokes as forceful as blows. Metal shone, bright as children's eyes and new-minted coins. As I stared at the men and their armor, the sun blazed off of the metal until it became impossible to tell warriors from breast-plates, skin from gold. Orestes laughed and stretched out his hand toward the shining ranks. They seemed an array of golden men, waiting to stretch their flaming limbs and dazzle into battle like animate rays of sunlight.

Left in the harbor with no one to fight, they were burning up fast. They couldn't survive without wind to stoke them, to blow them onto dry firewood. They needed new things to burn. They needed fuel.

You came to the tent where Iamas settled us to wait for the wedding. All three of us looked up at your approach. Orestes stretched his arms in the direction of your voice. You called only for Clytemnestra.

Mother slipped out of the tent, leaving Orestes and me to peer out from the shadows. Orestes fussed; I held him close. Mother's garment was bright against the dun ground, her sandaled feet pale and delicate. I heard cloth rustling as she embraced you.

"You've arrived." Your voice splintered with ambivalence.

"Come inside," mother said. "Iphigenia is wearing her wedding flowers. She'll want to see you. She looks radiant."

"I can't. I have things to attend to."

"Just come in for a moment. You have to see your Iphigenia one last time while she's still a maiden."

"I can't!" Your shout was sudden, anguished. "I must go. I'll return later."

Dust swirled around your retreating footsteps. I inhaled it, ready to choke.

Do you remember what happened later on that night when you led me out to see the soldiers in the fog? It has only just come back to me, how you took me by the hand and led me, walking this time, back out of the copse of trees and into the palace, up to my chamber where the other girls lay, half-awake, waiting for us to return.

I stared after your retreating form. I felt as if I were waking from a dream into my mundane existence. I wanted to run after you and make the dream last.

So I did.

Do you feel it now? The sky is darkening. My power grows. I feel the ruffle of waves beneath what has become of my spirit. They churn into tiny crests, surmounted with foam. Boats tremble beneath me. Sails billow with my breath. I tousle the hair of men who have set aside their helmets, and they totter, no longer sure of their footing.

I am still weak, my father. Soon, I will do more than wail in your ear.

Mother sat at the edge of the tent after you departed, staring out (as I stared after you when you left me to mundanity after showing me marvels). Perhaps she had begun to suspect something from your refusal to see me, from Iamas's shudder as he looked up at my wedding adornments.

Outside: a flash of gold.

Mother squeezed my hand. "That's Achilles's shield," she said. "Stay here. I'll ask your questions for you."

It was not like my stern, proper mother to expose herself to strange men.

I swung Orestes into my lap. I could only see a narrow slice of the camp from where I sat. I saw the arm and chest of the man who must be Achilles, his body rippling with muscles as sharply delineated as those on a statue. His helmet and breastplate were wrought of fine, detailed gold. His oiled brown skin shone as brightly as his armor.

Mother extended her hand. "Greetings, Achilles! May you and my daughter have the happiest of marriages."

Achilles eyed her fingers. Beneath his helmet, his eyes were dark and chary. (Fog, a branch, a dandelion mirroring the moon.) "Woman, why do you offer your hand to a stranger? You may be beautiful, but that is no excuse."

"Forgive me. I thought you'd recognize me from my description. I'm Agamemnon's wife."

"Are you? I would have thought such a powerful man would have better control of his women."

I could not see my mother's face, but I knew the taut smile she would wear in response to such an affront, the catlike stretch of her lips that would not reach her eyes. (Like the taut smile Helen flashed me in the courtyard, late that night when I had nine summers: "Come walk with me, niece.")

"We'll be related in a few days," said mother. "Just pretend we already are."

"Are you insane?" Achilles's dark eyes examined the length of my mother's body. "No one told me Agamemnon married a madwoman."

Mother's voice became dangerously low. "Young man. I am not mad."

"You must be. I'm the son of Thetis, goddess of the sea. I've slain a thousand men. I wear glory like other men wear scent. Why would I marry your daughter just because you tell me to?"

"My husband sent for us," said Clytemnestra. "He said that you wanted to marry my daughter."

"Why would I tell him that? I've never even seen her."

For a long moment, mother fell silent. (My head, ringing with emptiness, the sound of forgotten memories.)

"You'll forgive me if I sound skeptical," she said at last, "but either you are mistaken, or my husband is lying. What should a loyal wife believe?"

Achilles's eyes hardened like metal.

Before Achilles could speak, the slave Iamas pushed himself between the two of them. He turned toward Clytemnestra, panting, his face red with exertion.

Mother snapped, "What do you want?"

Iamas told them your plans. He revealed how the armies had delayed in the harbor, waiting for a wind. He told of how the goddess had demanded a sacrifice, and how the wedding was a ruse designed to lure us to my death.

All around us, the air was as still and expectant as a held breath. (Me, in my bed, forgetting green and figs and wool.)

"Tomorrow," Iamas said, "They will do it tomorrow at dawn."

*   *   *

My imagination caught on the moment when you forged your plan with Menelaus, Odysseus, and Calchas. My mind had become a scatter of half-forgotten fragments. Tatters of old memories hung in the places of things I could not recall. I couldn't remember Menelaus's face, so I saw my mother's instead, wearing the beard you had when I was younger, black through and through. A restless Achilles paced as Odysseus, sandals of gold kicking up dust as he paced the fog-filled copse. Calchas wore a thin linen robe instead of priestly raiment. He turned to you, and it was Helen's mouth sneering around his demands, her indigo eyes filled with visions of my blood.

Will you sacrifice your daughter?

I will.

Was your voice loud and resonant? Did mother-Menelaus clap you on the back? Achilles-Odysseus would have spoken with grudging respect, a flicker of admiration in his chary eyes. "You're a callous son of a bitch," he'd have said, "but you do what must be done."

Did you sink your head and whisper? Did Helen-Calchas crane her shapely neck to hear you, the red ribbons on her headband fluttering over her ear?

Tomorrow," Iamas said. "They will do it tomorrow at dawn."

He knelt before Clytemnestra.

"I wasn't sure whether I should tell you. A slave owes his loyalty to his master, but he owes his loyalty to his mistress, too. I came to Mycenae with your dowry. I was a young man then. I've always been yours."

"Why didn't you tell us before?" mother pleaded. "We could have ridden back to Mycenae. Agamemnon would never have known."

"I tried to," said Iamas. "I am a coward."

If it was necessary that you kill me, did you have to use a wedding as your ruse? Do you see how cruel it was to promise me all the treasures of womanhood that I would never possess?

Perhaps you thought you were marrying me off, after all, one way or another. As I if were Persephone, spending my youth on the arm of Hades. But there will be no spring for me.

Orestes struggled and cried in my arms. He could hear his mother. He reached for her voice. The sounds of Clytemnestra's weeping carried on the air, tiny pitiful sobs.

As for me, I felt airy, as if I were standing on the top of the limestone cliffs that surround Aulis harbor like the broken half of a bowl. Betrayal forced all our hearts to skip a beat, but mother and Orestes could still cry.

Parts of me were already gone. I knew there was no turning back.

Tomorrow," Iamas said. "They will do it tomorrow at dawn."

Mother's grip was painful on my arm. "Come on," she said, dragging me out of the tent. Orestes screamed as we went. It was the sound I would have made if I could have.

Achilles saw my unprotected face. He shielded his eyes (dark and chary, above a beard like adolescent scrub) with his sword arm. "Does the girl have to be here?"

"My husband has made fools of us all," said Clytemnestra. "He tricked me and used your name to do it. People will think you find it amusing to lure young girls to their deaths."

Achilles paced angrily. The slave, Iamas, flinched each time Achilles's sword clanked against his armor. "He had no right to use my name."

"You could make them stop this. They will listen to you. You're a hero. If you tell them to stop, they'll have to take heed."

Achilles halted. "You want me to tell Agamemnon to stop the sacrifice?"

"For the sake of your reputation!"

"But how will we get to Troy?"

Mother approached him. At once, the stern and proper woman I had known all my life vanished (Helen arraying herself on the bench, the folds of her garment decorating her languorous body). She became a softer, reticent figure, her eyes averted, her hands gentle and hesitant as they lifted her hem to show her plump calves. Her fingers fastened on the laces of Achilles's breastplate. Her lips moved near his neck, so close that her breath stirred the fine golden hair on his nape.

"You'll find a way," she murmured in his ear.

Achilles stayed silent. Mother lowered herself to her knees. She stared up at him, coy and alluring, through lowered lashes. Soft brown curls escaped from her braids to soften the angles of her face. Her breasts rose and fell with her breath.

"Do you want me to beg?" she asked. "My daughter and I are helpless. We have no choice but to implore you. Help us."

Achilles stepped back, repelled by her need. Mother held out her hands, her wrists upturned in supplication. ("My sister was born from an egg. I was born the normal way.")

"Do you want my daughter to beg instead? She will! She's always been virtuous, but what good will her honor do when they send her virgin to her grave?"

There was desire in Achilles's eyes. It was not for nothing that my mother was Helen's sister. But Achilles's gaze was hard and disdainful, too. For my mother was Helen's sister, and Helen was the whore who ran from Menelaus.

"Your daughter need not debase herself on my account. I will settle the matter of my honor with Agamemnon—"

Mother clasped her hands in gratitude. Achilles held out his hand to silence her.

"I will settle the matter of my honor with Agamemnon. And then *we will sail to Troy.*"

For the first time, Achilles's gaze came to rest on me. His eyes searched my face. I wondered what he saw there. I knew that I was not ugly. I thought, perhaps, in different circumstances he might have chosen to save a help-less woman with my youthful complexion and night-dark eyes. But to stir him that day, I would have had to be even more beautiful than Helen. Her beauty had gathered a thousand ships in the harbor. It would take some-thing even greater to convince them to sail home without their war.

Mother took me back to the tent. She tucked me beneath a blanket as if I were a child. She pulled the wedding adornments from my hair, and stroked my tresses until they lay smooth and shining across my shoulders. Orestes laid beside me. He curled toward my warmth like a sleeping cat, and wrapped his fists around my hair.

"Stay here," mother said. "Rest. Keep out of sight. Keep yourself pure. It will be harder for them to justify what they're doing if they know that you are innocent and obedient."

She ran her fingers across my cheek.

"Don't worry. They aren't monsters. They won't do this terrible thing."

My memories were tipping out of me more and more rapidly. My mind went dark with only a few memories lit up, like lamps casting small orbs of light along a corridor.

I wandered into a lamp of memory: I was trailing you as you left my room, down the steps and across the portico. I walked quietly behind so that you would not hear me. We emerged into the forest. The fog was dissipating from the copse, revealing men among the trees, their shouts and sword-clashes harsh in the cold, dim air. You were far ahead of me, already meeting with your hequetai, exchanging shouts and strategy.

Hands tightened on my shoulders. I looked up into their faces: two young men with patchy, adolescent beards. Their breath smelled of rotting fish. One stood in his nightclothes. The other wore a helmet and a breastplate but nothing else. Beneath the helmet's shadow, his eyes were dark and chary.

They spoke. Their voices were rapid, unintelligible, drowned out by the pounding of blood in my ears. Their eyes were enormous and sinister, large and white like the dandelion before I crushed it underneath my foot.

Smells: blood, musk, new sweat. A short, blunt limb – like the branch that you gave me to use as a sword – emerged from obscuring whiteness. It pushed blindly against my leg. "Stop," one boy commanded the other. "Here, swing at this. One strong, smooth motion." The breastplate clattered against my flesh with a sound like thunder. My belly, rotting like the stench of rotting fish, welling with tears of fright. (Helen in the courtyard: "Come walk with me, niece." Her daughter Hermione looking on, jealous and ignored.)

Rotting fish and sweat. The moon dwindling like a crushed dandelion. The branch swinging. The thin high wail that a girl makes when someone swings at her with a sword that is a branch that is neither thing at all.

"You're hopeless," said one boy to the other. "It's too bad you weren't born a girl."

Then another face, a hequetai in a tufted cloak, shouting like the clash of swords. "What's wrong with you two? Are you stupid? Don't you know who this is?"

The reek of shit and piss. The man's hand on my arm, tighter than the boys' had been.

"What are you doing here? Your father would kill you if he knew. He'd kill all of us. Be grateful I'm sending you back without shoving your slatternly face in the muck in front of him. Do you have any modesty at all? Your mother and her people. Brazen, the lot of you. Walking into men's camps like common whores. You may be beautiful, but that is no excuse. Go! Get out of here! Get back where you came from! Go!"

My feet, pounding on the path back home. The copse of trees; the grass; the empty mouth of the megaron where exhausted slaves tended the coals to keep them warm until morning.

The pounding of my heart as I lay down in bed for the third time that night. Memories of moons and fog and branches. Love for my father: flat like a branch, round like a dandelion, silver like the moon, welling up and out of me into a rush like the wind, but without the power to move a thousand ships.

Indigo shaded the sky to evening. Helen smiled a taut smile that I'd seen on my mother's face, one that did not reach her eyes.

She reached for my hand. "Come walk with me, niece."

Hermione watched us. Jealousy darkened her features. "Mother!" she exclaimed. "I have something to show you."

Helen did not look over at her daughter. "Later." She bent closer to me. "Iphigenia?"

I twisted the ribbon from Helen's headband around my fingers. I stepped toward her, but I didn't take her hand.

Hermione upturned the bench she'd been sitting on, and began to cry.

Helen led me past the canopy that sheltered the benches, and toward the black scratchings of the olive trees that stood, lonely, in the chilly air. Helen arrayed herself beneath one, her garment spreading around her in delicate, shadowed folds.

I heard footsteps behind us and turned to see Hermione peering from the shadows, hoping to overhear what her mother had to say to another girl. She was clutching something in her hand. I wondered what delicacy she'd brought to bribe her mother with this time. A honeyed fig? A flask of sweet wine?

I looked back to Helen. Her eyes changed hue with the setting sun, taking on a lighter shade like the gray of water beneath a cloudy sky. Firelight from the lamps near the benches cast flickers across her cheekbones, highlighting an undertone in her skin like bronze. She watched my gaze as it trailed over her features, and gave a little sigh of boredom.

"You'll be beautiful one day, too," she said patronizingly.

"Not as beautiful as you," I demurred.

"No one is as beautiful as I." Her voice was flat, but full of pride.

The night smelled of burning oil and women's bodies. A dandelion hung high in the sky, casting its light down on us. Helen's motives were obscured behind blankness, like soldiers' bodies disappearing into fog.

Helen distorts the world around her. Never look at her too closely. You'll go blind.

"I saw you holding your father's hand today," said Helen. "Do you feel safe with your father?"

I made a moue. I couldn't speak to my beautiful aunt without my mother beside me.

"What was that?"

"Yes," I mumbled.

Helen shifted. The folds of her garment rearranged themselves into new shimmers and shadows.

"There's something I think I should tell you, Iphigenia. About your father. Did your mother ever tell you that she was married before?"

I shook my head. Around and around, the ribbon wove through my fingers.

"She had a husband named Tantalus who was the king of Mycenae before your father came. They had a child together. A son."

Helen paused, scrutinizing my reaction. I didn't know what to do. I looked to the right and to the left. There was no one nearby.

"I know this is hard to hear, Iphigenia," said Helen, "but your father came to Mycenae and murdered Tantalus and then he—" She raised her sleeve over her mouth, and looked away. "He took the baby from your mother's arms and he dashed it to the stones and smashed it to pieces. My nephew."

With a quick glance over my shoulder, I saw that the servants were clearing out the benches and the canopy. Iamas helped a young girl douse the lamps. Behind me, there was safety, there was familiarity. I stepped back. Helen caught my hand.

"He was a round, happy baby. I only saw him once before—" She broke off. "After your father killed Tantalus, he forced Clytemnestra to marry him, and became king of Mycenae. I see him holding your hand and I worry. My sister doesn't want you to know, but you need to be warned. Your father isn't what he seems. He's the kind of man who would kill a baby."

I broke away and fled toward the bustling servants. My feet pounded past Hermione who glared at me, and then turned toward Helen, her expression aching with desire for her mother's attention.

Jealous woman. Vain woman. Boastful woman. I never believed her. I never believed you would kill a child.

After mother fell asleep, I took Orestes in my arms and crept out of the tent. We made our way to the shore where the night sea looked like obsidian, reflecting the glow of the dandelion overhead.

I broke off a piece of branch the length of Orestes's arm and gave it to him, but I couldn't remember why. He stared at me with puzzled eyes until I took it away again and threw it toward the boats.

"Why don't you speak?" I asked him. "You're old enough."

Orestes stretched out his chubby hands. He snuggled his face against my chin and throat, warm as a cat. He liked to snuggle when I was distressed. It made him feel powerful that he, too, could give comfort.

"I am dissolving into pieces," I told him. "I need you to remember me for me. Will you do that? Please?"

He stared up at me with sincere, sober eyes.

"I am your sister," I said. "My name is Iphigenia. I love our father very much. I am going to be murdered by our father, but you must not be angry with him for that. To be angry with our father is to be angry with everything. It's to be angry with wind and war and gods. Don't be angry with him.

"I was born on an autumn day when the rain fell, scented with the crisp aroma of falling leaves. I was born with the sound of thunder, but I was terrified of it anyway. When the palace rattled with strike and clash, I would run to hide behind mother's loom. She would glare at me and tell me to find something useful to do, but when I lay down beside her and stuck my thumb in my mouth, she would lean down to stroke my hair.

"I love music, but I can't sing. Our mother forever tells me to hush. I sang to you often anyway. When I sang, you laughed and clapped your hands. I taught you songs, but I don't remember them anymore. I want you to remember the things I taught you, whatever they were.

"Our grandmother was raped by Zeus when he turned into a swan, and our mother's sister was born out of an egg. Gods are our aunts and cousins, but we are only mortal. I am particularly mortal. I am weak and not very brave and I will die quickly, like those things they put in my hair for my wedding that never happened.

"I am afraid to die. I am afraid of losing simple things. Things like . . ." My memory cast a net through dark waters, coming up empty. I drew from what I saw. "Things like the smell of salt near a dark sea, and how warm your hand is, and how much you make me feel without ever speaking.

"I've lost so much already. I don't want to lose any more.

"Should I be glad that I'll never see the sun again so that Helen can be led like an errant child back to the marriage bed she desecrated? Should I rejoice that my death will enable my father to slaughter Trojans over a vixen that ran into the hills when she went into heat? Should my life dower the frigid air that passes between my uncle and his whore?

"I used to learn things, but now I forget them. I think I liked learning things. I need you to learn things for me now. Learn how to love some-one, and how to survive a tragedy. Learn how to swing a sword, and how to convince an opponent when you have no argument but justice. Learn how to polish your armor until you become a glowing golden man, and then learn to be a flame that fuels itself. Learn to be your own wind. Will you? Will you please?"

I felt my tears falling into Orestes's hair. He hugged me tighter. I breathed in his smell.

"When warm air rises, seeking the sun, cool air rushes in to replace it. That's the way of the world. Joy and youth and love flow ever upward. What they leave behind is the cold consolation of the wind."

Orestes pulled away from me. I studied his solemn face. His mouth opened. For a long second, I thought he would speak, but no words came. For once, I found him inscrutable.

I feel the sea beneath me. I inhale and it waits. I exhale and it tumbles. Can you feel the pressure of my anger as it blows fiercely across your skin? I am the sand in your eyes, and the reek of the camp's midden heap blowing toward the sea. I am the force that rocks you back on your heels so that you flail and stagger. My hatred whistles through the cliffs. It screeches across the rough timber of your boats.

I grow stronger with every moment. I will be wild. I will be brutal. I will encircle you and conquer you. I will be more powerful than your boats and your swords and your blood lust. I will be inevitable.

I brought Orestes back to the tent, and we laid down beside Clytemnestra. I stared, sleeplessly, into the dark.

Possible paths stretched before me. I could go to Achilles's tent and plead my case as a whore instead of a virgin. I imagined what Helen would have done in my place, how she would color her cheeks and set her hair. She would arrange herself to look like a dandelion, easily crushed, and easily conquered. Unlike my mother, she would not have halted her fingers at the laces of Achilles's breastplate. Unlike my mother, she would have let her lips do more than hover hotly by his ear. Unlike my mother, she would have convinced him.

I could plead my case to Menelaus as his niece and an innocent. Or if he did not care for virtue, I could venture a suit to replace his lost Helen. Such methods might work on Odysseus, too. Only I was not a practiced seductress. My clumsy attempts might only succeed in doing as my mother said they would, and make the monsters feel justified when they gave me to Calchas's knife.

I could have sought you out, in the hope that the eye of night would grant you mercy. But I already knew what you would do if you found me wandering alone through a camp of soldiers.

One path seemed best: I would run out into the cold and wake the first soldier I found. "Take me to Calchas," I would tell him, and march resolutely to my fate. It would give me a fast, honorable end. And there might be a chance, just a small one, that I could be killed without seeing your face and knowing how it changed after you betrayed me.

But Orestes whimpered and tossed beneath his little blanket. Sweat damped his brow. I'd kept him up too late, overwhelmed him with disturbing confidences. I stayed to soothe him until dawn neared and I was too tired to chase my death.

I was not brave. I was only a girl.

You came to fetch me. You didn't know we knew. You pretended to be over-joyed at the prospect of the wedding that would never happen. You took my hand and whirled me in a circle. "Oh, Iphigenia! You look so beautiful!"

I looked up into your eyes and saw that you were crying. Your smile felt as false as mother's. Your tears washed over the place where I'd once kept the day when Orestes was born.

"Stop this," said mother. She pulled me away from you and pushed me toward the other end of the tent. Orestes sat on the cushions beside me, a wooden toy in his hand, watching.

Mother turned to confront you. "I have heard a terrible thing. Tell me if it's true. Are you planning to kill our daughter?"

Your eyes went blank. "How can you accuse me of such a thing?"

"I'll ask again. Answer me plainly this time. Are you planning to kill our daughter?"

You had no answer. You gripped the hilt of your branch, and set your jaw. Tears remained immobile on your cheeks.

"Don't do this." Mother grasped at your shoulder. You wrenched away. "I've been a model wife. I've done everything you've asked of me. I ran your home and raised your children. I've been chaste and loyal and honorable. How can you repay me by killing my daughter?"

She snatched Orestes from the cushions and held him toward you. He began to cry and kick.

"Look at your son. How do you think he'll react when you murder Iphigenia? He'll shy away from you. He'll fear you." She turned the baby toward her. "Orestes, do you hear me? Do you want your father to take your sister away?"

You tried to grab my brother. Mother held him tight. Orestes screamed in pain and fear.

"He'll hate you or he'll imitate you," mother shouted over his wails. "You'll teach your son to be a murderer! Is that what you want?"

You pushed Orestes into his mother's arms and stormed away from her. You stopped a short distance from me and reached for my arm. I flinched away.

"Are you happy, Clytemnestra?" you asked. "You've scared the girl. She could have gone thinking that she was going to be married. Now she's going to be terrified."

You leaned close to touch my hair. (Tugging my ponytail: "It's a good thing you were born a girl.") You dropped a kiss on my brow. ("I know this is hard to hear," said Helen, "but your father is the kind of man who would kill a baby.") I wrenched backward.

"What do you want?" I asked. "Do you want me to take your hand, blithe and trusting as any goat that follows its master back to the camp to see men fighting in the fog? I'm not a little girl anymore."

I looked into your angry, sneering face.

"Or do I have it wrong?" I asked. "Do you want me to kick and scream? Do you want me to have a tantrum like Orestes so that later you can think back on my wailing and berate yourself about the terrible things you've done?"

You tossed your head like a disquieted horse. "You're acting mad."

I laughed. "So I'm right, am I? You're already beginning to make me into an idea. A difficult decision rendered by a great man. Well, stop now. This is only difficult because you make it so. All you have to do is break your vow and spare my life."

"Menelaus and Odysseus would take the armies and bring them to march against Mycenae. Don't you see? I have no choice."

"Don't *you* see? It should never have been your choice at all. My life isn't yours to barter. The choice should have been mine."

"You don't understand."

"I understand that you want me to pity you for my death."

Wind whistled through my brain. The edges of the tent rustled. Sand stirred. Strands of mother's hair blew out from her braids.

"You know, I never believed what Helen told me. Did he look like Orestes, father? Did my elder half-brother look like Orestes when you dashed him to the rocks?"

You glowered at my defiance. "This is how you beg me to save your life?"

"Is it sufficient?" I asked, but I already knew the answer. I inhaled deeply. "Don't kill me."

I had forgotten how to beg.

With almost nothing of myself remaining, I found myself reconsidering my conversation with Helen. Without my ego to distract me, I concentrated on different details, imagined different motivations behind her words. Did I think Helen was arrogant because that was what everyone said about her? Was she boastful or simply honest?

As Helen sat beneath the olive tree, watching me admire her face, she sighed. I'd always believed it was a sigh of pride. Perhaps it was weariness instead. Perhaps she was exhausted from always having to negotiate jealousy and desire when she wanted to do something as simple as hold her niece's hand.

"You'll be beautiful one day, too." Was she trying to reassure me?

"Not as beautiful as you," I demurred.

"No one is as beautiful as I."

Her voice was flat. How must it have felt, always being reduced to that single superlative?

After she told me the terrible things about my father, I fled into the crowd to search for my mother. I found her holding a stern conversation with one of Helen's women. She wouldn't budge when I tried to drag her away. She dabbed my tears and told me to find Iamas so he could calm me down.

It wasn't until I crumpled at her feet, distraught and wailing, that she realized I was suffering from more than a scrape.

She slipped her arms around me and helped me to stand, her embrace warm and comforting. She brought me to her rooms and asked what was wrong.

I repeated Helen's words. "It isn't true!" I cried. "She's mean and vain. Why would she lie about something like that? Tell me she's lying."

"Of course she is," said mother, patting me vaguely on the head. "No one would be monstrous enough to do that."

She pulled the blanket to my chin and sat beside me and stroked my hair (oh, mother, did you never learn another way to comfort a child?). I fell asleep, head tilted toward her touch.

Later, I woke to the sound of voices in the corridor. They drifted in, too quiet to hear. I tiptoed to the door and listened.

"I'm sorry," said Helen, her voice raw as if she'd been crying. "I didn't mean to scare her."

"Well, you did. She's inconsolable. She thinks her father kills babies."

"But Clytemnestra . . ."

"Stories like that have no place in this house. I don't understand what was going on in your head!"

"He's a killer. How can you stand to see him with that sweet little girl? I think of my nephew every time I look at her. He's a monster. He'd kill her in a moment if it suited him. How can you let him near her?"

"He won't hurt her. He's her father."

"Clytemnestra, she had to know."

"It wasn't your decision."

"It had to be someone's! You can't protect her from a little sadness now, and let him lead her into danger later. Someone had to keep your daughter safe."

Mother's voice dipped so low that it was barely more than a whisper. "Or maybe you couldn't stand to see that I can actually make my daughter happy."

Helen made a small, pained noise. I heard the rustling of her garment, her footsteps echoing down the painted clay corridor. I fled back to mother's blanket and tried to sleep, but I kept imagining your hands as you threw a baby down to his death on the stones. I imagined your fingers covered in blood, your palms blue from the cold in your heart. It couldn't be true.

You called two men to escort me to Calchas. One wore his nightclothes, the other a breastplate and nothing else. Patchy adolescent beards covered their chins.

Mother wept.

You stood beside me. "I have to do this."

"Do you?" I asked.

The soldiers approached. In a low voice, you asked them to be gentle.

My emotions lifted from me, one by one, like steam evaporating from a campfire.

Fear disappeared.

"Don't worry, mother," I said. "I will go with them willingly. It is only death."

Sadness departed.

"Don't grieve for me. Don't cut your hair. Don't let the women of the house cut their hair either. Try not to mourn for me at all. Crush dandelions. Run by the river. Wind ribbons around your fingers."

Empathy bled away.

"Father, I want you to think of all the suffering I've felt, and magnify it a thousand times. When you reach the shores of Troy, unleash it all on their women. Let my blood be the harbinger of their pain. Spear them. Savage them. Let their mothers' throats be raw with screaming. Let their elder brothers be dashed like infants on the rocks."

Love vanished. I turned on my mother.

"Why did you bring me here? You saw him kill your son, and still you let me hold his hand! Why didn't you remember what he is?"

I pushed my mother to the ground. Orestes tumbled from her arms. Bloody fingers on blue hands flashed past my vision in the instant before mother twisted herself to cushion his fall.

I forgot resignation.

"Why did you write that letter? Am I worth less to you than the hunk of wood they used to make your staff of office? Would it have been so bad to be the man who stayed home instead of fighting? Let Menelaus lead. Let him appease Artemis with Hermione's blood. If a girl must die to dower Helen, why shouldn't it be her own daughter?

"Did you raise me only so that you could trade me in for the best offer you could get? A wealthy husband? Influential children? A wind to push you across the sea?

"Mother, why didn't you take me to the hills? Helen went! Helen ran away! Why didn't we follow Helen?"

You uttered a command. The soldiers took my elbow. I forgot how to speak.

Your soldiers escorted me through the camp to the temple. Achilles found me on the way. "You're as beautiful as your aunt," he said.

The wind of my forgetfulness battered against him. Effortlessly, Achilles buffeted against its strength.

"I've changed my mind," he said. "It takes courage to walk calmly to your death. I wouldn't mind marrying you. Talk to me. I only need a little persuasion. Tell me why I should save your life."

Voiceless, I marched onward.

I forgot you.

They washed and perfumed me and decked me with the things that smell sweet. You came before me.

"My sweet Iphigenia," you said. "If there was anything I could do to stop it, I would, but I can't. Don't you see?"

You brushed your fingers along my cheek. I watched them, no longer certain what they were.

"Iphigenia, I have no right, but I've come to ask for your pardon. Can you forgive me for what I've done?"

I stared at you with empty eyes, my brows furrowed, my body cleansed and prepared. *Who are you?* asked my flesh.

They led me into Artemis's sacred space. Wild things clustered, lush and pungent, around the courtyard. The leaves tossed as I passed them, shuddering in my wind. Sunlight glinted off of the armor of a dozen men who were gathered to see the beginning of their war. Iamas was there, too, weeping as he watched.

Calchas pushed his way toward me as if he were approaching through a gale, his garment billowing around him. I recognized the red ribbons on his headband, his indigo eyes, his taut and joyless smile.

"You would have been beautiful one day, too," she said.

Not as beautiful as you.

"No one is as beautiful as I."

His breath stank with rotting fish, unless that was other men, another time. He held a jeweled twig in his hand – but I knew it would be your hand that killed me. Calchas was only an instrument, like Helen, like the twig.

He lifted the jeweled twig to catch the sun. I didn't move. He drew it across my throat.

My body forgot to be a body. I disappeared.

Artemis held me like a child holds a dandelion. With a single breath, she blew the wind in my body out of my girl's shape.

I died.

Feel me now. I tumble through your camp, upturning tents as a child knocks over his toys. Beneath me, the sea rumbles. Enormous waves whip across the water, powerful enough to drown you all.

"Too strong!" shouts Menelaus.

Achilles claps him on the back. "It'll be a son of a bitch, but it'll get us there faster!"

Mother lies by the remnants of the tent and refuses to move. Iamas tugs on her garment, trying to stir her. She cries and cries, and I taste her tears. They become salt on my wind.

Orestes wails for mother's attention. He puts his mouth to her breasts, but she cannot give him the comfort of suckling. I ruffle his hair and blow a chill embrace around him. His eyes grow big and frightened. I love him, but I can only hug him harder, for I am a wind.

Achilles stands at the prow of one of the ships, boasting of what he'll do to the citizens of Troy. Menelaus jabs his sword into my breeze and laughs. "I'll ram Paris like he's done to Helen," he brags. Odysseus laughs.

I see you now, my father, standing away from the others, your face turned toward Troy. I blow and scream and whisper.

You smile at first, and turn to Calchas. "It's my daughter!"

The priest looks up from cleaning his bloody dagger. "What did you say?"

I whip cold fury between your ears. Your face goes pale, and you clap your hands to the sides of your head, but my voice is the sound of the wind. It is undeniable.

Do you still want forgiveness, father?

"Set sail!" you shout. "It's time to get out of this harbor!"

I am vast and undeniable. I will crush you all with my strength and whirl your boats to the bottom of the sea. I'll spin your corpses through the air and dash them against the cliffs.

But no, I am helpless again, always and ever a hostage to someone else's desires. With ease, Artemis imposes her will on my wild fury. I feel the tension of her hands drawing me back like a bowstring. With one strong, smooth motion, she aims me at your fleet. Fiercely, implacably, I blow you to Troy.

Rachel Swirsky is on Destination Two of her bad-weather tour of the United States – Bakersfield, California, where the summer days regularly heat up to one hundred and fifteen degrees of desert sun.

Before moving west, she lived in Iowa City, where ice storms and blizzards provided a chilly background to her MFA studies at the Iowa Writers Workshop. Who knows where her next destination will be? Lava fields? The center of a black hole? An Alaskan shanty? She will sit, wrapped in synthetics and faux fur, shivering while she bangs out stories that appear in Tor .com, *Subterranean Magazine*, *Weird Tales*, and other venues, including year's best collections from Strahan, Horton, and the VanderMeers. A slim volume of her fiction and poetry, *Through the Drowsy Dark*, was published by Aqueduct Press in May and her second collection, *How the World Became Quiet: Myths of the Past, Present, and Future*, is forthcoming from Subterranean Press.

SINNER, BAKER, FABULIST, PRIEST; RED MASK, BLACK MASK, GENTLEMAN, BEAST

Eugie Foster

FROM THE AUTHOR: Like every writer, I'm keenly interested to hear readers' responses to my work, and "Sinner, Baker, Fabulist, Priest; Red Mask, Black Mask, Gentleman, Beast" has garnered quite a bit of commentary online. I find it fascinating, the different impressions and messages that people have come away with from it, and I've been tempted more than once to chime in at various forums or blogs to say, "I meant to show *this* when I wrote this passage"; or, "It's not gratuitous! I was foreshadowing *that* when I included scene X"; or, "no, no, the point I meant to convey was *this*." But I've refrained because I've always held that once a story is published, it must resonate with, captivate, and provoke thought (or fail to) on its own merits, without me hovering over it like some anxious helicopter parent. Now that I've been invited to discuss "Sinner" on a public platform, I find myself trying to find and keep to that line between authorial autocracy and abstruse rambling. No illusions that I'll succeed, but just wanted to let y'all know where I was coming from.

Some of my all-time most formative books – the ones that I read when I was in middle school and high school that made a lasting impression on me – are dystopias: George Orwell's *1984* and *Animal Farm*, Ray Bradbury's *Fahrenheit*

451, Margaret Atwood's *The Handmaid's Tale*. But "Sinner" is the first dystopian story I've written, and it didn't come about from some poignant sociological or societal message that I wanted to convey, but rather from a wish to explore the more personal themes of identity and self. While I do regard the dystopian setting as integral, I consider the true theme to revolve around an examination of identity: the choices we make or don't make, how our actions exemplify who we are against a backdrop of cultural roles and societal expectations, and the daily decisions that comprise our fundamental sense of self, as well as the external and internal influences that affect these decisions.

The individual has always interested me far more as both a writer and a reader – and as a person, really – than large group movements or overarching societal manifestos. As such, I think "Sinner" resonates the most with readers who come to it from a more intimate, psychological perspective rather than a world-building or sociopolitical outlook. In many respects, I think calling my novelette a dystopia is like calling the *Diary of Anne Frank* a war story. Neither classification is inaccurate, but the stories are more cogent as illustrations of an individual's introspection and reflection and their inner journeys rather than the strife and dysfunction of a ravaged or broken society. Although, having said that, if folks consider "Sinner" a good dystopia, I'm happy with that too.

EACH MORNING IS a decision. Should I put on the brown mask or the blue? Should I be a tradesman or an assassin today?

Whatever the queen demands, of course, I am. But so often she ignores me, and I am left to figure out for myself who to be.

Dozens upon dozens of faces to choose from.

1. Marigold is for Murder

The yellow mask draws me, the one made from the pelt of a mute animal with neither fangs nor claws – better for the workers to collect its skin. It can only glare at its keepers through the wires of its cage, and when the knives cut and the harvesters rip away its skin, no one is troubled by its screams.

I tie the tawny ribbons under my chin. The mask is so light, almost weightless. But when I inhale, a charnel stench redolent of outhouses, opened intestines, and dried blood floods my nose.

My wife's mask is so pretty, pink flower lips and magenta eyelashes that flutter like feathers when she talks. But her body is pasty and soft, the flesh of her thighs mottled with black veins and puckered fat.

Still, I want her.

"Darling, I'm sorry," I say. "They didn't have the kind you wanted. I bought what they had. There's Citrus Nectar, Iolite Bronze, and Creamy Illusion."

"Might as well bring me pus in a jar," she snaps. "Did you look on all the shelves?"

"N-no. But the shop girl said they were out."

"The slut was probably hoarding it for herself. You know they all skim the stuff. Open the pots and scoop out a spoonful here, a dollop there. They use it themselves or stick it in tawdry urns to sell at those independent markets."

"The shop girl looked honest enough." Her mask had been carved onyx with a brush of gold at temples and chin. She had been slim, her flesh taut where my wife's sagged, her skin flawless and golden. And she had moved with a delicate grace, totally unlike the lumbering woman before me.

"Looked honest?" My wife's eyes roll in the sockets of her mask. "Like you could tell Queen's Honey from shit."

"My love, I know you're disappointed, but won't you try one of these other ones? For me?" I pull a jar of Iolite Bronze from the sack and unscrew the lid.

Although hostility bristles from her – her scent, her stance, the glare of fury from the eyeholes of her mask – I dip a finger into the solution. It's true it doesn't have the same consistency, and the perfume is more musk than honey, but the tingle is the same.

With my Iolite Bronzed finger, I reach for the cleft between her doughy thighs.

"Don't touch me with that filth," she snarls, backing away.

If only she weren't so stubborn. I grease all the fingers of my hand with Iolite Bronze. The musk scent has roused me faster than Queen's Honey.

"Get away!"

I grab for her sex, clutching at her with my slick fingers. I am so intent that I do not see the blade, glowing in her fist. As my fingertips slip into her, she plunges the weapon into my chest, and I go down.

Lying in a pool of my own blood, the scent of Iolite Bronze turning rank, I watch the blade rise and fall as she stabs me again and again.

Her mask is so pretty.

2. Blue Is for Maidens

The next morning, I linger over my selection, touching one beautiful face, then another. There is a vacant spot where the yellow mask used to be, but I have many more.

Finally, I choose one the color of sapphires. The brow is sewn from satin smooth as water. I twine the velveteen ribbons in my hair, and the tassels shush around my ears like whispered secrets.

I don't think I'll ever marry," I say. "Why should I?"

The girl beside me giggles, slender fingers over her mouth opening. Her mask is hewn from green wood hardened by three days of fire. Once carved and finished, the wood takes on a glasslike clarity, the tracery of sepia veins like a thick filigree of lace.

"Mark my words," she says. "All the flirting you do will catch up to you one day. A man will steal your heart, and you'll come running to me to help with the wedding."

I laugh. "Not likely. The guys we know only think about Queen's Honey and getting me alone. I'd just as soon marry a Mask Maker as any of those meatheads."

"Eww, that's twisted." My girlfriend squeals and points. "Look! It's the new shipment. Didn't I tell you the delivery trucks come round this street first?"

We stand with our masks pressed against the shop window, ogling the display of vials.

"*Exotica, White Wishes Under a Black Moon.*" My friend rattles off the names printed in elegant fonts in the space beneath each sampler. "*Metallic Mischief, Homage to a Manifesto* – what do you suppose that one's like? – *Terracotta Talisman*, and *Dulcet Poison*. I like the sound of that last one."

"You would."

"Oh, hush. Let's go try them."

"That store's awfully posh. You think they'll let us try without buying?"

"Of course they will. We're customers, aren't we? They won't throw us out."

"They might."

My concerns fail to dampen her enthusiasm, and I let her tow me through the crystalline doors.

The mingled scents in the shop wash over us. My friend abandons me, rushing to join the jostling horde clustered around the new arrivals. While the mixture of emotive fumes makes my friend giddy and excited, they overwhelm me. I lean against a counter and take shallow breaths.

"You look lost." The man's mask is matte pewter, the metal coating so thin I can see the strokes from the artisan's paintbrush. A flame design swirls across both cheeks in variegated shades of purple.

"I'm just waiting for my friend." I gesture in the direction of the mob. There's a glint of translucent green, all I can see of her.

"You're not interested in trying this new batch?"

"Not really. I prefer the traditional distillations. I guess that makes me old-fashioned."

The man leans to conspiratorial closeness. "But you purchased those three new ones yesterday. I tried to warn you about the Iolite Bronze. It's not at all a proper substitute for Queen's Honey."

Memories of lust and violence fill me, musk and arousal, pain and blood. But they are wrong. I am someone else today. I shake my head.

"I don't know what you're talking about." I search for a hint of green glass or sepia lace. Where is she? "I'd never let someone use Iolite Bronze on me."

"Didn't you say it was a gift when I sold it to you?"

"What?"

"I was the shop girl in the onyx mask."

I am shocked beyond words, beyond reaction. It is the biggest taboo in our society, so profane and obscene that it is not even in our law books. We do not discuss the events and encounters of our other masks. It is not done. What if people started blaming one face for what another did, merely because the same citizen wore both?

The moment of speechless paralysis ends, and I run. I fly through the glittering doors, not caring that I've left my best friend behind, and run, run, run until I am back to the dormitory on Center at Corridor. I huddle in the lift, and it whisks me to my quarters. On my bed, I sob, the tears wetting the inside of my mask. A part of me worries that I will stain the satin, but it is a distant part.

When the tears run out, I am done with the day, done with this mask. But the unmasking time is still far off. If I'd only worn the tan mask today, with the bronze veneer and dripping beadwork, I wouldn't have fled from the pewter-masked deviant. I'd have punched him in the golden flesh of his gut or hauled him to the queen's gendarmes for a reckoning.

Then I realize what I'm thinking, what I'm wanting – another mask, but not during the morning selection, not during the unmasking – while I'm still wearing today's.

And I'm afraid.

3. Black Is for Sex

In the morning, as I stand barefaced among my masks, looking anywhere but at the tan one, I receive the queen's summons. It is delivered, as always, by a gendarme masked in thinly hammered silver. He rings my bell, waiting for me to acknowledge him over the intercom.

The gendarmes are the only citizens about during the early morning when the rest of us are selecting our daily masks, just as they are the only ones who patrol the thoroughfares after the unmasking hour, collecting retired masks and distributing new ones.

"Good morning, gendarme," I say.

"Good morning, citizen. You are called upon today to carry out your civic duty."

"I am pleased to oblige." A square of paper slips through my delivery slot and into my summons tray, bringing with it an elusive sweetness. The queen's writs are always scented like the honey named after her, both more insistent and more subtle than the stuff which circulates in the marketplaces.

Among my arrayed masks, raised above the others, is the sable mask – hammered steel painted with liquid ebony. It is the consort mask, worn only to honor the queen's summons. The paint is sheer, and glimmers of silver flicker through the color. The eyes are outlined in opaque kohl, a masked mask.

I lock the delicate chains with their delicate clasps around my head. For a moment, I am disoriented by the lenses over the eyes. It takes longer for me to adjust to the warp in my vision than to the feel and heft of the mask. But not much longer.

The music trills liquid and rich around us, and I concentrate on the steps. In her mask-like-stars, the queen swirls and glides across the ballroom in my arms. Caught in her beauty and my exertions, I have missed her words.

"I beg your pardon, my queen. What did you say?"

Her mask tilts up, and the piquant flavor of her amusement fills my senses. "I asked if you were enjoying the dance, whether you liked the refreshment."

"I have not sampled the buffet, but it looks lavish. As to the dance, I am worried that my clumsiness might offend you or that I might misstep."

"I've never danced with you before? That would explain your stiffness."

"I have not had the pleasure. I'm sorry."

"Don't be. It was only a whimsy. I don't dance with many. You probably won't dance with me again." The queen gestures, and the music stops. She leads me to her couch – crimson sheets and alabaster cushions. I am more familiar with this type of dance, but she isn't ready for me yet. Her scent, though heady, tells me it is not time to mate, although it will be soon.

It confuses me, this waiting. Why am I here, if not to do my duty?

She reclines on her couch but not in the position of copulation.

"Talk to me," she says.

"What would you like to speak on, my queen?"

"Do you have a favorite mask?"

It is an odd question, treading the boundary of indecency.

"No, my queen. They are all precious to me."

"Don't you wish you could discard some masks, perhaps the ones that you suffer in, and just wear the ones that are pleasurable?"

Was she testing me? "They are all precious to me," I say again. "Each in its wonderful variety. I would never presume to contravene the law."

"Not even to bend it a little? There are some citizens who wear just a few masks and don others only as often as they must in order to stay out of the purview of the gendarmes."

"But that's criminal."

"Technically, it's legal, although it defies the heart of the code. Generally, the number of their select rotation is large enough that no single mask becomes dominant. Do you find the prospect appealing?"

Dominant mask? What would be the purpose in limiting one's mask selection? Her words make no sense.

"No."

My answer pleases her. Her scent rises and with it, my arousal, and I cannot think clearly anymore. The queen is the font of desire and satisfaction – the perfume of true Queen's Honey between her legs, her need, mine – nothing exists but the urgency of mating. It eclipses mere copulation as the sun outshines the stars. I submerge in a tide of desire and completion and the rise of desire again, over and over, until the unmasking hour.

In the morning, barefaced and aching, I report to the Mask Makers galley. I avoid looking at their ugly, soft countenances. It's partly instinctive discomfort at being seen without a mask, but also, Mask Makers have always made me uneasy. I feel sorry for them, their faces so colorless and insipid. It's an irony that they wear such bland features and plain colors, yet they make such marvelous faces for us, each one unique in its brilliance. I pity them, and I'm glad I was not born to their caste.

I hand over my summons writ and accept my newest mask, my favor from the queen. It is glossy saffron with pointed wires to fasten it. It has no mouth opening, but it does not seem lacking for that. Like every face they craft, it is a feat of artistry.

4. Orange Is for Agony

I press the saffron mask to my face and wrap the barbed laces around my head. A fleeting touch, my fingertips on the painted metal tell me of thick runnels that dent the surface. Their unevenness makes the fit uncomfortable. For a moment.

Wire mesh presses above and below. If I lie down, I can stretch my neck, a little. But then the mesh cuts into my feet, my forearms, my chest. Standing, sitting, a few back-and-forth steps. But pacing only reminds me how small my cell is. And they do not like for us to pace. Exercise thins the fat between muscle and skin, making the harvest more difficult.

My neighbor wears a ginger mask dotted with cobalt sequins. He urinates, and it splashes through the mesh on me. I hiss my rage, crowded by the scent of his body, and return the favor.

I'm glad when the workers come for him and watch as they trap him in their loops. He tries to fight, but he has nothing sharp or hard to wield. Their wicked tools, edged with blue light, open him from neck to groin. He barely has time to bleed before they carve perpendicular incisions, flaps to better flay him in a single piece.

His eyes bulge as they tear away his skin, all the movement he is capable of. He's silent, for there is no mouth on his mask; he is as mute as I.

When they're done, they leave him writhing in the liquids of his body on the wire mesh floor. They take the heavy cloak of his skin with them.

Then it's my turn. The ginger planes of my neighbor's mask swivel to me, so he can watch.

There's no place to run in my tiny cell, and their loops pinion me. When they begin to cut away my skin, it is the most terrible pain I have ever known.

Their masks are lemon, daffodil, and butterscotch. Pretty and yellow, like sunshine.

5. Jasper Is for Jilting

The next morning, the choice is harder than usual. I flinch away from the saffron mask and stare for a long while at the tan one. But it feels inappropriate to select it.

Like a whiff of passing corruption, the notion of going without a mask today, simply staying in my quarters and not choosing a face, flits through my thoughts. It is too scandalous to contemplate; I feel guilty to have even considered it.

Without looking, I reach among the rows of empty faces and snatch the first one my hand falls upon.

It is brackish green, the color of stagnant water in a pool that never sees the sun. The chin and nose are gilded in dark velvet, and the lips shine, liquid silver hand-painted on silk. I tighten the woven cords around my head.

I hover beneath the window of my lover, she of the cerulean mask detailed in voile. She reclines on her balcony, and a song of courtship thrums from her dainty mouth. I inhale the delicate body scents her servant wafts out with a fan: enticement and temptation, innocence and promise.

"Do you love me?" my sweetheart calls.

"With all my soul. You are my everything."

"I don't believe you," she laughs. "How are you different from all the other men, just waiting for a chance to slather me with Queen's Honey?"

"How can you say that? I've asked you to marry me."

"What does that prove? Any meathead with a tongue can do that. And anyway, I don't want to marry at all. Marriage is a sorry state that leads to fighting and grief."

I pantomime exaggerated dismay for her benefit. "What can I do to convince you of my sincerity? Ask me for anything, and I'll give it to you."

"Do you have a jar of Queen's Honey?"

I hesitate. If I answer truthfully, she might accuse me again of being a libertine. But it is also my courting gift. She will feel slighted if I don't have anything to offer her.

I sigh and choose the better of my options. "A humble present to honor your loveliness."

"Good."

When I'm not immediately rebuffed, I dare to hope.

"I'm sending my girl down. Give the Queen's Honey to her, and we'll all play a game. She'll seal the jar so the contents may not be used without breaking it, and puncture its lid, freeing the scent. If you can spend the afternoon with me and my girl in my enclosed boudoir and keep from breaking the jar open, I'll believe that you love me and not simply the pleasures of copulation. But if you lose control and *do* break the jar, you can slake yourself on her, but you'll never get a word or whiff from me again."

"What, pray, do I get if I can restrain myself?"

Her laughter is like a teasing wind. "If you can check your desires until evening, I'll send her away and break the jar myself."

I'm both excited and dismayed by the prospect of her "game." My lover will ensure that our time is not spent on chaste recreations or thoughtful conversation. She will pose herself and her servant girl in all manner of ways suggestive of copulation. And she is probably already drenched in one of the trendy distillations – Passion Without Doubt or Exotica or Citrus Nectar – to madden me further. Still, the reward will be sweet. And at the very least (my love did not altogether peg me wrongly), I'll get to do the servant girl.

My prospective consolation prize opens the door. Her mask is a sage green that suggests transparency, the eyes rimmed in toffee lace. She snatches the Queen's Honey from me, but there the anticipated script ends. She twists off the lid and scoops the unguent out. Without embarrassment or coyness, she rubs it on herself, between her thighs. As I stare dumbfounded, she smears a glistening coating on me. Instantly, I'm aroused and eager.

"Want me?" she whispers.

"Yes." Flesh on flesh, the Queen's Honey brooks no denial.

"Then catch me." She sprints away.

I waver for only a breath. Above, my sweetheart calls down plaintively, wondering at our delay. But desire roars through me, and all I care about is the servant girl.

I chase her through the dormitory block as she weaves around crowds and over obstacles – sculptures, shops, new constructions. Sometimes men turn, catching the fleeting perfume of Queen's Honey mingled with her sex as she darts by.

I am enthralled. She fills every breath I take. I run until I'm a creature of fire – blazing lungs and burning limbs. But it is spice to my eagerness. I will catch her, and then we will copulate.

She leads me past the market district, past shop windows filled with citizens making purchases, and into the rural outskirts where the machines harvest our food and workers gather esoteric materials for the Mask Makers guild.

In a shaded copse of green wood trees, she drops to her knees. I'm upon her, not even waiting for her to assume the proper position. She opens to me, and I rush to join our bodies.

It is glorious, of course, the release all the more satisfying for the chase. But even as I spend myself, I notice something wrong. The girl is not making the right movements, and her scent, while intoxicating, is strange. Beneath the Queen's Honey she is impatient when she should be impassioned. As soon as I'm finished, she pulls away, and for the first time after a copulation, I'm not happy and languid, awash in the endorphins of sex. I feel awkward.

Before I can say anything, the girl tears off her mask. The horror of her unmasking paralyzes me; I'm unprepared for her next action. She lunges, ripping off the bindings of my mask, and yanks it free.

I am barefaced.

It's not the unmasking hour, not the time for emptiness and slumber. Without my mask, I don't know how to act or feel, or what to say. I don't even know if I *can* speak, for I never have without a mask. I'm lost, no one. The nucleus of my personality and intelligence is empty; the girl has stolen it.

6. White Is for Obedience

While I kneel, stupefied, the girl discards my mask, letting it fall among the long grasses where we loved. I don't even have the presence of will to retrieve it. She examines the inside of her mask. With infinite care, she peels a sheer membrane away. It is like a veil of gauze or chiffon, but this veil has a shape. There are nose, cheekbones, and chin.

It is a mask, but a mask unlike any I've seen. The fabric is unornamented and diaphanous white, like thin fog or still water, all but colorless. It doesn't conceal what it covers, only overlays it.

She takes this ghost of a mask and drapes it over my face. Without cord or chain, it fastens itself, clinging to my head. It is such relief to have my nakedness covered, I'm grateful when I should be outraged.

I wait for the mask to tell me who I am and what to do.

And I wait.

"There's not much oversoul there," the girl says. Without a mask, her features are too animated, obscenely so. I avert my gaze, wondering if the ghost mask exposes my expressions in such an indecent fashion.

"It's only a scaffold to help you get past the schizo-panic," she continues. "It doesn't have any personas or relationship scenarios to instill, and absolutely no emotives."

I don't like the ghost mask's vacancy. But at least I can think now, and it occurs to me to scramble for my own mask.

"Stop," she says.

I cannot move. My fingertips brush the darker green and glint of silver lying in the grass, but I can't pick it up.

"I'm afraid the scaffold does have an obedience imprint. I am sorry about that, but it's necessary. You wouldn't be able to access the oversoul in your mask anyway. The scaffold creates a barrier that mask imprints can't penetrate, and you won't be able to take the scaffold off. Go ahead, I know you want to. Try to remove it."

I grope my face, my head looking for something to undo. There's nothing to unknot, release, or unbuckle. I find the edge where the ghost mask, the scaffold, gives way to skin, but it's adhered to me. The memory from yesterday – the saffron mask, being skinned alive – is enough to deter me from anything drastic.

"What did you do to me?" I ask. "And why?"

"Good, you're questioning. I knew you'd acclimate quickly." A scent penetrates my distress. She is pleased. Except the tang isn't right. It's not feminine but not masculine either. She has no mask to tell me whether she's male or female. Should I continue thinking of her as a girl? And for that matter, the scaffold hasn't provided me with a gender. Am I a man or a woman, or am I neuter, or perhaps some sort of androgyne?

I feel lightheaded and ill. "If this is some perverted game," I say, "I'm not amused. I'll report this to the gendarmes. They'll confiscate all your masks for this crime, and—" I trail off. Her naked face is testimony of her indifference to the severest penalty of our society.

"Why are you doing this to me?" I whimper.

"Did you ever wonder who you are beneath your masks?" she says. "When you say 'me,' who is that?"

Hearing her voice the question that has lately made my mornings so troubling and the hours after unmasking so long is a kind of deliverance. I'm not the only citizen to have these thoughts; I'm not alone in my distress. But the guilt remains, along with an added unease. Is exposing my crime what this is about? Am I to be penalized?

"Don't be afraid," she says, "I'm not going to turn you over to the gendarmes or anything like that."

My breathing quickens. "Are you hearing my thoughts?"

"No, only watching your face."

"My face?"

"It conveys emotions. It's like smelling another's confusion or knowing that someone's angry by the tightness of their shoulders, only with facial musculature. Before long, you'll read it as instinctively as you do scents and stances."

"You say that as though you expect me to be pleased."

Her mouth curves and parts, revealing the whiteness of her teeth. Being witness to such an intimate view is both repulsive and fascinating.

"I know you don't think so now," she says, "but I've given you a gift, one very few people receive." She stands. "Walk with me."

I don't want to go anywhere with her, but the scaffold compels me to obey. We stroll deeper into the wilderness, leaving my mask in the grass. It is an uncomfortable sensation, having my will at odds with my body.

"I've been watching you for a while to make sure you were right," she says.

"Watching me?" Fragments of confusion knit into understanding. "You're the shop girl who sold me the Iolite Bronze and the deviant man with the pewter mask."

"And the customer at the bakery who bought a dozen egg tarts from you before that."

"The woman with the pink mask who asked for the recipe?"

"Yes. And before, when you wore your roan and iron mask, I was in the audience when you presented your new poem. And the day before that, I picked indigo with you for the Mask Makers."

We emerge into a clearing. A broken-down hut lists, obscured by over-grown foliage. Her sage and toffee mask still dangles from her fingertips. She passes its brim over the doorknob, and the door swings open.

"I'm glad to finally meet you," she says. "You can call me Pena."

The interior is dim, lit by stray sunbeams poking through holes in the ramshackle walls.

"Pena?" The word is meaningless. "Why?"

"It's my name, a word that means me, regardless of what mask I'm wearing or not wearing."

I snort. "Why stop at each citizen having their own name? Why not each tile or brick the builders use or every tree or blade of grass?"

"Every street has a name," Pena says. "And every shop."

"So we can tell one from the other. Otherwise, we couldn't say where a place was, or differentiate between one food market and another."

"Exactly." She runs her fingers over a floorboard, and I hear a click. In the far corner by the fireplace, flagstones part to expose steps.

"What's down there?" I ask.

"Answers. Come."

We descend, and the flagstones rumble shut overhead. Ambient light washes over us – dim and red, casting bloody shadows.

We're in a tunnel with rough, stone walls. The light extends ten paces before us; beyond is darkness. Pena strides toward this border, and I am obliged to accompany her. When we are within a pace of light's end, more red comes on to reveal another span of corridor. When we are within this new radius, the light behind us goes out.

And so we walk.

"Why do citizens need names?" I ask. "We change masks every day, unlike shops and streets which stay the same. What if I discover that my physician is the same citizen as my murderer? Or a citizen in one mask is my lover and in another, my enemy? If I call that citizen by a single word, it's like treating all their mask identities as the same person."

"That's the point," she says. "It lets us be who we truly are, underneath our masks."

I shake my head. "Without the masks, we're not anything."

"There was a time before the masks."

"And we were empty, primitive creatures, without will or purpose, until the First Queen created the First Mask to wear and carved faces for the citizens and—"

"And She designated the Guild of Mask Makers and tasked them with their sacred duty so that everyone would be imbued with souls, blah blah blah. I know the lies."

Her heresy is both disturbing and intriguing. "What do you believe, then?"

"That's what I'm going to show you."

"Why me?"

"There's a group of us named. We seek out others who harbor the same doubts and resentments we do, and we liberate them."

"I don't want to be liberated."

"Don't you? Haven't you wanted to be free of the daily selection routine? Or chafed against the mask, wishing the hour of unmasking came sooner? Don't you hover in indecision some mornings, not because the choosing is so hard, but because none of them appeal? Don't you wonder who you could be if you were left to decide for yourself?"

I am saved from having to answer by the appearance of something new when the next lights activate: a door.

7. Red Is for Revelation

"Where are we?"

"Beneath the palace at the Mask Makers guild."

She passes her mask over the door. Like the hut's, it opens.

I balk. "No. Absolutely not. It's prohibited."

She studies me. "I can make you, but I won't. It's your decision."

I open my mouth to repeat myself.

"But first, hear me out."

I exhale. "If I must. But it won't change my mind."

"You know I've been keeping by you as you've switched masks. I was also with you when you wore the saffron mask at the leather harvesters."

The memory is still raw. "So?"

"Do you know who I was?"

"One of the skinners, I presume."

"I was your neighbor in the adjoining cage."

Despite everything, I'm dismayed. "Didn't you know what they were going to do to you, to us?"

"I knew."

"And still you let them, willingly even. *Why*, in the name of the First Queen?"

"Because, to be with you, I could either hurt you or be hurt, and I chose not to hurt you."

"Am I someone to you? Have we been lovers or spouses or friends?"

"Not that I know of."

"Then why?"

"Because I know who I am, and my actions are a reflection of me. I don't skin people alive."

Her last sentence carries a conviction, a certainty that makes me envious.

"What would you do if you had to choose," she says, "if your decisions extended beyond what mask to wear any given day? Would you willingly inflict such suffering upon another?"

"I would . . . I-I don't know."

"Do you want to know?"

And I find I do.

The door opens upon a storage room jammed with row upon row of shelves. Bolts of multihued fabric, rolls of ribbon and lace, and jars of washes, dyes, and lacquers are piled together without any semblance of order. More rolls of textiles spill out of cubby holes and closets lining the room.

"This is their overflow storage, where they keep their excess," Pena says. "We raid it for our mask-making supplies. Named artisans can create near-perfect replicas of guild masks, but without the oversouls, of course."

"With added features that can unlock doors."

She displays her teeth again. Some part of me has learned to equate that facial configuration with positive emotion, even before I breathe the perfume of her approval.

"You noticed. Very good."

"How do they do it?"

She leads me through the jumble. "It's complicated to explain. All of our mask functions, including the scaffold you're wearing, are based on the Mask Makers' constructs. There's bits and pieces appliquéd, sewn, glued, or imbedded in all masks which stimulate thoughts, trigger emotions, assign personality traits, and so on. Named artisans have taken apart and put back together these pieces, realigning and modifying them until they've gained an understanding of their workings. In the process, they've discovered that the components can do much more than imprint oversouls, like lock and unlock doors. And there's still so much we haven't figured out yet."

The supply room exits upon a dark corridor that illuminates red at our approach. But unlike the one from the hut, the circle of light shows a cluster of turnings that fork in different directions.

"You make it sound like you named have been at this for a while," I say.

"We have." She sets off down one of the twisting tunnels. "Sometimes the gendarmes get wind of our activities, so we work exclusively in pairs – one mentor, one recruit. That way, the most named any of us knows is two, your mentor when you're recruited, and your recruit once you're ready to bring someone in. We disseminate information and requests through codes and drop-off points. It's slow but safer."

I've lost track of the bends and turns we've taken. "You must recruit pretty selectively, if each mentor can only take one."

"Mentors can take another recruit if theirs is apprehended by the gendarmes." The lighting casts deep shadows over the planes of her face, and for a moment, it seems that she's wearing a crimson mask. She brushes her fingers over her eyes, and they come away wet.

"What happens when the gendarmes catch you?"

"They kill us."

I shrug. "That's all? So you lose the day. In the morning—"

"No. They *kill* us. It's not like the petty murders citizens inflict upon each other. There's no waking up from the death the gendarmes deliver."

I stumble, shocked. "That's – that's *monstrous*. How is that possible? How can our laws permit it?"

"You said it yourself; without the masks, we're nothing. When the gendarmes execute one of us, they reassign all of that named's personas to the population at large. The oversouls continue, and there is no disruption among the citizenry. I think the gendarmes grieve more when they have to destroy a mask that has been 'murdered' than when they kill one of us."

Pena rounds a corner, and there is a wall. It's creamy smooth, as though stone workers spent hours painstakingly sanding it to perfect flatness.

"Did you make a wrong turn?" I ask.

"Afraid of getting lost?" Her tone is teasing. "Don't worry. Even if I had made a wrong turn, my mask contains the labyrinth's secrets. But I didn't."

I half expect her to wave the mask at the wall and a door to miraculously appear. She doesn't. Instead, Pena lifts a hand to her mouth and tears at it with her teeth. Dark blood oozes, and she smears this droplet on the wall.

Soundlessly, the wall glides up and disappears into the ceiling. White, not red, light comes on, blinding after the dimness.

Pena tugs me forward while I'm still blinking. I squint, eyes tearing and blurry, at the small room we have entered. The walls are polished metal, and they encircle us, curving outward so it feels like we're inside a cylinder. A closed one. While my eyes adjust, the door shuts itself.

In the room's center is an ornate chair of silver and gold. Resting upon its seat is a mask.

I recognize it, for it is the stuff of legend. Carved from a single diamond with a million-million facets, each representing a mask-to-be, the First Queen's Mask, the one She created with her own hands to bring enlightenment to us all.

8. Diamonds Are for Death

Pena touches my face, and the scaffold slips away. The anxiety of being barefaced is forgotten in the wonder of the First Mask.

"The truth, your answers, they're all in the oversoul of that mask," she says. "All you have to do is put it on."

"What if I don't?"

"Then we go back, and tomorrow morning you choose a mask to wear, like every other morning, and you never see me again."

"I might turn you over to the gendarmes."

Her lips part and flash teeth. "What will you tell them? That a citizen kidnapped you and filled your head with truth? How will you find me? And how do you know the gendarmes won't kill you simply for knowing this much?"

She's right, of course. "But I don't have to put on the First Mask?"

"What you do is up to you. Now and forever."

I hesitate for a heartbeat before striding to the chair and seizing the First Mask. It's so light. I'd expected it to be heavier. Holding it aloft, I realize the eyeholes are encased in nearly transparent lenses like my consort mask, except diamond instead of glass.

"You might want to sit before you put it on," Pena says. "I didn't and ended flat on my back."

I perch on the gold and silver chair, and set the mask over my face. There are segmented strands of diamond to wrap around my head that fasten with glittering diamond locks. The lenses warp my vision, disorienting me. But only for a moment.

Crowing exultation.

The war is finished! My last rival and her progeny are dead, and I reign in exclusive sovereignty.

My children, I am so proud of you. This is the dawn of a new age, a glorious and splendid age.

My scientists have conquered our only remaining enemy: time. They have found the key to unlocking the shackles of age and injury, and conquered the last disease. I am no longer chained by the dictates of perpetual reproduction. The years of my empire will be like a magnificent river, rippling past eon after eon, powerful and endless.

I do worry, however, that my soldiers will decline. They are the simplest of my children and only understand rigid procedures and physical contests. Perhaps I should manufacture a new corps of soldiers, an elite one. They can vie with each other in mock battles for the honor of being counted among my gendarmes.

The river of years is murky and deep, and I cannot see where it will take us.

I am stymied at an unanticipated quarter: my consorts. The noblest of my children, nearly my equals – clever and curious, independent and imaginative – I should have known they would feel neglected and adrift when I ceased summoning them to mate. They are creatures of great passion, as I am, and now they squabble, forming factions and carrying out vendettas.

I have started opening my body to them again, but I will ask the scientists to develop a synthetic pheromone so they may copulate amongst themselves.

I am despair.

A citizen killed another today, beyond what my scientists were able to restore. I must accept the truth; we are an aggressive people, not destined for peace, and all I have tried to build is in ruins.

If only there was a way for my consorts to expend their passions harmlessly.

I must confer with my scientists.

At last! I have devised an end to the chaos which blights my citizenry.

My scientists have developed a means of imprinting memories and eliciting emotions that may be interchanged, swapped out, and added upon with seemingly infinite variety. My consorts may oppose each other and mate with promiscuity, all without garnering rivals or blood feuds.

I have set my scientists to generate these oversoul masks in copious quantity and in wondrous variety.

This must work.

All is well. The activities of my children are once more in accord with my desiring, and eternity's river holds no more uncertainties.

There was a minor dilemma, but I have solved even that. It seems that I am not immune to the effect of the masks. I thought my royal will would safeguard my identity, but it is becoming a strain, sorting reality from fabrication.

I have had an oversoul commissioned. It will be a lasting record of all the tribulations I have confronted and my efforts to remedy them. This mask shall be sealed beneath my palace in a chamber secured by steel, and my blood shall be the only key that unlocks it.

I take off the mask of diamonds. Pena watches me, her lips parted.

I tumble out of the chair and fall to my knees. "I am your servant, First Queen."

Pena's eyes widen, and she laughs. "Oh, no, no." She is at my side and hauls me up. "I'm not the First Queen."

"But your blood opened the door."

"Don't you get it? We're all of her blood, each of us descended from the First Queen. Some joke on her, huh?"

I stay silent.

"Come," she says. "We need to get back before the hour of unmasking. If we're seen on the streets after, the gendarmes will take us."

I straggle after her, lost in my thoughts. I don't try to keep track of the red-lit corridors and notice only when we are among the fabrics and dyes of the storage room.

"Hsst." Pena gestures.

"What is it?"

Without warning, she shoves me, and I tumble into a closeted hole. Bolts of velvet and felt topple upon me. She flings an oversized bottle of jasmine oil after, engulfing me in cloying sweetness.

Then there is confusion. The red light extinguishes, and white beams flash in the darkness. They catch and glint off white metal – glittering eyes, gleaming brows – the silver masks of the gendarmes.

Hidden in my cubby, my scent as obscured as my body, they do not detect me. They converge on a single spot, Pena, huddled between shelves.

"By order of the queen, you are hereby accused and convicted of treason," one gendarme says.

I cannot smell anything over the sickening jasmine, but I can see the terror on her face. She glances at me, and there is a beseeching in her eyes, and a question, but she looks away before I can understand it.

"The penalty for treason is death, citizen," a gendarme, perhaps the same one, says. "Do you wish to repent? Identify your co-conspirators, and we will allow you to return to the way of the mask."

Pena lifts her head. "Never."

They don't ask again. They activate their loops, and I'm reminded of the day of the saffron mask. I'm ashamed of the gladness I felt then.

They don't skin her, but this is as gruesome, if swifter. A gendarme kneels over her as she is pinioned on her back by bands of blue. Bracing himself, he staves in her face with his fist. I want to look away. It is an obscene violation, a perverse defilement to damage a citizen *there* – to do any violence which might cause harm to a mask. But Pena isn't wearing a mask, and I don't look away.

He strikes again and again until there is nothing left of the front of her head but a wreckage of bone and pulped wetness.

9. The Last Mask

The gendarmes are as efficient in disposing of Pena's body as they were in dispatching her. When they have gone, the red light comes on, and I dare to creep out. As I untangle myself from a length of burgundy velvet, my hand falls upon an unmistakable shape – Pena's green and toffee mask. The sight of it, so soon after the atrocity of her execution, unhinges me. I start crying and I cannot stop. But it doesn't matter, because her mask will hide my tears.

Somehow, I make it to Center at Corridor and the familiar confines of my quarters. Safe.

But I am *not* safe. I cannot forget the First Queen's memories, which the gendarmes would surely kill me for having, and more, I cannot erase the beseeching question in Pena's eyes.

I tear off her mask. It's not the unmasking hour, but I don't care. I'm weary of masks, even a blameless one without an oversoul. Pena's death burdens me with shame and guilt – like being flayed again, but with the pain inside.

I am surrounded by masks. Each is a player in some fabricated theater – artist, victim, rake, entrepreneur, lover, spouse, friend. None of them is real, but I can put them on and escape these feelings.

But I won't.

One after the other, I destroy my masks. The ones that shatter are the easiest. I hurl them at the floor and shards spill across the tile. The ones that burn, I commit to fire. But the metal ones I must work at, smashing one upon another until they are twisted out of all recognition.

I save the sable mask for last out of a sense of propriety. Although it is metal, it is oddly malleable, and it crumbles between my hands. The lenses fall out of the eyeholes and tumble among the broken bits of ceramic and glass on my floor.

I stand amidst the debris that was my life and don the only mask I spared, Pena's green and toffee one.

My lover glances at me in her cerulean-with-voile mask and lets me in. She thinks I am her servant girl.

"Where did you go?" she demands. "Do you know how long I've been waiting for you? And where is my suitor?"

Her quarters are much like mine, much like every citizen's. There is a mask room, a kitchen, and a bedchamber. I brush past her and she follows, continuing to scold as we enter her kitchen. I find what I need in one of the drawers: a tenderizer mallet, heavy and solid. Even when I turn with it upraised, she doesn't relent.

"Are you ignoring me, you slut?" she shouts. "How dare you!"

Only when I yank off her mask does she become afraid, and by then, it's too late.

I smash the mallet into her face. She stumbles, and I ride her as she goes down, hammering the metal tool into her face over and over. Bones and flesh mash together into pulp, and still I persist. I must be thorough.

Pena did not have time to teach me the secrets of her league of named. But through her, I have learned enough. I have seen how the gendarmes kill. I do not have their loops or their strength, but I know how to murder so that my victims will not wake.

Pena also taught me to know who I am.

I am chaos in this ordered society, the flaw in a carefully wrought plan. I am turbulence in the queen's eternal river.

Eugie Foster calls home a mildly haunted, fey-infested house in metro Atlanta that she shares with her husband, Matthew. After receiving her master's degree in psychology, she retired from academia to pen flights of fancy. She also edits legislation for the Georgia General Assembly, which from time to time she suspects is another venture into flights of fancy.

In addition to receiving the Nebula Award for Best Novelette, she was named the 2009 Author of the Year by Bards and Sages. Her fiction has also received the 2002 Phobos Award; been translated into seven languages; and been a finalist for the Hugo, Black Quill, Bram Stoker, and BSFA Awards. Her publication credits number over one hundred and include stories in *Realms of Fantasy, Interzone, Cricket, Orson Scott Card's InterGalactic Medicine Show,* and *Fantasy Magazine;* podcasts *Escape Pod, Pseudopod,* and *PodCastle;* and anthologies *Best New Fantasy* and *Best New Romantic Fantasy 2.* Her short story collection, *Returning My Sister's Face: And Other Far Eastern Tales of Whimsy and Malice,* is available from Norilana Books. Visit her online at EugieFoster.com.

SFWA
DAMON
KNIGHT
GRAND
MASTER

SFWA DAMON KNIGHT GRAND MASTER: JOE HALDEMAN

Mark Kreighbaum

The author of twenty novels and five short story collections, Joe Haldeman's career spans over three and a half decades. His most famous novel, *The Forever War*, won both the Nebula and Hugo awards for best science fiction novel in 1975, and inspired two follow-up novels, *Forever Peace* (1998) and *Forever Free* (2000). In total, his writings have won him five Nebulas, five Hugos, three Rhyslings, and a host of other awards as well as numerous nominations. His latest book, *Starbound*, was published by Ace this January. He teaches writing as an adjunct professor at the Massachusetts Institute of Technology.

In one sense, summing up the career of Joe Haldeman to this point is as simple as that paragraph. He has been producing novels, short stories, and poems for over thirty-five years. Many of those works have won awards. He is a teacher.

But to say something deeper about his work is to grapple immediately with his biography. A veteran of the Vietnam War, his earliest works are informed by his experiences and memories as a demolition engineer in that conflict. Much of his best work draws deeply from the insights he learned there, and the wounds he suffered. Many of his stories are overtly about trauma, wounds, and death. But Haldeman's true concern is not merely a recitation of pain and tragedy, but transcendence over insults to the flesh and spirit.

Nowhere is that more clear than when Haldeman writes about cybernetics. Science fiction has a tradition of imagining the human body transformed by technology. Most stories on the subject treat the topic as a kind of evolution that leads to either utopia or dystopia. Haldeman is nearly unique in exploring not merely the technical aspects of prosthetics and cybernetic enhancements, but the psychological dimensions of what can be described as disfigurement by voluntary mutilation. In some of his stories, this dimension leads to alienation and madness. But he has also shown how they can be tools for overcoming various other forms of deficiency, especially self-doubt and loneliness. For a writer who is so adept at writing about cynicism and cruelty, it is moments of hope and connection that suffuse his most memorable tales.

Joe Haldeman is often described as a "hard s.f." writer, that is, someone who depends on a scientifically plausible idea to drive the plot of a book. Certainly, with his astronomy degree and background in engineering, he has the capability of delivering a rigorously extrapolated tale and has done so many times. In a recent novel, *The Accidental Time Machine*, Haldeman wove in a good deal of quantum physics and string theory, for example. So, the label is accurate, although its application to writers of a certain kind of genre fiction can mislead readers into thinking that to such writers, ideas are paramount and characters are only vectors for theories. Certainly, there are a few hard s.f. writers who fit such a stereotype. But the majority are far more interested in how the future will affect human beings. The best of them, like Joe Haldeman, are able to bring true passion and empathy to these stories, so that the clever concept, or ingenious device, become a means for understanding ourselves and others. And a Grand Master is SFWA's recognition of a writer who is the best of the best.

Beyond his many accomplishments as an author, Joe Haldeman has been a mentor and icon for other SFWAns and to writers in general. He is an avid cyclist, amateur astronomer, painter, musician, and enthusiastic cook. With his wife, Gay, who is his business partner and sometimes collaborator, he makes his home in Florida.

—Mark Kreighbaum

APPRECIATION

The following is a transcript of the speech Connie Willis delivered at the Nebula Awards Banquet, introducing Joe Haldeman.

Tonight it's my really exciting duty to present the Grand Master of Science Fiction Nebula Award to Joe Haldeman.

It's obvious why Joe was chosen for this honor. SFWA's Board of Directors and president and past presidents had more than ample reasons for honoring him.

I mean, he's won all sorts of awards – Hugos, Nebulas, the World Fantasy Award, the James Tiptree Award, the Ditmar and the Rhysling and dozens of others, and his novel *Forever Peace* was the first book to win the Triple Crown – the Nebula, the Hugo, and the Campbell.

His writing has covered the entire gamut of science fiction, from galactic war to time travel to telepathy, from space colonies to immortality to Ernest Hemingway.

His books and short stories – *Mindbridge*, "None So Blind," *All My Sins Remembered*, "Tricentennial," *The Accidental Time Machine*, "Graves," the WORLDS books, "The Hemingway Hoax," *Marsbound* – have been both critically acclaimed and bestsellers.

And he hasn't just written books. He's done all sorts of other things: screenplays and Star Trek novels and poetry and stage plays and graphic novels. He's gotten an MFA in creative writing, been an adjunct professor at MIT, fought in Vietnam, served as president of SFWA, and earned a Purple Heart (in Vietnam, not SFWA, although . . .)

He paints, cooks, writes poems, is an amateur astronomer, and plays the guitar. And poker.

SFWA could have decided to honor him for any – or all – of those reasons. Or maybe they just thought he was cute. I know that's how they pick the winners on *American Idol*. And the Nobel Prize winners in Physics.

But I know why *I* would have voted for him – besides his cuteness, which is, of course, a given.

Here are the reasons I would have voted for Joe to be made a Grand Master:

NUMBER 1: The incredible good sense he demonstrated in marrying Gay. She's not only been a wife and helpmate to Joe, but also a business manager, typist, publicist, and travel agent. And to everyone else in science fiction, she's been a dinner organizer, tour guide, translator, nursemaid, altercations-smoother-over, confidante, friend, and the most charming person in science fiction. Good call, Joe.

NUMBER 2: His bike riding. Joe was clearly out in front of all the rest of us on this global climate change, fossil-fuels-are-killing-our-planet thing. He's been riding his bike and working in longhand by the light of an oil lamp for years. And even though the war on the environment's going really well these days, with Joe on our side, it makes me think the planet might just survive after all.

NUMBER 3: Joe's teaching. Being a Grand Master isn't just about writing. It's about giving back, and over the years Joe has given back an enormous amount. He's shared his thoughts and his craft with hundreds of students, among them Eileen Gunn, Leslie What, Kim Stanley Robinson, Greg Frost, Cynthia Felice, and James Patrick Kelly. He's taught at Clarion and Clarion West, and for the last twenty-seven years has taught creative writing at MIT.

His students love him. James Patrick Kelly remembers him as one of the best instructors he ever had, not only for his insights on writing, but for his practical advice and attitude toward the enterprise of writing, from contracts to conventions.

NUMBER 4: Joe's consummate professionalism. Joe's books are meticulously thought out, crafted, and researched. Sheila Williams tells the story of having to call Joe and a new writer on the same day to ask for revisions to their stories in *Asimov's*. The new writer had made a glaring historical mistake about the moon landing.

Joe had *possibly* made a minor mistake on the technology in his story.

Joe said he'd check on it and call her back. The new writer ranted, raved, refused to change the error because it was too much work, and besides, nobody remembered the moon landing anyway, and then hung up on her. Joe called back a few hours later to say, "I'm sorry it took so long. I couldn't find it in MIT's library, so I had to ride my bike into Boston to the library there."

Which, as Sheila says, is why he's Joe Haldeman and why the new writer never sold another story to *Asimov's*.

NUMBER 5: *The Forever War*. (You were wondering when I'd get to that, weren't you?)

One of the hardest things for a writer is to write a great book early on in your career, let alone a classic. Most writers never recover from it. They either crack up under the pressure and go off to live in the woods, like J.D. Salinger. Or spend the rest of their life living off their fame, like Orson Welles. Or get enormously swelled heads and turn into complete jerks, like . . . oh, thousands I could name.

Joe didn't do any of those things. He kept on writing, experimenting with new styles and new subject matter, and producing a lifetime's worth of wonderful books.

But it doesn't change the fact that *The Forever War is* a classic, a thought-provoking work that uses science fiction to explore the harsh realities of war and the dehumanization and alienation it produces in those who fight it. It's also a harsh indictment of those who run the war and horrifyingly prophetic in its depiction of the directions warfare will take.

It may originally have been about Vietnam, but with its under-equipped soldiers and cynical, corporatized military, it's also clearly about Iraq and Blackwater. And wars we haven't even declared yet.

Which is why it began being on Top Ten Science Fiction Novels lists from the moment it was written and is still there. It's the real deal. And all by itself it would qualify Joe to be a Grand Master.

NUMBER 6: Finally, Joe, deserves this Grand Master Award for the person he is, and also the person he was. This was a kid who wanted to be an astronaut, who rode his bike to the public library, who saved up his paper-route money to buy a telescope, who studied astronomy and chemistry on his own, and read the encyclopedia for fun.

Kip Russell in the flesh – a true Heinlein hero.

All that's lacking is the slide rule.

Joe, I have something I want to give you. No, not the Grand Master Nebula. Not yet. This is a present from me.

It's not a K and E log log decitrig 4081-5 like Kip had in *Have Space Suit – Will Travel*, but it's the next best thing. It's a Pickett N600-ES, the same model of slide rule – excuse me, slipstick – that the NASA astronauts took to the Moon.

As a kid, you were a teenaged Heinlein hero. And now you're that Heinlein hero all grown up. And my hero. Our hero. And a Nebula Grand Master of Science Fiction.

Congratulations!

—Connie Willis

A !TANGLED WEB

JOE HALDEMAN

FROM THE AUTHOR: I chose this story because I think it's funny, and there isn't enough humor in SF anthologies.

You don't always know where a story comes from, but in this case I can pinpoint it exactly – August 26, 1981. The Jet Propulsion Laboratory in Pasadena had invited a bunch of science fiction writers to come witness the *Voyager 2* flyby of Saturn.

It was immensely exciting, but there were long periods when nothing was happening. Jerry Pournelle had a cooler full of iced beer in the back of his Jeep, and I was happy to join him for one in the California sun.

We got to talking about the movie *Star Wars*, and I expressed admiration for the tavern scene, all those weird aliens drinking impossible stuff, munching on raw meat, and so forth. Jerry said hell, that's nothing new. Every science fiction writer has done the aliens-in-a-bar scene a dozen times.

As a matter of fact, I hadn't. So I went home and did it.

YOUR SPACEPORT BARS fall into two distinct groups: the ones for the baggage and the ones for the crew. I was baggage, this trip, but didn't feel like paying the prices that people who space for fun can afford. The Facility Directory listed under "Food and Drink" four establishments: the Hartford Club (inevitably), the Silver Slipper Lounge, Antoine's, and Slim Joan's Bar & Grill.

I went to a currency exchange booth first, assuming that Slim Joan was no better at arithmetic than most bartenders, and cashed in a hundredth share of Hartford stock. Then I took the drop lift down to the bottom level. That the bar's door was right at the drop-lift exit would be a dead giveaway even if its name had been the Bell, Book, and Candle. Baggage don't generally like to fall ten stories, no matter how slowly.

It smelled right, stir-fry and stale beer, and the low lighting suggested economy rather than atmosphere. Slim Joan turned out to be about a hundred thousand grams of transvestite. Well, I hadn't come for the scenery.

The clientele seemed evenly mixed between humans and others, most of the aliens being !tang, since this was Morocho III. I've got nothing against the company of aliens, but if I was going to spend all next week wrapping my jaws around !tanglish, I preferred to mix my drinking with some human tongue.

"Speak English?" I asked Slim Joan.

"Some," he/she/it growled. "You would drink something?" I'd never heard a Russian-Brooklyn accent before. I ordered a double saki, cold, in Russian, and took it to an empty booth.

One of the advantages of being a Hartford interpreter is that you can order a drink in a hundred different languages and dialects. Saves money; they figure if you can speak the lingo you can count your change.

I was freelancing this trip, though, working for a real-estate cartel that wanted to screw the !tang out of a few thousand square kilometers of useless seashore property. It wouldn't stay useless, of course.

Morocho III is a real garden of a planet, but most people never see it. The tachyon nexus is down by Morocho I, which we in the trade refer to as "Armpit," and not many people take the local hop out to III (Armpit's the stopover on the Earth-Sammler run). Starlodge, Limited was hoping to change that situation.

I couldn't help eavesdropping on the !tangs behind me. (I'm not a snoop; it's a side effect of the hypnotic-induction learning process.) One of them was leaving for Earth today, and the other was full of useless advice. "He" – they have seven singular pronoun classes, depending on the individual's age and estrous condition – was telling "her" never to make any reference to human body odor, no matter how vile it may be. He should also have told her not to breathe on anyone. One of the byproducts of their metabolism is butyl nitrite, which smells like well-aged socks and makes humans get all faint and cross-eyed.

I've worked with !tangs a few times before, and they're some of my favorite people. Very serious, very honest, and their logic is closer to human logic than most. But they *are* strange-looking. Imagine a perambulating haystack with an elephant's trunk protruding. They have two arms under the pile of yellow hair, but it's impolite to take them out in public unless one is engaged in physical work. They do have sex in public, constantly, but it takes a zoologist with a magnifying glass to tell when.

He wanted her to bring back some Kentucky bourbon and Swiss chocolate. Their metabolisms part company with ours over protein and fats, but they love our carbohydrates and alcohol. The alcohol has a psychedelic effect on them, and sugar leaves them plastered.

A human walked in and stood blinking in the half-light. I recognized him and shrank back into the booth. Too late.

He strode over and stuck out his hand. "Dick Navarro!"

"Hello, Pete." I shook his hand once. "What brings you here? Hartford business?" Pete was also an interpreter.

—"Oh no," he said in Arabic. —"Only journeying."

—"Knock it off," I said in Serbian. —"Isn't your native language English?" I added in Greek.

"Sure it is. Yours?"

"English or Spanish. Have a seat."

I smacked my lips twice at Slim Joan, and she came over with a menu. "To be eating you want?"

"Nyet," he said. "Vodka." I told her I'd take another.

"So what are you doing here?" Pete asked.

"Business."

"Hartford?"

"Nope."

"Secret."

"That's right." Actually they hadn't said anything about its being secret. But I knew Peter Lafitte. He wasn't just passing through.

We both sat silently for a minute, listening to the !tangs. We had to smile when he explained to her how to decide which public bathroom to use when. . . . "This was important to humans," he said. Slim Joan came with the drinks and Pete paid for both, a bad sign.

"How did that Spica business finally turn out?" he asked.

"Badly." Lafitte and I worked together on a partition-of-rights hearing on Spica IV, with the Confederación actually bucking Hartford over an alien-rights problem. "I couldn't get the humans to understand that the minerals had souls, and I couldn't get the natives to believe that refining the minerals didn't affect their spiritual status. It came to a show of force, and the natives backed down. I wouldn't like to be there in twenty years, though."

"Yeah. I was glad to be recalled. Arcturus all over."

"That's what I tried to tell them." Arcturus wasn't a regular stop any more, not since a ship landed and found every human artistically dismembered. "You're just sightseeing?"

"This has always been one of my favorite planets."

"Nothing to do."

"Not for you city boys. The fishing is great, though."

Ah ha. "Ocean fishing?"

"Best in the Confederación."

"I might give it a try. Where do you get a boat?"

He smiled and looked directly at me. "Little coastal village, Pa'an!al."

Smack in the middle of the tribal territory I'd be dickering for. I dutifully repeated the information into my ring.

I changed the subject and we talked about nothing for a while. Then I excused myself, saying I was time-lagging and had to get some sleep. Which was true enough, since the shuttle had stayed on Armpit time, and I was eight hours out of phase with III. But I bounced straight into the Hartford courier's office.

The courier on duty was Estelle Dorring, whom I knew slightly. I cut short the pleasantries. "How long to get a message to Earth?"

She studied the clocks on the wall. "You're out of luck if you want it hand-carried. I'm not going to Armpit tomorrow. Two days on the shuttle and I'll miss the Earth run by half a day.

"If broadcast is all right, you can beam to Armpit and the courier there will take it on the Twosday run. That leaves in seventy-two minutes. Call it nineteen minutes' beam time. You know what you want to say?"

"Yeah. Set it up." I sat down at the customers' console.

STARLODGE LIMITED
642 EASTRIVER
NEW YORK, NEW YORK 10099-27654
ATTENTION: PATRICE DUVAL
YOU MAY HAVE SOME COMPETITION HERE. NOTHING OPEN YET BUT A
GUY WE CALL PETER RABBIT IS ON THE SCENE. CHECK INTERPRETERS
GUILD AND SEE WHO'S PAYING PETER LAFITTE. CHANGE TERMS OF
SALE? PLEASE SEND REPLY NEXT SAMMLER RUN – RICARDO NAVARRO/
RM2048/MOROCHO HILTON

I wasn't sure what good the information would do me, unless they also found out how much he was offering and authorized me to outbid him. At any rate, I wouldn't hear for three days, earliest. Sleep.

Morocho III – its real name is !ka'al – rides a slow sleeping orbit around Morocho A, the brighter of the two suns that make up the Morocho system (Morocho A is a close double star itself, but its white dwarf companion hugs so close that it's lost in the glare). At this time of day, Morocho B was visible low in the sky, a hard blue diamond too bright to stare at, and A was right overhead, a bloated golden ball. On the sandy beach below us the flyer cast two shadows, dark blue and faint yellow, which raced to come together as we landed.

Pa'an!al is a fishing village thousands of years old, on a natural harbor formed where a broad jungle river flows into the sea. Here on the beach were only a few pole huts with thatched roofs, where the fishers who worked the surf and shallow pools lived. Pa'an!al proper was behind a high stone wall, which protected it on one side from the occasional hurricane and on the other from interesting fauna of the jungle.

I paid off my driver and told him to come back at second sundown. I took a deep breath and mounted the steps. There was an open-cage Otis elevator beside the stairs, but people didn't use it, only fish.

The !tang are compulsive about geometry. This wall was a precise 1:2 rectangle, and the stairs mounted from one corner to the opposite in a satisfying Euclidian 30 degrees. A guardrail would have spoiled the harmony. The stairs were just wide enough for two !tang to pass, and the rise of each step was a good half meter. By the time I got to the top I was both tired and slightly terrified.

A spacefaring man shouldn't be afraid of heights, and I'm not, so long as I'm in a vehicle. But when I attained the top of the wall and looked down the equally long and perilous flight of stairs to ground level, I almost swooned. Why couldn't they simply have left a door in the wall?

I sat there for a minute and looked down at the small city. The geometric regularity *was* pleasing. Each building was either a cube or a stack of cubes, and the rock from which the city was built had been carefully sorted, so that each building was a uniform shade. They went from white marble through sandy yellow and salmon to pearly gray and obsidian. The streets were a regular matrix of red brick. I walked down, hugging the wall.

At the bottom of the steps a !tang sat on a low bench, watching the nonexistent traffic.

—*Greetings*, I clicked and snorted at him. —*It is certainly a pleasant day.*

—*Not everywhere*, he grunted and wheezed back. An unusually direct response.

—*Are you waiting for me?*

—*Who can say? I am waiting*. His trunk made a philosophical circle in the air. —*If you had not come, who knows for what I would have been waiting?*

—*Well, that's true*. He made a circle in the other direction, which I think meant What else? I stood there for a moment while he looked at me or the ground or the sky. You could never tell.

—*I hope this isn't a rude question*, he said. —*Will you forgive me if this is a rude question?*

—*I certainly will try.*

—*Is your name !ica'o *va!o?*

That was admirably close. —*It certainly is.*

—*You could follow me.* He got up. —*Or enjoy the pleasant day.*

I followed him closely down the narrow street. If he got in a crowd I'd lose him for sure. I couldn't tell an estrus-four female from a neuter, not having sonar (they tell each other apart by sensing body cavities, very romantic).

We went through the center of town, where the well and the market square were. A dozen !tang bargained over food, craft items, or abstractions. They were the most mercantile race on the planet, although they had sidestepped the idea of money in favor of labor equivalence: for those two ugly fish I will trade you an original sonnet about your daughter and three vile limericks for your next affinity-group meeting. Four limericks, tops.

We went into a large white building that might have been City Hall. It was evidently guarded, at least symbolically, since two !tang stood by the door with their arms exposed.

It was a single large room similar to a Terran mosque, with a regular pattern of square columns holding up the ceiling. The columns supported shelves in neat squares, up to about two meters; on the shelves were neat stacks of accordion-style books. Although the ceiling had inset squares of glass that gave adequate light, there was a strong smell of burnt fish oil, which meant the building was used at night. (We had introduced them to electricity, but they used it only for heavy machinery and toys.)

The !tang led me to the farthest corner, where a large haystack was bent over a book, scribbling. They had to read or write with their heads a few centimeters from the book, since their light-eyes were only good for close-work.

—*It has happened as you foretold, Uncle.* Not too amazing a prophecy, as I'd sent a messenger over yesterday.

Uncle waved his nose in my direction. —*Are you the same one who came in four days ago?*

—*No. I have never been to this place. I am Ricardo Navarro, from the Starlodge tribe.*

—*I grovel in embarrassment. Truly it is difficult to tell one human from another. To my poor eyes you look exactly like Peter Lafitte.*

(Peter Rabbit is bald and ugly, with terrible ears. I have long curly hair with only a trace of gray, and women have called me attractive.) —*Please do not be embarrassed. This is often true when different peoples meet. Did my brother say what tribe he represented?*

—I die. O my hair falls out and my flesh rots and my bones are cracked by the hungry ta!a'an. He drops me behind him all around the forest and nothing will grow where his excrement from my marrow falls. As the years pass the forest dies from the poison of my remains. The soil washes to the sea and poisons the fish, and all die. O the embarrassment.

—He didn't say?

—He did but said not to tell you.

That was that. *—Did he by some chance say he was interested in the small morsel of land I mentioned to you by courier long ago?*

—No, he was not interested in the land.

—Can you tell me what he was interested in?

—He was interested in buying *the land.*

Verbs. *—May I ask a potentially embarrassing question?*

He exposed his arms. *—We are businessmen.*

—What were the terms of his offer?

—I die. I breathe in and breathe in and cannot exhale. I explode all over my friends. They forget my name and pretend it is dung. They wash off in the square and the well becomes polluted. All die. O the embarrassment.

—He said not to tell me?

—That's right.

—Did you agree to sell him the land?

—That is a difficult question to answer.

—Let me rephrase the question: is it possible you might sell the land to my tribe?

—It is possible, if you offer better terms. But only possible, in any case.

—This is embarrassing. I, uh, die and, um, the last breath from my lungs is a terrible acid. It melts the seaward wall of the city and a hurricane comes and washes it away. All die. O the embarrassment.

—You're much better at it than he was.

—Thank you. But may I ask you to amplify the possibility?

—Certainly. Land is not a fish or an elevator. Land is something that keeps you from falling all the way down. It gives the sea a shore and makes the air stop. Do you understand?

—So far. Please continue.

—Land is time, but not in a mercantile sense. I can say "In return for the time it takes me to decide which one of you is the guilty party, you must give me so-and-so." But how can I say "In return for the land I am standing on you must give me this-and-that?" Nobody can step off the time, you

*see, but I can step off the land, and then what is it? Does it even exist?
In a mercantile sense? These questions and corollaries to them have been
occupying some of our finest minds ever since your courier came long ago.*

—*May I make a suggestion?*

—*Please do. Anything might help.*

—*Why not just sell it to the tribe that offers you the most?*

—*No, you don't see.* Forgive me, you Terrans are very simpleminded
people, for all your marvelous Otis elevators and starships (this does not
embarrass me to say because it is meant to help you understand yourself;
if you were !tang you would have to pay for it). *You see, there are three
mercantile classes. Things and services may be of no worth, of measurable
worth, or of infinite worth. Land has never been classified before, and it
may belong in any of the categories.*

—*But Uncle! The Lafitte and I have offered to buy the land. Surely
that eliminates the first class.*

—*O you poor Terran. I would hate to see you try to buy a fish. You
must think of all the implications.*

—*I die.* I, uh, have a terrible fever in my head and it gets hotter and
hotter until my head is on fire, a forge, a star. I set the world on fire and
everybody dies. O the embarrassment. *What implications?*

—*Here is the simplest. If the land has finite value, when at best all it
does is keep things from falling all the way down, how much is air worth?
Air is necessary for life, and it make fires burn. If you pay for land do you
think we should let you have air for free?*

—*An interesting point,* I said, thinking fast and !tangly. —*But you
have answered it yourself. Since air is necessary for life, it is of infinite
value, and not one breath can be paid for with all the riches of the universe.*

—*O poor one, how can you have gotten through life without losing
your feet? Air would be of infinite worth thus only if life were of infinite
worth, and even so little as I know of your rich and glorious history proves
conclusively that you place very little value on life. Other people's lives,
at any rate. Sad to say, our own history contains a similarly bonehungry
period.*

—*Neither are we that way now, Uncle.*

—*I die. My brain turns to maggots. . . .*

I talked with Uncle for an hour or so but got nothing out of it but a sore
soft palate. When I got back to the hotel there was a message from Peter
Lafitte, asking whether I would like to join him at Antoine's for dinner.
No, I would not *like* to, but under the circumstances it seemed prudent.
I had to rent a formal tunic from the bellbot.

Antoine's has all the *joie de vivre* of a frozen halibut, which puts it on par with every other French restaurant off Earth. We started with an artichoke vinaigrette that should have been left to rot in the hydroponics tank. Then a filet of "beef" from some local animal that I doubt was even warm blooded. All this served by a waiter who was a Canadian with a fake Parisian accent.

But we also had a bottle of phony Pouilly-Fuissé followed by a bottle of ersatz Burgundy followed by a bottle of synthetic Château-d'Yquem. Then they cleared the table and set a bottle of brandy between us, and the real duel began. Short duel, it turned out.

"So how long is your vacation going to last?" I made a gesture that was admirably economical. "Not long at these prices."

"Well, there's always Slim Joan's." He poured himself a little brandy and me a lot. "How about yourself?"

"Ran into a snag," I said. "Have to wait until I hear from Earth."

"They're not easy to work with, are they?"

"Terrans? I'm one myself."

"The !tang, I mean." He stared into his glass and swirled the liquor. "Terrans as well, though. Could I set to you a hypothetical proposition?"

"My favorite kind," I said. The brandy stung my throat.

"Suppose you were a peaceable sort of fellow."

"I am." Slightly fuzzy, but peaceable.

"And you were on a planet to make some agreement with the natives."

I nodded seriously.

"Billions of bux involved. Trillions."

"That would really be something," I said.

"Yeah. Now further suppose that there's another Terran on this planet who, uh, is seeking to make the same sort of agreement."

"Must happen all the time."

"For trillions, Dick? Trillions?"

"Hyp'thetical trillions." Bad brandy, but strong.

"Now the people who are employing you are ab-so-lute-ly ruthless."

"*Ma!ryso'ta,*" I said, the !tang word for "bonehungry." Close to it, anyway.

"That's right." He was starting to blur. More wine than I'd thought. "Stop at nothing. Now how would you go about warning the other Terran?"

My fingers were icy cold and the sensation was crawling toward my elbows. My chin slipped off my hand and my head was so heavy I could hardly hold it up. I stared at the two fuzzy images across the table. "Peter." The words came out slowly, then not at all: "You aren't drinking. . . ."

"Terrible brandy, isn't it?" My vision went away, although it felt as if my eyes were still open. I heard my chin hit the table.

"Waiter?" I heard the man come over and make sympathetic noises. "My friend has had a little too much to drink. Would you help me get him to the bellbot?" I couldn't even feel them pick me up. "I'll take this brandy. He might want some in the morning." Jolly.

I finally lapsed into unconsciousness while we were waiting for the elevator, the bellbot lecturing me about temperance. I woke up the next afternoon on the cold tile floor of my suite's bathroom. I felt like I had been taken apart by an expert surgeon and reassembled by an amateur mechanic. I looked at the tile for a long time. Then I sat for a while and studied the interesting blotches of color floating between my eyes and my brain. When I thought I could survive it, I stood up and took four Hangaways.

I sat and started counting. Hangaways hit you like a pile driver. At eighty the adrenaline shock came. Tunnel vision and millions of tiny needles being pushed out through your skin. Rivers of sweat. Cathedral bells tolling, your head the clapper. Then the dry heaves and it was over.

I staggered to the phone and ordered some clear soup and a couple of cold beers. Then I stood in the shower and contemplated suicide. By the time the soup came I was contemplating homicide.

The soup stayed down and by the second beer I was feeling almost human. Neanderthal, anyhow. I made some inquiries. Lafitte had checked out. No shuttle had left, so he was either still on the planet or he had his own ship, which was possible if he was working for the outfit I suspected he was working for. I invoked the holy name of Hartford, trying to find out to whom his expenses had been billed. Cash.

I tried to order my thoughts. If I reported Lafitte's action to the Guild he would be disbarred. Either he didn't care, because they were paying him enough to retire in luxury – for which I knew he had a taste – or he actually thought I was not going to get off the planet alive. I discarded the dramatic second notion. Last night he could have more easily killed me than warned me. Or had he actually *tried* to kill me, the talk just being insurance in case I didn't ingest a fatal dose? I had no idea what the poison could have been. That sort of knowledge isn't relevant to my line of work.

I suppose the thoroughly rational thing would have been to sit tight and let him have the deal. The fortunes of Starlodge were infinitely less important to me than my skin. He could probably offer more than I could, anyhow.

The phone chimed. I thumbed the vision button and a tiny haystack materialized over the end table.

—*Greetings. How is the weather?*

—*Indoors, it's fine. Are you* Uncle?

—*Not now.* Inside *the Council Building I am Uncle.*

—*I see. Can I perform some worthless service for you?*

—*For yourself, perhaps.*

—*Pray continue.*

—*Our Council is meeting with Lafitte this evening, with the hope of resolving this question about the mercantile nature of land. I would be embarrassed if you did not come, too. The meeting will be at* *ala'ang *in the Council Building.*

—*I would not cause embarrassment. But could it possibly be postponed?*

He exposed his arms. —*We are meeting.*

He disappeared and I spent a few minutes translating *ala'ang into human time. The !tang divide their day into a complicated series of varying time intervals depending on the position of the suns and state of appetite and estrous condition. Came to a little before ten o'clock, plenty of time.

I could report Lafitte, and probably should, but decided I'd be safer not doing so, retaining the threat of exposure for use as a weapon. I wrote a brief description of the situation – and felt a twinge of fear on writing the word *Syndicate* – and sealed it in an envelope. I wrote the address of the Hartford Translators' Guild across the seal and bounced up to the courier's office.

Estelle Dorring stared at me when I walked into the office. "Ricardo! You look like a corpse warmed over!"

"Rough night," I said. "Touch of food poisoning."

"I never eat that tang stuff."

"Good policy." I set the envelope in front of her. "I'm not sure whether to send this or not. If I don't come get it before the next shuttle, take it to Armpit and give it to the next Earth courier."

She nodded slowly and read the address. "Why so mysterious?"

"Just a matter of Guild ethics. I wanted to write it down while it was still fresh. Uh . . ." I'd never seen a truly penetrating stare before. "But I might have more information tonight that would invalidate it."

"If you say so, Ricardo." She slipped the envelope into a drawer. I backed out, mumbling something inane.

Down to Slim Joan's for a sandwich of stir-fried vegetables in Syrian bread. Slightly rancid and too much curry, but I didn't dare go to the Council meeting on an empty stomach; !tang sonar would scan it and they would make a symbolic offer of bread, which wouldn't be refused. Estelle was partly right about the "tang" food: one bite of the bread contained enough mescaline to make you see interesting things for hours. I'd had enough of that for a while.

I toyed with the idea of taking a weapon. There was a rental service in the pharmacy, to accommodate the occasional sporting type, and I could pick up a laser or tranquilizer there. But there would be no way to conceal it from the !tang sonar. Besides, Lafitte wasn't the kind of person who would employ direct violence.

But if it actually were the Syndicate behind Lafitte, they might well have sent more than one person here; they certainly could afford it. A hitter. But then why would Lafitte set up the elaborate poisoning scheme? Why not simply arrange an accident?

My feet were taking me toward the pharmacy. Wait. Be realistic. You haven't fired a gun in twenty years. Even then, you couldn't hit the ground with a rock. If it came to a burnout, you'd be the one who got crisped. Better to leave their options open.

I decided to compromise. There was a large clasp knife in my bag; that would at least help me psychologically. I went back up to my room.

I thumbed the lock and realized that the cube I'd heard playing was my own. The door slid open and there was Lafitte, lounging on my sofa, watching an old movie.

"Dick. You're looking well."

"How the hell did you get in here?"

He held up his thumb and ripped a piece of plastic off the fleshy part. "We have our resources." He sat up straight. "I hear you're taking a flyer out to Pa'an!al. Shall we divide the cost?"

There was a bottle of wine in a bucket of ice at his feet. "I supposed you charged this to my room." I turned off the cube.

He shrugged. "You poked me for dinner last night, *mon frère*. Passing out like that."

I raised the glass to my lips, flinched, and set it down untouched. "Speaking of resources, what was in that brandy? And who are these resourceful friends?"

"The wine's all right. You seemed agitated; I gave you a calmative."

"A *horse* calmative! Is it the Syndicate?"

He waved that away. "The Syndicate's a myth. You—"

"Don't take me for an idiot. I've been doing this for almost as long as you have." Every ten years or so there was a fresh debunking. But the money and bodies kept piling up.

"You have indeed." He concentrated on picking at a hangnail. "How much is Starlodge willing to pay?"

I tried not to react. "How much is the Syndicate?"

"If the Syndicate existed," he said carefully, "and if it were they who had retained me, don't you think I would try to use that fact to frighten you away?"

"Maybe not directly . . . last night, you said 'desperate men.' "

"I was drunk." No, not Peter Rabbit, not on a couple of bottles of wine. I just looked at him. "All right," he said, "I was told to use any measures short of violence—"

"Poisoning isn't violence?"

"Tranquilizing, not poisoning. You couldn't have died." He poured himself some wine. "Top yours off?"

"I've become a solitary drinker."

He poured the contents of my glass into his. "I might be able to save you some trouble, if you'll only tell me what terms—"

"A case of Jack Daniel's and all they can eat at Slim Joan's."

"That might do it," he said unsmilingly, "but I can offer fifteen hundred shares of Hartford."

That was $150 million, half again what I'd been authorized. "Just paper to them."

"Or a million cases of booze, if that's the way they want it." He checked his watch. "Isn't our flyer waiting?"

I supposed it would be best to have him along, to keep an eye on him. "The one who closes the deal pays for the trip?"

"All right."

On the hour-long flyer ride I considered various permutations of what I could offer. My memory had been jammed with the wholesale prices of various kinds of machinery, booze, candy, and so forth, along with their mass and volume, so I could add in the shipping costs from Earth to Armpit to Morocho III. Lafitte surely had similar knowledge; I could only hope his figure of 1500 shares was a bluff.

(I had good incentive to bargain well. Starlodge would give me a bonus of up to 10 percent of the difference between a thousand shares and whatever the settlement came to. If I brought it in at 900, I'd be a millionaire.)

We were turning inland; the walls of the city made a pink rectangle against the towering jungle. I tapped the pilot on the shoulder. "Can you land inside the city?"

"Not unless you want to jump from the top of a building. I can set you on the wall, though." I nodded.

"Can't take the climb, Dick? Getting old?"

"No need to waste steps." The flyer was a little wider than the wall, and it teetered as we stepped out. I tried to look just at my feet.

"Beautiful up here," Lafitte said. "Look at that sunset." Half the large sun's disk was visible on the jungle horizon, a deeper red than Earth's sun ever shone. The bloody light stained the surf behind us purple. It was already dark in the city below; the smell of rancid fish oil burning drifted up to us.

Lafitte managed to get the inside lane of the staircase. I tried to keep my eyes on him and the wall as we negotiated the high steps.

"Believe me," he said (a phrase guaranteed to inspire trust), "it would make both our jobs easier if I could tell you who I'm representing. But I really am sworn to secrecy."

An oblique threat deserves an oblique answer. "You know I can put you in deep trouble with the Standards Committee. Poisoning a Guild brother."

"Your word against mine. And the bellbot's, the headwaiter's, the wine steward's . . . you did have quite a bit to drink."

"A couple of bottles of wine won't knock me out."

"Your capacity is well known. I don't think you want a hearing investigating it, though, not at your age. Two years until retirement?"

"Twenty months."

"I was rounding off," he said. "Yes, I did check. I wondered whether you might be in the same position as I am. My retirement's less than two months away; this is my last big-money job. So you must understand my enthusiasm."

I didn't answer. He wasn't called Rabbit for lack of "enthusiasm."

As we neared the bottom, he said, "Suppose you weren't to oppose me too vigorously. Suppose I could bring in the contract at a great deal less than—"

"Don't be insulting."

In the dim light from the torches sputtering below, I couldn't read his expression. "Ten percent of my commission wouldn't be insulting."

I stopped short. He climbed another step. "I can't believe even *you*—"

"*Verdad.* Just joking." He laughed unconvincingly. "Everyone knows how starchy you are, Dick. I know better than most." I'd fined him several times during the years I was head of the Standards Committee.

We walked automatically through the maze of streets, our guides evidently having taken identical routes. Both of us had eidetic memories, of course, that being a minimum prerequisite for the job of an interpreter. I was thinking furiously. If I couldn't outbargain the Rabbit

I'd have to somehow finesse him. Was there anything I knew about the !tang value system that he didn't? Assuming that this council would decide that land was something that could be bought and sold.

I did have a couple of interesting proposals in my portfolio, that I'd written up during the two-week trip from Earth. I wondered whether Lafitte had seen them. The lock didn't appear to have been tampered with, and it was the old-fashioned magnetic key type. You can pick it but it won't close afterward.

We turned a corner and there was the council building at the end of the street, impressive in the flickering light, its upper reaches lost in darkness. Lafitte put his hand on my arm, stopping. "I've got a proposition."

"Not interested."

"Hear me out, now; this is straight. I'm empowered to take you on as a limited partner."

"How generous. I don't think Starlodge would like it."

"What I *mean* is Starlodge. You hold their power of attorney, don't you?"

"Unlimited, on this planet. But don't waste your breath; we get an exclusive or nothing at all." Actually, the possibility had never been discussed. They couldn't have known I was going into a competitive bidding situation. If they had, they certainly wouldn't have sent me here slow freight. For an extra fifty shares I could have gone first class and been here a week before Peter Rabbit; could have sewn up the thing and been headed home before he got to the Armpit.

Starlodge had a knack of picking places that were about to become popular – along with impressive media power, to make sure they did – and on dozens of worlds they did have literally exclusive rights to tourism. Hartford might own a spaceport hotel, but it wasn't really competition, and they were usually glad to hand it over to Starlodge anyhow. Hartford, with its ironclad lock on the tachyon drive, had no need to diversify.

There was no doubt in my mind that this was the pattern Starlodge had in mind for Morocho III. It was a perfect setup, the beach being a geologic anomaly: there wasn't another spot for a hotel within two thousand kilometers of the spaceport. Just bleak mountaintops sprouting occasionally out of jungles full of large and hungry animals. But maybe I could lead the Rabbit on. I leaned up against a pot that supported a guttering torch. "At any rate, I certainly couldn't consider entering into an agreement without knowing who you represent."

He looked at me stone-faced for a second. "Outfit called A.W. Stoner Industries."

I laughed out loud. "Real name, I mean." I'd never heard of Stoner, and I do keep in touch.

"That's the name I know them by."

"No concern not listed in *Standard, Poor and Tueme* could come up with nine figures for extraterrestrial real-estate speculation. No legitimate concern, I mean."

"There you go again," he said mildly. "I believe they're a coalition of smaller firms."

"I don't. Let's go."

Back in my luggage I had a nasal spray that deadened the sense of smell. Before we even got inside, I knew I should have used it.

The air was gray with fish-oil smoke, and there were more than a hundred !tang sitting in neat rows. I once was treated to a "fish kill" in Texas, where a sudden ecological disaster had resulted in windrows of rotting fish piled up on the beach. This was like walking along that beach using an old sock for a muffler. By Lafitte's expression, he was also unprepared. We both walked forward with slightly green cheerfulness.

A !tang in the middle of the first row stood up and approached us.— *Uncle?* I ventured, and he waved his snout in affirmation.

— *We have come to an interim decision*, he said.

— *Interim?* Lafitte said. — *Were my terms unacceptable?*

— I die. My footprints are cursed. I walk around the village not knowing that all who cross where I will, stay in estrous zero and bear no young. Eventually, all die. O the embarrassment. We want to hear the terms of Navarro's tribe. Then perhaps a final decision may be made.

This was frighteningly direct. I'd tried for an hour to tell him our terms before, but he'd kept changing the subject.

— *May I hear the terms of Lafitte's tribe?* I asked.

— *Certainly. Would Lafitte like to state them, or should I?*

— *Proceed, Uncle*, Lafitte said, and then, in Spanish, — "Remember the possibility of a partnership. If we get to haggling . . ."

I stopped listening to the Rabbit as Uncle began a long litany of groans, creaks, pops and whistles. I kept a running total of the wholesale prices and shipping costs. Bourbon, rum, brandy, gin. Candy bars, raw sugar, honey, pastries. Nets, computers, garbage compactors, water-purifying plant, hunting weapons. When he stopped, I had a total of only H620.

— *Your offer, Navarro? Could it include these things as a subset?*

I had to be careful. Lafitte was probably lying about the 1500, but I didn't want to push him so hard he'd be able to go over a thousand on the next round. And I didn't want to bring out my big guns until the very end.

— *I can offer these things and three times the specified quantity of rum* – (the largest distillery on Earth was a subsidiary of Starlodge) – *and furthermore free you from the rigors of the winter harvest, with twenty-six fully programmed mechanical farm laborers.* (The winters here were not even cool by Earth standards, but something about the season made the local animals restless enough to occasionally jump over the walls that normally protected farmland.)

— *These mechanical workers would not be good to eat? For the animals?*

— *No, and they would be very hard for the animals even to damage.*

There was a lot of whispered conversation. Uncle conferred with the !tang at the front of each row, then returned.

— I die. Before I die my body turns hair-side-in. People come from everywhere to see the insides of themselves. But the sight makes them lose the will, and all die. O the embarrassment. The rum is welcome, but we cannot accept the mechanical workers. When the beast eats someone he sleeps, and can be killed, and eaten in turn. If he does not eat he will search, and in searching destroy crops. This we know to be true.

— *Then allow me to triple the quantities of gin, bourbon, and brandy. I will add two tons each of vermouth and hydrochloric acid, for flavoring.* (That came to about H710.)

— *This is gratefully accepted. Does your tribe, Lafitte, care to include these as a subset of your final offer?*

— *Final offer, Uncle?*

— Two legs, two arms, two eyes, two mouths, two offers.

— I die, Lafitte said. — When they bury me, the ground caves in. It swallows up the city and all die. O the embarrassment. *Look, Uncle, that's the market law for material objects. You can't move land around; its ownership is an abstraction.*

Uncle exposed one arm – the Council tittered – and reached down and thumped the floor twice. — *The land is solid, therefore material. You can move it around with your machines; I myself saw you do this in my youth, when the spaceport was built. The market law applies.*

Lafitte smiled slowly. — *Then the Navarro's tribe can no longer bid. He's had two.*

Uncle turned toward the Council and gestured toward Rabbit, and said, — *Is he standing on feet?* And they cracked and snuffled at the joke. To Lafitte, he said, — *The Navarro's offer was rejected, and he made a substitution. Yours was not rejected. Do you care to make his amended offer a subset of yours?*

— *If mine is rejected, can I amend it?*

This brought an even louder reaction. — *Poor one*, Uncle said. — *No feet, no hands. That would be a third offer. You must see that.*

—All right. Lafitte began pacing. He said he would start with my amended offer and add the following things. The list was very long. It started with a hydroelectric generator and proceeded with objects of less and less value until he got down to individual bottles of exotic liqueurs. By then I realized he was giving me a message: he was coming down as closely as he could to exactly a thousand shares of Hartford. So we both had the same limit. When he finished he looked right at me and raised his eyebrows.

Victory is sweet. If the Rabbit had bothered to spend a day or two in the market, watching transactions, he wouldn't have tried to defeat me by arithmetic; he wouldn't have tried by accretion to force me into partnership.

Uncle looked at me and bared his arms for a split second. —*Your tribe, Navarro? Would you include this offer as a subset to your final offer?*

What Rabbit apparently didn't know was that this bargaining by pairs of offers was a formalism: if I did simply add to his last offer, the haggling would start over again, with each of us allowed another pair. I unlocked my briefcase and took out two documents.

—*No. I merely wish to add two inducements to my own previous offer* (sounds of approval and expectation).

Lafitte stared, his expression unreadable.

—*These contracts are in Spanish. Can you read them, Uncle?*

—*No, but there are two of us who can.*

—*I know how you like to travel.* (I handed him one of the documents.) —*This allows each of five hundred !tang a week's vacation on the planet of its choice, any planet where Starlodge has facilities.*

"What?" Lafitte said, in English. "How the hell can you do that?"

"Deadheading," I said.

One of the Council abruptly rose. "Pardon me," he said in a weird parody of English. "We have to be dead to take this vacation? That seems of little value."

I was somewhat startled at that, in view of the other inducement I was going to offer. I told them it was an English term that had nothing to do with heads or death. —*Most of the Hartford vessels that leave this planet are nearly empty. It is no great material loss to Hartford to take along nonpaying guests, so long as they do not displace regular passengers. And Hartford will ultimately benefit from an increase in tourism to !ka'al, so they were quite willing to make this agreement with my tribe.*

—*The market value of this could be quite high,* Uncle said.

—*As much as five or six hundred shares,* I said, —*depending on how distant each trip is.*

—Very well. And what is your other inducement?

—I won't say. (I had to grin.) —It is a gift.

The Council chattered and tweeted in approval. Some even exposed their arms momentarily in a semi-obscene gesture of fellowship. "What kind of game are you playing?" Peter Rabbit said.

"They like surprises and riddles." I made a polite sound requesting attention and said, *—There is one thing I will tell you about this gift: it belongs to all three mercantile classes. It is of no value, of finite value, and infinite value, all at once, and to all people.*

—When considered as being of finite value, Uncle said, *—how much is it worth in terms of Hartford stock?*

—Exactly one hundred shares.

He rustled pleasantly at that and went to confer with the others.

"You're pretty clever, Dick," Rabbit said. "What, they don't get to find out what the last thing is unless they accept?"

"That's right. It's done all the time; I was rather surprised that you didn't do it."

He shook his head. "I've only negotiated with !tang off-planet. They've always been pretty conventional."

I didn't ask him about all the fishing he had supposedly done here. Uncle came back and stood in front of us.

—There is unanimity. The land will go to Navarro's tribe. Now what is the secret inducement, please? How can it be every class at once, to all people?

I paused to parse out the description in !tanglish. *—Uncle, do you know of the Earth corporation, or tribe, Immortality Unlimited?*

—No.

Lafitte made a strange noise. I went on. *—This Immortality Unlimited provides a useful service to humans who are apprehensive about death. They offer the possibility of revival. A person who avails himself of this service is frozen solid as soon as possible after death. The tribe promises to keep the body frozen until such time as science discovers a way to revive it.*

—The service is expensive. You pay the tribe one full share of Hartford stock. They invest it, and take for themselves one-tenth of the income, which is their profit. A small amount is used to keep the body frozen. If and when revival is possible, the person is thawed, and cured of whatever was killing him, and he will be comparatively wealthy.

—This has never been done with nonhumans before, but there is nothing forbidding it. Therefore I purchased a hundred "spaces" for !tang; I leave it to you to decide which hundred will benefit.

—You see, this is of no material value to any living person, because you must die to take advantage of it. However, it is also of finite worth, since each space costs one share of Hartford. It is also of infinite worth, because it offers life beyond death.

The entire Council applauded, a sound like a horde of locusts descending. Peter Rabbit made the noise for attention, and then he made it again, impolitely loud.

—This is all very interesting, and I do congratulate the Navarro for his cleverness. However, the bidding is not over.

There was a low, nervous whirring. "Better apologize first, Rabbit," I whispered.

He bulled ahead. *—Let me introduce a new mercantile class: negative value.*

"Rabbit, don't—"

—This is an object or service that one does not want to have. I will offer not to give it to you if you accept my terms rather than the Navarro's.

—Many kilometers up the river there is a drum full of a very powerful poison. If I touch the button that opens it, all of the fish in the river, and for a great distance out to sea, will die. You will have to move or . . . He trailed off.

One by one, single arms snaked out, each holding a long sharp knife.

"Poison again, Rabbit? You're getting predictable in your old age."

"Dick," he said hoarsely, "they're completely nonviolent. Aren't they?"

"Except in matters of trade." Uncle was the last one to produce a knife. They moved toward us very slowly. "Unless you do something fast, I think you're about to lose your feet."

"My God! I thought that was just an expression."

"I think you better start apologizing. Tell them it was a joke."

—I die! He shouted, and they stopped advancing. —I, um . . .

— "You play a joke on your friends and it backfires," I said in Greek. Rapidly: *—I play a joke on my good friend and it backfires. I, uh . . .*

"Christ, Dick, help me."

"Just tell the truth and embroider it a little. They know about negative value, but it's an obscenity."

—I was employed by . . . a tribe that did not understand mercantilism. They asked me, of all things, to introduce the terms of negative value into a trivial transaction. My friends know I must be joking and they laugh. They laugh so much they forget to eat. All die. O the embarrassment.

Uncle made a complicated pass with his knife and it disappeared into his haybale fur. All the other knives remained in evidence, and the !tang moved into a circle around us.

—*This machine in your pocket*, Uncle said, —*it is part of the joke?*

Lafitte pulled out a small gray box. —*It is. Do you want it?*

—*Put it on the floor. The fun would be complete if you stayed here while the Navarro took one of your marvelous floaters up the river. How far would he have to go to find the rest of the joke?*

—*About twelve kilometers. On an island in midstream.*

Uncle turned to me and exposed his arms briefly. —*Would you help us with our fun?*

The air outside was sweet and pure. I decided to wait a few hours, for light.

That was some years ago, but I still remember vividly going into the Council Building the next day. Uncle had divined that Peter Rabbit was getting hungry, and they'd filled him up with !tang bread. When I came in, he was amusing them with impersonations of various Earth vegetables. The effect on his metabolism was not permanent, but when he left Morocho III he was still having mild attacks of cabbageness.

By the time I retired from Hartford, Starlodge had finished its hotel and sports facility on the beach. I was the natural choice to manage it, of course, and though I was wealthy enough not to need employment, I took the job with enthusiasm.

I even tried to hire Lafitte as an assistant – people who can handle !tang are rare – but he had dropped out of sight. Instead, I found a young husband-and-wife team who have so much energy that I hardly have to work at all.

I'm not crazy enough to go out in the woods, hunting. But I do spend a bit of time fishing off the dock, usually with Uncle, who has also retired. Together we're doing a book that I think will help our two cultures understand one another. The human version is called *Hard Bargain*.

NOVELLA

THE WOMEN OF NELL GWYNNE'S

Kage Baker

ONE:
In Which It Is Established That

In the city of Westminster, in the vicinity of Birdcage Walk, in the year of our Lord 1844 . . . There was once a private residence with a view of St. James's Park. It was generally known, among the London tradesmen, that a respectable widow resided there, upon whom it was never necessary to call for overdue payment. Beggars knew she could be relied upon for charity, if they weren't too importunate, and they were careful never to be so; for she was one of their own, in a manner of speaking, being as she was blind.

Now and again Mrs. Corvey could be observed, with her smoked goggles and walking stick, on the arm of her adolescent son Herbert, taking the pleasant air in the park. It was known that she had several daughters also, though the precise number was unclear, and that her younger sister was in residence there as well. There may even have been a pair of younger sisters, or perhaps there was an unmarried sister-in-law, and though the daughters had certainly left the schoolroom their governess seemed to have been retained.

In any other neighborhood, perhaps, there would have been some uncouth speculation about the inordinate number of females under one roof. The lady of the house by Birdcage Walk, however, retained her reputation for spotless respectability, largely because no gentlemen visitors were ever seen arriving or departing the premises, at any hour of the day or night whatsoever.

Gentlemen were unseen because they never went to the house near Birdcage Walk. They went instead to a certain private establishment

known as Nell Gwynne's, two streets away, which connected to Mrs.
Corvey's cellar by an underground passage and which was in the basement of a fairly exclusive dining establishment. The tradesmen never
came near *that* place, needless to say. Had any one of them ever done
so, he'd have been astonished to meet there Mrs. Corvey and her entire
household, including Herbert, who under this separate roof was transformed, Harlequin-like, into Herbertina. The other ladies resident were
likewise transformed from Ladies into Women, brandishing riding crops,
birch rods, and other instruments of their profession.

Nell Gwynne's clientele were often statesmen, who found the place
convenient to Whitehall. They were not infrequently members of other
exclusive clubs. Some were journalists. Some were notable persons in the
sciences or the arts. All were desperately grateful to have been accorded
membership at Nell Gwynne's, for it was known – among the sort of
gentlemen who know such things – that there was no use whining for a
sponsor. Membership was by invitation only, and entirely at the discre-
tion of the lady whose establishment it was.

Now and again, in the hushed and circumspect atmosphere of the
Athenaeum (or the Carlton Club, or the Traveller's Club) someone
might imbibe enough port to wonder aloud just what it took to get an
invitation from Mrs. Corvey.

The answer, though quite simple, was never guessed.

One had to know secrets.

Secrets were, in fact, the principal item retailed at Nell Gwynne's, with
entertainments of the flesh coming in a distant second. Secrets were
teased out of sodden members of Parliament, coaxed from lustful cabinet ministers, extracted from talkative industrialists, and finessed from
members of the Royal Society as well as the British Association for the
Advancement of Science.

Information so acquired was not, as you might expect, sold to the
highest bidder. It went directly across Whitehall and up past Scotland
Yard, to an unimposing-looking brick edifice in Craig's Court, wherein
was housed Redking's Club. Membership at Redking's was composed
equally of other MPs, ministers, industrialists, and Royal Society
members, and a great many other clever fellows beside. However, there
were many more clever fellows beneath Redking's, for *its* secret cellars
went down several storeys, and housed an organization known publicly –
but to very few – as the Gentlemen's Speculative Society.

In return for the secrets sent their way by Mrs. Corvey, the GSS under-
wrote her establishment, enabling all ladies present to live pleasantly

when they were not engaged in the business of gathering intelligence. Indeed, once a year Nell Gwynne's closed its premises when its residents went on holiday. The more poetical of the ladies preferred the Lake District, but Mrs. Corvey liked nothing better than a month at the seaside, so they generally ended up going to Torbay.

Life for the ladies of Nell Gwynne's was, placed in the proper historical, societal, and economic context, quite tolerably nice.

Now and then it did have its challenges, however.

TWO:
In Which Our Heroine
Is A Witness To History

We will call her Lady Beatrice, since that was the name she chose for herself later.

Lady Beatrice's Papa was a military man, shrewd and sober. Lady Beatrice's Mamma was a gently bred primrose of a woman, demure, proper, perfectly genteel. She was somewhat pained to discover that the daughter she bore was rather more bold and direct than became a little girl.

Lady Beatrice, encountering a horrid great spider in the garden, would not scream and run. She would stamp on it. Lady Beatrice, on having her doll snatched away by a bullying cousin, would not weep and plead; she would take back her doll, even at the cost of pulled hair and torn lace. Lady Beatrice, upon falling down, would never lie there sobbing, waiting for an adult to comfort her. She would pick herself up and inspect her knees for damage. Only when the damage amounted to bloody painful scrapes would she perhaps cry, as she limped off to the ayah to be scolded and bandaged.

Lady Beatrice's Mamma fretted, saying such brashness ill became a little lady. Lady Beatrice's Papa said he was damned glad to have a child who never wept unless she was really hurt.

"My girl's true as steel, ain't she?" he said fondly. Whereupon Lady Beatrice's Mamma would purse her lips and narrow her eyes.

Presently Lady Beatrice's Mamma had another focus for her attention, however, for walking out in the cabbage patch one day she found a pair of twin baby girls, as like her and each other as it was possible to be. Lady Beatrice hadn't thought there was a cabbage patch in the garden. She went out and searched diligently, and found not so much as a Brussels sprout, which fact she announced loudly at dinner that evening. Lady Beatrice's Mamma turned scarlet. Lady Beatrice's Papa roared with laughter.

Thereafter Lady Beatrice was allowed a most agreeable childhood, by her standards, Mamma being preoccupied with little Charlotte and Louise. She was given a pony, and was taught to ride by their Punjabi groom. She was given a bow and arrows and taught archery. She was taught her letters, and read as many books as she liked. When she asked for her own regimental uniform, Mamma told her such a thing was wicked, and retired with a fainting fit, but Papa gave her a little red coat on her next birthday.

The birthdays came and went. Just after Lady Beatrice turned seventeen, Lady Beatrice's Grandmamma was taken ill, and so Lady Beatrice's Mamma took the twins and went back to England for a visit. Lady Beatrice was uninterested in going, having several handsome young officers swooning for her at the time, and Mamma was quite content to leave her in India with Papa.

Grandmamma had been expected to die rather soon, but for some reason lingered, and Lady Beatrice's Mamma found one reason after another to postpone returning. Lady Beatrice relished running Papa's house by herself, especially presiding over dinners, where she bantered with all the handsome young officers and not a few of the old ones. One of them wrote poetry in praise of her gray eyes. Two others dueled on her account.

Then Papa's regiment was ordered to Kabul.

Lady Beatrice was left alone with the servants for some months, bored beyond anything she had believed possible. One day word came that all the wives and children of the married officers were to be allowed to go to Kabul as well, as a way to keep up the troops' morale. Lady Beatrice heard nothing directly from Papa, as it happened, but she went with all the other families. After two months of miserably difficult travel through all the red dust in the world, Lady Beatrice arrived in Kabul.

Papa was not pleased to see her. Papa was horrified. He sat her down and in few words explained how dangerous their situation was, how unlikely it was that the Afghanis would accept the British-backed ruler. He told her that rebellion was likely to break out any moment, and that the order to send for wives and children had been perfectly insane folly.

Lady Beatrice had proudly told Papa that she wasn't afraid to stay in Kabul; after all, all her handsome suitors were there! Papa had given a bitter laugh and replied that he didn't think it was safe now to send her home alone in any case.

So Lady Beatrice had stayed in Kabul, hosting Papa's dinners for increasingly glum and uninterested young suitors. She remained there until the end, when Elphinstone negotiated the retreat of the British garrison, and was one of the doomed sixteen thousand who set off from Kabul for the Khyber Pass.

Lady Beatrice watched them die, one after another after another. They died of the January cold; they died when Ghilzai snipers picked them off, or rode down in bands and skirmished with the increasingly desperate army. Papa died in the Khoord Kabul gorge, during one such skirmish, and Lady Beatrice was carried away screaming by a Ghilzai tribesman.

Lady Beatrice was beaten and raped. She was left tied among the horses. In the night she tore through the rope with her teeth and crawled into the shelter where her captors slept. She took a knife and cut their throats, and did worse to the last one, because he woke and attempted to break her wrist. She swathed herself in their garments, stole a pair of their boots. She stole their food. She took their horses, riding one and leading the others, and went down to find Papa's body.

He was frozen stiff when she found him, so she had to give up any idea of tying him across the saddle and taking him away. Instead she buried him under a cairn of stones, and scratched his name and regiment on the topmost rock with the knife with which she had killed her rapists. Then Lady Beatrice rode away, weeping; but she felt no shame weeping, because she was really hurt.

All along the Khyber Pass she counted the British and Indian dead. On three separate occasions she rode across the body of one and then another and another of her handsome young suitors. Lady Beatrice looked like a gray-eyed specter, all her tears wept out, by the time she rode into Jellalabad.

No one quite knew what to do with her there. No one wanted to speak of what had happened, for, as one of the officers who had known her family explained, her father's good name was at stake. Lady Beatrice remained with the garrison all through the siege of Jellalabad that followed, cooking for them and washing clothes. In April, just after the siege had been raised, she miscarried.

Her father's friends saw to it that Lady Beatrice was escorted back to India. There she sold off the furniture, dismissed the servants, closed up the house, and bought herself passage to England.

*   *   *

Once she had arrived, it took Lady Beatrice several weeks to find Mamma and the twins. Grandmamma had died at last, and upon receiving word of the massacre in Afghanistan, Mamma had bought mourning and thrown herself upon the mercy of her older brother, a successful merchant. She and the twins were now living as dependents in his household.

Lady Beatrice arrived on their doorstep and was greeted by shrieks of horror. Apparently Lady Beatrice's letters had gone astray in the mail. Her mother fainted dead away. Uncle Frederick's wife came in and fainted dead away as well. Charlotte and Louise came running down to see what had happened and, while they did not faint, they screamed shrilly. Uncle Frederick came in and stared at her as though his eyes would burst from his face.

Once Mamma and Aunt Harriet had been revived, to cling to each other weeping on the settee, Lady Beatrice explained what had happened to her.

A lengthy and painful discussion followed. It lasted through tea and dinner. It was revealed to Lady Beatrice that, though she had been sincerely mourned when Mamma had been under the impression she was dead, her unexpected return to life was something more than inconvenient. Had she never considered the disgrace she would inflict upon her family by returning, after all that had happened to her? What were all Aunt Harriet's neighbors to think?

Uncle Frederick as good as told her to her face that she must have whored herself to the men of the 13th Foot, during all those months in Jellalabad; and if she hadn't, she might just as well have, for all that anyone would believe otherwise.

At this point Mamma fainted again. While they were attempting to revive her, Charlotte and Louise reproached Lady Beatrice in bluntest terms for her selfishness. Had she never thought for a moment of what the scandalous news would do to *their* marriage prospects? Mamma, sitting up at this point, tearfully begged Lady Beatrice to enter a convent. Lady Beatrice replied that she no longer believed in God.

Whereupon Uncle Frederick, his face black with rage, rose from the table (the servants were in the act of serving the fish course) and told Lady Beatrice that she would be permitted to spend the night under his roof, for her Mamma's sake, but in the morning he was personally taking her to the nearest convent.

At this point Aunt Harriet pointed out that the nearest convent was in France, and he would be obliged to drive all day and hire passage on a boat, which hardly seemed respectable. Uncle Frederick shouted that he didn't give a damn. Mamma fainted once more.

Lady Beatrice excused herself and rose from the table. She went upstairs, found her mother's room, ransacked her jewel box, and left the house by the back door.

She caught the night coach in the village and went to London, where she pawned a necklace of her mother's and paid a quarter's rent on a small room in the Marylebone Road. Having done that, Lady Beatrice went to a dressmaker's and had an ensemble made in the most lurid scarlet silk the seamstress could find on her shelves. Afterward she went to a milliner's and had a hat made up to match.

The next day she went shopping for shoes and found a pair of ready-mades in her size that looked as though they would bear well with prolonged walking. Lady Beatrice purchased cosmetics also.

When her scarlet raiment was ready Lady Beatrice collected it. She took it back to her room, put it on, and stood before the cracked glass above her washstand. Holding her head high, she rimmed her gray eyes with blackest kohl.

What else was there to do, but die?

THREE:
In Which She Gets On With Her Life

The work seemed by no means as dreadful as Lady Beatrice had heard tell. She realized, however, that her point of view was somewhat unusual. The act was never pleasurable for her but it was at least not painful, as it had been in the Khyber Pass. She took care to carry plenty of lambskin sheaths in her reticule. She worked her body like a draft horse. It obeyed her patiently and earned her decent meals and a clean place in which to sleep, and books. Lady Beatrice found that she still enjoyed books.

She felt nothing, neither for nor against, regarding the men who lay with her.

Lady Beatrice learned quickly where the best locations were for plying one's trade, if one didn't wish to be brutalized by drunken laborers: outside theaters, outside the better restaurants and wine bars. She discovered that her looks and her voice gave her an advantage over the other working women, who were for the most part desperate country girls or Cockneys. She watched them straggle through their nights, growing steadily drunker and more hoarse, sporting upper-arm bruises ever more purple.

They regarded her with disbelief and anger, especially when an old cove with a diamond stickpin could walk their importuning gauntlet unmoved, shaking off their hands, deaf to their filthiest enticements, but stop in his tracks when Lady Beatrice stepped out in front of him. "Oi! Milady's stole another one!" someone would cry. She liked the name.

One night three whores lay for her with clubs in an alley off the Strand. She pulled a knife – for she carried one – and held them at bay, and told them what she'd done to the Ghilzai tribesmen. They backed away, and fled. They spread the word that Milady was barking mad.

Lady Beatrice wasn't at all mad. It was true that the snows of the Khyber Pass seemed to have settled around her heart and left it incapable of much emotion, but her mind was sharp and clear as ice. It was difficult even to feel contempt for her fellow whores, though she saw plainly enough that many were ignorant, that they drank too much, that they habitually fell in love with men who beat them, that they wallowed in self-pity and festering resentments.

Lady Beatrice never drank. She lived thriftily. She opened a bank account and saved the money she made, reserving out enough to remain well-dressed and buy a novel now and again. She calculated how much she would need to save in order to retire and live quietly, and she worked toward that goal. She kept a resolute barrier between her body and her mind, only nominally resident in the one, only truly living in the other.

One evening she was strolling the pavement outside the British Museum (an excellent place to do business, judging from all the wealthy clientele she picked up there) when a previous customer recognized her and engaged her services for a gentlemen's party on the following night. Lady Beatrice dressed in her best evening scarlets for the occasion, and paid for a cab.

She recognized some of her better-dressed rivals at the party, at which some sporting victory was being celebrated, and they nodded to one another graciously. One by one, each portly financier or baronet paired off with a courtesan, and Lady Beatrice was just thinking that she could do with more of this sort of engagement when she heard her name called, in a low voice.

She turned and beheld an old friend of her father's, whom she had once charmed with an hour's sprightly conversation. Lady Beatrice stepped close to him, quickly.

"That is not the name I use now," she said.

"But – my dear child – how could you come to this?"

"Do you truly wish to hear the answer?"

He cast a furtive look around and, taking her by the wrist, led her into an antechamber and shut the door after them, to general laughter from those not too preoccupied to notice.

Lady Beatrice told him her story, in a matter-of-fact way, seated on a divan as he paced and smoked. When she had finished he sank into a chair opposite, shaking his head.

"You deserved better in life, my dear."

"No one deserves good or evil fortune," said Lady Beatrice. "Things simply happen, and one survives them the best one can."

"God! That's true; your father used to say that. He never flinched at unpleasantness. You are very like him, in that sense. He always said you were as true as steel."

Lady Beatrice heard the phrase with a sense of wonder, remembering that long-ago life. It seemed to her, now, as though it had happened to some other girl.

The old friend was regarding her with a strange mixture of compassion and a certain calculation. "For your father's sake, and for your own, I should like to assist you. May I know where you live?"

Lady Beatrice gave him her address readily enough. "Though I do not advise you to visit," she said. "And if you have any gallant ideas about rescuing me, think again. No lady in London would receive me, after what I endured, and you know that as well as I do."

"I know, my dear." He stood and bowed to her. "But women true as steel are found very rarely, after all. It would be shameful to waste your excellent qualities."

"How kind," said Lady Beatrice.

She expected nothing from the encounter; and so Lady Beatrice was rather surprised when someone knocked at the door of her lodging three days thereafter.

She was rather more surprised when, upon opening the door, she beheld a blind woman, who asked for her by her name.

"I am she," admitted Lady Beatrice.

"May I come in for a moment, miss, and have a few words with you?"

"As many as you wish," said Lady Beatrice. Swinging her cane before her, the blind woman entered the room. Seemingly quite by chance she encountered a chair and lowered herself into it. Despite her infirmity, she was not a beggar; indeed, she was well-dressed and well-groomed, resembling, if not a lady, certainly someone's respectable mother. Her accents indicated that she had come from the lower classes, but she spoke quietly, with precise diction. She drew off her gloves and bonnet, and held them in her lap, with her cane crooked over one arm.

"Thank you. I'll introduce myself, if I may: Mrs. Elizabeth Corvey.

We have a friend in common." She uttered the name of the gentleman who had known Lady Beatrice in her former life.

"Ah," said Lady Beatrice. "And I expect you administer some sort of charity for fallen women?"

Mrs. Corvey chuckled. "I wouldn't say that, miss, no." She turned her goggled face toward Lady Beatrice. The smoked goggles were very black, and quite prominent. "None of the ladies in my establishment require charity. They're quite able to get on in the world. As you seem to be. Your friend told me the sort of things you've seen and done. What's done can't be undone, more's the pity, but there it is.

"That being the case, may I ask you whether you'd consider putting your charms to better use than streetwalking?"

"Do you keep a house of prostitution, madam?"

"I do and I don't," said Mrs. Corvey. "If it was a house of prostitution, you may be sure it would be of the very best sort, with girls as beautiful and clever as you, and some of them as well-bred. I am not, myself; I was born in the workhouse.

"When I was five years old they sold me to a pin factory. Little hands are needed for the making of pins, you see, and little keen eyes. Little girls are preferred for the work; so much more painstaking than little boys, you know. We worked at a long table, cutting up the lengths of wire and filing the points, and hammering the heads flat. We worked by candlelight when it grew dark, and the shop-mistress read to us from the Bible as we worked. I was blind by the age of twelve, but I knew my Scripture, I can tell you.

"And then, of course, there was only one work I was fit for, wasn't there? So I was sold off into a sort of specialty house.

"You meet all kinds of odd ducks in a place like that. Sick fellows, and ugly fellows, and shy fellows. I was got with child twice, and poxed, too. I do hope I'm not shocking you, am I? Both of us being women of the world, you see. I lost track of the years, but I think I was seventeen when I got out of there. Should you like to know how I got out?"

"Yes, madam, I should."

"There was this fellow came to see me. He paid specially to have me to himself a whole evening and I thought, *oh, Lord, no*, because you get so weary of it, and the gentlemen don't generally like it if you seem as though you're not paying proper attention, do they? But all this fellow wanted to do was talk.

"He asked me all sorts of questions about myself – how old I was, where had I come from, did I have any family, how did I come to be blind. He told me he belonged to a club of scientific gentlemen. He said they thought they might have a way to cure blindness. If I was willing to let this Gentlemen's Speculative Society try it out on me, he'd buy me out of the house I was in and see that I was physicked for the pox as well, and found an honest living.

"He did warn me I'd lose my eyes. I said I didn't care – they weren't any use anyhow, were they? And he said I might find myself disfigured, and I said I didn't mind that – what had my looks ever gotten me?

"To be brief, I went with him and had it done. And I did lose my eyes, and I was disfigured, but I haven't regretted it a day since."

"You don't appear to be disfigured," said Lady Beatrice. "And clearly they were unable to cure your blindness."

Mrs. Corvey smiled. "Oh, no? The clock says half-past-twelve, and you're wearing such a lovely scarlet dressing-gown, miss, and you have such striking gray eyes – quite unlike mine. You're made of stern stuff, I know, so you won't scream now." Having said that, she slid her goggles up to reveal her eyes.

Lady Beatrice, who had been standing upright, took a step backward and clutched the edge of the table behind her.

"Dear me, you have gone quite pale," said Mrs. Corvey in amusement. "Sets off that scarlet mouth of yours a treat. House of Rimmel Red No. 3, isn't it? Not so pink as their No. 4. And, let me see, why, what a lot of books you have! *Sartor Resartus, Catherine, Falkner* – that's her last one, isn't it? – and, what's that on your bedside table?" The brass optics embedded in Mrs. Corvey's face actually protruded forward, with a faint whirring noise, and swiveled in the direction of Lady Beatrice's bed. "*Nicholas Nickleby.* Yes, I enjoyed that one, myself.

"I do hope I have proven my point now, miss."

"What a horror," said Lady Beatrice faintly.

"Oh, I shouldn't say that at all, miss! My condition is so much improved from my former state that I would go down on my knees and thank God morning and night, if I thought He ever took notice of the likes of me. I have my sight back, after all. I have my health – for I may say the Gentlemen's Speculative Society has an excellent remedy for the pox – and agreeable employment. I am here to offer you the same work."

"Would I pay for it with my eyes?" Lady Beatrice inquired.

"Oh, dear me, no. It would be a crime to spoil *your* looks, especially when they might be so useful. You were a soldier's daughter, as I understand it, miss. What would you think of turning your dishonor into a weapon, in a just cause?

"The Society's very old, you see. In the old days they had to work secretly, or folk would have burnt them for witchcraft, with all the astonishing things they invented. The secrecy was still useful even when times became more enlightened. There are all manner of devices that make our lives less wretched, that first came from the Society. They work to make the world better still.

"Now, it helps them in their work, miss, to have some sway with ministers and members of Parliament. And who better controls a man than a pretty girl, eh? A girl with sufficient charm can unlock a man's tongue and find out all sorts of things the Society needs to know. A girl with sufficient charm can persuade a man to do all sorts of things he'd never dream of doing, if he thought anyone else could see.

"And *I* can't see, of course, or so he thinks, for I never let my secret slip. When a man is a cabinet minister it reassures him to believe that the lady proprietress of his favorite brothel couldn't identify his face in a court of law. All the easier for us to trap him later. All the easier to persuade him to sign a law into being or vote a certain way, which benefits the Society.

"You and I both know how little it takes to ruin a girl, when a man can make the same mistakes and the world smiles indulgently at him. Wouldn't you like to make the world more just?

"You and I both know how little our bodies matter, for all the fuss men make over them. Wouldn't you like to put yours to good use? There are other girls like you – clever girls, well-bred girls. They did one unwise thing, or perhaps, like you, they were unlucky, and the world sent them down to the pavement. But they found they needn't stay there.

"You needn't stay there either, miss. We can offer you a clean, quiet room of your own, with a view of St. James's Park – I never tire of looking at it, myself – and a quiet life, except when working. We need never fear being beaten, or taking ill. We are paid very well. Shall you join us, miss?"

Lady Beatrice considered it.

"I believe I shall," said she.

And she did, to the great relief of the other streetwalkers.

FOUR:
In Which She Settles In
And Learns Useful Things

Lady Beatrice discovered that Mrs. Corvey had spoken perfect truth. The house near Birdcage Walk was indeed pleasant, commodious, and adjacent to St. James's Park. Her private room was full of the best air and light to be had in London. It had, moreover, ample shelves for her books, a capacious wardrobe, and a clean and comfortable bed.

She found her sister residents agreeable as well.

Mrs. Otley was, near Birdcage Walk, a rather studious young lady with fossils she had collected at Lyme Regis and a framed engraving of a scene in Pompeii in her room. At Nell Gwynne's, however, she generally dressed like a jockey, and had moreover a cabinet full of equestrian paraphernalia with which to pander to the tastes of gentlemen who enjoyed being struck with a riding crop while being forced to wear a bit between their teeth.

Miss Rendlesham, though quiet, bespectacled and an enthusiastic gardener, was likewise in the Discipline line, both general and (as needed) specialized. As a rule she dressed in a manner suggesting a schoolmistress, and was an expert at producing the sort of harsh interrogatory tones that made a member of Parliament regress to the age of the schoolroom, where he had been a very naughty boy indeed.

Herbertina Lovelock, on the other hand, was a very good boy, with the appearance of a cupid-faced lad fresh from a public school whereat a number of outré vices were practiced. She wore male attire exclusively, cropped hair pomaded sleek. She also smoked cigars, read the sporting papers with her feet on the fender, and occasionally went to the races. At Nell Gwynne's she had a wardrobe full of military uniforms both Army and Navy, all with very tight trousers with padding sewn into the knees.

The Misses Devere were three sisters, Jane, Dora, and Maude, blonde, brunette, and auburn-haired respectively. Their work at Nell Gwynne's consisted of unspecialized harlotry and also, when required, group engagements in which they worked as a team.

They alone were forthcoming to Lady Beatrice on the subject of their pasts: it seemed their Papa had been a gentleman, but ruined himself in the customary manner by drinking, gambling, and speculating in a joint stock company. Depending on whether one heard the story from Jane, Dora, or Maude, their Papa had then either blown his brains out, run away to the Continent with a mistress, or become an opium-smoker in a den in Limehouse and fallen to depths of degradation too appalling to describe. Jane played the pianoforte, Dora played the concertina, and Maude sang. They were equally versatile in other matters.

All ladies resident at the house near Birdcage Walk proved good-natured upon further acquaintance. Lady Beatrice found it pleasant to sit in the common parlour after dinner on Sundays (for Nell Gwynne's did no business on the Sabbath) and attend to her mending while Herbertina read aloud to them all, or the Misses Devere performed a medley of popular songs, as Miss Rendlesham arranged a vase of flowers from the garden. It was agreed that Lady Beatrice ought not alter her scarlet costume in any respect, since it had such a galvanic effect on customers, but Mrs. Corvey and Herbertina went with her to the shops and the dressmaker's to have a few ensembles made up, in rather more respectable colors, for day wear. Mrs. Otley presented her with a small figure of the goddess Athena from her collection of antiquities, for, as she said, "You are so very like her, my dear, with those remarkable eyes!"

All in all, Lady Beatrice thought her new situation most agreeable.

Oh, Major, sir, you wouldn't cane me, would you?" squeaked Herbertina. "Not for such a minor infraction?"

"I'll do worse than cane you, you young devil," leered the Major, or rather the Member of Parliament wearing a major's uniform. He grabbed Herbertina by the arm and dragged her protesting to a plush-upholstered settee. "Drop those breeches and bend over!"

"Oh, Major, sir, must I?"

"That's an order! By God, sir, I'll teach you what obedience means!"

"Look through this eyepiece and adjust the lens until the image comes into focus," said Mrs. Corvey in a low voice, from the adjacent darkened room. Lady Beatrice peered into the camera and beheld the slightly blurry Major gleefully dropping his own breeches.

"How does one adjust it?" Lady Beatrice inquired.

"This ring turns," explained Mrs. Corvey, pointing. Lady Beatrice turned it and immediately the Major came into focus, very much *in flagrante delicto*, with Herbertina looking rather bored as she cried out in boyish horror.

"Now squeeze the bulb," said Mrs. Corvey. Lady Beatrice did so. The gas-jets flared in the room for a moment, but the Major was far too busy to be distracted by the sudden intense brightness, or the faint *click*.

"Have we produced a daguerreotype?" inquired Lady Beatrice, rather intrigued, for she had just been reading about them in a scientific periodical to which Miss Rendlesham subscribed.

"Oh, no, dear; this is a much more advanced process. Something the Society gave us." Mrs. Corvey slid out the plate and slipped in another. "It produces an image that can be printed on paper. That shot was simply for our files. We'll have to wait until he's a bit quieter for an image we can really use. Herbertina will give you the signal."

Lady Beatrice watched carefully as the Major rode to his frenzy and at last collapsed over Herbertina. They ended up reclining on the settee, somewhat scantily clad.

"Now," said the Major, wheezing somewhat, "Tell me how enormous I was, and how overpowered you were."

"Oh, Major, sir, how could you do such a thing to a young man? I've never felt so helpless," said Herbertina tearfully, making a sign behind her back. Lady Beatrice saw it and squeezed the bulb again. Once more the lamps flared. The Major squinted irritably but paid no further heed, for Herbertina quite held his attention over the next five minutes with her imaginative account of how terrified and submissive the young soldier felt, and how gargantuan were the Major's personal dimensions.

Sadly, neither Mrs. Corvey nor Lady Beatrice heard her inspired improvisations, for they had both retreated to a small room, lit with red De la Rue's lamps and fitted up like a chemist's laboratory. There they had fastened cloth masks over their mouths and noses and were busily developing the plates.

"Oh, these are very good," said Mrs. Corvey approvingly. "Upon my soul, dear, you have a talent for photography."

"Are they to be used for blackmail?"

"Beg pardon? Oh, no; which is to say, only if it should become necessary. And if it should, this one – " she held up the second photograph, with the Major lying on the settee – "can be copied over onto a daguerreotype, and presented as an inducement to cooperate. For the present, the pictures will go into his file. We keep a file, you see, on each of the customers. So useful, when business is brisk, to have a record of each gentleman's likes and dislikes."

"I expect it is indeed. When does it become necessary to blackmail, if I may ask?"

"Why, when the Society requires it. I must say, it isn't necessary often. They're quite persuasive on their own account, and seldom have to resort to such extreme measures. Still, one never knows." Mrs. Corvey hung the prints up to dry. She turned the lever that switched off the De la Rue's lamp and they left the room, carefully shutting the door behind them. The two women walked out into the hidden corridor that ran between the private chambers. From the rooms to either side of the corridor could be heard roars of passion, or pleading cries, and now and again the rhythmic swish and crack of a birch rod over ardent confessions of wickedness.

"Are all of the customers men of rank?" Lady Beatrice inquired, raising her voice slightly to be heard over a baritone bawling *Yes, yes, I did steal the pies!*

"Yes, as a rule; though now and again we treat members of the Society. The fellows whose business it is to go out and manage the Society's affairs, mostly; the rank and file, if you like. They want their pleasures as much as the next man, and most of them have to work a good deal harder to earn them, so we oblige. That is rather a different matter, however, from servicing statesmen and the like.

"In fact, there's rather a charming custom – at least I find it so – of treating the new fellows, before they're first sent on the Society's business. Give them a bit of joy before they go out traveling, poor things, because now and again they do fall in the line of duty. So sad."

"Is it dangerous work?"

"It can be." Mrs. Corvey gave a vague wave of her hand. They entered the private chamber that served as Mrs. Corvey's office, stepping through the sliding panel and closing it just as Violet, the maid-of-all-work, entered from the reception area beyond.

"If you please, Mrs. Corvey, Mr. Felmouth's just stepped out of the Ascending Room this minute to pay a call. He's got his case with him."

"He'll want his tea, then. How nice! I was hoping we'd be allotted a few new toys." Mrs. Corvey lifted a device from her desk, a sort of speaking-tube of brass and black wax, and after a moment spoke into it: "Tea, please, with a tray of savories. The reception room. Thank you."

She set the device down. Lady Beatrice regarded it with quiet wonder. "And that would be another invention from the Society?"

"Only made by them; it was one of our own ladies invented it. Miss Gleason. Since retired to a nice little cottage in Scotland on the bonus, I am pleased to say. Sends us a dozen grouse every Christmas. Now, come with me, dear, and I'll introduce you to Mr. Felmouth. Such an obliging man!"

FIVE:
In Which Ingenious Devices
Are Introduced

The reception room was rather larger than a private parlor, with fine old dark paneling on the walls and a thick carpet. It was lit by more De la Rue's lamps, glowing steadily behind tinted shades of glass. A middle-aged gentleman had already removed his coat and hat and hung them up, and rolled up his shirtsleeves; he was perched on the edge of a divan, leaning down to rummage in an open valise, but he jumped to his feet as they entered.

"Mr. Felmouth," said Mrs. Corvey, extending her hand.

"Mrs. Corvey!" Mr. Felmouth bowed and, taking her hand, kissed it.

"And may I introduce our latest sister? Lady Beatrice. Lady Beatrice, Mr. Felmouth, from the Society. Mr. Felmouth is one of the Society's artificers."

"How do you do, sir?"

"Enchanted to make your acquaintance, Ma'am," Mr. Felmouth said, stammering rather. He coughed, blushed, and tugged self-consciously at his rolled-up sleeves. "I do hope you'll excuse the liberty, my dear – one gets so caught up in one's work."

"Pray, be seated," said Mrs. Corvey, gliding to her own chair. At that moment a chime rang and a hitherto concealed door in the paneling opened. A pair of respectably clad parlormaids bore in the tea things and arranged them on a table by Mrs. Corvey's chair before exiting again through the same door. Tea was served, accompanied by polite conversation on trivial matters, though the whole time Mr. Felmouth's glance kept wandering from Lady Beatrice to the floor, and hence to his open valise, and then on to Mrs. Corvey.

At last he set his cup and saucer to one side. "Delightful refreshment. My compliments to your staff, Ma'am. Now, I must inquire – how are the present optics suiting you, my dear?"

"Very well," said Mrs. Corvey. "I particularly enjoy the telescoping feature. It's quite useful at the seaside, though of course one must take care not to be noticed."

"Of course. And the implant continues comfortable? No irritation?"

"None nowadays, Mr. Felmouth."

"Very good. Happy to hear it." Mr. Felmouth rubbed his hands together. "However, I have been experimenting with an improvement or two . . . may I demonstrate?"

"By all means, Mr. Felmouth."

At once he delved into his valise and brought up a leatherbound box about the size of a spectacle case. He opened it with a flourish. Lady Beatrice saw a set of optics very similar to those revealed when Mrs. Corvey had removed her goggles, as she did now. Lady Beatrice involuntarily looked away, then looked back as Mr. Felmouth presented the case to Mrs. Corvey.

"You will observe, Ma'am, that these are a good deal lighter. Mr. Stubblefield in Fabrication discovered a new alloy," said Mr. Felmouth, unrolling a case of small tools. Mrs. Corvey's optics extended outward with a whirr as she examined the new apparatus.

"Yes indeed, Mr. Felmouth, they are lighter. And seem more complicated."

"Ah! That is because . . . if I may . . ." Mr. Felmouth leaned forward and applied a tiny screwdriver to Mrs. Corvey's present set of optics, losing his train of thought for a moment as he worked carefully. Lady Beatrice found herself unable to watch as the optics were removed. "Because they are greatly improved, or at least that is my hope. Now then . . . my apologies, Ma'am, the blindness is entirely temporary . . . I will just fasten in the new set, and I think you will be pleased with the result."

Lady Beatrice made herself look up, and saw Mrs. Corvey patiently enduring having a new set of optics installed in her living face.

"There," said Mrs. Corvey, "I can see again."

"Splendid," said Mr. Felmouth, tightening the last screw. He sat back. "I trust you find them comfortable?"

"Quite," said Mrs. Corvey, turning her face from side to side. "Oh!" Her optics telescoped outward, a full two inches farther than the range of the previous set, and the whirring sound they produced was much quieter. "Oh, yes, greatly improved!"

"It was my thought that if you held your hands up to obscure them at full extension, you could give anyone observing you the impression that you are looking through a pair of opera glasses," said Mr. Felmouth. "However, permit me to demonstrate the *real* improvement."

He rose to his feet and, going to the nearest lamp, extinguished it by turning a key at its base. He did this with each of the lamps in turn. When he had extinguished the last lamp the room was plunged into Stygian blackness. His voice came out of the darkness:

"Now, Ma'am, if you will give the left-hand lens casing a three-quarter turn . . ."

Lady Beatrice heard a faint *click*, and then a cry of delight from Mrs. Corvey.

"Why, the room is quite light! Though everything appears green. Ought it?"

"That is the effect of the filter," said Mr. Felmouth in satisfaction, as he switched on the lamp again. "But it was, I think, bright enough to read by? Yes, that was what I'd hoped for. We will improve it, of course, but from this moment I may confidently assert that you need never endure another moment of darkness, if you are not so inclined."

"How very useful this should prove," said Mrs. Corvey, in satisfaction. "My compliments, Mr. Felmouth! And please extend my thanks to the other kind gentlemen in Fabrication."

"Of course. As it happens, I do have one or two other small items," said Mr. Felmouth, as he went from one lamp to another, switching them back on. He sat down once more and, reaching into his bag, drew out what appeared to be a locket. "Here we are!"

He held it up for their inspection. "Now, ladies, wouldn't you say that was a perfectly ordinary ornament?" Lady Beatrice leaned close to see it; Mrs. Corvey merely extended her optics.

"I should have said so, yes," said Lady Beatrice. Mr. Felmouth raised his index finger, revealing the small hole in the locket's side, with a smaller protrusion a half-inch below.

"No indeed, ladies. This is, rather, positively the last word in miniaturization. Behold." He opened it to reveal a tiny portrait. "And—" Mr. Felmouth thumbed a catch and the portrait swung up, to display a compartment beyond, in which were a minute steel barrel and spring mechanism. "A pistol! The trigger is this knob just below the muzzle. Hold it *so* – aim and fire. Though for best results I recommend firing point-blank, if at all possible."

"Ingenious, I must say," said Mrs. Corvey. To Lady Beatrice she added, a little apologetically, "We do find ourselves in need of self-defense, now and then, you see."

"But surely the bullet must be too small to do much harm," said Lady Beatrice.

"You might think so," said Mr. Felmouth. He brought up an ammunition case, no bigger than a pillbox, and opened it to reveal a dozen tiny pin cartridges ranged in a rack, with a pair of tweezers for loading. "No bigger than flies, are they? However – one point three seconds after lodging in the target, they explode. Not with a quarter of the force of a Guy Fawkes squib, but should the bullet happen to be lodged in the brain or heart at the time, that would be quite enough to drop an assailant in his tracks."

"I would fire into my assailant's ear," said Lady Beatrice thoughtfully. "The entrance wound would be undetectable, and anyone looking at him would suppose the man had died of a stroke."

Mrs. Corvey and Mr. Felmouth stared at her. "I see you are not disposed to be squeamish, dear," said Mrs. Corvey at last. "You'll do very well."

The Misses Devere came wandering sadly into the reception area, dressed in costumes representing a doll, Puss in Boots and a harlequin respectively. "Our four o'clock gentleman sent word to say he is unavoidably detained and can't come until tomorrow," said Jane, "and we can't get the catch on the back of Dora's costume unfastened. Lady Beatrice, will you see what you can do? Oh! Hello, Mr. Felmouth!" Jane skipped across the room and sat on his knee. "Have you brought us any toys, Father Christmas?"

Mr. Felmouth, who had gone quite scarlet, sputtered a moment before managing to say "Er – yes, as it happens, I do have one or two more items. H'em! If you'll permit me . . ." He pulled the bag up on his other knee and took out a couple of the pasteboard cards of buttons generally to be found at notions shops. There were approximately a dozen buttons on each card. One set resembled oystershell pearl buttons; the others appeared to be amber glass.

"The very thing for unruly customers," Mr. Felmouth said, waving the pearl buttons. "Sew them onto a garment, and they appear indistinguishable from ordinary buttons. They are, however, a profoundly strong sedative in a hard sugar shell. You have only to drop one of these in a glass of port wine, or indeed any beverage, and within seconds the button will dissolve. Any gentleman imbibing a wineglassful will fall into a profound sleep within minutes."

"And the amber buttons?" inquired Lady Beatrice, who had risen and was unworking the catch on the back of the Puss in Boots costume.

"Ah! *These* are really useful. One button, dissolved in a man's drink, will induce a state of talkative idiocy. Gently questioned, he will tell you anything, everything. Not all of it will be truthful, I suspect, but I am confident in your powers of discernment. When the drug wears off he will have absolutely no memory of the episode." Mr. Felmouth presented the cards to Mrs. Corvey.

"Splendid," said Mrs. Corvey.

"Oh, won't the amber ones look lovely on my yellow satin?" cried Dora, popping out of the top of her costume as Lady Beatrice freed her hair from the catch. Mr. Felmouth coughed and averted his eyes.

"They would, dear, but they really ought to go to Miss Rendlesham. She would make the best use of them, after all," said Mrs. Corvey. Dora pouted.

"Dear Mr. Felmouth, can't you make up some more in different colors? Miss Rendlesham never wears yellow." Dora leaned close and tickled Mr. Felmouth under his chin with her paw-gloved hand. "Please, Mr. Felmouth? Pussy will catch you a nice fish."

"It, er, ought to be quite easy," said Mr. Felmouth, breathing a little heavily. "Yes, I'm sure I should find nothing easier. Rely on me, ladies."

"As ever, Mr. Felmouth," said Mrs. Corvey.

SIX:
In Which Disquieting Intelligence
Is Conveyed

Sir Richard H. was of advanced years, quite stout, and so he preferred to lie on his back and engage the angels of bliss, as he called them, astraddle. He lay now groaning with happiness as Lady Beatrice rode away, her gray gaze fixed on the brass rail of the bed, her red mouth curved in a professional smile in which there was something faintly mocking. Her mind was some distance off, wondering how *The Luck of Barry Lyndon* was going to turn out, for she had not yet seen a copy of the latest *Fraser's Magazine*.

At some point her musings were interrupted by the realization that Sir Richard had stopped moving. Lady Beatrice's mind consented to return to the vicinity of her flesh long enough to determine that Sir Richard was, in fact, still alive, if drenched with sweat and puffing like a railway engine. "Are you quite all right, my dear?" she inquired. Sir Richard nodded feebly. She swung herself off him and down, lithe as though he were a particularly well-upholstered vaulting horse, and checked his pulse nevertheless. Having determined that he was unlikely to expire in the immediate future, Lady Beatrice gave him a brief, brisk sponging off with eau de cologne. He was snoring by the time she drew the blanket up over him and went off to bathe in the adjacent chamber.

Lady Beatrice tended her own body with the same businesslike impartiality. During her bout with Sir Richard, her nether regions might have been made of cotton batting like a doll's, for all the sensation she had derived from the act. Even now there was only a minor soreness from chafing. Applying lotion, she marveled once again at the absurd fuss everyone made, swooning over flesh, fearing it, dreading it, lusting after it, when none of it really mattered at all . . .

She knew there had been a time when the sight of Sir Richard's naked body with its purple tool would have caused her to scream in maidenly dismay; now the poor old thing seemed no more lewd or horrid than a broken-down cart horse. And what had her handsome suitors been but so many splendid racing animals, until they lay blue and stiff in a mountain gorge, when they were even less? They might have had shining souls that ascended to Heaven; it was certainly comforting to imagine so. *Bodies* in general, however, being so impermanent, were scarcely worth distressing oneself.

Lady Beatrice got dressed and returned to the boudoir, where she settled into an armchair and retrieved a copy of *Oliver Twist* from its depths. She read quietly until Sir Richard woke with a start, in the midst of a snore. Sitting up, he asked foggily where his trousers were. Lady Beatrice set her book aside and helped him dress himself, after which she took his arm and escorted him out to the reception area, where he toddled off into the ascending room without so much as a backward glance at her.

"He might have said 'thank you,'" observed Mrs. Corvey, from her chair by the tea-table.

"A little befuddled this evening, I think," said Lady Beatrice, leaning down to adjust her stocking. "Have I anyone else scheduled tonight?"

"No, dear. Mrs. Otley is entertaining his lordship until midnight; then we may all go home to our beds."

"Oh, good. May I ask a favor? Will you remind me to look for the latest number of *Fraser's* tomorrow? The last installment—" Lady Beatrice broke off, and Mrs. Corvey turned her head, for both had heard the distinct chime that indicated the ascending room was coming back down with a passenger.

"How curious," said Mrs. Corvey. "Generally the dining area closes at ten o'clock."

"I'll take him," said Lady Beatrice, assuming her professional smile and seating herself on the divan.

"Would you, dear? Miss Rendlesham had such a lot of cleaning up to do, after the duke left, that I gave her the rest of the evening off. You're very kind."

"It is no trouble," Lady Beatrice assured her. The panel slid open and a gentleman emerged. He was bespectacled and balding, with the look of a senior bank clerk, and in fact carried a file case under his arm. He swept his gaze past Lady Beatrice, with no more than a perfunctory nod, focusing his attention on Mrs. Corvey.

"Ma'am," he said.

"Mr. Greene?" Mrs. Corvey rose to her feet. "What an unexpected pleasure, Sir. And what, may one ask, is *your* pleasure?"

"Not here on my own account," said Mr. Greene, going a little red. "Though, er, of course I should like to have the leisure to visit soon. Informally. You know. Hem. In any case, Ma'am, may we withdraw to your office? There is a matter I wish to discuss."

"Of course," said Mrs. Corvey.

"I don't mind sitting up. Shall I watch for any late guests?" Lady Beatrice inquired of Mrs. Corvey. Mr. Greene turned and looked at her again, more closely now.

"Ah. The new member. I knew your father, my dear. Please, join us. I think perhaps you ought to hear what I have to say as well."

Mr. Green, having accepted a cup of cocoa in the inner office, drank, set it aside, and cleared his throat.

"I don't suppose either of you has ever met Lord Basmond?"

"No indeed," said Mrs. Corvey.

"Nor have I," said Lady Beatrice.

"Quite an old family. Estate in Hertfordshire. Present Lord, Arthur Rawdon, is twenty-six. Last of the line. Unmarried, did nothing much at Cambridge, lived in town until two years ago, when he returned to the family home and proceeded to borrow immense sums of money. Hasn't gambled; hasn't been spending it on a mistress; hasn't invested it. Has given out that he's making improvements on Basmond Hall, though why such inordinate amounts of rare earths should be required in home repair, to say nothing of such bulk quantities of some rather peculiar chemicals, is a mystery.

"There were workmen on the property, housed there, and they won't talk and they can't be bribed to. The old gardener does visit the local public house, and was overheard to make disgruntled remarks about his lordship destroying the yew maze, but on being approached, declined to speak further on the subject."

"What does it signify, Mr. Greene?" said Mrs. Corvey.

"What indeed? The whole business came to our attention when he purchased the rare earths and chemicals; for, you know, we have men who watch the traffic in certain sorts of goods. When an individual exceeds a certain amount in purchases, we want to know the reason why. Makes us uneasy.

"We set a man on it, of course. His reports indicate that Lord Basmond, despite his poor showing at university, nevertheless seems to have turned inventor. Seems to have made some sort of extraordinary discovery. Seems to have decided to keep it relatively secret. And most certainly *has* sent invitations to four millionaires, three of them foreign nationals I might add, inviting them to a private auction at Basmond Park."

"He intends to sell it, then," said Lady Beatrice. "Whatever it is. And imagines he can get a great deal of money for it."

"Indeed, miss," said Mr. Greene. "The latest report from our man is somewhat overdue; that, and the news of this auction (which came to us from another source) have us sufficiently alarmed to take steps. Fortunately, Lord Basmond has given us an opportunity. It will, however, require a certain amount of, ah, immoral behavior."

"And so you have come to us," said Mrs. Corvey, with a wry smile.

"It will also require bravery. And quick wits," Mr. Greene added, coloring slightly. "Lord Basmond sent out a request to a well-known establishment for a party of four, er, girls to supply entertainment for his guests. We intercepted the request. We require four volunteers from amongst your ladies here, Mrs. Corvey, to send to the affair."

"And what are we to do, other than service millionaires?" asked Lady Beatrice. Mr. Greene coughed.

"You understand, it is strictly voluntary – but we want to know what sort of invention could fetch a price only a millionaire could pay. Is it, for example, something that touches on our national security? And we need to know what has become of the man we got inside."

"We shall be happy to oblige," said Mrs. Corvey, with a graceful wave of her hand.

"We would be profoundly grateful, ma'am." Mr. Greene stood and bowed, offering her the file case. "All particulars are here. Communication on the usual frequency. I shall leave the matter in your capable hands, ma'am."

He turned to depart, and abruptly turned back. Very red in the face now, he took Lady Beatrice's hand and, after a fumbling moment of indecision, shook it awkwardly.

"God bless you, my dear," he blurted. "First to volunteer. You do your father credit." He fled for the reception chamber, and a moment later they heard him departing in the ascending room.

"Am I to assume there are certain dangers we may face?" said Lady Beatrice.

"Of course, dear," said Mrs. Corvey, who had opened the file case and was examining the documents within. "But then, what whore does not endure hazards?"

"And do we do this sort of work very often?"

"We do." Mrs. Corvey looked up at her, smiling slightly. "We are no *common* whores, dear."

SEVEN:
In Which Visitors Arrive At Basmond Hall

As the village of Little Basmond was some distance from the nearest railway line, they took a hired coach into Hertfordshire. Mrs. Corvey sat wedged into a corner of the coach, studying the papers in the file case, as the Devere sisters chattered about every conceivable subject. Lady Beatrice gazed out the window at the rolling hills, green even in winter, unlike any that she had ever known. The streets of London were a realm out of nature, easy to learn, since one city is in its essentials like any other; but the land was another matter. Lady Beatrice found it all lovely, in its greenness, in the vastness of the tracts of woodland with their austere gray branches; but her senses were still attuned to a hotter, dryer, brighter place. She wondered whether she would come in time to grow accustomed to – she very nearly said *Home* to herself, and then concluded that the word had lost any real meaning.

". . . but it was only fifty-four inches wide, and so I was obliged to buy fifteen yards rather than what the pattern called for—" Jane was saying, when Mrs. Corvey cleared her throat. All fell silent at once, looking at her expectantly.

"Arthur Charles Fitzhugh Rawdon," she said, and drew out a slip of pasteboard the size of a playing card. Lady Beatrice leaned forward to peer at it. It appeared to be a copy of a daguerreotype. Its subject, holding his lapels and looking self-important, stood beside a Roman column against a painted backdrop of Pompeii. Lord Basmond was slender and pale, with small regular features and eyes of liquid brilliance; Lady Beatrice had thought him handsome, but for the fact that his eyes were set somewhat close together.

"Our host," said Mrs. Corvey. "Or our employer, if you like; one or all of you may be required to do him."

"What a pretty fellow!" said Maude.

"He looks bad-tempered, though," observed Dora.

"And I am quite sure all of you are practiced enough in the art of being agreeable to avoid provoking him," said Mrs. Corvey. "Your work will be to discover what, precisely, is being auctioned at this affair. We may be fortunate enough to have it spoken of in our presence, with no more thought of our understanding than if we were dogs. *He* may be more discreet, and in that case you will need to get it out of the guests. I suspect the lot of you will be handed around like bonbons, but if any one of them takes any one of you to his bedroom, then I strongly recommend the use of one of Mr. Felmouth's nostrums."

"Oh, jolly good," said Dora in a pleased voice, lifting the edge of her traveling cloak to admire the amber buttons on her yellow satin gown.

"Our other objective . . ." Mrs. Corvey sorted through the case and drew out a second photograph. "William Reginald Ludbridge." She held up the image. The subject of the portrait faced square ahead, staring into the camera's lens. He was a man of perhaps forty-five, with blunt pugnacious features rendered slightly diabolical by a moustache and goatee. His gaze was shrewd and leonine.

"One of our brothers in the Society," said Mrs. Corvey. "The gentleman sent to Basmond Park before us, in the guise of a laborer. He seems to have gone missing. We are to find him, if possible, and render any assistance we may. I expect that will be my primary concern, while you lot concentrate on the other gentlemen."

At that moment the coach slowed and, shortly, stopped. The coach-man descended and opened the door. "The Basmond Arms, ladies," he informed them, offering his arm to Mrs. Corvey.

"Mamma, the kind man has put out his arm for you," said Maude. Mrs. Corvey pretended to grope, located the coachman's arm, and allowed herself to be helped down from the coach.

"So very kind!" she murmured, and stood there feeling about in her purse while the other ladies were assisted into Basmond High Street, and their trunks lifted down. Temporarily anonymous and respectable, they stood all together outside the Basmond Arms, regarded with mild interest by passersby. At length the publican ventured out and inquired whether he might be of service.

"Thank you, good man, but his lordship is sending a carriage to meet us," said Mrs. Corvey, just as Jane pointed and cried, "Oooh, look at the lovely barouche!" The publican, having by this time noticed their paint and the general style of their attire, narrowed his eyes and stepped back.

"Party for the Hall?" inquired the grinning driver. He pulled up before the public house. "Scramble up, girls!"

Muttering, the publican turned and went back indoors as the ladies approached the carriage. The driver jumped down, loaded on their trunks, and sprang back into his seat. "How about the redhead sits beside me?" said the driver, with a leer.

"How about you give us a hand up like a gentleman, duckie?" retorted Maude.

"Say no more." The driver obliged by giving them each rather more than a hand up, after which Maude obligingly settled beside him and submitted herself to a kiss, a series of pinches and a brief covert exploration of her ankle. Lady Beatrice, observing this, fingered her pistol-locket thoughtfully, but Maude seemed equal to defending herself.

"Naughty boy!" said Maude, giving the driver an openly intimate fondle in return. The driver blushed and sat straight. He shook the reins and the carriage moved off along the high street, running a gauntlet of disgusted looks from such townsfolk as happened to be lounging on their front steps or leaning over their garden walls.

"My gracious, they ain't quite a friendly lot here, are they?" Maude inquired pertly, in rather coarser accents than was her wont. "Doesn't his lordship have working girls to call very often?"

"You're the first," said the driver, who had recovered a little of his compo-sure. Looking over his shoulder to be certain they had passed the last of the houses, he slipped his arm around Maude's waist.

"The first! And here we thought he was a right sporting buck, didn't we, girls? What's your name, by-the-bye?"

"Ralph, miss – I mean – my dear."

"Well, you're a handsome chap, Ralph, and I'm sure we'll get on." Maude leaned into his arm. "So his lordship ain't a bit of an exquisite, I hope? Seems a bit funny him hiring us on if he is."

Ralph guffawed. "Not from what I heard. He ain't no sporting buck, but he did get a girl with child when he was at Cambridge. Sent her back here to wait it out, but the little thing died in any case."

"What, the girl?"

"No! The baby. It wasn't right. His lordship's been more careful since, I reckon."

"Well, what's he want with us, then?" Maude reached up and stroked Ralph's cheek, tracing a line with her fingertip down to his collar. "A big stout man like you, I know *you* know what to do with a girl. His lordship don't fancy funny games?"

"I reckon you're for his party," said Ralph, shivering. "For the guests."

"Oooh! We likes parties, girls, don't we?" Maude looked over her shoulder. As she looked back Ralph grabbed her chin and gave her a violent kiss of some length, until Jane was obliged to tell him rather sharply to mind the horse.

"It's all right," said Maude, surfacing for air with a gasp. "Look here, girls, I've taken such a fancy to our dear friend Ralph, would you ever mind very much if we pulled up a moment?"

"Please yourself," said Mrs. Corvey. The carriage happened to be proceeding down a long private drive along an aisle of trees at that moment, and Ralph steered the carriage to one side before taking Maude's hand and leaping down. They disappeared into the shrubbery. Lady Beatrice looked at Mrs. Corvey and raised an eyebrow in inquiry. Mrs. Corvey shrugged. "Helps to have friends and allies, doesn't it?" she said.

"Is that Basmond Hall?" Dora stood and peered up the aisle at a gray bulk of masonry just visible on a low hill beyond rhododendrons. Mrs. Corvey glanced once toward the shrubbery and, removing her goggles a moment, extended her optics for a closer look at the building.

"That would be it," she said, replacing her goggles. "Historic place. Dates back to the Normans and such."

"An old family, then," said Lady Beatrice.

"And his lordship the last of them," said Mrs. Corvey. "Interesting, isn't it? I do wonder what sort of fellow he is."

In due course Maude and Ralph emerged from the bushes, rather breathless. Ralph swept Maude up on the seat with markedly more gallantry than before, jumping up beside her bright-eyed.

"Had a nice rattle, did you?" inquired Mrs. Corvey. Ralph ducked his head sheepishly, but Maude patted his arm in a proprietary way.

"He's a jolly big chap, dear Ralph is. But we shan't mention our little tumble to his lordship, shall we? Wouldn't want you to lose your place, Ralph dear."

"No, ma'am," said Ralph. "Very kind of you, I'm sure."

They proceeded up the drive and beheld Basmond Hall in all its gloomy splendor. If Lord Basmond had given home improvement as his reason for borrowing money, it was certainly a plausible excuse; for the Hall was an ancient motte and bailey of flints, half-buried under a thick growth of ivy. No Tudor-era Rawdons had enlarged it with halftimbering and windows; no Georgian Rawdons had given it any Palladian grace or statues. Nor did it seem now that the Rawdon of the present age had any intention of making the place over into respectable Gothic Revival; there was no sign that so much as a few pounds had been spent to repoint the masonry.

Ralph drove the carriage up the slope, over the crumbling causeway that had replaced the drawbridge, and so under the portcullis into the courtyard.

"How positively medieval," observed Dora.

"And a bit awkward to get out of, if one had to," murmured Mrs. Corvey under her breath. "Caution is called for, ladies."

Lady Beatrice nodded. It all looked like an illustration from one of her schoolbooks, or perhaps *Ivanhoe*; the courtyard scattered with straw, the stables under the lowering wall, the covered well, the Hall with its steep-pitched roof and the squat castle behind it. All it wanted was a churl polishing armor on a bench.

Instead, a black-suited butler emerged from the great front door and gestured frantically at Ralph. "Take them to the trade entrance!"

Ralph shrugged and drove the wagon around to a small door at the rear of the Hall. Here he stopped and helped the ladies down as grandly as any knight-errant, while the butler popped out of the trade door and stood there wringing his hands in detestation.

"Here you go, Pilkins," said Ralph. "Fresh-delivered roses!"

Pilkins shooed them inside and they found themselves in the back-entryway to the kitchens, amid crates of wines and delicacies ordered from some of the finest shops in London. Some two or three parlormaids were peering around a door frame at them, only to be ordered away in a hoarse bawl by the cook, who came and stared.

"I never thought I'd see the day," she said, shaking her head grimly. "Common whores in Lord Basmond's very house!"

"I beg your pardon," said Mrs. Corvey, tapping her cane sharply on the flagstones. "Very high-priced *and* quality whores, ordered special, and my girls would be obliged to you for a nice cup of tea after such a long journey, I'm sure."

"Fetch them something, Mrs. Duncan," said Pilkins. Pursing his mouth, he turned to Mr. Corvey. "I assume you are their . . . proprietress, madam?"

"That's right," said Mrs. Corvey. "And am in charge of their finances as well. We was promised a goodly sum for this occasion, and I'm sure his lordship won't be so mean as to renege."

"His lordship will, in fact, be here presently to see whether your – your girls – are satisfactory," said Pilkins, his elocution a little hampered by the difficulty he had unpursing his lips.

"Of course they're satisfactory! Girls, drop your cloaks," said Mrs. Corvey.

They obeyed her. The plain gray traveling gear fell away to reveal the ladies in all their finery. Lady Beatrice wore her customary scarlet, and the Devere sisters had affected jewel tones: Maude in emerald green, Jane in royal blue, and Dora in golden yellow satin. The effect of such voluptuous color in such a drab chamber was breathtaking and a little barbaric. Pilkins, for one, found himself recalling certain verses of Scripture. To his horror, he became aware that his manhood was asserting itself.

"If that ain't what his lordship ordered, I'm sure I don't know what is," said Mrs. Corvey. Pilkins was unable to reply, for several reasons that need not be given here, and in the poignant silence that followed they heard footsteps hurrying down the stairs and along the corridor.

"Are those the whores?" cried an impatient voice. Arthur Rawdon, Lord Basmond, entered the room.

"None other," said Mrs. Corvey. Lord Basmond halted involuntarily, with a gasp of astonishment upon seeing them.

"By God! I'm getting my money's worth, at least!"

"I should hope so. My girls are very much in demand, you know," said Mrs. Corvey. "And they don't do the commoner sort of customer."

"Ah." Lord Basmond gawked at her. "Blind. And you would be their . . ."

"Procuress, my lord."

"Yes." Lord Basmond rubbed his hands together as he walked slowly round the ladies, who obligingly struck attitudes of refined invitation. "Yes, well. They're not poxed, I hope?"

"If you was at all familiar with my establishment, sir, you would know how baseless any allegations of the sort must be," said Mrs. Corvey.

"Only look, my lord! Bloom of youth, pink of health, and not so much as a crablouse between the four of 'em."

"We'd be happy to give his lordship a closer look at the goods," said Dora, fingering her buttons suggestively. "What about a nice roll between the sheets before tea, dear, eh?" But Lord Basmond backed away from her.

"No! No thank you. Y-you must be fresh for my guests. Have they been told about the banquet?"

"Not yet, my lord," said Pilkins, blotting sweat from his face with a handkerchief.

"Well, tell them! Get them into their costumes and rehearse them! The business must proceed perfectly, do you understand?"

"Yes, my lord."

"And where are my girls to lodge, your lordship?" Mrs. Corvey inquired. Lord Basmond, who had turned as though to depart, halted with an air of astonishment.

"Lodge? Er – I assume they will lie with the guests."

"I ain't, however," said Mrs. Corvey. "And do require a decent place to sleep and wash, you know."

"I suppose so," said Lord Basmond. "Well then. Hem. We'll just have a bed made up for you in . . . erm . . ." He turned his back on the ladies and gestured wildly at Pilkins, mouthing in silence *The closet behind the stables*, and pointed across the yard to be sure Pilkins got the point. "A nice little room below the coachman's, quite cozy."

"How very kind," said Mrs. Corvey.

But the window looks out on the— mouthed Pilkins, with an alarmed gesture. Lord Basmond grimaced and, with his index finger, drew Xs in the air before his eyes.

She won't see anything, you idiot, he mouthed. Pilkins looked affronted, but subsided.

"Certainly, my lord. I'll have Daisy see to it at once," he replied.

"See that you do." Lord Basmond turned and strode from the room.

EIGHT:
In Which Proper Historical Costuming
Is Discussed

They were grudgingly served tea in the pantry, and then ushered into another low dark room wherein were a great number of florist's boxes and a neatly folded stack of bedsheets.

"Those are your costumes," said Pilkins, with a sniff.

"Rather too modest, aren't they?" remarked Lady Beatrice. "Or not modest enough. What are we intended to do with them?"

Pilkins studied the floor. "His lordship wishes you to fashion them into, er, togas. The entertainment planned is to resemble, as closely as possible, a – hem – bacchanal of the ancient Romans. And he wishes you to resemble, ah, nymphs dressed in togas."

"But the toga was worn by men," Lady Beatrice informed him. Pilkins looked up, panic-stricken, and gently Lady Beatrice pressed on: "I suspect that what his lordship requires is the chiton, as worn by the ancient hetaerae."

"If you say so," stammered Pilkins. "With laurel wreaths and all."

"But the laurel wreath was rather worn by—"

"Bless your heart, dear, if his lordship wishes the girls to wear laurel wreaths on their heads, I'm sure they shall," said Mrs. Corvey. "And what must they do, besides the obvious? Dance, or something?"

"In fact, they are to bear in the dessert," said Pilkins, resorting to his handkerchief once more. "Rather a large and elaborate refreshment on a pallet between two poles. And if they could somehow contrive to dance whilst bringing it in, his lordship would prefer it."

"We'll do our best, ducks," said Maude dubiously.

"And there are some finger cymbals in that red morocco case, and his lordship wishes that they might be played upon as you enter."

"In addition to dancing and carrying in the dessert," said Lady Beatrice.

"Perhaps you might practice," said Pilkins. "It is now half past noon and the dinner will be served at eight o'clock precisely."

"Never you fear," said Mrs. Corvey. "My girls is nothing if not versatile."

At that moment they heard the sound of a coach entering the courtyard. "The first of the guests," exclaimed Pilkins, and bolted for the door, where he halted and called back "Sort out the costumes for yourselves, please," before closing the door on them.

"Nice," said Mrs. Corvey. "Jane, dear, just open the window for us?"

Jane turned and obliged, exerting herself somewhat to pull the swollen wood of the casement free. The light so admitted was not much improved, for the window was tiny and blocked by a great deal of ivy. "Shall I try to pull a few leaves?" Jane asked.

"Not necessary, dear." Mrs. Corvey stepped close to the window and, removing her goggles, extended her optics through the cover of the vines.

"What do you see?"

"I expect this is the Russian," said Mrs. Corvey. "At least, that's a Russian crest on his coach. Prince Nakhimov, that was the name. Mother was Prussian; inherited businesses from her and invested, and it's made him very rich indeed. Well! And there he is."

"What's he look like?" asked Maude.

"He's quite large," said Mrs. Corvey. "Has a beard. Well dressed. Footman, coachman, valet. There they go – he's been let off at the front door, I expect. Well, and who's this? Another carriage! Ah, now that must be the Turk. Ali Pasha."

"Oh! Has he got a turban on?"

"No, dear, one of those red sugar-loaf hats. And a military uniform with a lot of ornament. Some sort of official that's made a fortune in the Sultan's service."

"Has he got a carriage full of wives?"

"If he had, I should hardly think he'd bring them to a party of this sort. No, same as the other fellow: footman, driver, valet. And here's the next one! This would be the Frenchman, now. Count de Mortain, the brief said; I expect that's his coat-of-arms. Millionaire like the others, because his family did some favors for Bonaparte, but mostly the wealth's in his land. A bit cash-poor. Wonder if Lord Basmond knows?

"And here's the last one. Sir George Spiggott. No question *he's* a millionaire; pots of money from mills in the north. Bad-tempered-looking man, I must say. Well, ladies, one for each of you; and I doubt you'll get to choose."

"I suppose Lord Basmond is a bit of a fairy prince after all," said Maude.

"Might be, I suppose." Mrs. Corvey turned away from the window. "Notwithstanding, if he *does* require your services in the customary way, any one of you, be sure to oblige and see if you can't slip him something to make him talkative into the bargain."

Having been left to fend for themselves, the ladies spent an hour or two devising chitons out of the bed sheets. Fortunately Jane had a sewing kit in her reticule, and found moreover a spool of ten yards of peacock blue grosgrain ribbon in the bottom of her trunk, so a certain amount of tailoring was possible. The florist's boxes proved to contain laurel leaves indeed, but also maidenhair fern and pink rosebuds, and Lady Beatrice was therefore able to produce chaplets that better suited her sense of historical accuracy.

They were chatting pleasantly about the plot of Dickens's latest literary effort when Mrs. Duncan opened the door and peered in at them.

"I don't suppose one of you girls would consider doing a bit of honest work," she said.

"Really, madam, how much more honest could our profession be?" said Lady Beatrice. "We dissemble about nothing."

"What's the job?" inquired Mrs. Corvey.

Mrs. Duncan grimaced. "Churning the ice cream. The swan mold arrived by special post this morning, and it's three times the size we thought it was to be, and the girls and I have about broke our arms trying to make enough ice cream to fill the damned thing."

"As it's in aid of the general entertainment for which we was engaged, my girls will be happy to assist at no extra charge," said Mrs. Corvey. "Our Maude does a lot of heavy lifting and is quite strong, ain't you, dear?"

"Yes, ma'am," replied Maude, dropping a curtsey. Mrs. Duncan, with hope dawning in her face, ventured further:

"And, er, if some of you wouldn't mind – there's some small work with the sugar paste, and the jellied Cupids want a steady hand in turning out . . ."

Aprons were found for them and the ladies ventured forth to assist with the Dessert.

A grain-sack carrier had been set across a pair of trestles, with a vast pewter tray fastened atop it, and a massive edifice of cake set atop that. One of the maids was on a stepladder, crouched over the cake with a piping-bag full of icing, attempting to decorate it with a frieze of scallop shells. As they entered, she dropped the bag and burst into tears.

"Oh! There's another one crooked! Oh, I'll lose my place for certain! Mrs. Duncan, I ain't no pastry cook, and my arm hurts like anything. Why don't I just go out and drown myself?"

"No need for theatrics," said Lady Beatrice, taking up the piping-bag. "Ladies? Forward!"

There was, it seemed, a great deal more to be done on the Dessert. There was sugar paste to press into pastillage forms to make all manner of decorations, including a miniature Roman temple, doves, a chariot, and bows and arrows. There were indeed Cupids of rose-flavored jelly to be turned out of their molds, resulting in rather horrible-looking little things like pinkly transparent babies. They wobbled, heads drooping disconcertingly as real infants, once mounted at the four corners of the cake. There were pots and pots of muscadine-flavored cream to be poured into the sorbetière and churned, with grinding effort, before scraping it into the capacious hollow of an immense swan mold. When it was filled at last it took both Maude and Dora to lift it into the ice locker.

"And that goes on top of the cake?" Lady Beatrice asked.

"It's supposed to," said Mrs. Duncan plaintively, avoiding her gaze.

"And we're to carry that in and dance too, are we?" said Jane, pointing with her thumb at the main mass of the Dessert, which was now creaking on its supports with the weight of all the temples, Cupids, doves, and other decorations, to say nothing of the roses and ferns trimming its bearer-poles.

"Well, that was what his lordship said," Mrs. Duncan replied. "And I'm sure you're all healthy young girls, ain't you? And it ain't like he ain't paying you handsome."

NINE:
In Which The Object Of Particular Interest Appears

Any further concerns were stilled, a half-hour into the dinner service, when Pilkins and Ralph entered the kitchen, bearing between them an object swathed in sacking. Ralph stopped short, gaping at the ladies in their chitons, and Pilkins swore as the object they carried fell to the kitchen flagstones with a clatter. Lady Beatrice glimpsed the corner of a long flat box like a silverware case, before Pilkins hurriedly covered it over again with the sacking.

"You great oaf! Mind what you're about," said Pilkins. "And you, you – girls, clear out of here. You, too, Cook. Go wait in the pantry until I call."

"Well, I like that! This ain't your kitchen, you know," cried Mrs. Duncan.

"Lordship's orders," said Pilkins. "And you can go with them, Ralph."

"Happy to oblige," said Ralph, sidling up to Maude.

"If you please," said Mrs. Corvey, "My rheumatism is painful, now that night's drawn on, and I find it troublesome to move. Mightn't I just bide here by the fire?"

Pilkins glanced at her. "I don't suppose *you'll* matter. Very well, stay there; but into the pantry with the rest of you, and be quick about it."

The ladies obeyed, with good grace, and Mrs. Duncan with markedly less enthusiasm. Ralph stepped after them and pulled the door shut.

"Heigh-ho! 'Here I stand like the Turk, with his doxies around,' " he chortled. "Saving your presence, Cook," he added, but she slapped him anyway.

Mrs. Corvey, meanwhile, watched with interest as Pilkins unwrapped the box – rather heavier, apparently, than its appearance indicated – and grunted with effort as he slid it across the floor to the creaking trestle that supported the Dessert. Mrs. Corvey saw what appeared to be a row of dials and levers along its nearer edge.

Pilkins pushed it underneath the trestle and fumbled with it a moment. Mrs. Corvey heard a faint humming sound, then saw the box rise abruptly through the air, as though it fell *upward*. It struck the underside of the tray with a crash and remained there, apparently, while Pilkins crouched on the flagstones and massaged his wrists, muttering to himself.

Then, almost imperceptibly at first but with increasing violence, the Dessert began to tremble. The jellied Cupids shook their heads, as though in disbelief. As Mrs. Corvey watched in astonishment, the Dessert on its carrier lifted free of the trestles and rose jerkily through the air. It was within a hand's breadth of the ceiling when Pilkins, having exclaimed an oath and scrambled to his feet, reached up frantically and made some sort of adjustment with the dials and levers. One end of the carrier dipped, then the other; the whole affair leveled itself, like a newly launched ship, and settled gently down until it bobbed no more than an inch above its former resting place on the trestles. The flat box was so well screened by drooping ferns and flowers as to be quite invisible.

Pilkins sagged onto a stool and drew a flask from his pocket.

"Are you quite all right, Mr. Pilkins?" said Mrs. Corvey.

"Well enough," said Pilkins, taking a drink and tucking the flask away.

"I only wondered because I heard you lord mayoring there, in a temper."

"None of your concern if I was."

"I reckon his lordship must be a trial to work for, sometimes," said Mrs. Corvey, in the meekest possible voice. Pilkins glared at her sidelong.

"An old family, the Rawdons. If they've got strange ways about them, it's not my place to talk about 'em with folk from outside."

"Well, I'm sure I meant no harm—" began Mrs. Corvey, as Mrs. Duncan threw the pantry door open with a crash.

"I'll see you get your notice, Ralph, you mark my words!" she cried. "I ain't staying in there with him another minute. He's a fornicating disgrace!"

"Indeed, I think he does a very creditable job." Maude's voice drifted from the depths of the pantry. Ralph emerged from the pantry smirking, followed by the ladies. Upon seeing the floating Dessert, Ralph pointed and exclaimed:

"Hi! That's what it does, is it? I been going mad wondering—"

Mrs. Duncan, noticing the Dessert's new state, gave a little scream and backed away. "Marry! He's done it again, hasn't he? That unnatural—"

"Hold your noise!" Pilkins told her.

"Whatever's the matter?" said Mrs. Corvey.

"The Dessert appears to be levitating," Lady Beatrice said.

"Oh, stuff and nonsense! I'm sure it's just a conjuror's trick," said Mrs. Corvey. Pilkins gave her a shrewd look.

"That's it, to be sure; nothing but a stage trick, as his lordship likes to impress people."

"So the Dessert isn't really floating in midair?" Jane poked one of the Cupids with a fingertip, causing it to writhe. "Just as you say; I'm only grateful we shan't kill ourselves carrying it in."

A bell rang then. Pilkins jumped to his feet. "That's his lordship signaling for the next course! Get those finger cymbals on, you lot! Where's the bloody swan?"

The swan was heaved out in its mold and upended over the cake, and a screw turned to let air into its vacuum; the swan unmolded and plopped into its place on the cake with an audible thud, sending the Cupids into quivering agonies.

"Right! Pick the damned thing up! He wants you *smiling* and . . . and exercising your wiles when you go out there!" cried Pilkins.

"We strive to please, sir," said Lady Beatrice, taking her place on one of the carrier poles. The Devere sisters took their places as well. They found that the Dessert lifted quite easily, for it now seemed to weigh scarcely more than a few ounces. Lady Beatrice struck up a rhythm on the finger cymbals, the Devere sisters cut a few experimental capers, and Pilkins ran before them up the stairs and so to the vast banqueting table of Basmond Hall.

"I could do with a dram of gin, after all that," said Mrs. Duncan, collapsing into her chair.

"I could, too," said Ralph.

"Well, you can just take yourself off to the stables!"

"Perhaps you'd be so kind as to guide me to my room?" asked Mrs. Corvey. "I'm rather tired."

TEN:
In Which A Proposition Is Advanced

Lord Basmond had spared no expense in the pursuit of his chosen *motif*; an oilcloth had been laid down over the flagstones and painted with a design resembling tiled mosaic on a villa floor. Hothouse palms had been carried about and placed in decorative profusion, as had an abundance of aspidistra. Five chaise longues had been set around the great central table on which Lady Beatrice spied the remains of the grand dishes that had preceded the Dessert from the kitchen: A roast suckling pig, a roast peacock with decorative tail, a dish of ortolans, a mullet in orange and lemon sauce.

On the chaise longues reclined Lord Basmond and his four guests. The gentlemen were flushed, all, with repletion. Lord Basmond, alone pale and sweating, sat up as the ladies entered and flung out an arm.

"Now, sirs! For your amusement, I present these lovely nymphs bearing a delectable and mysterious treat. The nymphs, being pagan spirits, have absolutely no morals whatsoever and will happily entertain your attentions in every respect. As for the other treat . . . you may have heard of a dish called 'Floating Island.' That is a mere metaphor. Behold the substance! Nymphs, free yourselves of your burden!"

Lady Beatrice let go her corner of the Dessert and essayed a Bacchic dance, drawing on her memories of India. She glimpsed Maude and Dora pirouetting and Jane performing something resembling a frenzied polka, finger cymbals clanging madly. Alas, all terpsichorean efforts were going unnoticed, for the banqueters had riveted their stares on the Dessert, which drifted gently some four feet above the oilcloth. Lord Basmond, having assured himself that all was as he had intended, turned his gaze on the faces of his guests, and hungrily sought to interpret their expressions. Lady Beatrice considered them, one after the other.

Prince Nakhimov had lurched upright into a sitting position, gaping at the unexpected vision, and now began to laugh and applaud. Ali Pasha had glanced once at the Dessert, was distracted by Jane's breasts (which had emerged from the top of her chiton like rabbits bounding from a fox's den) and then, as what he had seen registered in his mind, turned his head back to the Dessert so sharply he was in danger of dislocating his neck.

Count de Mortain watched keenly and got to his feet, seemingly with the intention of going closer to the Dessert to see what the trick might be. He got as far as the end of his chaise longue before Dora leapt into his arms – her ribbons and securing stitches had all come unfastened, with results that had been catastrophic, were the party of another sort – and they plumped down together on the lounge. The Count applied himself to an energetic appreciation of Dora's charms, but continued to steal glances at the Dessert. Sir George Spiggott's mouth was wide in an O of surprise, his eyes round, too, but there was a scowl beginning to form.

"What d'you call this, then—" he exclaimed, ending in a *whoof* as Maude jumped astride him and emulated a few of Lady Beatrice's movements.

"What do I call it?" replied Lord Basmond, in rather a theatrical voice. "A demonstration, gentlemen. Here I come to the point and purpose of your presences here. All of you are men of means and influence; you would know whether your respective governments would be interested in a discovery so momentous it may grant ultimate power to its owner."

"What do you mean?" demanded Sir George, who had got his breath back, as he peered around Maude. Lord Basmond cleared his throat and struck an attitude.

"When I was at Cambridge, gentlemen, I studied the vanished civilization of Egypt. I chanced to be taking a holiday in France when I was approached by an elderly beggar, a former member of the late emperor's army and a veteran of the Egyptian campaign. In his destitution he was obliged to offer for sale certain papyrus scrolls he had looted, from what source he was unable to recall, in the land of the pharaohs.

"I purchased the scrolls and returned with them to England. When they yielded up their secrets to translation, I was astonished to discover therein the method by which the very pyramids themselves were built! The ancient priests had developed a means of circumventing the force of gravity itself, gentlemen, and not with charms or spells but by the application of sound scientific principles! Vast blocks of stone were made to float, as light as balloons. Sadly, the scrolls were later lost in a fire, but fortunately not before I had committed their texts to memory.

"Consider the confection floating before you. Do you see any wires? Any props? You do not, because there are none. I have been able to reproduce the device used by the Egyptians, and I intend to sell my secret to the highest bidder.

"Now, consider the applications! Any nation owning my device must swiftly outpace its rivals for dominance. Think of the speed and ease in public works, when a single workman may lift slabs of stone as though they were feathers. Think of the industrial uses to which this may be put, gentlemen. And – dare I say it – the uses for national defense? Envision cannons or supply wagons that might be floated with the ease of soap bubbles and the speed of sleds. Imagine floating platforms from which enemy positions may be spied out, or even fired upon.

"And he who offers the highest bid gains this splendid advantage, gentlemen!"

"What is your reserve?" inquired Prince Nakhimov.

"Two million pounds, sir," replied Lord Basmond, as Sir George uttered an oath.

"You ought to have offered it to your own countrymen first, you swine!"

"You were invited, weren't you? If you want it, you're free to outbid the others," said Lord Basmond coolly. "But, please! I perceive the ice cream is melting. Let us enjoy our treat, and hope that its effects will sweeten your temper. Pleasure before business, gentlemen; tomorrow you will be given a tour of my laboratory and witness further astonishing demonstrations of levitation. Bidding will commence at precisely two in the afternoon. Tonight, you will enjoy my hospitality and the ministrations of these charming females. Pilkins? Serve the sweet course, please."

"At once, sir," said Pilkins, climbing onto a chair.

An orgy commenced.

ELEVEN:
In Which Our Heroine And Her Benefactress Make Discoveries

Having bid Ralph a civil good-night, Mrs. Corvey edged past her trunk and seated herself on the narrow bed that had been made up for her. Her hearing was rather acute, an advantage gained from the years of her darkness, and so she listened patiently as Ralph climbed the creaking stairs that led to his room above the stables. He undressed himself, he climbed into bed, he indulged in a prolonged episode of onanism (if Mrs. Corvey was any judge of the audible indicators of male solitary passion) and, finally, he snored.

When she was assured Ralph was unlikely to wake, Mrs. Corvey rose and walked to the end of her room, where a single small window admitted the light of the moon. She looked out and beheld a view down the steep slope to the gardens behind Basmond Hall. Perhaps *garden* was an ambitious term; there appeared to be an old orchard and a few rows of park. Directly below, however, was a modern structure of brick and slate, perhaps twice the size of a coachhouse, and in sharp contrast to the general air of picturesque ruin characteristic of Basmond Hall.

Mrs. Corvey regarded it thoughtfully a moment, before turning from the window and opening her trunk. She undressed quickly and drew forth a boy's clothing, simple dark trousers and a knitted jersey. Donning this attire, she opened a hidden panel in the trunk's lid and revealed a box containing a dozen brass shells, roughly the size of rifle ammunition. Taking her cane, she made certain alterations to it and loaded the shells

into the chamber revealed thereby. So prepared, Mrs. Corvey crept from
her room and into the courtyard, keeping to the shadows along its eastern edge.

It somewhat discomfited her to discover that the portcullis had been
lowered. A moment's study of the grate, however, revealed that its iron
gridwork had been constructed to block the entrance of great-thewed
knights of old. Mrs. Corvey, by contrast, being female and considerably
undernourished in her younger years, was sufficiently small enough to
writhe through without much difficulty. She scrambled down the hillside and into the dry moat, and so made her way around to the gardens.

There she stepped out upon a short space of level lawn, somewhat
ill cared-for. Beyond it was the new structure, built close against the
hillside. Mrs. Corvey wondered briefly whether it might be a hothouse,
for the north face was almost entirely windows. Circling around it, she
was surprised to note no door in evidence, nor did the windows appear
to open.

Mrs. Corvey removed her goggles and extended her optics against the
glass. Moonlight was illuminating the building's interior clearly. She saw
no plants of any kind; rather, several tables upon which were glass vessels
of the sort associated with chemists' laboratories. Upon other tables
were tools and small machinery, at the purpose of which she could only
speculate. The dark bulk of a steam engine crouched in one corner. In
the other corner Mrs. Corvey spotted a door, and realized that the only
entrance to the laboratory was from within; for the door was in the wall
that backed up to the hill behind, and must communicate with a tunnel
beyond that led upward into the tower above.

Nodding to herself, Mrs. Corvey proceeded to study the leading
around the window panes. Near the ground she found a spot in which
the pane had, apparently, been recently replaced, for the lead solder was
brighter there. Drawing a long pin from her hair, she busied herself for
a few minutes prizing down the lead, and after diligent work slipped
out the glass and set it carefully to one side. Crawling through the gap
thereby created was no more difficult than going through the portcullis had been; indeed, Mrs. Corvey mused to herself that she might
have made a first-rate burglar, had fate decreed other than her present
situation.

For the next while she examined the laboratory at some length,
committing its details to memory and wishing that Mr. Felmouth would
exert himself to build a camera small enough to be carried on such occasions. In vain she looked for any notes, papers, or journals that might
illuminate the purpose of the machines. At last Mrs. Corvey addressed

the door with her hairpin, and a long moment later stood gazing into the utter darkness of the tunnel on the other side.

In retrospect, Lady Beatrice was obliged to admit that bedsheets made an admirably practical costume for the evening's festivities. In the course of her employment she had become liberally smeared with ice cream, sugar icing, cake crumbs, rose petals, and spilled wine. The last item had fountained over her breasts, not in an excess of Bacchic enthusiasm, but when Prince Nakhimov had been startled into dropping his glass by the sight of Sir George swallowing one of the jellied Cupids whole. ("The damned press claim I eat workers' babies for breakfast," Sir George had said smugly. "Let's see if I can open my jaws wide enough!")

Lady Beatrice serviced each of the guests in turn during the amusements, for they were, one and all, inclined to share the ladies' favors. Lord Rawdon unbent so far as to permit himself to be fellatiated, when his guests insisted he partake of the carnal blisses available, but declined to retire with anyone when the long evening drew to its close. Rather, Lady Beatrice found herself claimed by Prince Nakhimov; Ali Pasha took Dora off to his bed. Jane was taken, in a brisk and businesslike manner, by Sir George Spiggott, and Maude retired on the arm of Count de Mortain.

In the privacy of the bedchamber Prince Nakhimov divested himself of his garments, and proved to be a veritable Russian Bear for hairiness and animal spirits. The sheer athleticism required left Lady Beatrice somewhat fatigued, and therefore she was more than a little discountenanced when, after two hours of his attentions, the prince pulled the blankets up, rolled away from her, and said: "Thank you. You may go now."

"But am I not to sleep here?"

"*Shto?*" The prince looked over his shoulder at her, surprised. "Sleep here? You? I never sleep with, please pardon my frankness, whores." He turned back toward his pillow and Lady Beatrice, profoundly irritated, picked up the sticky remnants of her costume and held it against herself as she left his room.

She faced now the choice of wandering downstairs in her present state of undress and searching for her trunk, there to change into a robe, and afterward to seek repose on one of the chaise longues in the dining room until morning, or simply opening one of the other bedroom doors and seeing if any of the other couples had room in bed for a third party. Being desirous of sleep, Lady Beatrice opted for the chaise longue.

She descended the stairs and made her way along the gallery that led to the grand staircase. Strong moonlight slanted in through the windows at this hour, throwing patches of brilliant illumination on several of the portraits that hung along the walls. Lady Beatrice slowed to examine them. It was plain that Lord Basmond was a true Rawdon; here in face after face were the same lustrous eyes and delicate features, to say nothing of a certain chilly hauteur common to all the portraits' subjects. Lady Beatrice remarked particularly one painting, upon which the moonlight fell directly. It was of a child, she supposed, a miniature beauty in Elizabethan costume. The wide lace collar framed the heart-shaped face. A silver net bound the hair, so fair as to appear white, and the contrast of the dark eyes with such ethereal pallor was striking indeed. *Hellspeth Rawdon, Lady Basmond*, read the brass plate on the lower frame.

Lady Beatrice, conscious of the cold, walked on. She had passed the last of the portraits when she spied a door ajar, through which the corner of a bed could be glimpsed. Hopeful of finding a warmer resting place for the night, Lady Beatrice opened the door and peered within.

The room was feebly lit by a single candle, much reduced in height, beside the bed. Lord Basmond lay across the bed, still fully dressed. His eyes were open and glistening in the candlelight. Lady Beatrice saw at once that he was dead. Nonetheless, she stepped across the threshold and had a closer look.

His mouth was open in a silent cry of protest. No wounds were in evidence; rather the unnatural angle of his neck told plainly what had effected Lord Basmond's dispatch. He couldn't have been dead no more than two hours, and yet in that time seemed to have shrunken within his evening clothes. He looked frail and pathetic. Lady Beatrice thought of the ancestral portraits, all the centuries fallen down to this sad creature lying sprawled and broken, last of the long line.

Lady Beatrice swept the room with a glance, looking for obvious clues, but found none. She stepped back into the corridor and stood pensive a moment, considering what she ought to do next.

TWELVE:
In Which Still More Discoveries Are Made

Lady Beatrice decided fairly quickly that nothing much could be accomplished in her present state of undress, and therefore she went down to the kitchen. The fire there was banked, the range still radiating pleasant warmth, and so she pumped a few gallons of water and heated them sufficiently to bathe herself by the hearth.

Having located her trunk, she dressed herself in the firelight and went out by the side door, making her way across the courtyard to the stables. She found the room that had been assigned to Mrs. Corvey and knocked softly, intending to report her discovery. When no reply came to her knock she opened the door and saw the empty bed. Returning to the kitchens, Lady Beatrice encountered Dora, just coming down the stairs in a state of sticky nudity, trailing what remained of her costume.

"Oh, good, the fire's lit," Dora exclaimed, tossing aside her costume and going to the sink to pump water. "If I don't bathe I shall simply scream. Did yours snore, too?"

"No; he pitched me out."

"Ah! They do, sometimes, don't they? My pasha went at it like a stoat in rut until he fell asleep, and then he snored so loud the bed curtains trembled."

"You never got a chance to drug him, then?"

"What, with my little buttons? No. In the first place he wouldn't drink any wine, and anyway, what would have been the point of drugging him? *We* know as much as *he* does. If we want to find out any more about the levitation device, the one to drug would be Lord Basmond."

"That would be rather difficult now, I'm afraid," said Lady Beatrice, and told what she had found on entering his lordship's bedchamber. Dora's eyes widened.

"No! You're sure?"

"I know a dead man when I see one," said Lady Beatrice.

"Damn and blast! *So* convenient to murder someone when there are whores about to blame for it. I suppose now we'll have to run all screaming and hysterical to the butler and report it. Jane and Maude will have firm alibis, at least. First, however, we'll need to report to the missus." Dora set a bucket of water on the fire.

"She isn't in her room," explained Lady Beatrice.

"No? I suppose it's possible *she* did for his lordship."

"Would she?"

"You never know; I should think it was a bit treasonous, wouldn't you, offering an invention like that to other empires? She may have made the decision to do for him and confiscate the thing for the Society. If she did, she may be out making arrangements to cover our tracks."

"Let's not go running to Pilkins yet, then," said Lady Beatrice. "What became of the rest of the Dessert?"

"That's a good question," said Dora. "Pantry?"

They left the silent kitchen and, following a trail of cake crumbs and blobs of crème anglaise, located the remaining Dessert in the pantry, as expected. Thoroughly ruined now, it lay spilt sideways on the flagstones, its grain carrier leaning against the wall.

"Once more, damn and blast," said Dora. "Where's the marvelous flying thing? The box or plank or whatever it was Pilkins carried in?"

"Not here, at any rate," said Lady Beatrice.

"You don't suppose the missus took it?"

"Might have, but—" Lady Beatrice began, as a prolonged bumping crash came from above. They looked at each other and ran upstairs, Lady Beatrice lifting her skirts to hurry. Dora, being nimbler in her present state of undress, arrived in the great hall first. Lady Beatrice heard her exclaim a fairly shocking oath, and upon joining her discovered why; for Arthur Fitzhugh Rawdon, Lord Basmond, lay in a crumpled heap at the foot of the great staircase.

The two ladies stood there considering his corpse for a long moment.

"Frightfully convenient accident," said Lady Beatrice at last.

"I think it will look better if you do the screaming," said Dora, with a gesture indicating her nudity.

"Very well," said Lady Beatrice. Dora retreated to the kitchen. Lady Beatrice cleared her throat and, drawing a deep breath, uttered the piercing shriek of a terrified female.

Mrs. Corvey paused only to switch on the night-vision feature of her optics before advancing down the tunnel. Instantly she beheld the tunnel walls and floor, stretching ahead into a green obscurity. She had expected the same neat brickwork that distinguished the laboratory building, but the tunnel appeared to be of some antiquity: haphazardly mortared with flints, here and there buttressed with timbers, and penetrated with roots throughout, threadlike white ones or gnarled and black subterranean limbs.

As she proceeded along the tunnel's length, Mrs. Corvey noted in several places the print of shoes. Most were small, not much bigger than her own, but twice she saw a much larger track, a man's certainly. Moreover she perceived strange and shifting currents of air in the tunnel. About a hundred yards in she spotted what must be their source, for a second tunnel opened where some of the flint and mortar had fallen in, creating a narrow gap in the wall.

Mrs. Corvey studied the tunnel floor in front of the gap. Someone had gone through in the recent past, to judge from the way the earth was disturbed. She turned and considered the main course of the tunnel, which ended a few yards ahead where a ladder ascended, doubtless to the tower above. Yielding to her intuition, however, she turned back and slipped through the gap into the second tunnel.

Here the walls seemed of greater antiquity still, indeed, scarcely as though shaped by human labors at all; rather burrowed by some great animal. There was an earthy damp smell and, distantly echoing, the sound of trickling water. Mrs. Corvey peered into the depths and spotted something scarlet ahead in the green gloom, an irregular mass against one wall.

She lifted her cane to her shoulder and went forward cautiously, five feet, ten feet, and then there was a sudden burst of hectic illumination and a blare of – sound? No, not sound; Mrs. Corvey was at a loss to say what sensation it was that affected her nerves so painfully. She swayed for a moment before regaining her balance. Two or three deep breaths restored her composure before she heard a groan in the darkness ahead. And then:

"You know," said a male voice, "if I'm to die here I'd much rather be shot. All this blinding me and chaining me to walls and so forth is becoming tedious."

THIRTEEN:
In Which Mr. Ludbridge
Tells A Curious Story

The scarlet mass had shifted, and resolved itself now into the shape of a man, slumped against the wall of the tunnel with one arm flung up awkwardly. As she neared him, Mrs. Corvey saw that he was in fact pinioned in place by a manacle whose chain had been passed about one of the ancient roots.

"Mr. Ludbridge?" she inquired.

His head came up sharply and he turned his face in her direction.

"Is that a lady?"

"I am, sir. William Reginald Ludbridge?"

"Might be," he said. She was within a few paces of him now and, opening a compartment in her cane, drew forth a lucifer and struck it for his benefit. The circle of dancing light so produced proved to her satisfaction that the prisoner was indeed the missing man Ludbridge. "Who's that?"

"I am Elizabeth Corvey, Mr. Ludbridge. From Nell Gwynne's."

"Are you? What becomes of illusions?"

"We dispel them," she replied, relieved to remember the countersign, for she was seldom required to give it.

"And we are everywhere. If you're wondering why your match isn't producing any light, it's because of that damned – excuse me – that device you tripped just now. It'll be at least an hour before we can see anything again."

"In fact, I can see now, Mr. Ludbridge." She blew out the tiny flame.

"I beg your pardon? Oh! *Mrs.* Corvey. You're the lady with the . . . do forgive me, madam, but I hardly expected the GSS to send the ladies' auxiliary to my aid. So the flash hasn't affected your, er, eyes?"

"It does not appear to have, sir."

"That's something, anyway. Er . . . I trust you weren't sent alone?"

"I was not, sir. Some of my girls are upstairs, I suppose you'd say, entertaining Lord Basmond and his guests."

"Ha! Ingenious. I don't suppose you happen to have a hacksaw with you, Mrs. Corvey?"

"No, sir, but let me try what I might do with a bullet." Mrs. Corvey set the end of her cane against the root where the manacle's chain passed over it, and pressed the triggering mechanism. With a *bang* the chain parted, and white flakes of root drifted down like snow. Ludbridge's arm fell, a dead weight.

"I am much obliged to you," said Ludbridge, gasping as he attempted to massage life back into the limb. "What have you found out?"

"We know about the levitation device."

"Good, but that isn't all. Not by a long way. There's this thing in the tunnel that makes such an effective burglar catcher, and I suspect there's more still."

"What precisely is it, Mr. Ludbridge?"

"Damned if I know, beg your pardon. You saw the laboratory, did you?"

"Indeed, Mr. Ludbridge, I entered that way."

"So did I. Crawled through and had a good look round. Took notes and made sketches, which I still have here somewhere . . ." Ludbridge felt about inside his coat. "Yes, to be sure. Had started up the other tunnel when I heard the trap opening above and someone starting down the ladder. Put out my light in a hurry and ducked into what I'd assumed was an alcove in the wall, hoping to avoid notice. Bloody thing crumbled backward under my weight and I fell in here.

"I heard quick footsteps hurry past, in the main tunnel without. When I felt safe I lit my candle again and looked around me. This place is only the entrance to a great network of tunnels, you know, quite a warren; it's a wonder Basmond Hall hasn't sunk into the hill. I could hear water and felt the rush of air, so I thought I'd explore and see if I could find myself a discreet exit.

"That was two weeks ago, I think. I never found an exit, though I did find a great deal else, some of it very queer indeed. There's a spring-fed subterranean lake, ma'am, and what looks to be some of the ancestral tombs of the Rawdons – at least, I hope that's what they are. Midden heaps full of rather strange things. Someone lived in this place long before the Rawdons came with William the Conqueror, I can tell you that! I'm ashamed to admit I became lost more than once. If not for the spring and my field rations I'd have died down there.

"Having found my way back up at last, I was proceeding in triumph down this passageway when I ran slap into the – the whatever-it-is that makes such a flash-bang. I was knocked unconscious the first time. When I woke I discovered I'd been chained up as you found me. That was . . . yesterday? Not very clear on the passage of time, I'm afraid."

"Clearly Lord Basmond had noticed someone was trespassing," said Mrs. Corvey.

"Too right. Haven't seen him, though. He hasn't even come down to gloat, which honestly I'd have welcomed; always the chance I could persuade him to join the GSS, after all. Just as well it was you, perhaps."

"And what are we to do now, Mr. Ludbridge?"

"What indeed? I am entirely at your disposal, ma'am."

Mrs. Corvey turned and looked intently at the floor of the tunnel. She saw, now, the braided wire laid across their path, and the metal box to which it was anchored.

"I think we had better escape, Mr. Ludbridge."

FOURTEEN:
In Which Lord Basmond Is Mourned,
With Apparent Sincerity

He must have fallen," declared Sir George Spiggott.

"A lamentable accident," said Ali Pasha, looking very hard at Sir George. So did Jane, who had trailed after them clutching her chiton to herself.

"What becomes of the auction now, may I ask?" said Prince Nakhimov.

"He had bones like sugar-sticks," said Pilkins through his tears. He was on his knees beside Lord Basmond's body. "Always did. Broke his arm three times when he was a boy. Oh, Lord help us, what are we to do? He was the only one with . . . I mean to say . . ."

"The only one with the plans for the levitation device?" said Lady

Beatrice. Pilkins looked up at her, startled, and then his face darkened with anger.

"That's enough of your bold tongue," he shouted. "I'm not having the constable see you lot here! I want you downstairs, all of you whores, now! Get down there and keep still, if you know what's good for you!" He turned to glare at Dora, who had just come up in a state of respectable dress from the kitchens.

"Suit yourself; we'll go," she said. Looking around, she added "But where's Maude?"

"Where is the Count de Mortain? He cannot have slept through such screams," said Prince Nakhimov.

"Perhaps I'd better go fetch her," said Lady Beatrice, starting up the stairs.

"No! I said you were . . . were to . . . oh, damned fate," said Pilkins, drooping with fresh tears. "Go on, get up there and wake them up. And then I want to see the back of you all."

"Happy to oblige," said Jane, striding past him to go downstairs. Lady Beatrice, meanwhile, ran up the grand staircase and along the gallery, where the faces of Rawdons past watched her passage. The moonlight had shifted from her portrait, but Hellspeth Rawdon still seemed to glimmer with unearthly luminescence.

Lady Beatrice knocked twice at the door of the bedroom that had been allotted to the Count de Mortain, but received no response. At last, opening the door and peering in, she beheld one candle burning on the dresser and Maude alone in the bed, deeply asleep.

"Maude!" Lady Beatrice hurried in and shook Maude's shoulder. "Wake up! Where is the count?"

Maude remained unconscious, despite Lady Beatrice's best efforts. Lady Beatrice sniffed at the dregs remaining in the wine glass on the bedside table, and thought she detected some medicinal odor. There was no sign of Count de Mortain in the room.

When this fact was communicated to the parties downstairs, Sir George Spiggott exclaimed, "It's the damned frog! I'll wager a thousand pounds *he* pushed Lord Basmond down the stairs!"

"You had better send for your constabulary now, rather than wait for morning," Ali Pasha told Pilkins.

"In the meanwhile, perhaps someone would assist me in getting Maude downstairs?" Lady Beatrice inquired. Prince Nakhimov volunteered and brought Maude, limp as a washrag, down as far as the Great Hall; from there Lady Beatrice and Dora carried her between them down to the kitchen.

"How awfully embarrassing," said Jane, from the hearthrug where she was bathing. "We were supposed to be the ones administering drugs!"

"We ought to have expected this," said Lady Beatrice grimly. She went to the sink and pumped a bucketful of cold water. "I should think the count drugged her and then killed Lord Basmond, meaning to steal the device."

"What?" Jane looked up from soaping herself. "I thought his lordship fell down the stairs."

Dora explained that Lady Beatrice had found Lord Basmond dead in his bedroom before his body had been flung down the stairs. Jane's eyes narrowed.

"Don't be so sure the count was his murderer," she said. "Mine was in a towering temper – did me only once, quite rough and nasty, and kept telling me it was a damned good thing I was English. At last he got out of bed and left. I asked him where he was going and he told me to mind my own business. He wasn't gone above ten minutes. When he came back he looked a different man – white and shaking. I pretended to be asleep, because I was tired of his nonsense, but he didn't try to wake me for any more fun. He tossed and turned for about twenty more minutes and then leaped out of bed and ran from the room. He was only gone about five minutes this time, and very much out of breath when he came back. Jumped into bed and pulled the covers up. It seemed only a moment later we heard you screaming."

"Did he ever seem as though he paused to hide something in the bedroom?" asked Lady Beatrice, upending the bucket's contents over Maude, who groaned and tried to sit up.

"No, never."

"He might have killed his lordship, but that doesn't mean the device has been stolen," said Dora, crouching beside Maude and waving a bottle of smelling salts under her nose. Maude coughed feebly and opened her eyes.

"Damn and blast," she murmured.

"Wake up, dear."

"That bastard slipped me a powder!"

"Yes, dear, we'd guessed."

"And we'd had such a lovely time in bed." Maude leaned forward, massaging her temples. "Such a jolly and amusing man. He's got no money, though. Told me he was delighted to accept a night of free food and copulation, but isn't in any position to bid on the levitation device."

"Have you any idea where he's got to?"

"None. What's been going on?"

The other ladies gave her a brief summary of what had occurred. In the midst of it, Mrs. Duncan came shuffling downstairs in tears, clutching a candlestick.

"Oh, it's too cruel," she sobbed. "What'll become of us now? And the Basmonds! What of the Basmonds?"

"Bugger the Basmonds," said Maude, who was still feeling rather ill.

"How dare you, you chit! They're one of the oldest families in the land!" cried Mrs. Duncan. "Ruined now, ruined! And there he went and spent all the trust fund— What's to happen now?" She sank down on a stool and indulged in furious tears.

"Trust fund?" asked Lady Beatrice.

"None of your bloody business. It's the end of the Basmonds, that's all."

"There aren't any cousins to inherit?" inquired Dora sympathetically.

"No." Mrs. Duncan blew her nose. "And poor Master Arthur never married, on account of him being – well—"

"A fairy prince?" said Jane, toweling herself off. Lady Beatrice winced, for it was hardly a tactful remark, but Mrs. Duncan lifted her head sharply.

"You been reading in the library? You wasn't allowed in there!"

"No, I haven't read anything. I don't know what you mean," said Jane.

"That's in a book in the library," said Mrs. Duncan. "About the Rawdons having fairy blood. Old Sir Robert finding a girl sitting up there on the hill in the moonlight, and she putting a spell on him. And that was why, ever since . . ." She trailed off into tears again.

"What a charming story," said Lady Beatrice. "Now, if you'll pardon a change of subject, my dear: I notice the levitation device has been removed from under the cake. Do you happen to know where it was put?"

"Wasn't put anywhere," said Mrs. Duncan. "I pushed the nasty thing into the pantry like it was and left it for morning. You mean to say it's gone?"

FIFTEEN:
In Which Our Heroine Is Obliged
To Exert Herself

Mrs. Corvey, upon inspecting the box on the passage floor, discovered a switch on one end. Cautiously, using her cane, she pushed the switch to its opposite position. A humming noise ceased, so faint it had been imperceptible until it stopped.

"I believe we may now pass safely, Mr. Ludbridge."

"Glad to hear it," Ludbridge said, wheezing as he tried to get to his feet. "Oh – ow – oh, bloody hell, I'm half crippled."

"You may lean on me," said Mrs. Corvey, taking his hand and pulling his arm around her shoulders. "Not to worry, dear; I'm a great deal stronger than I look."

"As yet I've no idea what you look like at all," replied Ludbridge. "Ha! The blind leading the blind, although in our case it makes excellent sense. Lead on, dear lady."

They made their way out again into the main tunnel, and hurriedly down it to the laboratory. Ludbridge was able to crawl through the hole in the window easily enough, but was obliged afterward to sit and catch his breath.

"It seems a lifetime ago I went in there," he said, gasping. "By God, the night air smells sweet! Rather odd nobody noticed the pane missing in all that time, though."

"In fact, someone did," said Mrs. Corvey. "It had been replaced when I found it this evening."

"Really? Well, that's enough to lend new vigor to my wasted limbs," said Ludbridge, getting up with a lurch. "Let's get the hell out of here, shall we?"

Mrs. Corvey led him out through the hedge and around the moat. She had a moment of worry about getting through the portcullis, for Ludbridge was a man of respectable girth. However, just as they came to the causeway the portcullis came rattling up. Someone drove the carriage forth in great haste; the portcullis was left open behind them. Mrs. Corvey looked after the carriage in keen interest, thinking she recognized Ralph gripping the reins. She wondered what might have happened, to send him out at such speed.

"We had best hurry, Mr. Ludbridge," she said.

"Swiftly as I may, ma'am," he replied, crawling after her on hands and knees. When they reached the courtyard Mrs. Corvey was disconcerted to see lights blazing in the Great Hall. She endeavored to pull Ludbridge along after her, and was greatly relieved when they tumbled together through the door into her room.

Forty years I've worked here," said Mrs. Duncan, somewhat indistinctly, for she was now on her third glass of gin. The scullery and parlor maids, all in their nightgowns, were huddled around her like chicks around a hen, in varying degrees of tearful distress.

"Well, consider: you are now at liberty to travel," said Jane helpfully. Mrs. Duncan gave her a dark look and two of the maids were provoked into fresh weeping.

"I've just remembered," said Lady Beatrice. "I left something in Prince Nakhimov's room. I wouldn't wish to be so indiscreet as to take the front stairs, when the constable may arrive any moment . . . Are there back stairs, Mrs. Duncan?"

The cook pointed at a doorway beyond the pantry. "Mind you be quick about it."

"I shall endeavor to be," said Lady Beatrice. With a significant glance at the Devere sisters, she hastened up the back stairs.

"Lordship's good name at stake and all . . ." muttered Mrs. Duncan, and had another dram of gin.

Lady Beatrice ran at her best speed, and arrived at last in the gallery. She paused a moment, catching her breath, listening. She heard Prince Nakhimov telling a long anecdote, to which Sir George, Pilkins, Ali Pasha, and several valets were listening. Creeping to the edge of the grand staircase she beheld them through a fog of cigar smoke, seated around Lord Basmond's corpse.

Turning, she crossed the gallery and went up to the guests' rooms. She opened the count's door and stepped within. The candle still illuminated the room. By its light Lady Beatrice made a quick and thorough search for the levitation device. Opening the count's trunk, she dug through folded garments. Upon encountering a book she drew it forth and examined it. It was merely a popular novel, but stuck within were a number of papers. One in particular bore an official seal, and appeared to have been signed by Metternich. Lady Beatrice's grasp of French was imperfect, but sufficient for her to make out a phrase here and there. *You will attempt by any means possible to see if his lordship would be agreeable . . . do not need to remind you of the consequences if you fail . . .*

"I did not know that whores were fond of reading."

Lady Beatrice looked up. A man stood in the doorway of the antechamber connecting to Count de Mortain's room. His accent was harsh, Germanic; he appeared to be the count's valet. He was holding a knife. Lady Beatrice considered her options, which were few.

"We aren't," she replied. "I was looking for the count; did you know there's been an accident? Lord Basmond is dead."

The valet had started toward her, menace in his eyes, but at her news he stopped in astonishment. "Dead!"

She hurled herself at him and bore him backward. They fell across the bed. The valet struck at her with the knife. Lady Beatrice experienced then an eerie sense of stepping away from herself, of watching as the patient draft animal of her body bared its teeth and fought for its life. The struggle was a vicious one, as any fight between animals must be. Lady Beatrice was pleased to observe that her flesh had not lost the strength it had drawn upon in the Khyber Pass. She was particularly pleased to see herself wrenching the knife from the valet's hand and stunning him with a sharp downward strike of the pommel. He sagged backward, momentarily unconscious.

So far sheer instinct had preserved her; now Lady Beatrice picked herself up, poured a glass of water from the carafe on the bedside table, and dropped into it a button torn from her blouse. The button dissolved with a gentle hiss. She lifted the valet's head, murmuring to him in a soothing voice, and held the glass to his lips. He drank without thinking, before opening his eyes.

"*Danke, Mutter . . .*" he whispered. He opened his eyes, looked up at Lady Beatrice, and started. "Filthy bitch! I'll kill you—"

"Bitch, unfortunately, yes. Filthy? Certainly not." Lady Beatrice held him down without much effort, as the drug took its swift effect. "And certainly not the sort of bitch who allows herself to be killed by men like you. Yes, you do feel unaccountably sleepy now, don't you? You can barely move. Just close your eyes and go back to Dreamland, dear. It will be so much easier."

When he lay unconscious at last, and having verified by lifting his eyelid that he was, in fact, unconscious, Lady Beatrice rose and considered him coldly. She lifted his legs onto the bed, removed his shoes, and moreover made certain adjustments to his clothing in order to suggest the lewdest possible scenario to anyone discovering him later. Then Lady Beatrice retrieved the papers she had dropped from the floor and secreted them in her bodice.

She left the room and closed the door quietly.

SIXTEEN:
In Which A Curious Creature Is Introduced

You know, I believe my sight has returned," said Ludbridge, blinking and rubbing his eyes. Mrs. Corvey, who had just finished changing her clothing while explaining how matters presently stood, turned to raise an eyebrow at him.

"My congratulations, Mr. Ludbridge. Lovely feeling, isn't it?"

"It is indeed, Mrs. Corvey."

"Now, Mr. Ludbridge, I believe I'll just go see how my ladies are getting on. Like to know why all the lights are burning at the Hall, as well. I suggest you avail yourself of the soap and the washbasin and polish yourself up a bit, eh? So you don't look quite so much as though you'd spent the last fortnight mucking about in caves. There's a hairbrush and a comb on the table you can use, too."

"Thank you, ma'am, I certainly shall."

Mrs. Corvey drew her shawl around her shoulders and stepped out into the courtyard. She walked briskly toward the Great Hall, watching the lit windows, and consequently was startled when she trod on something unexpected. She looked down. She stared for a long moment at what lay in the courtyard. Then Mrs. Corvey turned around and walked back to the room behind the stables. She opened the door and beheld Ludbridge in the act of washing his face. When, puffing and blowing like a walrus, he reached for a towel, she said:

"If you please, Mr. Ludbridge, there's a dead Frenchman outside. I wonder if you would be so kind as to come have a look at him?"

"Happy to oblige," said Ludbridge, and followed her out into the courtyard. When they reached the corpse he drew a small cylindrical object from his pocket and adjusted a switch on it. A thin beam of brilliant light shot from one end, occasioning a cry of admiration from Mrs. Corvey.

"Oh, I do hope Mr. Felmouth makes up a few of those for me!"

"We call them electric candles; very useful. Let's see the beggar . . ." Ludbridge shone the light on the dead man's face, and winced. Count de Mortain's features were still recognizable, for all that they were distorted and frozen in a grimace of fear; quite literally frozen, too, blue with cold, glittering with frost. His arms were stretched above his head like a diver's, his fingers crooked as though clawing.

"What the deuce! This is Emile Frochard!"

"Not the Count de Mortain?"

"Not half. This fellow's a spy in the pay of the Austrians! But they've been blackmailing the real Count. Shouldn't be surprised if they hadn't intercepted the invitation to this auction. Well, well. Damned odd. I wonder how he died?"

"I believe I have an idea," said Mrs. Corvey, glancing at the house. "I'll know more presently."

"Ought we to do anything with him?"

"No! Let him lie for now, Mr. Ludbridge."

Lady Beatrice stood still a moment in the corridor outside the bedchambers, listening intently. Prince Nakhimov had apparently launched into another anecdote, something to do with hunting wolves. An icy gust of wind crossed the floor, so unexpected as to make Lady Beatrice start. Were she a less ruthlessly pragmatic woman, she had imagined some spectral origin to the chill. A moment's keen examination of the hallway revealed that a tapestry hung at the rear of the hall, moving as though stirred by a breeze. Lady Beatrice glimpsed the bottom of a door in the wall.

She approached it warily and drew the tapestry aside. The revealed door was ajar. Lady Beatrice saw beyond a short corridor, lit by moonlight through unglazed slit-windows, with another door at its end.

Venturing into the corridor, Lady Beatrice peered through one of the windows and saw that it was high in the air, in effect an enclosed bridge connecting the rear of the house with the tower atop the motte. She hurried across bare wooden planks and tried the door at the other end. It opened easily, for the lock was broken.

Lady Beatrice stood blinking a moment in the brilliant light of the room beyond. The light came not from candles or oil lamps, but from something very like an immense battery of De la Rue's vacuum lamps; and this astonished Lady Beatrice, for, as far as she had been aware, no one but the Gentlemen's Speculative Society had been able to build practical vacuum lamps.

Her astonishment was as nothing, however, compared to that of the room's occupant. He turned, saw her, and froze a moment. He might have been Lord Basmond's ghost, so like him he was; but smaller, paler, infinitely more fragile-looking. His hands and naked feet were white as chalk, and too long to seem graceful. In the way of clothing he wore only trousers with braces and a shirt, cuffs rolled up prodigiously, and a leather band about his nearly hairless head. Clipped to the band were several pairs of spectacles of different sorts, on swiveling brackets, and a tiny vacuum lamp that presently threw a flood of ghastly light upon his terrified face.

He screamed, shrill as a rabbit in a trap, and scuttled out of sight.

Lady Beatrice stepped forward into the circular chamber. Against the far wall was a small bed, a dresser, and a washstand. In the midst of the room was a trap door, firmly shut and locked. Beside it was a sort of workbench, on which was what appeared to be a disassembled clock, and it was plain from the tools scattered about that the creature had been working on it when Lady Beatrice entered. The most remarkable thing about the room, however, was its decoration. All around the room's white plaster, reaching as high as ten to twelve feet, were charcoal drawings of machines: gears, pulleys, pistons, springs, wires. Here and there were what seemed to be explanatory notes in shorthand, quite illegible to Lady Beatrice. Nor was she able to discern any purpose or plan to the things depicted.

She walked around the workbench, searching for the room's inhabitant. He was nowhere in sight now, but there beyond the trap door was a chest roughly the size and shape of a blanket-press. Lady Beatrice knelt beside the chest.

"You needn't be afraid, Mr. Rawdon," she said.

From within the chest came a gibbering shriek, which cut off abruptly.

"Leave him alone," said another voice, seemingly out of midair. The illusion was so complete Lady Beatrice looked very hard at the wall, half-expecting to see a speaking tube. "Can't you see you can't talk to Hindley? Go talk to Arthur instead."

"I'm afraid Arthur is dead, Hindley."

"I'm not Hindley! I'm Jumbey. Arthur isn't dead. How ridiculous! Now, you run along and leave poor Hindley alone. He's far too busy to deal with distractions."

"May I speak with you, then, Jumbey? If I promise to leave Hindley alone?"

"You must promise. And keep your promise!"

"I do. I will. Tell me, Jumbey: Hindley builds things, doesn't he?"

"Of course he does! He's a genius."

"Yes, I can see that he must be. He built the levitation device, didn't he?"

"You saw it, did you? Yes. Arthur took it, but Hindley didn't mind. He can always make another."

"Did Arthur ask Hindley to make a levitation device for him?"

"Arthur? No! Arthur's the stupid one. He'd never have come up with such an idea on his own. Hindley was being kept in the little room with the wardrobe. His toys kept rolling under the wardrobe, and poor Hindley couldn't reach them, and nasty Pilkins wouldn't come fetch them for him anymore. So Hindley made something to make the wardrobe float, you see, and then he could always rescue his own toys.

"And then Arthur came home and the servants told on Hindley, and he was so frightened, poor thing, because he was sure it would be the little dark room and the cold water again. But Arthur told Hindley he'd give him a nice big room and a laboratory of his own, if Hindley would make things for him. And Hindley could have all the candy floss he wanted. And Arthur would keep all the strangers away. But he didn't!" The last words were spat out with remarkable venom.

"Didn't he, Jumbey?"

"No! Not a scrap nor a shred of candy floss has Hindley tasted. And there was a big blundering nosey-parker spying on Hindley, down in the

tunnels. Hindley had to deal with him all by himself, which was so difficult for poor Hindley, because he can't be seen by people, you know."

"I am so sorry to hear it, Jumbey."

"Arthur is *supposed* to look after Hindley and protect him! Mummy
said so. Always."

"Well, Jumbey dear, I'm afraid Arthur can't do that anymore. We will
have to make some other arrangement for Hindley."

"Has Arthur gone away to school again?"

Lady Beatrice thought carefully before she spoke. "Yes. He has."

"An-an-and poor Hindley will be left with Pilkins again?" The confident voice wavered. "Hindley doesn't want that. Hindley doesn't like the
little room and the cold water!"

"I believe we can help Hindley, Jumbey."

"How?"

SEVENTEEN:
In Which The Ladies Triumph

Bloody hell!" exclaimed Mrs. Corvey. Dora, who had just concluded
explaining the events of the last two hours, reeled at her language. She
glanced around, grateful that Mrs. Duncan had drunk herself into insensibility and the maids had all gone back to their beds, and said: "I'm sure
we did our best, ma'am."

"I'm sure you did; but this is a complication, as now there'll be an
inquiry. We ain't getting the levitating thing either; I rather suspect
it's well on its way to the moon by this time. At least none of that lot
upstairs will get it either. Dear, dear, what a puzzle. Where's Lady
Beatrice?"

"Here," said she, hurrying down the back stairs quick as a cat. "I am so
glad to see you well, ma'am. Did you discover anything?"

"I did, as it happens."

"So did I." Lady Beatrice drew up a kitchen chair and, leaning
forward, told her a great deal in an admirably brief time. Mrs. Corvey
then returned the favor. Jane, Dora, and Maude listened intently, now
and then exclaiming in amazement or dismay.

"Well!" said Mrs. Corvey at last. "I think I see a way through our
difficulties. Jane, my dear, just go out to the room behind the stable and
knock. Ask Mr. Ludbridge if he would be so kind as to step across, and
bring the dead Frenchman with him."

*   *   *

Pilkins looked up with a scowl as Lady Beatrice entered the Great Hall.

"Didn't I tell you hussies to keep to your places belowstairs?" he cried. "The constable will be here any minute!"

"If you please, sir, there's a gentleman arrived in the courtyard, but it's not the constable," said Lady Beatrice. "And I was wondering, sir, if we mightn't just take ourselves off to London tonight, so as to avoid scandal?"

"For all I care you can go to—" said Pilkins, before a solemn knock sounded at the door. He rose to open it. Mr. Ludbridge stood there with a grave expression on his face.

"Good evening; Sir Charles Haversham, Special Investigator for Her Majesty's Office of Frauds and Impostures. I have a warrant for the arrest of Arthur Rawdon, Lord Basmond."

Pilkins gaped. "He – he's dead," he said.

"A likely story! I demand you produce him at once."

"No, he really is dead," said Prince Nakhimov, standing and lifting a corner of the blanket that had been thrown over Lord Basmond's corpse. Ludbridge, who had walked boldly into the Great Hall, peered down at the dead man.

"Dear, dear. How inconvenient. Oh, well; I do hope none of you gentlemen had paid him any considerable sums of money?"

"What d'you mean?" said Sir George Spiggott.

"I mean, sir, that my department has spent the last six months carefully building a case against his late lordship. We have the sworn testimony of no fewer than three conjurors, most notably one Dr. Marvello of the Theater Royal, Drury Lane, that his lordship paid them to teach him common tricks to produce the illusion of levitation. We also intercepted correspondence that led us to believe his lordship intended to use this knowledge to defraud a person or persons unknown."

"But – but—" said Pilkins.

"Good God!" cried Sir George. "A confidence trickster! I knew it! I told him to his face he was a damned un-English bounder—"

"Do you mean to say you quarreled with his lordship, sir?" inquired Lady Beatrice quietly.

"Er," said Sir George. "No! Not exactly. I implied it. I mean to say, I was going to tell him that. In the morning. Because I was, er, suspicious, yes, damned suspicious of his proposal. Yes. I know a liar when I see one!"

"So do I," said Ludbridge, giving him a stern look, at which he wilted somewhat. "And I take it his lordship has died as the result of misadventure?"

"We are waiting for your constabulary to arrive, but *it would appear*

Lord Basmond fell down the stairs and broke his neck," said Ali Pasha, with a glance at Sir George.

"Shame," said Ludbridge. "Still, Providence has a way of administering its own justice. None of you were defrauded, I hope?"

"We had as yet not even bid," said Prince Nakhimov.

"Capital! You've had a narrow escape, then. I suspect that my work is done," said Ludbridge. "Much as I would have liked to bring the miscreant into a court of law, he is presently facing a far sterner tribunal."

"If you please, sir," said Pilkins, in a trembling voice. "My lordship wasn't no fraud—"

Ludbridge held up his hand in an imperious gesture. "To be sure; your loyalty to an old family fallen on evil times is commendable, but it won't do, my good man. We have proof that his lordship was heavily in debt. Do you deny it?"

"No, sir." Pilkins' shoulders sagged. The sound of wheels and hoofbeats came from the courtyard. "Oh; that'll be our Ralph bringing the constable, I reckon."

"Very good." Ludbridge surveyed them all. "Gentlemen, in view of the tragic circumstances of this evening, and considering the Rawdons' noble history – to say nothing of your own reputations as shrewd men of the world – I do think nothing is to be gained by bruiting this scandal abroad. Perhaps I ought to quietly withdraw."

"If you only would, sir—" said Pilkins, weeping afresh.

"The kitchens are down here, sir," said Lady Beatrice, leading the way. As they descended, they heard the constable's knock and Ali Pasha saying, "Should someone not go waken the count?"

A splendid farrago of lies, sir," said Lady Beatrice, as they descended.

"Thank you. Perhaps we ought to quicken our pace," said Ludbridge. "I should like to be well clear of the house before anyone goes in search of the Frenchman."

"Where did you put him, sir, if I may ask?"

"In his bed, where else? And a nice job someone did on his partner, I must say. Let the Austrians clean that up!"

"Thank you, sir."

"Did anyone hear us?" asked Dora, as they entered the kitchen. "I had to get Jane to help me lift it – not heavy, you know, but awkward."

"They didn't hear a thing," said Lady Beatrice, kneeling beside the chest. "Jumbey? Jumbey, dear, is poor Hindley all right?"

"He's frightened," said the eerie voice. "He can tell there are strangers about."

"Tell him he needn't worry. No one will disturb him, and soon he'll have a bigger and better laboratory to play in."

"Maude, just you go catch your Ralph before he puts the horses away," said Mrs. Corvey, and Maude went running out crying:

"Ralph, my love, would you oblige us ever so much? We just need a ride to the village."

The tragedy of Lord Basmond's death set tongues wagging in Little Basmond, but what really scandalized the village was the death of the French count at the hands of his Austrian valet; a crime of passion, apparently, though no one could quite determine how the valet had managed to break all the count's bones. The local magistrate was secretly grateful when an emissary of the Austrian government showed up with a writ of extradition and took the valet away in chains. More: in a handsome gesture, the Austrians paid to have the count's corpse shipped back to France.

Ali Pasha and Prince Nakhimov returned alive to their respective nations, wiser men. Sir George Spiggott returned to his vast estate in Northumberland, where he took to drink and made, in time, a bad end.

When Lord Basmond's solicitors looked through his papers and discovered the extent of his debts, they shook their heads sadly. The staff was paid off and dismissed; every stick of furniture was auctioned in an attempt to satisfy the creditors, and when even this proved inadequate, Basmond Park itself was forfeit. Here complications ensued, with the two most importunate creditors wrangling over whose claim took precedence. In the end the case was tied up in chancery for thirty years.

EIGHTEEN:
In Which It Is Summed Up

I say, ladies!" Herbertina tilted her chair back and rested her feet on the fender. "Here's a bit of news; Basmond Hall has collapsed."

"How awfully sad," said Jane, looking up from the pianoforte.

"Indeed," said Miss Otley. "It was an historic site of great interest."

"It says here it fell in owing to the collapse of several hitherto unsuspected mine shafts beneath the property," said Herbertina.

"I don't doubt it," remarked Mrs. Corvey, with a shudder. "I'm surprised the place didn't fall down with us in it."

"And soon, no doubt, shall be a moldering and moss-grown mound haunted by the spectres of unquiet Rawdons," said Lady Beatrice, snipping a thread of scarlet embroidery floss. "Speaking of whom, has there been any word of poor dear Jumbey?"

"Not officially," said Mrs. Corvey. "There wouldn't be, would there? But Mr. Felmouth has intimated that the present Lord Basmond is developing a number of useful items for Fabrication."

"Happily, I trust?"

"As long as he gets his candy floss regular, yes."

"Jolly good!" Maude played a few experimental notes on her concertina. "Who's for a song? Shall we have 'Begone, Dull Care,' ladies?"

A note about the story: Kage Baker wrote science fiction and fantasy, but what she loved to read was history. The Women of Nell Gwynne's *(Subterranean Press, 2009) was born from a vignette in Kage Baker's steampunk novel* Not Less Than Gods *(Tor, 2010). Kage had built the Gentlemen's Speculative Society, a Victorian predecessor to Dr. Zeus, Inc. in the Company stories. She wanted a player she could send into that Great Game of top hats and aetheric energies and geared death ray machines; the eponymous ladies of Nell Gwynne's were intended to provide a saucy little interlude for her novice spies. But then they got away from her. She said their voices would not fall silent.*

Kage had an enormous background in stage management and improvisation. That contributed a lot to the genteelly perverse theater of Nell Gwynne's. The demimondaines of Nell's were inspired by backstage lunacy at the Dickens Fair where Kage spent every December; it all drew on every desperately under-provisioned show she ever wrote, directed, or performed in. And because Kage was Kage, there was a wide streak of rather black humor in all this. There's an undeniable element of farce in the business of a brothel anyway: so much strained fantasy and desperate make-believe! A Victorian whorehouse, she said, was a perfect place wherein to poke fun at authority with its breeches round its knees.

Kage Baker (1952 to 2010) was a daughter of Hollywood. She grew up in the Hollywood Hills, as close as the modern world can come to the Border of Faerieland – the Wild Hunt came to cocktail parties in her mother's rose garden, and Kage got to eat the fruit spears out of their drinks.

All this gave her a unique vision of what was real and what was not, and how the many realities of the world blend together. She was fascinated with the layers of reality, and how strangeness peeks out between those layers to confound everyday life. Often, in fact, strangeness stands up and shouts and waves its arms to get our attention – then life gets very odd indeed. Those were the moments she liked the best: the collision between mundane and fantastic. How every elfin prince has to worry about how to pay the rent; how even a Dark Lord's fortress needs functional plumbing; how immortality can only be endured by clinging to mortal appetites. How you make a living home on Mars.

Kage started writing about all this when she was nine years old, and she wrote until the week before her death from cancer in January 2010. What Kage mostly *did* was write. Everything else she did – acting, painting, one-thousand-mile-a-weekend commutes up and down California – poured straight into her stories. Once the stories and novels began to sell, she rebuilt her life around writing – ecstatic to be making her living doing what she loved best. By the last year of her life, she couldn't write fast enough to keep up with the demands; many notes and story lines are still waiting in her files. She ran out of time before she ran out of ideas.

Kage was lucky, and she knew it. She said that writing never failed, that there was nothing as satisfying as sitting down and falling into the world behind the keyboard. She had a clear picture of her muse – her very male muse – and she said she could always feel his hand on the nape of her neck, urging her on as she wrote. That may have been why she wrote so constantly, at such a breakneck speed – like a runner chasing the rising sun, like a woman running toward her lover. And in the end, I think she caught him.

—Kathleen Bartholomew

RHYSLING AWARDS

RHYSLING AWARDS

Since 1978, when Suzette Haden Elgin founded the Science Fiction Poetry Association, its members have recognized achievement in the field of speculative poetry by presenting the Rhysling Awards, named after the blind bard protagonist of Robert A. Heinlein's "The Green Hills of Earth."

Every year, each SFPA member is allowed to nominate two poems from the previous year for the Rhysling Awards: one in the "long" category (50+ lines) and one in the "short" category (1–49 lines). Because it's practically impossible for each member to have read every nominated poem in the various publications where they originally appeared, the nominees are all collected into one volume, called *The Rhysling Anthology*. Copies of this anthology are mailed to all the members, who read it and vote for their favorites. The top vote-getters in each of the two categories become the Rhysling winners. Past winners have included Michael Bishop, Bruce Boston, Tom Disch, Joe Haldeman, Alan P. Lightman, Ursula K. Le Guin, Susan Palwick, Lucius Shepard, Jeff VanderMeer, Gene Wolfe, and Jane Yolen. In 2006, the SFPA created a new award, the Dwarf Stars Award, to honor poems of 10 lines or less.

SONG FOR AN ANCIENT CITY

Amal El-Mohtar

Merchant, keep your attar of roses,
your ambers, your oud,
your myrrh and sandalwood. I need
nothing but this dust
palmed in my hand's cup
like a coin, like a mustard seed,
like a rusted key.
I need
no more than this, this earth
that isn't earth, but breath,
the exhalation of a living city, the song
of a flute-boned woman,
air and marrow on her lips. This dust,
shaken from a drum, a door opening, a girl's heel
on stone steps, this dust
like powdered cinnamon, I would wear
as other girls wear jasmine and lilies,
that a child with seafoam eyes
and dusky skin might cry, *There
goes a girl with seven thousand years
at the hollow of her throat, there
goes a girl who opens her mouth to pour
caravans, mamelukes, a Mongolian horde
from lips that know less of roses
than of temples in the rising sun!*

Damascus, Dimashq
is a song I sing to myself. I would find
where she keeps her mouth, meet it with mine,
press my hand against her palm

and see if our fingers match. She
is the sound, the feel
of coins shaken in a cup, of dice,
the alabaster clap of knight claiming rook,
of kings castling – she is the clamour
of tambourines and dirbakki,
nays sighing, qanouns musing, the complaint
of you merchants with spice-lined hands,
and there is dust in her laughter.

I would drink it, dry my tongue
with this noise, these narrow streets,
    until she is a parched pain in my throat, a thorned rose
growing outward from my belly's pit, aching fragrance
into my lungs. I need no other. I
would spill attar from my eyes,
mix her dust with my salt,
steep my fingers in her stone
and raise them to my lips.

SEARCH

Geoffrey A. Landis

Jeremiah sits in a room at Cornell
Lit by fluorescent lights
His ears are covered by headphones, and he's bopping along as
   he searches
   (He doesn't look anything like Jodie Foster)
He's not listening to the telescope – his headphones are blasting
   Queen
The telescope sends to him nothing but a string of numbers
His fingertips are doing the search
Writing a new algorithm to implement frequency-domain filtering
Sorting out a tiny signal of intelligence
   (hypothetical intelligence)
from the thousand thousand thousand sources of noise from the sky
It's four a.m., his favorite time of night
No distractions
Outside, the stars are bright
Inside, the stars sing to him alone.

Nine hundred light years away
In the direction of Perseus
Intelligent creatures are wondering why they hear nothing from
   the skies
They are sending out messages,
Have been sending out messages for hundreds of years
One of their number, renowned for his clear thinking,
Has an electromagnetic pickup on his head
   (or, what would pass for a head)
He is thinking clear, simple thoughts
   $1 + 1 = 2$
   $1 + 2 = 3$
   $1 + 3 = 4$

And the electromagnetic signals of his brain
  (or, what would pass for a brain)
Are being amplified and beamed into the sky
In the direction of Earth
It is the simplest signal they know
A brain thinking
   $1 + 1 = 2$
   $2 + 2 = 4$

Jeremiah has been searching for years
He has a beard like Moses
Glasses like Jerry Garcia
A bald head like Jesse Ventura
Patience like Job
They are out there
If only the telescope arrays were larger . . .
if only they could search deeper . . .
If only his filtering algorithms were more incisive.

Nine hundred light years away
In the direction of Perseus
The aliens are patient
They are sending their thoughts to the stars
Clear, simple thoughts
  We are here
  We are here
  We are here
  Where are you?

FIREFLIES

Geoffrey A. Landis

---

flashing in a summer field against twilight sky-dark. Drifting shifting sparkle flashes, ever-changing patterns of writing in some
unknowable language of streaks and flashes, constellations
blinking on and off. Fireflies dance below us, fireflies behind
us, fireflies above us; their silent mating calls a symphony of
light. A million flashes a minute, we are immersed in a sea of
flickering light.

Just so, the immortals look out across the universe, as stars and
galaxies flick into life
fade into dark.

OTHER AWARDS

NEBULA AWARD FOR BEST NOVEL

THE WINDUP GIRL
PAOLO BACIGALUPI

FROM THE AUTHOR: The Windup Girl *was an experiment in risk for me. I bit off more than I could chew, with its many characters and cultures, its distorted world, and a plot structure that always felt one notch too complicated for me to keep in my head. That it's on the Nebula ballot with so much other very fine work, by writers who I respect so much . . . It's a gift. I'd like to thank my editor Juliet Ulman for guiding me across thin ice, the crew at Charles Coleman Finlay's Blue Heaven for their help, and Jeremy Lassen, my publisher at Night Shade, who was willing to take a risk on a book that had such uncertain potential. I'd also like to thank Maureen McHugh for giving me the shove I needed to start on something that scared me. I doubt she remembers the conversation, but it made all the difference.*

ANDRE NORTON AWARD FOR YOUNG ADULT
SCIENCE FICTION AND FANTASY

This literary award recognizes outstanding science fiction and fantasy novels that are written for the young adult market. The award has been named in honor of the late Andre Norton, a SFWA Grand Master and author of more than one hundred novels, including the acclaimed Witch World series, many of them for young adult readers. Ms. Norton's work has influenced generations of young people, creating new fans of the fantasy and science fiction genres and setting the standard for excellence in fantasy writing.

2009 Winner:
The Girl Who Circumnavigated Fairyland in a Ship of Her Own Making, Catherynne M. Valente

THE RAY BRADBURY AWARD FOR
OUTSTANDING DRAMATIC PRESENTATION

The Ray Bradbury Award is presented by SFWA at the Nebula ceremonies to recognize excellence in screenwriting.

2009 Winner:
District 9, Neill Blomkamp and Terri Tatchell

SOLSTICE AWARD

SFWA's Solstice Award was created in 2008 for individuals who have had a significant impact on the science fiction or fantasy landscape, and is particularly intended for those who have consistently made a major, positive difference within the speculative fiction field.

2009 Honorees:
Tom Doherty
Terri Windling
Donald A. Wollheim

SFWA SERVICE AWARD

The SFWA Service Award is presented to recognize those individuals who have performed particularly noteworthy service to the organization.

2009 Honorees:
Vonda N. McIntyre
Keith Stokes

ABOUT THE SCIENCE FICTION AND FANTASY WRITERS OF AMERICA

SFWA is a nonprofit organization of professional writers of science fiction, fantasy, and related genres. Founded in 1965 by Damon Knight, the organization now includes over one thousand five hundred speculative authors, artists, editors, and allied professionals. SFWA presents the prestigious Nebula Awards, assists members in legal disputes with publishers, and hosts the well-known Writer Beware website. SFWA administers a number of benevolent funds, including the Emergency Medical Fund, the Legal Fund, and a Literacy Fund intended to encourage genre reading and literacy in general. Online discussion forums, member directories, and private convention suites help its members keep in touch with each other and stay abreast of new developments in the field.

ABOUT THE
NEBULA AWARDS

Since 1965, the Nebula Awards have been presented yearly for the best works of science fiction or fantasy published in the United States. The winners are chosen by a vote of the active members of SFWA; awards are made in the categories of novel, novella, novelette, short story, and script. The award itself was originally designed by Judy Blish. Over the years additional awards are now presented at the Nebula Awards ceremony, honoring those who have contributed to science fiction and fantasy in other ways. These include such awards as Grand Master, Solstice, and Author Emeritus.

COMPLETE LIST OF PAST NEBULA WINNERS

2008 Nebula Awards

Best Novel: *Powers* by Ursula K. Le Guin

Best Novella: *The Spacetime Pool* by Catherine Asaro

Best Novelette: "Pride and Prometheus" by John Kessel

Best Short Story: "Trophy Wives" by Nina Kiriki Hoffman

Script: *WALL-E* Screenplay by Andrew Stanton, Jim Reardon, Original story by Andrew Stanton, Pete Docter

Andre Norton Award: *How a Girl of Spirit Gambles All to Expand Her Vocabulary, Confront a Bouncing Boy Terror, and Try to Save Califa from a Shaky Doom (Despite Being Confined to Her Room)* by Ysabeau S. Wilce

Solstice Award: Kate Wilhelm, A.J. Budrys and Martin H. Greenberg

SFWA Service Award: Victoria Strauss

Bradbury Award: Joss Whedon

Grand Master: Harry Harrison

Author Emerita: M.J. Engh

2007 Nebula Awards

Best Novel: *The Yiddish Policeman's Union* by Michael Chabon

Best Novella: *Fountain of Age* by Nancy Kress

Best Novelette: "The Merchant and the Alchemist's Gate" by Ted Chiang

Best Short Story: "Always" by Karen Joy Fowler

Best Script: *Pan's Labyrinth* by Guillermo del Toro

Andre Norton Award: *Harry Potter & the Deathly Hallows* by JK Rowling

Grand Master: Michael Moorcock

Author Emerita: Ardath Mayhar

SFWA Service Award: Melisa Michaels and Graham P. Collins

2006 Nebula Awards

Best Novel: *Seeker* by Jack McDevitt

Best Novella: *Burn* by James Patrick Kelly

Best Novelette: "Two Hearts" by Peter S. Beagle

Best Short Story: "Echo" by Elizabeth Hand

Best Script: *Howl's Moving Castle* by Hayao Miyazaki, Cindy Davis Hewitt, and Donald H. Hewitt

Andre Norton Award: *Magic or Madness* by Justine Larbalestier

Grand Master: James Gunn

Author Emeritus: D.G. Compton

SFWA Service Award: Brook West and Julia West jointly

2005 Nebula Awards

Best Novel: *Camouflage* by Joe Haldeman

Best Novella: *Magic for Beginners* by Kelly Link

Best Novelette: "The Faery Handbag" by Kelly Link

Best Short Story: "I Live with You" by Carol Emshwiller

Best Script: *Serenity* by Joss Whedon

Andre Norton Award: *Valiant: A Modern Tale of Faerie* by Holly Black

Grand Master: Harlan Ellison

Author Emeritus: William F. Nolan

2004 Nebula Awards

Best Novel: *Paladin of Souls*, by Lois McMaster Bujold

Best Novella: *The Green Leopard Plague* by Walter Jon Williams

Best Novelette: "Basement Magic" by Ellen Klages

Best Short Story: "Coming to Terms" by Eileen Gunn

Best Script: *The Lord of the Rings: The Return of the King* by Fran Walsh & Philippa Boyens & Peter Jackson; based on *The Lord of the Rings* by J.R.R. Tolkien

Grand Master: Anne McCaffrey

Service to SFWA Award: Kevin O'Donnell, Jr.

2003 Nebula Awards

Best Novel: *The Speed of Dark* by Elizabeth Moon

Best Novella: *Coraline* by Neil Gaiman

Best Novelette: "The Empire of Ice Cream" by Jeffrey Ford

Best Short Story: "What I Didn't See" by Karen Joy Fowler

Best Script: *The Lord of the Rings: The Two Towers* by Fran Walsh & Philippa Boyens & Stephen Sinclair & Peter Jackson; based on *The Lord of the Rings* by J.R.R. Tolkien

Grand Master: Robert Silverberg

Author of Distinction: Charles Harness

Service to SFWA Award: Michael Capobianco & Ann Crispin jointly

2002 Nebula Awards

Best Novel: *American Gods: A Novel* by Neil Gaiman

Best Novella: *Bronte's Egg* by Richard Chwedyk

Best Novelette: "Hell is the Absence of God" by Ted Chiang

Best Short Story: "Creature" by Carol Emshwiller

Best Script: *The Lord of the Rings: The Fellowship of the Ring* by Fran Walsh & Philippa Boyens & Peter Jackson; based on *The Lord of the Rings* by J.R.R. Tolkien

Grand Master: Ursula K. Le Guin

Author Emeritus: Katherine MacLean

2001 Nebula Awards

Best Novel: *The Quantum Rose* by Catherine Asaro

Best Novella: *The Ultimate Earth* by Jack Williamson

Best Novelette: "Louise's Ghost" by Kelly Link

Best Short Story: "The Cure for Everything" by Severna Park

Best Script: *Crouching Tiger, Hidden Dragon* by James Schamus, Kuo Jung Tsai, and Hui-Ling Wang; from the book by Du Lu Wang

President's Award: Betty Ballantine

2000 Nebula Awards

Best Novel: *Darwin's Radio* by Greg Bear

Best Novella: *Goddesses* by Linda Nagata

Best Novelette: "Daddy's World" by Walter Jon Williams

Best Short Story: "macs" by Terry Bisson

Best Script: *Galaxy Quest* by Robert Gordon and David Howard

Grand Master: Philip José Farmer

Bradbury Award: *2000X – Tales of the Next Millennia* by Yuri Rasovsky and Harlan Ellison

Author Emeritus: Robert Sheckley

1999 Nebula Awards

Best Novel: *Parable of the Talents* by Octavia E. Butler

Best Novella: *Story of Your Life* by Ted Chiang

Best Novelette: "Mars is No Place for Children" by Mary A. Turzillo

Best Short Story: "The Cost of Doing Business" by Leslie What

Best Script: *The Sixth Sense* by M. Night Shyamalan

Grand Master: Brian W. Aldiss

Author Emeritus: Daniel Keyes

Service to SFWA Award: George Zebrowski and Pamela Sargent jointly

1998 Nebula Awards

Best Novel: *Forever Peace* by Joe Haldeman

Best Novella: *Reading the Bones* by Sheila Finch

Best Novelette: "Lost Girls" by Jane Yolen

Best Short Story: "Thirteen Ways to Water" by Bruce Holland Rogers

Grand Master: Hal Clement (Harry Stubbs)

Bradbury Award: *Babylon 5* by J. Michael Straczynski

Author Emeritus: William Tenn (Phil Klass)

1997 Nebula Awards

Best Novel: *The Moon and the Sun* by Vonda N. McIntyre

Best Novella: *Abandon in Place* by Jerry Oltion

Best Novelette: "The Flowers of Aulit Prison" by Nancy Kress

Best Short Story: "Sister Emily's Lightship" by Jane Yolen
Grand Master: Poul Anderson
Author Emeritus: Nelson Slade Bond
Service to SFWA Award: Robin Wayne Bailey

1996 Nebula Awards

Best Novel: *Slow River* by Nicola Griffith
Best Novella: *Da Vinci Rising* by Jack Dann
Best Novelette: "Lifeboat on a Burning Sea" by Bruce Holland Rogers
Best Short Story: "A Birthday" by Esther M. Friesner
Grand Master: Jack Vance
Author Emeritus: Judith Merril
Service to SFWA Award: Sheila Finch

1995 Nebula Awards

Best Novel: *The Terminal Experiment* by Robert J. Sawyer
Best Novella: *Last Summer at Mars Hill* by Elizabeth Hand
Best Novelette: "Solitude" by Ursula K. Le Guin
Best Short Story: "Death and the Librarian" by Esther Friesner
Grand Master: A. E. Van Vogt
Author Emeritus: Wilson "Bob" Tucker
Service to SFWA Award: Chuq Von Rospach

1994 Nebula Awards

Best Novel: *Moving Mars: A Novel* by Greg Bear
Best Novella: *Seven Views of Olduvai Gorge* by Mike Resnick

Best Novelette: "The Martian Child" by David Gerrold
Best Short Story: "A Defense of the Social Contracts" by Martha Soukup
Grand Master: Damon Knight
Author Emeritus: Emil Petaja

1993 Nebula Awards

Best Novel: *Red Mars* by Kim Stanley Robinson
Best Novella: *The Night We Buried Road Dog* by Jack Cady
Best Novelette: "Georgia on My Mind" by Charles Sheffield
Best Short Story: "Graves" by Joe Haldeman

1992 Nebula Awards

Best Novel: *Doomsday Book* by Connie Willis
Best Novella: *City of Truth* by James Morrow
Best Novelette: "Danny Goes to Mars" by Pamela Sargent
Best Short Story: "Even the Queen" by Connie Willis
Grand Master: Frederik Pohl

1991 Nebula Awards

Best Novel: *Stations of the Tide* by Michael Swanwick
Best Novella: *Beggars in Spain* by Nancy Kress
Best Novelette: "Guide Dog" by Mike Conner
Best Short Story: "Ma Qui" by Alan Brennert
Bradbury Award: *Terminator 2: Judgment Day* by James Cameron

1990 Nebula Awards

Best Novel: *Tehanu: The Last Book of Earthsea* by Ursula K. Le Guin
Best Novella: *The Hemingway Hoax* by Joe Haldeman
Best Novelette: "Tower of Babylon" by Ted Chiang
Best Short Story: "Bears Discover Fire" by Terry Bisson
Grand Master: Lester Del Rey

1989 Nebula Awards

Best Novel: *Healer's War* by Elizabeth Ann Scarborough
Best Novella: *The Mountains of Mourning* by Lois McMaster Bujold
Best Novelette: "At the Rialto" by Connie Willis
Best Short Story: "Ripples in the Dirac Sea" by Geoffrey Landis

1988 Nebula Awards

Best Novel: *Falling Free* by Lois McMaster Bujold
Best Novella: *The Last of the Winnebagos* by Connie Willis
Best Novelette: "Schrodinger's Kitten" by George Alec Effinger
Best Short Story: "Bible Stories for Adults, No. 17: The Deluge" by James Morrow
Grand Master: Ray Bradbury

1987 Nebula Awards

Best Novel: *The Falling Woman* by Pat Murphy
Best Novella: *The Blind Geometer* by Kim Stanley Robinson
Best Novelette: "Rachel in Love" by Pat Murphy
Best Short Story: "Forever Yours, Anna" by Kate Wilhelm
Grand Master: Alfred Bester

1986 Nebula Awards

Best Novel: *Speaker for the Dead* by Orson Scott Card
Best Novella: *R&R* by Lucius Shepard
Best Novelette: "The Girl Who Fell Into the Sky" by Kate Wilhelm
Best Short Story: "Tangents" by Greg Bear
Grand Master: Isaac Asimov

1985 Nebula Awards

Best Novel: *Ender's Game* by Orson Scott Card
Best Novella: *Sailing to Byzantium* by Robert Silverberg
Best Novelette: "Portraits of His Children" by George R. R. Martin
Best Short Story: "Out of All Them Bright Stars" by Nancy Kress
Grand Master: Arthur C. Clarke

1984 Nebula Awards

Best Novel: *Neuromancer* by William Gibson
Best Novella: *Press Enter* by John Varley
Best Novelette: "Bloodchild" by Octavia Butler
Best Short Story: "Morning Child" by Gardner Dozois

1983 Nebula Awards

Best Novel: *Startide Rising* by David Brin
Best Novella: *Hardfought* by Greg Bear
Best Novelette: "Blood Music" by Greg Bear
Best Short Story: "The Peacemaker" by Gardner Dozois
Grand Master: Andre Norton

1982 Nebula Awards

Best Novel: *No Enemy But Time* by Michael Bishop

Best Novella: *Another Orphan* by John Kessel

Best Novelette: "Fire Watch" by Connie Willis

Best Short Story: "A Letter from the Clearys" by Connie Willis

1981 Nebula Awards

Best Novel: *Claw of the Conciliator* by Gene Wolfe

Best Novella: *The Saturn Game* by Poul Anderson

Best Novelette: "The Quickening" by Michael Bishop

Best Short Story: "The Bone Flute" by Lisa Tuttle (award declined)

1980 Nebula Awards

Best Novel: *Timescape* by Gregory Benford

Best Novella: *The Unicorn Tapestry* by Suzy McKee Charnas

Best Novelette: "The Ugly Chickens" by Howard Waldrop

Best Short Story: "Grotto of the Dancing Bear" by Clifford D. Simak

Grand Master: Fritz Leiber

1979 Nebula Awards

Best Novel: *The Fountains of Paradise* by Arthur C. Clarke

Best Novella: *Enemy Mine* by Barry Longyear

Best Novelette: "Sandkings" by George R.R. Martin

Best Short Story: "giANTS" by Edward Bryant

1978 Nebula Awards

Best Novel: *Dreamsnake* by Vonda N. McIntyre

Best Novella: *The Persistence of Vision* by John Varley

Best Novelette: "A Glow of Candles, a Unicorn's Eye" by Charles L. Grant

Best Short Story: "Stone" by Edward Bryant

Grand Master: L. Sprague de Camp

1977 Nebula Awards

Best Novel: *Gateway* by Frederik Pohl

Best Novella: *Stardance* by Spider and Jeanne Robinson

Best Novelette: "The Screwfly Solution" by Raccoona Sheldon

Best Short Story: "Jeffty is Five" by Harlan Ellison

Special Award: *Star Wars*

1976 Nebula Awards

Best Novel: *Man Plus* by Frederik Pohl

Best Novella: *Houston, Houston, Do You Read?* by James Tiptree, Jr.

Best Novelette: "The Bicentennial Man" by Isaac Asimov

Best Short Story: "A Crowd of Shadows" by Charles L. Grant

Grand Master: Clifford D. Simak

1975 Nebula Awards

Best Novel: *The Forever War* by Joe Haldeman

Best Novella: *Home Is the Hangman* by Roger Zelazny

Best Novelette: "San Diego Lightfoot Sue" by Tom Reamy

Best Short Story: "Catch That Zeppelin!" by Fritz Leiber

Best Dramatic Writing: Mel Brooks and Gene Wilder for *Young Frankenstein*

Grand Master: Jack Williamson

1974 Nebula Awards

Best Novel: *The Dispossessed* by Ursula K. Le Guin

Best Novella: *Born with the Dead* by Robert Silverberg

Best Novelette: "If the Stars Are Gods" by Gordon R. Eklund and Gregory Benford

Best Short Story: "The Day Before the Revolution" by Ursula K. Le Guin

Best Dramatic Presentation: *Sleeper* by Woody Allen

Grand Master: Robert A. Heinlein

1973 Nebula Awards

Best Novel: *Rendezvous with Rama* by Arthur C. Clarke

Best Novella: *The Death of Doctor Island* by Gene Wolfe

Best Novelette: "Of Mist, and Grass, and Sand" by Vonda N. McIntyre

Best Short Story: "Love is the Plan, the Plan is Death" by James Tiptree, Jr.

Best Dramatic Presentation: *Soylent Green*, Stanley R. Greenberg for Screenplay (based on the novel *Make Room! Make Room!* by Harry Harrison)

1972 Nebula Awards

Best Novel: *The Gods Themselves* by Isaac Asimov

Best Novella: *A Meeting with Medusa* by Arthur C. Clarke

Best Novelette: "Goat Song" by Poul Anderson

Best Short Story: "When it Changed" by Joanna Russ

1971 Nebula Awards

Best Novel: *A Time Of Changes* by Robert Silverberg

Best Novella: *The Missing Man* by Katherine MacLean

Best Novelette: "The Queen of Air and Darkness" by Poul Anderson

Best Short Story: "Good News from the Vatican" by Robert Silverberg

1970 Nebula Awards

Best Novel: *Ringworld* by Larry Niven

Best Novella: *Ill Met in Lankhmar* by Fritz Leiber

Best Novelette: "Slow Sculpture" by Theodore Sturgeon

Best Short Story: None

1969 Nebula Awards

Best Novel: *The Left Hand of Darkness* by Ursula K. Le Guin

Best Novella: *A Boy and His Dog* by Harlan Ellison

Best Novelette: "Time Considered as a Helix of Semi-Precious Stones" by Samuel R. Delany

Best Short Story: "Passengers" by Robert Silverberg

1968 Nebula Awards

Best Novel: *Rite of Passage* by Alexei Panshin

Best Novella: *Dragonrider* by Anne McCaffrey

Best Novelette: "Mother to the World" by Richard Wilson

Best Short Story: "The Planners" by Kate Wilhelm

1967 Nebula Awards

Best Novel: *The Einstein Intersection* by Samuel R. Delany

Best Novella: *Behold the Man* by Michael Moorcock

Best Novelette: "Gonna Roll the Bones" by Fritz Leiber

Best Short Story: "Aye, and Gormorrah" by Samuel R. Delany

1966 Nebula Awards

Best Novel: *Flowers for Algernon* by Daniel Keyes and *Babel-17* by Samuel Delany

Best Novella: *The Last Castle* by Jack Vance

Best Novelette: "Call Him Lord" by Gordon R. Dickson

Best Short Story: "The Secret Place" by Richard McKenna

1965 Nebula Awards

Best Novel: *Dune* by Frank Herbert

Best Novella: *The Saliva Tree* by Brian W. Aldiss and *He Who Shapes* by Roger Zelazny

Best Novelette: "The Doors of His Face, the Lamps of His Mouth" by Roger Zelazny

Best Short Story: "Repent, Harlequin!" "Said the Ticktockman" by Harlan Ellison

The Mammoth Book of Mindblowing SF

Edited by Mike Ashley

ISBN: 978-1-84529-891-3
Price: £7.99

Unmissable and thrilling SF – 21 stories to blow you away

Science fiction at its best can inspire a sense of wonder – bringing about that magic moment when our minds open to new perceptions and amazing possibilities. Here in one giant volume are 21 of the most visionary and thought-provoking SF short stories ever collected, by Stephen Baxter, Alastair Reynolds, Robert Silverberg, Gregory Benford, Robert Reed and more. They include two remarkable works from the 1950s by Arthur C. Clarke and James Blish, as well as five specially commissioned new stories . . .

- A discovery on the Moon that allows us to revisit our past

- Explorers in an alien world trapped beneath the surface whose only way out is down

- A future in which death has been eradicated, but returns to fulfil its destiny

- The very last moments on planet Earth and the fate of the last inhabitants

Visit www.constablerobinson.com for more information

The Mammoth Book of Best Short SF Novels

Edited by Gardner Dozois

ISBN: 978-1-84529-923-1
Price: £9.99

**In one great volume – the very best science fiction
novellas of modern times**

Science fiction is ideally suited to the short novel form: long
enough to conjure an alien or future society in our imaginations,
yet elegant and powerful – free of padding. Award-winning editor
Gardner Dozois presents here the 13 finest science fiction novellas
of the last two decades, including

Robert Silverberg's "Sailing to Byzantium", in
which a man from the 1980s is set adrift in a future so
remote that technology has become magic

Michael Swanwick's "Griffin's Egg", which holds
out the promise – or threat – of new brain chemicals
that will enable the evolution of the mind to be controlled

Alastair Reynolds's "Turquoise Days", an extension
of his far-future Demarchist/Conjoiner universe

Ursula K. Le Guin's "Forgiveness Day", a return to
the planets Werel and Yeowe, and their populations
descended from South Africans

"Outstanding . . . pays homage to the science fiction
novellas of the past two decades and by extension to
the entire genre in all its varied glory."
Publisher's Weekly

Visit www.constablerobinson.com for more information

The Mammoth Book of Best New SF 24

Edited by Gardner Dozois

ISBN: 978-1-84901-373-4
Price: £9.99

**Seventeen-times winner of the Locus Award
for the Year's Best Anthology**

For over twenty years, Gardner Dozois's compelling annual has
deservedly remained the single must-have collection for science
fiction fans around the world. Unfailingly offering the very best
new stories of the year, it showcases up-and-coming stars alongside
established masters of the genre. This year's collection includes the
work of over thirty writers, including Robert Reed, Nina Allan, Kage
Baker, Yoon Ha Lee, Ian R. MacLeod, Joe Haldeman,
Naomi Novik, Cory Doctorow and Aliette de Bodard.

In addition to over 3000,000 words of fantastic fiction,
the anthology includes bonus features such as Dozois's insightful
round-up of the year in SF and an extensive recommended
reading guide.

"For over two decades, Gardner Dozois's *Mammoth Book of
Best New SF* has defined the field. It is the most important
anthology, not only annually, but overall."
Charles N. Brown, publisher of *Locus*

"Dozois's definitive must-read short story anthology takes
the pulse of science fiction today."
Publishers Weekly

Visit www.constablerobinson.com for more information

The Mammoth Book of Apocalyptic SF

Edited by Mike Ashley

ISBN: 978-1-84901-305-5
Price: £7.99

Apocalypse Now?

Have the last days begun?

Humankind has long been fascinated by the precarious vulnerability of civilization and of the Earth itself. When our fragile civilizations finally go, will it be as a result of nuclear war, or some cosmic catastrophe? The impact of global warming, or a terrorist atrocity? Genetic engineering, or some modern plague more virulent even than HIV or Ebola?

Mike Ashley's gripping anthology of short stories explores the destruction of civilization and looks at how humanity might strive to survive such a crisis, including the end of the Earth.

- A vaccine threatens to turn into a virus that could wipe out mankind in "Bloodletting" by Kate Wilhelm

- Will the internet destroy civilization, or save it? "When Sysadmins Ruled the Earth" by Cory Doctorow

- In "Guardians of the Phoenix", Eric Brown depicts a world in the grip of climate change

How will the end come, and will you be there to witness it?

Visit www.constablerobinson.com for more information

To order other books in the Mammoth series from **Constable & Robinson** simply contact The Book Service (TBS) by phone, email or by post. Alternatively visit our website at www.constablerobinson.com.

No. of copies	Title	RRP	ISBN	Total
	The Mammoth Book of Best New SF 24	£9.99	978-1-84901-373-4	
	The Mammoth Book of Apocalyptic SF	£7.99	978-1-84901-305-5	
	The Mammoth Book of Mindblowing SF	£7.99	978-1-84529-891-3	
	The Mammoth Book of Best Short SF Novels	£9.99	978-1-84529-923-1	
			P&P: £	
			Grand Total: £	

FREEPOST RLUL-SJGC-SGKJ, Cash Sales Direct Mail Dept.,
The Book Service, Colchester Road, Frating, Colchester, CO7 7DW

Tel: +44 (0) 1206 255 800
Fax: +44 (0) 1206 255 930

Email: sales@tbs-ltd.co.uk

UK customers: please allow £1.00 p&p for the first book, plus 50p
for the second, and an additional 30p for each book thereafter,
up to a maximum charge of £3.00.

Overseas customers (incl. Ireland): please allow £2.00 p&p for the first book,
plus £1.00 for the second, plus 50p for each additional book.

NAME (block letters): _____
ADDRESS: _____
_____
_____ POSTCODE: _____

I enclose a cheque/PO (payable to 'TBS Direct') for the amount of £_____
I wish to pay by Switch/Credit Card
Card number: _____
Expiry date:_____ Switch issue number:_____